Books by Sidney Sheldon

Rage of Angels
Bloodline
A Stranger in the Mirror
The Other Side of Midnight
The Naked Face

*Published by
WARNER BOOKS

RAGE of ANGELS

Sidney Sheldon

WARNER BOOKS

A Warner Communications Company

This book is dedicated with love
to Mary
The Eighth Wonder of the World

The characters and events in this novel are fictional. The background, however, is real, and I am indebted to those who generously helped to fill it in for me. In a few instances I have taken what I believe to be necessary dramatic license. Any legal or factual errors are mine alone.

My deep gratitude for sharing with me their courtroom lives and experiences goes to F. Lee Bailey, Melvin Belli, Paul Caruso, William Hundley, Luke McKissack, Louis Nizer, Jerome Shestack and Peter Taft.

In California, the Honorable Wm. Matthew Byrne, of the United States District Court, was most helpful.

In New York, I owe special thanks to Mary de Bourbon of the New York District Attorney's office for showing me the inner workings of the court system; to Phil Leshin, former Assistant Commissioner for Public Affairs of the New York City Department of Correction, for escorting me through Riker's Island; and to Pat Perry, the Assistant Deputy Warden at Riker's Island.

Barry Dastin's legal supervision and counsel have proved invaluable.

My appreciation to Alice Fisher for her assistance in researching this book.

And finally, a thank you to Catherine Munro, who patiently and cheerfully transcribed and typed what began as a thousand-page manuscript, more than a dozen times over a period of almost three years.

—SIDNEY SHELDON

". . . Tell us of the secret hosts of evil, O Cimon   ."
"Their names may not be spake aloud
lest they profane mortal lips,
for they came out of unholy darknesses
and attacked the heavens,
but they were driven away by the rage of angels . . ."
—from *Dialogues of Chios*

RAGE of ANGELS

BOOK
I

1

The hunters were closing in for the kill.

Two thousand years ago in Rome, the contest would have been staged at the Circus Neronis or the Colosseum, where voracious lions would have been stalking the victim in an arena of blood and sand, eager to tear him to pieces. But this was the civilized twentieth century, and the circus was being staged in the Criminal Courts Building of downtown Manhattan, Courtroom Number 16.

In place of Suetonius was a court stenographer, to record the event for posterity, and there were dozens of members of the press and visitors attracted by the daily headlines about the murder trial, who queued up outside the courtroom at seven o'clock in the morning to be assured of a seat.

The quarry, Michael Moretti, sat at the defendant's table, a silent, handsome man in his early thirties. He was tall and lean, with a face formed of converging planes that gave him a rugged, feral look. He had fashionably styled black hair, a prominent chin with an unexpected dimple in it and deeply

set olive-black eyes. He wore a tailored gray suit, a light
blue shirt with a darker blue silk tie, and polished, custom-
made shoes. Except for his eyes, which constantly swept over
the courtroom, Michael Moretti was still.

The lion attacking him was Robert Di Silva, the fiery District Attorney for the County of New York, representative of
The People. If Michael Moretti radiated stillness, Robert Di
Silva radiated dynamic movement; he went through life as
though he were five minutes late for an appointment. He was
in constant motion, shadowboxing with invisible opponents.
He was short and powerfully built, with an unfashionable
graying crew cut. Di Silva had been a boxer in his youth and
his nose and face bore the scars of it. He had once killed a
man in the ring and he had never regretted it. In the years
since then, he had yet to learn compassion.

Robert Di Silva was a fiercely ambitious man who had
fought his way up to his present position with neither money
nor connections to help him. During his climb, he had assumed the veneer of a civilized servant of the people; but
underneath, he was a gutter fighter, a man who neither forgot
nor forgave.

Under ordinary circumstances, District Attorney Di Silva
would not have been in this courtroom on this day. He had a
large staff, and any one of his senior assistants was capable
of prosecuting this case. But Di Silva had known from the
beginning that he was going to handle the Moretti case himself.

Michael Moretti was front-page news, the son-in-law of
Antonio Granelli, *capo di capi*, head of the largest of the five
eastern Mafia Families. Antonio Granelli was getting old and
the street word was that Michael Moretti was being groomed
to take his father-in-law's place. Moretti had been involved
in dozens of crimes ranging from mayhem to murder, but no
district attorney had ever been able to prove anything. There
were too many careful layers between Moretti and those

who carried out his orders. Di Silva himself had spent three frustrating years trying to get evidence against Moretti. Then, suddenly, Di Silva had gotten lucky.

Camillo Stela, one of Moretti's *soldati*, had been caught in a murder committed during a robbery. In exchange for his life, Stela agreed to sing. It was the most beautiful music Di Silva had ever heard, a song that was going to bring the most powerful Mafia Family in the east to its knees, send Michael Moretti to the electric chair, and elevate Robert Di Silva to the governor's office in Albany. Other New York governors had made it to the White House: Martin Van Buren, Grover Cleveland, Teddy Roosevelt and Franklin Roosevelt. Di Silva intended to be the next.

The timing was perfect. The gubernatorial elections were coming up next year.

Di Silva had been approached by the state's most powerful political boss. "With all the publicity you're getting on this case, you'll be a shoo-in to be nominated and then elected governor, Bobby. Nail Moretti and you're our candidate."

Robert Di Silva had taken no chances. He prepared the case against Michael Moretti with meticulous care. He put his assistants to work assembling evidence, cleaning up every loose end, cutting off each legal avenue of escape that Moretti's attorney might attempt to explore. One by one, every loophole had been closed.

It had taken almost two weeks to select the jury, and the District Attorney had insisted upon selecting six "spare tires" —alternate jurors—as a precaution against a possible mistrial. In cases where important Mafia figures were involved, jurors had been known to disappear or to have unexplained fatal accidents. Di Silva had seen to it that this jury was sequestered from the beginning, locked away every night where no one could get to it.

The key to the case against Michael Moretti was Camillo

Stela, and Di Silva's star witness was heavily protected. The District Attorney remembered only too vividly the example of Abe "Kid Twist" Reles, the government witness who had "fallen" out of a sixth-floor window of the Half Moon Hotel in Coney Island while being guarded by half a dozen policemen. Robert Di Silva had selected Camillo Stela's guards personally, and before the trial Stela had been secretly moved to a different location every night. Now, with the trial under way, Stela was kept in an isolated holding cell, guarded by four armed deputies. No one was allowed to get near him, for Stela's willingness to testify rested on his belief that District Attorney Di Silva was capable of protecting him from the vengeance of Michael Moretti.

It was the morning of the fifth day of the trial.

It was Jennifer Parker's first day at the trial. She was seated at the prosecutor's table with five other young assistant district attorneys who had been sworn in with her that morning.

Jennifer Parker was a slender, dark-haired girl of twenty-four with a pale skin, an intelligent, mobile face, and green, thoughtful eyes. It was a face that was attractive rather than beautiful, a face that reflected pride and courage and sensitivity, a face that would be hard to forget. She sat ramrod straight, as though bracing herself against unseen ghosts of the past.

Jennifer Parker's day had started disastrously. The swearing-in ceremony at the District Attorney's office had been scheduled for eight A.M. Jennifer had carefully laid out her clothes the night before and had set the alarm for six so that she would have time to wash her hair.

The alarm had failed to go off. Jennifer had awakened at seven-thirty and panicked. She had gotten a run in her stocking when she broke the heel of her shoe, and had had to change clothes. She had slammed the door of her tiny apartment at the same instant she remembered she had left her keys inside. She had planned to take a bus to the Criminal Courts Building, but now that was out of the question, and she had raced to get a taxi she could not afford and had been trapped with a cab driver who explained during the entire trip why the world was about to come to an end.

When Jennifer had finally arrived, breathless, at the Criminal Courts Building at 155 Leonard Street, she was fifteen minutes late.

There were twenty-five lawyers gathered in the District Attorney's office, most of them newly out of law school, young and eager and excited about going to work for the District Attorney of the County of New York.

The office was impressive, paneled and decorated in quiet good taste. There was a large desk with three chairs in front of it and a comfortable leather chair behind it, a conference table with a dozen chairs around it, and wall cabinets filled with law books.

On the walls were framed autographed pictures of J. Edgar Hoover, John Lindsay, Richard Nixon and Jack Dempsey.

When Jennifer hurried into the office, full of apologies, Di Silva was in the middle of a speech. He stopped, turned his attention on Jennifer and said, "What the hell do you think this is—a tea party?"

"I'm terribly sorry, I—"

"I don't give a damn whether you're sorry. Don't you ever be late again!"

The others looked at Jennifer, carefully hiding their sympathy.

Di Silva turned to the group and snapped, "I know why you're all here. You'll stick around long enough to pick my brains and learn a few courtroom tricks, and then when you think you're ready, you'll leave to become hotshot criminal lawyers. But there may be one of you—maybe—who will be good enough to take my place one day." Di Silva nodded to his assistant. "Swear them in."

They took the oath, their voices subdued.

When it was over, Di Silva said, "All right. You're sworn officers of the court, God help us. This office is where the action is, but don't get your hopes up. You're going to bury your noses in legal research, and draft documents—subpoenas, warrants—all those wonderful things they taught you in law school. You won't get to handle a trial for the next year or two."

Di Silva stopped to light a short, stubby cigar. "I'm prosecuting a case now. Some of you may have read about it." His voice was edged with sarcasm. "I can use half a dozen of you to run errands for me." Jennifer's hand was the first one up. Di Silva hesitated a moment, then selected her and five others.

"Get down to Courtroom Sixteen."

As they left the room, they were issued identification cards. Jennifer had not been discouraged by the District Attorney's attitude. *He has to be tough*, she thought. *He's in a tough job.* And she was working for him now. She was a member of the staff of the District Attorney of the County of New York! The interminable years of law school drudgery were over. Somehow her professors had managed to make the law seem abstract and ancient, but Jennifer had always managed to glimpse the Promised Land beyond: the real law that dealt with human beings and their follies. Jennifer had been graduated second in her class and had been on Law Review. She had passed the bar examination on the first try, while a third of those who had taken it with her had failed. She felt that she understood Robert Di Silva, and she was sure she would be able to handle any job he gave her.

Jennifer had done her homework. She knew there were four different bureaus under the District Attorney—Trials,

Appeals, Rackets and Frauds—and she wondered to which one she would be assigned. There were over two hundred assistant district attorneys in New York City and five district attorneys, one for each borough. But the most important borough, of course, was Manhattan: Robert Di Silva.

Jennifer sat in the courtroom now, at the prosecutor's table, watching Robert Di Silva at work, a powerful, relentless inquisitor.

Jennifer glanced over at the defendant, Michael Moretti. Even with everything Jennifer had read about him, she could not convince herself that Michael Moretti was a murderer. *He looks like a young movie star in a courtroom set,* Jennifer thought. He sat there motionless, only his deep, black eyes giving away whatever inner turmoil he might have felt. They moved ceaselessly, examining every corner of the room as though trying to calculate a means of escape. There was no escape. Di Silva had seen to that.

Camillo Stela was on the witness stand. If Stela had been an animal, he would have been a weasel. He had a narrow, pinched face, with thin lips and yellow buckteeth. His eyes were darting and furtive and you disbelieved him before he even opened his mouth. Robert Di Silva was aware of his witness's shortcomings, but they did not matter. What mattered was what Stela had to say. He had horror stories to tell that had never been told before, and they had the unmistakable ring of truth.

The District Attorney walked over to the witness box where Camillo Stela had been sworn in.

"Mr. Stela, I want this jury to be aware that you are a reluctant witness and that in order to persuade you to testify, the State has agreed to allow you to plead to the lesser charge of involuntary manslaughter in the murder you are charged with. Is that true?"

"Yes, sir." His right arm was twitching.

"Mr. Stela, are you acquainted with the defendant, Michael Moretti?"

"Yes, sir." He kept his eyes away from the defendant's table where Michael Moretti was sitting.

"What was the nature of your relationship?"

"I worked for Mike."

"How long have you known Michael Moretti?"

"About ten years." His voice was almost inaudible.

"Would you speak up, please?"

"About ten years." His neck was twitching now.

"Would you say you were close to the defendant?"

"Objection!" Thomas Colfax rose to his feet. Michael Moretti's attorney was a tall, silver-haired man in his fifties, the *consigliere* for the Syndicate, and one of the shrewdest criminal lawyers in the country. "The District Attorney is attempting to lead the witness."

Judge Lawrence Waldman said, "Sustained."

"I'll rephrase the question. In what capacity did you work for Mr. Moretti?"

"I was kind of what you might call a troubleshooter."

"Would you be a little more explicit?"

"Yeah. If a problem comes up—someone gets out of line, like—Mike would tell me to go straighten this party out."

"How would you do that?"

"You know—muscle."

"Could you give the jury an example?"

Thomas Colfax was on his feet. "Objection, Your Honor. This line of questioning is immaterial."

"Overruled. The witness may answer."

"Well, Mike's into loan-sharkin', right? A coupla years ago Jimmy Serrano gets behind in his payments, so Mike sends me over to teach Jimmy a lesson."

"What did that lesson consist of?"

"I broke his legs. You see," Stela explained earnestly, "if

you let one guy get away with it, they're all gonna try it."

From the corner of his eye, Robert Di Silva could see the shocked reactions on the faces of the jurors.

"What other business was Michael Moretti involved in besides loan-sharking?"

"Jesus! You name it."

"I would like *you* to name it, Mr. Stela."

"Yeah. Well, like on the waterfront, Mike got a pretty good fix in with the union. Likewise the garment industry. Mike's into gamblin', juke boxes, garbage collectin', linen supplies. Like that."

"Mr. Stela, Michael Moretti is on trial for the murders of Eddie and Albert Ramos. Did you know them?"

"Oh, sure."

"Were you present when they were killed?"

"Yeah." His whole body seemed to twitch.

"Who did the actual killing?"

"Mike." For a second, his eyes caught Michael Moretti's eyes and Stela quickly looked away.

"Michael Moretti?"

"That's right."

"Why did the defendant tell you he wanted the Ramos brothers killed?"

"Well, Eddie and Al handled a book for—"

"That's a bookmaking operation? Illegal betting?"

"Yeah. Mike found out they was skimmin'. He had to teach 'em a lesson 'cause they was his boys, you know? He thought—"

"Objection!"

"Sustained. The witness will stick to the facts."

"The facts was that Mike tells me to invite the boys—"

"Eddie and Albert Ramos?"

"Yeah. To a little party down at The Pelican. That's a private beach club." His arm started to twitch again and Stela, suddenly aware of it, pressed against it with his other hand.

Jennifer Parker turned to look at Michael Moretti. He was watching impassively, his face and body immobile.

"What happened then, Mr. Stela?"

"I picked Eddie and Al up and drove 'em to the parkin' lot. Mike was there, waitin'. When the boys got outta the car, I moved outta the way and Mike started blastin'."

"Did you see the Ramos brothers fall to the ground?"

"Yes, sir."

"And they were dead?"

"They sure buried 'em like they was dead."

There was a ripple of sound through the courtroom. Di Silva waited until there was silence.

"Mr. Stela, you are aware that the testimony you have given in this courtroom is self-incriminating?"

"Yes, sir."

"And that you are under oath and that a man's life is at stake?"

"Yes, sir."

"You witnessed the defendant, Michael Moretti, cold-bloodedly shoot to death two men because they had withheld money from him?"

"Objection! He's leading the witness."

"Sustained."

District Attorney Di Silva looked at the faces of the jurors and what he saw there told him he had won the case. He turned to Camillo Stela.

"Mr. Stela, I know that it took a great deal of courage for you to come into this courtroom and testify. On behalf of the people of this state, I want to thank you." Di Silva turned to Thomas Colfax. "Your witness for cross."

Thomas Colfax rose gracefully to his feet. "Thank you, Mr. Di Silva." He glanced at the clock on the wall, then turned to the bench. "If it please Your Honor, it is now almost noon. I would prefer not to have my cross-examination interrupted.

Might I request that the court recess for lunch now and I'll cross-examine this afternoon?"

"Very well." Judge Lawrence Waldman rapped his gavel on the bench. "This court stands adjourned until two o'clock."

Everyone in the courtroom rose as the judge stood up and walked through the side door to his chambers. The jurors began to file out of the room. Four armed deputies surrounded Camillo Stela and escorted him through a door near the front of the courtroom that led to the witness room.

At once, Di Silva was engulfed by reporters.

"Will you give us a statement?"

"How do you think the case is going so far, Mr. District Attorney?"

"How are you going to protect Stela when this is over?"

Ordinarily Robert Di Silva would not have tolerated such an intrusion in the courtroom, but he needed now, with his political ambitions, to keep the press on his side, and so he went out of his way to be polite to them.

Jennifer Parker sat there, watching the District Attorney parrying the reporters' questions.

"Are you going to get a conviction?"

"I'm not a fortune teller," Jennifer heard Di Silva say modestly. "That's what we have juries for, ladies and gentlemen. The jurors will have to decide whether Mr. Moretti is innocent or guilty."

Jennifer watched as Michael Moretti rose to his feet. He looked calm and relaxed. *Boyish* was the word that came to Jennifer's mind. It was difficult for her to believe that he was guilty of all the terrible things of which he was accused. *If I had to choose the guilty one*, Jennifer thought, *I'd choose Stela, the Twitcher*.

The reporters had moved off and Di Silva was in conference with members of his staff. Jennifer would have given anything to hear what they were discussing.

Jennifer watched as a man said something to Di Silva, detached himself from the group around the District Attorney, and hurried over toward Jennifer. He was carrying a large manila envelope. "Miss Parker?"

Jennifer looked up in surprise. "Yes."

"The Chief wants you to give this to Stela. Tell him to refresh his memory about these dates. Colfax is going to try to tear his testimony apart this afternoon and the Chief wants to make sure Stela doesn't foul up."

He handed the envelope to Jennifer and she looked over at Di Silva. *He remembered my name*, she thought. *It's a good omen.*

"Better get moving. The D.A. doesn't think Stela's that fast a study."

"Yes, sir." Jennifer hurried to her feet.

She walked over to the door she had seen Stela go through. An armed deputy blocked her way.

"Can I help you, miss?"

"District Attorney's office," Jennifer said crisply. She took out her identification card and showed it. "I have an envelope to deliver to Mr. Stela from Mr. Di Silva."

The guard examined the card carefully, then opened the door, and Jennifer found herself inside the witness room. It was a small, uncomfortable-looking room containing a battered desk, an old sofa and wooden chairs. Stela was seated in one of them, his arm twitching wildly. There were four armed deputies in the room.

As Jennifer entered, one of the guards said, "Hey! Nobody's allowed in here."

The outside guard called, "It's okay, Al. D.A.'s office."

Jennifer handed Stela the envelope. "Mr. Di Silva wants you to refresh your recollection about these dates."

Stela blinked at her and kept twitching.

2

As Jennifer was making her way out of the Criminal Courts Building on her way to lunch, she passed the open door of a deserted courtroom. She could not resist stepping inside the room for a moment.

There were fifteen rows of spectators' benches on each side of the rear area. Facing the judge's bench were two long tables, the one on the left marked *Plaintiff* and the one on the right marked *Defendant*. The jury box contained two rows of eight chairs each. *It's an ordinary courtroom*, Jennifer thought, *plain—even ugly—but it's the heart of freedom*. This room and all the courtrooms like it represented the difference between civilization and savagery. The right to a trial by a jury of one's peers was what lay at the heart of every free nation. Jennifer thought of all the countries in the world that did not have this little room, countries where citizens were taken from their beds in the middle of the night and tortured and murdered by anonymous enemies for undisclosed reasons: Iran,

Uganda, Argentina, Peru, Brazil, Romania, Russia, Czecho-slovakia . . . the list was depressingly long.

If the American courts were ever stripped of their power, Jennifer thought, *if citizens were ever denied the right to a trial by jury, then America would cease to exist as a free nation.* She was a part of the system now and, standing there, Jennifer was filled with an overwhelming feeling of pride. She would do everything she could to honor it, to help preserve it. She stood there for a long moment, then turned to leave.

From the far end of the hall there was a distant hum that got louder and louder, and became pandemonium. Alarm bells began to ring. Jennifer heard the sound of running feet in the corridor and saw policemen with drawn guns racing toward the front entrance of the courthouse. Jennifer's instant thought was that Michael Moretti had escaped, had somehow gotten past the barrier of guards. She hurried out into the corridor. It was bedlam. People were racing around frantically, shouting orders over the din of the clanging bells. Guards armed with riot guns had taken up positions at the exit doors. Reporters who had been telephoning in their stories were hurrying into the corridor to find out what was happening. Far down the hall, Jennifer saw District Attorney Robert Di Silva wildly issuing instructions to half a dozen policemen, his face drained of color.

My God! He's going to have a heart attack, Jennifer thought.

She pushed her way through the crowd and moved toward him, thinking that perhaps she could be of some use. As she approached, one of the deputies who had been guarding Camillo Stela looked up and saw Jennifer. He raised an arm and pointed to her, and five seconds later Jennifer Parker found herself being grabbed, handcuffed and placed under arrest.

There were four people in Judge Lawrence Waldman's chambers: Judge Waldman, District Attorney Robert Di Silva, Thomas Colfax, and Jennifer.

"You have the right to have an attorney present before you make any statement," Judge Waldman informed Jennifer, "and you have the right to remain silent. If you—"

"I don't need an attorney, Your Honor! I can explain what happened."

Robert Di Silva was leaning so close to her that Jennifer could see the throbbing of a vein in his temple. "Who paid you to give that package to Camillo Stela?"

"Paid me? Nobody paid me!" Jennifer's voice was quavering with indignation.

Di Silva picked up a familiar looking manila envelope from Judge Waldman's desk. "*No one* paid you? You just walked up to my witness and delivered *this*?" He shook the envelope and the body of a yellow canary fluttered onto the desk. Its neck had been broken.

Jennifer stared at it, horrified. "I—one of your men—gave me—"

"Which one of my men?"

"I—I don't know."

"But you know he was one of my men." His voice rang with disbelief.

"Yes. I saw him talking to you and then he walked over to me and handed me the envelope and said you wanted me to give it to Mr. Stela. He—he even knew my name."

"I'll bet he did. How much did they pay you?"

It's all a nightmare, Jennifer thought. *I'm going to wake up any minute and it's going to be six o'clock in the morning, and I'm going to get dressed and go to be sworn in on the District Attorney's staff.*

"*How much?*" The anger in him was so violent that it forced Jennifer to her feet.

"Are you accusing me of—?"

"Accusing you!" Robert Di Silva clenched his fists. "Lady, I haven't even started on you. By the time you get out of prison you'll be too old to spend that money."

"There is no money." Jennifer stared at him defiantly.

Thomas Colfax had been sitting back, quietly listening to the conversation. He interrupted now to say, "Excuse me, Your Honor, but I'm afraid this isn't getting us anywhere."

"I agree," Judge Waldman replied. He turned to the District Attorney. "Where do you stand, Bobby? Is Stela still willing to be cross-examined?"

"Cross-examined? He's a basket case! Scared out of his wits. He won't take the stand again."

Thomas Colfax said smoothly, "If I can't cross-examine the prosecution's chief witness, Your Honor, I'm going to have to move for a mistrial."

Everyone in the room knew what that would mean: Michael Moretti would walk out of the courtroom a free man.

Judge Waldman looked over at the District Attorney. "Did you tell your witness he can be held in contempt?"

"Yes. Stela's more scared of them than he is of us." He turned to direct a venomous look at Jennifer. "He doesn't think we can protect him anymore."

Judge Waldman said slowly, "Then I'm afraid this court has no alternative but to grant the defense's request and declare a mistrial."

Robert Di Silva stood there, listening to his case being wiped out. Without Stela, he had no case. Michael Moretti was beyond his reach now, but Jennifer Parker was not. He was going to make her pay for what she had done to him.

Judge Waldman was saying, "I'll give instructions for the defendant to be freed and the jury dismissed."

Thomas Colfax said, "Thank you, Your Honor." There was no sign of triumph in his face.

"If there's nothing else . . ." Judge Waldman began.

"There is something else!" Robert Di Silva turned to Jennifer Parker. "I want her held for obstructing justice, for tampering with a witness in a capital case, for conspiracy, for . . ." He was incoherent with rage.

In her anger, Jennifer found her voice. "You can't prove a single one of those charges because they're not true. I—I may be guilty of being stupid, but that's *all* I'm guilty of. No one bribed me to do anything. I thought I was delivering a package for you."

Judge Waldman looked at Jennifer and said, "Whatever the motivation, the consequences have been extremely unfortunate. I am going to request that the Appellate Division undertake an investigation and, if it feels the circumstances warrant it, to begin disbarment proceedings against you."

Jennifer felt suddenly faint. "Your Honor, I—"

"That is all for now, Miss Parker."

Jennifer stood there a moment, staring at their hostile faces. There was nothing more she could say.

The yellow canary on the desk had said it all.

3

Jennifer Parker was not only on the evening news—she *was* the evening news. The story of her delivering a dead canary to the District Attorney's star witness was irresistible. Every television channel had pictures of Jennifer leaving Judge Waldman's chambers, fighting her way out of the courthouse, besieged by the press and the public.

Jennifer could not believe the sudden horrifying publicity that was being showered on her. They were hammering at her from all sides: television reporters, radio reporters and newspaper people. She wanted desperately to flee from them, but her pride would not let her.

"Who gave you the yellow canary, Miss Parker?"

"Have you ever met Michael Moretti?"

"Did you know that Di Silva was planning to use this case to get into the governor's office?"

"The District Attorney says he's going to have you disbarred. Are you going to fight it?"

To each question Jennifer had a tight-lipped "No comment."

On the CBS evening news they called her "Wrong-Way Parker," the girl who had gone off in the wrong direction. An ABC newsman referred to her as the "Yellow Canary." On NBC, a sports commentator compared her to Roy Riegels, the football player who had carried the ball to his own team's one-yard line.

In Tony's Place, a restaurant that Michael Moretti owned, a celebration was taking place. There were a dozen men in the room, drinking and boisterous.

Michael Moretti sat alone at the bar, in an oasis of silence, watching Jennifer Parker on television. He raised his glass in a salute to her and drank.

Lawyers everywhere discussed the Jennifer Parker episode. Half of them believed she had been bribed by the Mafia, and the other half that she had been an innocent dupe. But no matter which side they were on, they all concurred on one point: Jennifer Parker's short career as an attorney was finished.

She had lasted exactly four hours.

She had been born in Kelso, Washington, a small timber town founded in 1847 by a homesick Scottish surveyor who named it for his home town in Scotland.

Jennifer's father was an attorney, first for the lumber companies that dominated the town, then later for the workers in the sawmills. Jennifer's earliest memories of growing up were filled with joy. The state of Washington was a storybook place for a child, full of spectacular mountains and glaciers and national parks. There were skiing and canoeing and, when she was older, ice climbing on glaciers and pack trips to places with wonderful names: Ohanapecosh and Nisqually and Lake

Cle Elum and Chenuis Falls and Horse Heaven and the Yakima Valley. Jennifer learned to climb on Mount Rainier and to ski at Timberline with her father.

Her father always had time for her, while her mother, beautiful and restless, was mysteriously busy and seldom at home. Jennifer adored her father. Abner Parker was a mixture of English and Irish and Scottish blood. He was of medium height, with black hair and green-blue eyes. He was a compassionate man with a deep-rooted sense of justice. He was not interested in money, he was interested in people. He would sit and talk to Jennifer by the hour, telling her about the cases he was handling and the problems of the people who came into his unpretentious little office, and it did not occur to Jennifer until years later that he talked to her because he had no one else with whom to share things.

After school Jennifer would hurry over to the courthouse to watch her father at work. If court was not in session she would hang around his office, listening to him discuss his cases and his clients. They never talked about her going to law school; it was simply taken for granted.

When Jennifer was fifteen she began spending her summers working for her father. At an age when other girls were dating boys and going steady, Jennifer was absorbed in lawsuits and wills.

Boys were interested in her, but she seldom went out. When her father would ask her why, she would reply, "They're all so *young*, Papa." She knew that one day she would marry a lawyer like her father.

On Jennifer's sixteenth birthday, her mother left town with the eighteen-year-old son of their next-door neighbor, and Jennifer's father quietly died. It took seven years for his heart to stop beating, but he was dead from the moment he heard the news about his wife. The whole town knew and was sympathetic, and that, of course, made it worse, for Abner Parker was a proud man. That was when he began to drink. Jennifer did everything she could to comfort him but it was no use, and nothing was ever the same again.

The next year, when it came time to go to college, Jennifer wanted to stay home with her father, but he would not hear of it.

"We're going into partnership, Jennie," he told her. "You hurry up and get that law degree."

When she was graduated she enrolled at the University of Washington in Seattle to study law. During the first year of school, while Jennifer's classmates were flailing about in an impenetrable swamp of contracts, torts, property, civil procedure and criminal law, Jennifer felt as though she had come home. She moved into the university dormitory and got a job at the Law Library.

Jennifer loved Seattle. On Sundays, she and an Indian student named Ammini Williams and a big, rawboned Irish girl named Josephine Collins would go rowing on Green Lake in the heart of the city, or attend the Gold Cup races on Lake Washington and watch the brightly colored hydroplanes flashing by.

There were great jazz clubs in Seattle, and Jennifer's favorite was Peter's Poop Deck, where they had crates with slabs of wood on top instead of tables.

Afternoons, Jennifer, Ammini and Josephine would meet at The Hasty Tasty, a hangout where they had the best cottage-fried potatoes in the world.

There were two boys who pursued Jennifer: a young, attractive medical student named Noah Larkin and a law student named Ben Munro; and from time to time Jennifer would go out on dates with them, but she was far too busy to think about a serious romance.

The seasons were crisp and wet and windy and it seemed to rain all the time. Jennifer wore a green-and-blue-plaid lumber jacket that caught the raindrops in its shaggy wool and made her eyes flash like emeralds. She walked through the rain, lost in her own secret thoughts, never knowing that all those she passed would file away the memory.

In spring the girls blossomed out in their bright cotton dresses. There were six fraternities in a row at the university, and the fraternity brothers would gather on the lawn and watch the girls go by, but there was something about Jennifer that made them feel unexpectedly shy. There was a special quality about her that was difficult for them to define, a feeling that she had already attained something for which they were still searching.

Every summer Jennifer went home to visit her father. He had changed so much. He was never drunk, but neither was he ever sober. He had retreated into an emotional fortress where nothing could touch him again.

He died when Jennifer was in her last term at law school. The town remembered, and there were almost a hundred people at Abner Parker's funeral, people he had helped and advised and befriended over the years. Jennifer did her grieving in private. She had lost more than a father. She had lost a teacher and a mentor.

After the funeral Jennifer returned to Seattle to finish school. Her father had left her less than a thousand dollars and she had to make a decision about what to do with her life. She knew that she could not return to Kelso to practice law, for there she would always be the little girl whose mother had run off with a teen-ager.

Because of her high scholastic average, Jennifer had interviews with a dozen top law firms around the country, and received several offers.

Warren Oakes, her criminal law professor, told her: "That's a real tribute, young lady. It's very difficult for a woman to get into a good law firm."

Jennifer's dilemma was that she no longer had a home or roots. She was not certain where she wanted to live.

Shortly before graduation Jennifer's problem was solved for her. Professor Oakes asked her to see him after class.

"I have a letter from the District Attorney's office in Manhattan, asking me to recommend my brightest graduate for his staff. Interested?"

New York. "Yes, sir." Jennifer was so stunned that the answer just popped out.

She flew to New York to take the bar examination, and returned to Kelso to close her father's law office. It was a bittersweet experience, filled with memories of the past and it seemed to Jennifer that she had grown up in that office.

She got a job as an assistant in the law library of the university to tide her over until she heard whether she had passed the New York bar examination.

"It's one of the toughest in the country," Professor Oakes warned her.

But Jennifer *knew*.

She received her notice that she had passed and an offer from the New York District Attorney's office on the same day.

One week later, Jennifer was on her way east.

She found a tiny apartment (*Spc W/U fpl gd loc nds sm wk,* the ad said) on lower Third Avenue, with a fake fireplace in a steep fourth-floor walk-up. *The exercise will do me good,* Jennifer told herself. There were no mountains to climb in Manhattan, no rapids to ride. The apartment consisted of a small living room with a couch that turned into a lumpy bed, and a tiny bathroom with a window that someone long ago had painted over with black paint, sealing it shut. The furniture looked like something that could have been donated by the Salvation Army. *Oh, well, I won't be living in this place long.* Jennifer thought. *This is just temporary until I prove myself as a lawyer.*

* * *

That had been the dream. The reality was that she had been in New York less than seventy-two hours, had been thrown off the District Attorney's staff and was facing disbarment.

Jennifer quit reading newspapers and magazines and stopped watching television, because wherever she turned she saw herself. She felt that people were staring at her on the street, on the bus, and at the market. She began to hide out in her tiny apartment, refusing to answer the telephone or the doorbell. She thought about packing her suitcases and returning to Washington. She thought about getting a job in some other field. She thought about suicide. She spent long hours composing letters to District Attorney Robert Di Silva. Half the letters were scathing indictments of his insensitivity and lack of understanding. The other half were abject apologies, with a plea for him to give her another chance. None of the letters was ever sent.

For the first time in her life Jennifer was overwhelmed with a sense of desperation. She had no friends in New York, no one to talk to. She stayed locked in her apartment all day, and late at night she would slip out to walk the deserted streets of the city. The derelicts who peopled the night never accosted her. Perhaps they saw their own loneliness and despair mirrored in her eyes.

Over and over, as she walked, Jennifer would envision the courtroom scene in her mind, always changing the ending.

A man detached himself from the group around Di Silva and hurried toward her. He was carrying a manila envelope.

Miss Parker?

Yes.

The Chief wants you to give this to Stela.

Jennifer looked at him coolly. Let me see your identification, please.

The man panicked and ran.

* * *

*A man detached himself from the group around Di Silva
and hurried toward her. He was carrying a manila envelope.
Miss Parker?*

Yes.

*The Chief wants you to give this to Stela. He thrust the en-
velope into her hands.*

*Jennifer opened the envelope and saw the dead canary in-
side. I'm placing you under arrest.*

*A man detached himself from the group around Di Silva
and hurried toward her. He was carrying a manila envelope.
He walked past her to another young assistant district attorney and handed him the envelope. The Chief wants you to
give this to Stela.*

She could rewrite the scene as many times as she liked, but
nothing was changed. One foolish mistake had destroyed her.
And yet—who said she was destroyed? The press? Di Silva?
She had not heard another word about her disbarment, and
until she did she was still an attorney. *There are law firms that
made me offers,* Jennifer told herself.

Filled with a new sense of resolve, Jennifer pulled out the
list of the firms she had talked to and began to make a series
of telephone calls. None of the men she asked to speak to was
in, and not one of her calls was returned. It took her four days
to realize that she was the pariah of the legal profession. The
furor over the case had died down, but everyone still remembered.

Jennifer kept telephoning prospective employers, going
from despair to indignation to frustration and back to despair
again. She wondered what she was going to do with the rest
of her life, and each time it came back to the same thing: All
she wanted to do, the one thing she really cared about, was
to practice law. She was a lawyer and, by God, until they

stopped her she was going to find a way to practice her profession.

She began to make the rounds of Manhattan law offices. She would walk in unannounced, give her name to the receptionist and ask to see the head of personnel. Occasionally she was granted an interview, but when she was, Jennifer had the feeling it was out of curiosity. She was a freak and they wanted to see what she looked like in person. Most of the time she was simply informed there were no openings.

At the end of six weeks, Jennifer's money was running out. She would have moved to a cheaper apartment, but there *were* no cheaper apartments. She began to skip breakfast and lunch, and to have dinner at one of the little corner dinettes where the food was bad but the prices were good. She discovered the Steak & Brew and Roast-and-Brew, where for a modest sum she was able to get a main course, all the salad she could eat, and all the beer she could drink. Jennifer hated beer, but it was filling.

When Jennifer had gone through her list of large law firms, she armed herself with a list of smaller firms and began to call on them, but her reputation had preceded her even there. She received a lot of propositions from interested males, but no job offers. She was beginning to get desperate. *All right*, she thought defiantly, *if no one wants to hire me, I'll open my own law office*. The catch was that that took money. Ten thousand dollars, at least. She would need enough for rent, telephone, a secretary, law books, a desk and chairs, stationery . . . she could not even afford the stamps.

Jennifer had counted on her salary from the District Attorney's office but that, of course, was gone forever. She could forget about severance pay. She had not been severed; she had been beheaded. No, there was no way she could afford to open her own office, no matter how small. The answer was to find someone with whom to share offices.

Jennifer bought a copy of *The New York Times* and began to search through the want ads. It was not until she was near the bottom of the page that she came across a small advertisement that read: *Wanted:/Prof man sh sm off w/2 oth/prof men. Rs rent.*

The last two words appealed to Jennifer enormously. She was not a professional man, but her sex should not matter. She tore out the ad and took the subway down to the address listed.

It was a dilapidated old building on lower Broadway. The office was on the tenth floor and the flaking sign on the door read:

KENNETH BAILEY
ACE INVEST GA IONS

Beneath it:

ROCKEFELLER C LLECTION AG NCY

Jennifer took a deep breath, opened the door and walked in. She was standing in the middle of a small, windowless office. There were three scarred desks and chairs crowded into the room, two of them occupied.

Seated at one of the desks was a bald, shabbily dressed, middle-aged man working on some papers. Against the opposite wall at another desk was a man in his early thirties. He had brick-red hair and bright blue eyes. His skin was pale and freckled. He was dressed in tight-fitting jeans, a tee shirt, and white canvas shoes without socks. He was talking into the telephone.

"Don't worry, Mrs. Desser, I have two of my best operatives working on your case. We should have news of your husband any day now. I'm afraid I'll have to ask you for a little more expense money . . . No, don't bother mailing it. The mails are terrible. I'll be in your neighborhood this afternoon. I'll stop by and pick it up."

He replaced the receiver and looked up and saw Jennifer.

He rose to his feet, smiled and held out a strong, firm hand. "I'm Kenneth Bailey. And what can I do for you this morning?"

Jennifer looked around the small, airless room and said uncertainly, "I—I came about your ad."

"Oh." There was surprise in his blue eyes.

The bald-headed man was staring at Jennifer.

Kenneth Bailey said, "This is Otto Wenzel. He's the Rockefeller Collection Agency."

Jennifer nodded. "Hello." She turned back to Kenneth Bailey. "And you're Ace Investigations?"

"That's right. What's your scam?"

"My—?" Then, realizing, "I'm an attorney."

Kenneth Bailey studied her skeptically. "And you want to set up an office *here*?"

Jennifer looked around the dreary office again and visualized herself at the empty desk, between these two men.

"Perhaps I'll look a little further," she said. "I'm not sure—"

"Your rent would only be ninety dollars a month."

"I could *buy* this building for ninety dollars a month," Jennifer replied. She turned to leave.

"Hey, wait a minute."

Jennifer paused.

Kenneth Bailey ran a hand over his pale chin. "I'll make a deal with you. Sixty. When your business gets rolling we'll talk about an increase."

It was a bargain. Jennifer knew that she could never find any space elsewhere for that amount. On the other hand, there was no way she could ever attract clients to this hellhole. There was one other thing she had to consider. She did not have the sixty dollars.

"I'll take it," Jennifer said.

"You won't be sorry," Kenneth Bailey promised. "When do you want to move your things in?"

"They're in."

Kenneth Bailey painted the sign on the door himself. It read:

JENNIFER PARKER

ATTORNEY AT LAW

Jennifer studied the sign with mixed feelings. In her deepest depressions it had never occurred to her that she would have her name under that of a private investigator and a bill collector. Yet, as she looked at the faintly crooked sign, she could not help feeling a sense of pride. She was an attorney. The sign on the door proved it.

Now that Jennifer had office space, the only thing she lacked was clients.

Jennifer could no longer afford even the Steak & Brew. She made herself a breakfast of toast and coffee on the hot plate she had set up over the radiator in her tiny bathroom. She ate no lunch and had dinner at Chock Full O'Nuts or Zum Zum, where they served large pieces of wurst, slabs of bread and hot potato salad.

She arrived at her desk promptly at nine o'clock every morning, but there was nothing for her to do except listen to Ken Bailey and Otto Wenzel talking on the telephone.

Ken Bailey's cases seemed to consist mostly of finding runaway spouses and children, and at first Jennifer was convinced that he was a con man, making extravagant promises and collecting large advances. But Jennifer quickly learned that Ken Bailey worked hard and delivered often. He was bright and he was clever.

Otto Wenzel was an enigma. His telephone rang constantly. He would pick it up, mutter a few words into it, write something on a piece of paper and disappear for a few hours.

"Oscar does repo's," Ken Bailey explained to Jennifer one day.

"Repo's?"

"Yeah. Collection companies use him to get back automobiles, television sets, washing machines—you name it." He looked at Jennifer curiously. "You got *any* clients?"

"I have some things coming up," Jennifer said evasively.

He nodded. "Don't let it get you down. Anyone can make a mistake."

Jennifer felt herself flushing. So *he* knew about her.

Ken Bailey was unwrapping a large, thick roast-beef sandwich. "Like some?"

It looked delicious. "No, thanks," Jennifer said firmly. "I never eat lunch."

"Okay."

She watched him bite into the juicy sandwich. He saw her expression and said, "You sure you—?"

"No, thank you. I—I have an appointment."

Ken Bailey watched Jennifer walk out of the office and his face was thoughtful. He prided himself on his ability to read character, but Jennifer Parker puzzled him. From the television and newspaper accounts he had been sure someone had paid this girl to destroy the case against Michael Moretti. After meeting Jennifer, Ken was less certain. He had been married once and had gone through hell, and he held women in low esteem. But something told him that this one was special. She was beautiful, bright and very proud. *Jesus!* he said to himself. *Don't be a fool! One murder on your conscience is enough.*

Emma Lazarus was a sentimental idiot, Jennifer thought.

"Give me your tired, your poor, your huddled masses yearning to breathe free . . . Send these, the homeless, tempesttossed, to me." Indeed! Anyone manufacturing welcome mats in New York would have gone out of business in an hour. In New York no one cared whether you lived or died. *Stop feeling sorry for yourself!* Jennifer told herself. But it was difficult. Her resources had dwindled to eighteen dollars, the rent on her apartment was overdue, and her share of the office rent was due in two days. She did not have enough money to stay in New York any longer, and she did not have enough money to leave.

Jennifer had gone through the Yellow Pages, calling law offices alphabetically, trying to get a job. She made the calls from telephone booths because she was too embarrassed to let Ken Bailey and Otto Wenzel hear her conversations. The results were always the same. No one was interested in hiring her. She would have to return to Kelso and get a job as a legal aide or as a secretary to one of her father's friends. How he would have hated that! It was a bitter defeat, but there were no choices left. She would be returning home a failure. The immediate problem facing her was transportation. She looked through the afternoon *New York Post* and found an ad for someone to share driving expenses to Seattle. There was a telephone number and Jennifer called it. There was no answer. She decided she would try again in the morning.

The following day, Jennifer went to her office for the last time. Otto Wenzel was out, but Ken Bailey was there, on the telephone, as usual. He was wearing blue jeans and a veeneck cashmere sweater.

"I found your wife," he was saying. "The only problem, pal, is that she doesn't want to go home. . . . I know. Who can figure women out? . . . Okay. I'll tell you where she's staying and you can try to sweet-talk her into coming back."

He gave the address of a midtown hotel. "My pleasure." He hung up and swung around to face Jennifer. "You're late this morning."

"Mr. Bailey, I—I'm afraid I'm going to have to be leaving. I'll send you the rent money I owe you as soon as I'm able to."

Ken Bailey leaned back in his chair and studied her. His look made Jennifer uncomfortable.

"Will that be all right?" she asked.

"Going back to Washington?"

Jennifer nodded.

Ken Bailey said, "Before you leave, would you do me a little favor? A lawyer friend's been bugging me to serve some subpoenas for him, and I haven't got time. He pays twelve-fifty for each subpoena plus mileage. Would you help me out?"

One hour later Jennifer Parker found herself in the plush law offices of Peabody & Peabody. This was the kind of firm she had visualized working in one day, a full partner with a beautiful corner suite. She was escorted to a small back room where a harassed secretary handed her a stack of subpoenas.

"Here. Be sure to keep a record of your mileage. You do have a car, don't you?"

"No, I'm afraid I—"

"Well, if you use the subway, keep track of the fares."

"Right."

Jennifer spent the rest of the day delivering subpoenas in the Bronx, Brooklyn and Queens in a downpour. By eight o'clock that evening, she had made fifty dollars. She arrived back at her tiny apartment chilled and exhausted. But at least she had earned some money, her first since coming to New York. And the secretary had told her there were plenty more subpoenas to serve. It was hard work, running all over town, and it was humiliating. She had had doors slammed in her face, had been cursed at, threatened, and propositioned twice. The prospect of facing another day like that was dismaying; and yet, as long as she could remain in New York there was hope, no matter how faint.

Jennifer ran a hot bath and stepped into it, slowly sinking down into the tub, feeling the luxury of the water lapping over her body. She had not realized how exhausted she was. Every muscle seemed to ache. She decided that what she needed was a good dinner to cheer her up. She would splurge. *I'll treat myself to a real restaurant with tablecloths and napkins,* Jennifer thought. *Perhaps they'll have soft music and I'll have a glass of white wine and—*

Jennifer's thoughts were interrupted by the ringing of the doorbell. It was an alien sound. She had not had a single visitor since she had moved in two months earlier. It could only be the surly landlady about the overdue rent. Jennifer lay still, hoping she would go away, too weary to move.

The doorbell rang again. Reluctantly, Jennifer dragged herself from the warm tub. She slipped on a terry-cloth robe and went to the door.

"Who is it?"

A masculine voice on the other side of the door said, "Miss Jennifer Parker?"

"Yes."

"My name is Adam Warner. I'm an attorney."

Puzzled, Jennifer put the chain on the door and opened it a crack. The man standing in the hall was in his middle thirties, tall and blond and broad-shouldered, with gray-blue inquisitive eyes behind horn-rimmed glasses. He was dressed in a tailored suit that must have cost a fortune.

"May I come in?" he asked.

Muggers did not wear tailored suits, Gucci shoes and silk ties. Nor did they have long, sensitive hands with carefully manicured nails.

"Just a moment."

Jennifer unfastened the chain and opened the door. As Adam Warner walked in, Jennifer glanced around the one-room apartment, seeing it through his eyes, and winced. He looked like a man who was used to better things.

"What can I do for you, Mr. Warner?"

Even as she spoke, Jennifer suddenly knew why he was there, and she was filled with a quick sense of excitement. It was about one of the jobs she had applied for! She wished that she had on a nice, dark blue tailored robe, that her hair was combed, that—

Adam Warner said, "I'm a member of the Disciplinary Committee of the New York Bar Association, Miss Parker. District Attorney Robert Di Silva and Judge Lawrence Waldman have requested the Appellate Division to begin disbarment proceedings against you."

4

The law offices of Needham, Finch, Pierce and Warner were located at 30 Wall Street, occupying the entire top floor of the building. There were a hundred and twenty-five lawyers in the firm. The offices smelled of old money and were done in the quiet elegance befitting an organization that represented some of the biggest names in industry.

Adam Warner and Stewart Needham were having their ritual morning tea. Stewart Needham was a dapper, trim man in his late sixties. He had a neat Vandyke beard and wore a tweed suit and vest. He looked as though he belonged to an older era, but as hundreds of opponents had learned to their sorrow through the years, Stewart Needham's mind belonged very much to the twentieth century. He was a titan, but his name was known only in the circles where it mattered. He preferred to remain in the background and use his considerable influence to affect the outcome of legislation, high government appointments and national politics. He was a New Englander, born and reared taciturn.

Adam Warner was married to Needham's niece Mary Beth, and was Needham's protégé. Adam's father had been a respected senator. Adam himself was a brilliant lawyer. When he had been graduated *magna cum laude* from Harvard Law School, he had had offers from prestigious law firms all over the country. He chose Needham, Finch and Pierce, and seven years later became a partner. Adam was physically attractive and charming, and his intelligence seemed to add an extra dimension to him. He had an easy sureness about himself that women found challenging. Adam had long since developed a system for dissuading overamorous female clients. He had been married to Mary Beth for fourteen years and did not approve of extramarital affairs.

"More tea, Adam?" Stewart Needham asked.

"No, thanks." Adam Warner hated tea, and he had been drinking it every morning for the last eight years only because he did not want to hurt his partner's feelings. It was a brew that Needham concocted himself and it was dreadful.

Stewart Needham had two things on his mind and, typically, he began with the pleasant news. "I had a meeting with a few friends last night," Needham said. *A few friends* would be a group of the top power brokers in the country. "They're considering asking you to run for United States senator, Adam."

Adam felt a sense of elation. Knowing Stewart Needham's cautious nature, Adam was certain that the conversation had been more than casual or Needham would not have brought it up now.

"The big question, of course, is whether you're interested. It would mean a lot of changes in your life."

Adam Warner was aware of that. If he won the election, it would mean moving to Washington, D.C., giving up his law practice, starting a whole new life. He was sure that Mary Beth would enjoy it; Adam was not so sure about himself. And yet, he had been reared to assume responsibility. Also, he had to admit to himself that there was a pleasure in power.

"I'd be very interested, Stewart."

Stewart Needham nodded with satisfaction. "Good. They'll be pleased." He poured himself another cup of the dreadful brew and casually broached the other subject that was on his mind. "There's a little job the Disciplinary Committee of the Bar Association would like you to handle, Adam. Shouldn't take you more than an hour or two."

"What is it?"

"It's the Michael Moretti trial. Apparently, someone got to one of Bobby Di Silva's young assistants and paid her off."

"I read about it. The canary."

"Right. Judge Waldman and Bobby would like her name removed from the roster of our honorable profession. So would I. It reeks."

"What do they want me to do?"

"Just make a quick check, verify that this Parker girl behaved illegally or unethically, and then recommend disbarment proceedings. She'll be served with a notice to show cause and they'll handle the rest of it. It's just routine."

Adam was puzzled by something. "Why me, Stewart? We have a couple of dozen young lawyers around here who could handle this."

"Our revered District Attorney specifically asked for you. He wants to make sure nothing goes wrong. As we're both aware," he added dryly, "Bobby's not the most forgiving man in the world. He wants the Parker woman's hide nailed up on his wall."

Adam Warner sat there, thinking about his busy schedule.

"You never know when we might need a favor from the D.A.'s office, Adam. Quid pro quo. It's all cut and dried."

"All right, Stewart." Adam rose to his feet.

"Sure you won't have some more tea?"

"No, thanks. It was as good as always."

* * *

When Adam Warner returned to his office he rang for one of his paralegal assistants, Lucinda, a bright, young Black woman.

"Cindy, get me all the information you can on an attorney named Jennifer Parker."

She grinned and said, "The yellow canary."

Everybody knew about her.

Late that afternoon Adam Warner was studying the transcript of the court proceedings in the case of *The People of New York* v. *Michael Moretti*. Robert Di Silva had had it delivered by special messenger. It was long past midnight when Adam finished. He had asked Mary Beth to attend a dinner party without him, and had sent out for sandwiches. When Adam was through reading the transcript, there was no doubt in his mind that Michael Moretti would have been found guilty by the jury if fate had not intervened in the form of Jennifer Parker. Di Silva had prosecuted the case flawlessly.

Adam turned to the transcript of the deposition that had been taken in Judge Waldman's chambers afterward.

DI SILVA: *You are a college graduate?*

PARKER: *Yes, sir.*

DI SILVA: *And a law school graduate?*

PARKER: *Yes, sir.*

DI SILVA: *And a stranger hands you a package, tells you to deliver it to a key witness in a murder trial and you just do it? Wouldn't you say that went beyond the bounds of stupidity?*

PARKER: *It didn't happen that way.*

DI SILVA: *You said it did.*

PARKER: *What I mean is, I didn't think he was a stranger. I thought he was on your staff.*

DI SILVA: *What made you think that?*

PARKER: *I've told you. I saw him talking to you and then he came over to me with this envelope and he called me by name, and he said you wanted me to deliver it to the witness. It all happened so fast that—*

DI SILVA: *I don't think it happened that fast. I think it took time to set it up. It took time to arrange for someone to pay you off to deliver it.*

PARKER: *That's not true. I—*

DI SILVA: *What's not true? That you didn't know you were delivering the envelope?*

PARKER: *I didn't know what was in it.*

DI SILVA: *So it's true that someone paid you.*

PARKER: *I'm not going to let you twist my words around. No one paid me anything.*

DI SILVA: *You did it as a favor?*

PARKER: *No. I thought I was acting on your instructions.*

DI SILVA: *You said the man called you by name.*

PARKER: *Yes.*

DI SILVA: *How did he know your name?*

PARKER: *I don't know.*

DI SILVA: *Oh, come on. You must have some idea. Maybe it was a lucky guess. Maybe he just looked around that courtroom and said, There's someone who looks like her name could be Jennifer Parker. Do you think that was it?*

PARKER: *I've told you. I don't know.*

DI SILVA: *How long have you and Michael Moretti been sweethearts?*

PARKER: *Mr. Di Silva, we've gone all over this. You've been questioning me now for five hours. I'm tired. I have nothing more to add. May I be excused?*

DI SILVA: *If you move out of that chair I'll have you placed under arrest. You're in big trouble, Miss Parker. There's only one way you're going to get out*

> *of it. Stop lying and start telling the truth.*
>
> PARKER: *I've told you the truth. I've told you everything I know.*
>
> DI SILVA: *Except the name of the man who handed you the envelope. I want his name and I want to know how much he paid you.*

There were thirty more pages of transcript. Robert Di Silva had done everything but beat Jennifer Parker with a rubber hose. She had stuck to her story.

Adam closed the transcript and wearily rubbed his eyes. It was two A.M.

Tomorrow he would dispose of the Jennifer Parker matter.

To Adam Warner's surprise, the Jennifer Parker case would not be disposed of so easily. Because Adam was a methodical man he ran a check on Jennifer Parker's background. As far as he could determine, she had no crime connections, nor was there anything to link her with Michael Moretti.

There was something about the case that disturbed Adam. Jennifer Parker's defense was too flimsy. If she were working for Moretti, he would have protected her with a reasonably plausible story. As it was, her story was so transparently naïve that it had a ring of truth about it.

At noon Adam received a call from the District Attorney. "How goes it, Adam?"

"Fine, Robert."

"I understand you're handling the hatchet-man job on the Jennifer Parker matter."

Adam Warner winced at the phrase. "I've agreed to make a recommendation, yes."

"I'm going to put her away for a long time." Adam was taken aback by the hatred in the District Attorney's voice.

"Easy, Robert. She's not disbarred yet."

Di Silva chuckled. "I'll leave that to you, my friend." His

tone changed. "I hear on the grapevine that you may be moving to Washington soon. I want you to know that you can count on my full support."

Which was considerable, Adam Warner knew. The District Attorney had been around a long time. He knew where the bodies were buried and he knew how to squeeze the most out of that information.

"Thanks, Robert. I appreciate that."

"My pleasure, Adam. I'll wait to hear from you."

Meaning Jennifer Parker. The quid pro quo Stewart Needham had mentioned, with the girl used as a pawn. Adam Warner thought about Robert Di Silva's words: *I'm going to put her away for a long time.* From reading the transcript, Adam judged that there was no real evidence against Jennifer Parker. Unless she confessed, or unless someone came forward with information that proved criminal complicity, Di Silva would not be able to touch the girl. He was counting on Adam to give him his vengeance.

The cold, harsh words of the transcript were clear-cut, and yet Adam wished he could have heard the tone of Jennifer Parker's voice when she denied her guilt.

There were pressing matters claiming Adam's attention, important cases involving major clients. It would have been easy to go ahead and carry out the wishes of Stewart Needham, Judge Lawrence Waldman and Robert Di Silva, but some instinct made Adam Warner hesitate. He picked up Jennifer Parker's file again, scribbled some notes and began to make some long-distance telephone calls.

Adam had been given a responsibility and he intended to carry it through to the best of his ability. He was all too familiar with the long, back-breaking hours of study and hard work it took to become an attorney and to pass the bar. It was a prize that took years to attain, and he was not about to deprive someone of it unless he was cerain there was justification.

The following morning Adam Warner was on a plane to

Seattle, Washington. He had meetings with Jennifer Parker's law professors, with the head of a law firm where she had clerked for two summers, and with some of Jennifer's former classmates.

Stewart Needham telephoned Adam in Seattle. "What are you doing up there, Adam? You've got a big case load waiting for you back here. That Parker thing should have been a snap."

"A few questions have arisen," Adam said carefully. "I'll be back in a day or so, Stewart."

There was a pause. "I see. Let's not waste any more time on her than we have to."

By the time Adam Warner left Seattle, he felt he knew Jennifer Parker almost as well as she knew herself. He had built up a portrait of her in his mind, a mental identikit, with pieces filled in by her law professors, her landlady, members of the law firm where she had served as a clerk, and classmates. The picture that Adam had acquired bore no resemblance to the picture Robert Di Silva had given him. Unless Jennifer Parker was the most consummate actress who ever lived, there was no way she could have been involved in a plot to free a man like Michael Moretti.

Now, almost two weeks after he had had that morning conversation with Stewart Needham, Adam Warner found himself facing the girl whose past he had been exploring. Adam had seen newspaper pictures of Jennifer, but they had not prepared him for the impact she made in person. Even in an old robe, without makeup, and her dark brown hair bath-damp, she was breathtaking.

Adam said, "I've been assigned to investigate your part in the Michael Moretti trial, Miss Parker."

"Have you now!" Jennifer could feel an anger rising in her. It started as a spark and became a flame that exploded inside her. They still were not through with her. They were going to make her pay for the rest of her life. Well, she had had enough.

When Jennifer spoke, her voice was trembling. "I have nothing to say to you! You go back and tell them whatever you please. I did something stupid, but as far as I know, there's no law against stupidity. The District Attorney thinks someone paid me off." She waved a scornful hand in the air. "If I had any money, do you think I'd be living in a place like this?" Her voice was beginning to choke up. "I—I don't care what you do. All I want is to be left alone. Now please go away!"

Jennifer turned and fled into the bathroom, slamming the door behind her.

She stood against the sink, taking deep breaths, wiping the tears from her eyes. She knew she had behaved stupidly. *That's twice,* she thought wryly. She should have handled Adam Warner differently. She should have tried to explain, instead of attacking him. Maybe then she would not be disbarred. But she knew that was wishful thinking. Sending someone to question her was a charade. The next step would be to serve her with an order to show cause, and the formal machinery would be set in motion. There would be a trial panel of three attorneys who would make their recommendation to the Disciplinary Board which would make its report to the Board of Governors. The recommendation was a foregone conclusion: disbarment. She would be forbidden to practice law in the state of New York. Jennifer thought bitterly, *There's one bright side to this. I can get into the* Guinness Book of Records *for the shortest law career in history.*

She stepped into the bath again and lay back, letting the still-warm water lap at her, soothing away her tension. At this moment she was too tired to care what happened to her. She closed her eyes and let her mind drift. She was half asleep when the chill of the water awakened her. She had no idea how long she had lain in the tub. Reluctantly she stepped out and began toweling herself dry. She was no longer hungry. The scene with Adam Warner had taken her appetite away.

Jennifer combed her hair and creamed her face and decided she would go to bed without dinner. In the morning she would telephone about the ride to Seattle. She opened the bathroom door and walked into the living room.

Adam Warner was seated in a chair, leafing through a magazine. He looked up as Jennifer came into the room, naked.

"I'm sorry," Adam said. "I—"

Jennifer gave a small cry of alarm and fled to the bathroom, where she put on her robe. When she stepped out to confront Adam again, Jennifer was furious.

"The inquisition is over. I asked you to leave."

Adam put the magazine down and said quietly, "Miss Parker, do you think we could discuss this calmly for a moment?"

"No!" All the old rage boiled up in Jennifer again. "I have nothing more to say to you or your damned disciplinary committee. I'm tired of being treated like—like I'm some kind of criminal!"

"Have I said you were a criminal?" Adam asked quietly.

"You—isn't that why you're here?"

"I told you why I'm here. I'm empowered to investigate and recommend for or against disbarment proceedings. I want to get your side of the story."

"I see. And how do I buy you off?"

Adam's face tightened. "I'm sorry, Miss Parker." He rose to his feet and started for the door.

"Just a minute!" Adam turned. "Forgive me," she said. "I—everybody seems to be the enemy. I apologize."

"Your apology is accepted."

Jennifer was suddenly aware of the flimsy robe she was wearing. "If you still want to ask me questions, I'll put some clothes on and we can talk."

"Fair enough. Have you had dinner?"

She hesitated. "I—"

"I know a little French restaurant that's just perfect for inquisitions."

It was a quiet, charming bistro on 56th Street on the East Side.

"Not too many people know about this place," Adam Warner said when they had been seated. "It's owned by a young French couple who used to work at Les Pyrénées. The food is excellent."

Jennifer had to take Adam's word for it. She was incapable of tasting anything. She had not eaten all day, but she was so nervous that she was unable to force any food down her throat. She tried to relax, but it was impossible. No matter how much he pretended, the charming man seated opposite her was the enemy. And he *was* charming, Jennifer had to admit. He was amusing and attractive, and under other circumstances Jennifer would have enjoyed the evening enormously; but these were not other circumstances. Her whole future was in the hands of this stranger. The next hour or two would determine in which direction the rest of her life would move.

Adam was going out of his way to try to relax her. He had recently returned from a trip to Japan where he had met with top government officials. A special banquet had been prepared in his honor.

"Have you ever eaten chocolate-covered ants?" Adam asked.

"No."

He grinned. "They're better than the chocolate-covered grasshoppers."

He talked about a hunting trip he had taken the year before in Alaska, where he had been attacked by a bear. He talked about everything but why they were there.

Jennifer had been steeling herself for the moment when

Adam would begin to interrogate her, yet when he finally brought up the subject, her whole body went rigid.

He had finished dessert and he said quietly, "I'm going to ask you some questions, and I don't want you to get upset. Okay?"

There was a sudden lump in Jennifer's throat. She was not sure she would be able to speak. She nodded.

"I want you to tell me exactly what happened in the courtroom that day. Everything you remember, everything you felt. Take your time."

Jennifer had been prepared to defy him, to tell him to do whatever he pleased about her. But somehow, sitting across from Adam Warner, listening to his quiet voice, Jennifer's resistance was gone. The whole experience was still so vivid in her mind that it hurt just to think about it. She had spent more than a month trying to forget it. Now he was asking her to go through it again.

She took a deep, shaky breath and said, "All right."

Haltingly, Jennifer began to recount the events in the courtroom, gradually speaking more rapidly as it all came to life again. Adam sat there quietly listening, studying her, saying nothing.

When Jennifer had finished, Adam said, "The man who gave you the envelope—was he in the District Attorney's office earlier that morning when you were sworn in?"

"I've thought about that. I honestly don't remember. There were so many people in the office that day and they were all strangers."

"Had you ever seen the man before, anywhere?"

Jennifer shook her head helplessly. "I can't recall. I don't think so."

"You said you saw him talking to the District Attorney just before he walked over to give you the envelope. Did you see the District Attorney hand him the envelope?"

"I—no."

"Did you actually see this man talking to the District Attorney, or was he just in the group around him?"

Jennifer closed her eyes for a second, trying to bring back that moment. "I'm sorry. Everything was so confused. I—I just don't know."

"Do you have any idea how he could have known your name?"

"No."

"Or why he selected you?"

"That one's easy. He probably knew an idiot when he saw one." She shook her head. "No. I'm sorry, Mr. Warner, I have no idea."

Adam said, "A lot of pressure is being brought to bear on this. District Attorney Di Silva has been after Michael Moretti for a long time. Until you came along, he had an airtight case. The D.A.'s not very happy with you."

"I'm not very happy with me, either." Jennifer could not blame Adam Warner for what he was about to do. He was just carrying out his job. They were out to get her and they had succeeded. Adam Warner was not responsible; he was merely the instrument they were using.

Jennifer felt a sudden, overwhelming urge to be alone. She did not want anyone else to see her misery.

"I'm sorry," she apologized. "I—I'm not feeling very well. I'd like to go home, please."

Adam studied her a moment. "Would it make you feel any better if I told you I'm going to recommend that disbarment proceedings against you be dropped?"

It took several seconds for Adam's words to sink in. Jennifer stared at him, speechless, searching his face, looking into those gray-blue eyes behind the horn-rimmed glasses. "Do—do you really mean that?"

"Being a lawyer is very important to you, isn't it?" Adam asked.

Jennifer thought of her father and his comfortable little law office, and of the conversations they used to have, and the long years of law school, and their hopes and dreams. *We're going into partnership. You hurry up and get that law degree.*

"Yes," Jennifer whispered.

"If you can get over a rough beginning, I have a feeling you'll be a very good one."

Jennifer gave him a grateful smile. "Thank you. I'm going to try."

She said the words over again in her mind. *I'm going to try!* It did not matter that she shared a small and dingy office with a seedy private detective and a man who repossessed cars. It was a *law* office. She was a member of the legal profession, and they were going to allow her to practice law. She was filled with a feeling of exultation. She looked across at Adam and knew she would be forever grateful to this man.

The waiter had begun to clear the dishes from the table. Jennifer tried to speak, but it came out a cross between a laugh and a sob. "Mr. Warner—"

He said gravely, "After all we've been through together, I think it should be Adam."

"Adam—"

"Yes?"

"I hope it won't ruin our relationship, but—" Jennifer moaned, "I'm starved!"

5

The next few weeks raced by. Jennifer found herself busy from early morning until late at night, serving summonses—court orders to appear to answer a legal action—and subpoenas—court orders to appear as a witness. She knew that her chances of getting into a large law firm were nonexistent, for after the fiasco she had been involved in, no one would dream of hiring her. She would just have to find some way to make a reputation for herself, to begin all over.

In the meantime, there was the pile of summonses and subpoenas on her desk from Peabody & Peabody. While it was not exactly practicing law, it was twelve-fifty and expenses.

Occasionally, when Jennifer worked late, Ken Bailey would take her out to dinner. On the surface he was a cynical man, but Jennifer felt that it was a facade. She sensed that he was lonely. He had been graduated from Brown University and was bright and well-read. She could not imagine why he was satisfied to spend his life working out of a dreary office, trying to locate stray husbands and wives. It was as though he had resigned himself to being a failure and was afraid to try for success.

Once, when Jennifer brought up the subject of his marriage, he growled at her, "It's none of your business," and Jennifer had never mentioned it again.

Otto Wenzel was completely different. The short, potbellied little man was happily married. He regarded Jennifer as a daughter and he constantly brought her soups and cakes that his wife made. Unfortunately, his wife was a terrible cook, but Jennifer forced herself to eat whatever Otto Wenzel brought in, because she did not want to hurt his feelings. One Friday evening Jennifer was invited to the Wenzel home for dinner. Mrs. Wenzel had prepared stuffed cabbage, her specialty. The cabbage was soggy, the meat inside was hard, and the rice half-cooked. The whole dish swam in a lake of chicken fat. Jennifer attacked it bravely, taking small bites and pushing the food around on her plate to make it seem as though she were eating.

"How do you like it?" Mrs. Wenzel beamed.

"It—it's one of my favorites."

From that time on, Jennifer had dinner at the Wenzel's every Friday night, and Mrs. Wenzel always prepared Jennifer's favorite dish.

Early one morning, Jennifer received a telephone call from the personal secretary of Mr. Peabody, Jr.

"Mr. Peabody would like to see you this morning at eleven o'clock. Be prompt, please."

"Yes, ma'am."

In the past, Jennifer had only dealt with secretaries and law clerks in the Peabody office. It was a large, prestigious firm, one that young lawyers dreamed of being invited to join. On the way to keep her appointment, Jennifer began to fantasize. If Mr. Peabody himself wanted to see her, it had to be about something important. He probably had seen the light and was going to offer her a job as a lawyer with his firm, to give her a chance to show what she could do. She was going to surprise all of them. Some day it might even be Peabody, Peabody & Parker.

Jennifer killed thirty minutes in the corridor outside the office, and at exactly eleven o'clock, she entered the reception room. She did not want to seem too eager. She was kept waiting for two hours, and was finally ushered into the office of Mr. Peabody, Jr. He was a tall, thin man wearing a vested suit and shoes that had been made for him in London.

He did not invite her to sit down. "Miss Potter—" He had an unpleasant, high-pitched voice.

"Parker."

He picked up a piece of paper from his desk. "This is a summons. I would like you to serve it."

At that instant, Jennifer sensed that she was not going to become a member of the firm.

Mr. Peabody, Jr., handed Jennifer the summons and said, "Your fee will be five hundred dollars."

Jennifer was sure she had misunderstood him. "Did you say five hundred dollars?"

"That is correct. If you are successful, of course."

"There's a problem," Jennifer guessed.

"Well, yes," Mr. Peabody, Jr., admitted. "We've been trying to serve this man for more than a year. His name is William Carlisle. He lives on an estate in Long Island and he never leaves his house. To be quite truthful, a dozen people have tried to serve him. He has a bodyguard-butler who keeps everyone away."

Jennifer said, "I don't see how I—"

Mr. Peabody, Jr. leaned forward. "There's a great deal of money at stake here. But I can't get William Carlisle into court unless I can serve him, Miss Potter." Jennifer did not bother to correct him. "Do you think you can handle it?"

Jennifer thought about what she could do with five hundred dollars. "I'll find a way."

At two o'clock that afternoon, Jennifer was standing outside the imposing estate of William Carlisle. The house itself was Georgian, set in the middle of ten acres of beautiful, carefully tended grounds. A curving driveway led to the front of the house, which was framed by graceful fir trees. Jennifer had given a lot of thought to her problem. Since it was impossible to get into the house, the only solution was to find a way to get Mr. William Carlisle to come out.

Half a block down the street was a gardener's truck. Jennifer studied the truck a moment, then walked over to it, looking for the gardeners. There were three of them at work, and they were Japanese.

Jennifer walked up to the men. "Who's in charge here?"

One of them straightened up. "I am."

"I have a little job for you . . ." Jennifer began.

"Sorry, miss. Too busy."

"This will only take five minutes."

"No. Impossible to—"

"I'll pay you one hundred dollars."

The three men stopped to look at her. The chief gardener said, "You pay us one hundred dollars for five minutes' work?"

"That's right."

"What we have to do . . . ?"

Five minutes later, the gardener's truck pulled into the driveway of William Carlisle's estate and Jennifer and the three gardeners got out. Jennifer looked around, selected a beautiful tree next to the front door and said to the gardeners, "Dig it up."

They took their spades from the truck and began to dig. Before a minute had gone by, the front door burst open and an enormous man in a butler's uniform came storming out.

"What the hell do you think you're doing?"

"Long Island Nursery," Jennifer said crisply. "We're takin' out all these trees."

The butler stared at her. "You're *what*?"

Jennifer held up a piece of paper. "I have an order here to dig up these trees."

"That's impossible! Mr. Carlisle would have a fit!" He turned to the gardeners. "You stop that!"

"Look, mister," Jennifer said, "I'm just doin' my job." She looked at the gardeners. "Keep diggin', fellas."

"No!" the butler shouted. "I'm telling you there's been a mistake! Mr. Carlisle didn't order any trees dug up."

Jennifer shrugged and said, "My boss says he did."

"Where can I get in touch with your boss?"

Jennifer looked at her watch. "He's out on a job in Brooklyn. He should be back in the office around six."

The butler glared at her, furious. "Just a minute! Don't do anything until I return."

"Keep diggin'," Jennifer told the gardeners.

The butler turned and hurried into the house, slamming the door behind him. A few moments later the door opened and the butler returned, accompanied by a tiny middle-aged man.

"Would you mind telling me what the devil is going on here?"

"What business is it of yours?" Jennifer demanded.

"I'll tell you what business it is of mine," he snapped. "I'm William Carlisle and this happens to be my property."

"In that case, Mr. Carlisle," Jennifer said, "I have something for you." She reached in her pocket and put the summons in his hand. She turned to the gardeners. "You can stop digging now."

Early the next morning Adam Warner telephoned. Jennifer recognized his voice instantly.

"I thought you would like to know," Adam said, "that the

disbarment proceedings have been officially dropped. You have nothing more to worry about."

Jennifer closed her eyes and said a silent prayer of thanks. "I—I can't tell you how much I appreciate what you've done."

"Justice isn't always blind."

Adam did not mention the scene he had had with Stewart Needham and Robert Di Silva. Needham had been disappointed, but philosophical.

The District Attorney had carried on like a raging bull. "You let that bitch get away with this? Jesus Christ, she's Mafia, Adam! Couldn't you see that? She's conning you!"

And on and on, until Adam had tired of it.

"All the evidence against her was circumstantial, Robert. She was in the wrong place at the wrong time and she got mousetrapped. That doesn't spell Mafia to me."

Finally Robert Di Silva had said, "Okay, so she's still a lawyer. I just hope to God she practices in New York, because the minute she sets foot in any of my courtrooms, I'm going to wipe her out."

Now, talking to Jennifer, Adam said nothing of this. Jennifer had made a deadly enemy, but there was nothing that could be done about it. Robert Di Silva was a vindictive man, and Jennifer was a vulnerable target. She was bright and idealistic and achingly young and lovely.

Adam knew he must never see her again.

There were days and weeks and months when Jennifer was ready to quit. The sign on the door still read *Jennifer Parker, Attorney at Law*, but it did not deceive anyone, least of all Jennifer. She was not practicing law: Her days were spent running around in rain and sleet and snow, delivering subpoenas and summons to people who hated her for it. Now and then she accepted a *pro bono* case, helping the elderly get food stamps, solving various legal problems of ghetto Blacks and

Puerto Ricans and other underprivileged people. But she felt trapped.

The nights were worse than the days. They were endless, for Jennifer had insomnia and when she did sleep, her dreams were filled with demons. It had begun the night her mother had deserted Jennifer and her father, and she had not been able to exorcise whatever it was that was causing her nightmares.

She was consumed by loneliness. She went out on occasional dates with young lawyers, but inevitably she found herself comparing them to Adam Warner, and they all fell short. There would be dinner and a movie or a play, followed by a struggle at her front door. Jennifer was never sure whether they expected her to go to bed with them because they had bought her dinner, or because they had had to climb up and down four steep flights of stairs. There were times when she was strongly tempted to say *Yes*, just to have someone with her for the night, someone to hold, someone to share herself with. But she needed more in her bed than a warm body that talked; she needed someone who cared, someone for whom she could care.

The most interesting men who propositioned Jennifer were all married, and she flatly refused to go out with any of them. She remembered a line from Billy Wilder's wonderful film *The Apartment*: "When you're in love with a married man you shouldn't wear mascara." Jennifer's mother had destroyed a marriage, had killed Jennifer's father. She could never forget that.

Christmas came and New Year's Eve, and Jennifer spent them alone. There had been a heavy snowfall and the city looked like a gigantic Christmas card. Jennifer walked the streets, watching pedestrians hurrying to the warmth of their homes and families, and she ached with a feeling of emptiness.

She missed her father terribly. She was glad when the holidays were over. *Nineteen seventy is going to be a better year,* Jennifer told herself.

On Jennifer's worst days, Ken Bailey would cheer her up. He took her out to Madison Square Garden to watch the Rangers play, to a disco club and to an occasional play or movie. Jennifer knew he was attracted to her, and yet he kept a barrier between them.

In March, Otto Wenzel decided to move to Florida with his wife.

"My bones are getting too old for these New York winters," he told Jennifer.

"I'll miss you." Jennifer meant it. She had grown genuinely fond of him.

"Take care of Ken."

Jennifer looked at him quizzically.

"He never told you, did he?"

"Told me what?"

He hesitated, then said, "His wife committed suicide. He blames himself."

Jennifer was shocked. "How terrible! Why—why did she do it?"

"She caught Ken in bed with a young blond man."

"Oh, my God!"

"She shot Ken and then turned the gun on herself. He lived. She didn't."

"How awful! I had no idea that . . . that—"

"I know. He smiles a lot, but he carries his own hell with him."

"Thanks for telling me."

When Jennifer returned to the office, Ken said, "So old Otto's leaving us."

"Yes."

Ken Bailey grinned. "I guess it's you and me against the world."

"I guess so."

And in a way, Jennifer thought, *it is true.*

Jennifer looked at Ken with different eyes now. They had lunches and dinners together, and Jennifer could detect no signs of homosexuality about him but she knew that Otto Wenzel had told her the truth: Ken Bailey carried his own private hell with him.

A few clients walked in off the street. They were usually poorly dressed, bewildered and, in some instances, out-and-out nut cases.

Prostitutes came in to ask Jennifer to handle their bail, and Jennifer was amazed at how young and lovely some of them were. They became a small but steady source of income. She could not find out who sent them to her. When she mentioned it to Ken Bailey, he shrugged in a gesture of ignorance and walked away.

Whenever a client came to see Jennifer, Ken Bailey would discreetly leave. He was like a proud father, encouraging Jennifer to succeed.

Jennifer was offered several divorce cases and turned them down. She could not forget what one of her law professors had once said: *Divorce is to the practice of law what proctology is to the practice of medicine.* Most divorce lawyers had bad reputations. The maxim was that when a married couple saw red, lawyers saw green. A high-priced divorce lawyer was known as a *bomber,* for he would use legal high explosives to win a case for a client and, in the process, often destroyed the husband, the wife and the children.

A few of the clients who came into Jennifer's office were different in a way that puzzled her.

They were well dressed, with an air of affluence about them, and the cases they brought to her were not the nickel-and-dime cases Jennifer had been accustomed to handling. There were estates to be settled that amounted to substantial sums of money, and lawsuits that any large firm would have been delighted to represent.

"Where did you hear about me?" Jennifer would ask.

The replies she got were always evasive. From a friend . . . I read about you . . . your name was mentioned at a party . . . It was not until one of her clients, in the course of explaining his problems, mentioned Adam Warner that Jennifer suddenly understood.

"Mr. Warner sent you to me, didn't he?"

The client was embarrassed. "Well, as a matter of fact, he suggested it might be better if I didn't mention his name."

Jennifer decided to telephone Adam. After all, she did owe him a debt of thanks. She would be polite, but formal. Naturally, she would not let him get the impression that she was calling him for any reason other than to express her appreciation. She rehearsed the conversation over and over in her mind. When Jennifer finally got up enough nerve to telephone, a secretary informed her that Mr. Warner was in Europe and was not expected back for several weeks. It was an anticlimax that left Jennifer depressed.

She found herself thinking of Adam Warner more and more often. She kept remembering the evening he had come to her apartment and how badly she had behaved. He had been wonderful to put up with her childish behavior when she had taken out her anger on him. Now, in addition to everything else he had done for her, he was sending her clients.

Jennifer waited three weeks and then telephoned Adam again. This time he was in South America.

"Is there any message?" his secretary asked.

Jennifer hesitated. "No message."

Jennifer tried to put Adam out of her mind, but it was impossible. She wondered whether he was married or engaged. She wondered what it would be like to be Mrs. Adam Warner. She wondered if she were insane.

From time to time Jennifer came across the name of Michael Moretti in the newspapers or weekly magazines. There was an in-depth story in the *New Yorker* magazine on Antonio Granelli and the eastern Mafia Families. Antonio Granelli was reported to be in failing health and Michael Moretti, his son-in-law, was preparing to take over his empire. *Life* magazine ran a story about Michael Moretti's lifestyle, and at the end of the story it spoke of Moretti's trial. Camillo Stela was serving time in Leavenworth, while Michael Moretti was free. It reminded its readers how Jennifer Parker had destroyed the case that would have sent him to prison or the electric chair. As Jennifer read the article, her stomach churned. The electric chair? She could cheerfully have pulled the switch on Michael Moretti herself.

Most of Jennifer's clients were unimportant, but the education was priceless. Over the months, Jennifer came to know every room in the Criminal Courts Building at 100 Centre Street and the people who inhabited them.

When one of her clients was arrested for shoplifting, mugging, prostitution or drugs, Jennifer would head downtown to arrange bail, and bargaining was a way of life.

"Bail is set at five hundred dollars."

"Your Honor, the defendant doesn't have that much money. If the court will reduce bail to two hundred dollars, he can go back to work and keep supporting his family."

"Very well. Two hundred."

"Thank you, Your Honor."

Jennifer got to know the supervisor of the complaint room, where copies of the arrest reports were sent.

"You again, Parker! For God's sake, don't you ever sleep?"

"Hi, Lieutenant. A client of mine was picked up on a vagrancy charge. May I see the arrest sheet? The name is Connery. Clarence Connery."

"Tell me something, honey. Why would you come down here at three A.M. to defend a vagrant?"

Jennifer grinned. "It keeps me off the streets."

She became familiar with night court, held in Room 218 of the Centre Street courthouse. It was a smelly, overcrowded world, with its own arcane jargon. Jennifer was baffled by it at first.

"Parker, your client is booked on bedpain."

"My client is booked on *what*?"

"Bedpain. Burglary, with a Break, Enter, Dwelling, Person, Armed, Intent to kill, at Night. Get it?"

"Got it."

"I'm here to represent Miss Luna Tarner."

"Jesus H. Christ!"

"Would you tell me what the charges are?"

"Hold on. I'll find her ticket. Luna Tarner. That's a hot one . . . here we are. Pross. Picked up by CWAC, down below."

"*Quack?*"

"You're new around here, huh? *CWAC* is the City-Wide Anti-Crime unit. A *pross* is a hooker, and *down below* is south of Forty-Second Street. Capish?"

"Capish."

Night court depressed Jennifer. It was filled with a human tide that ceaselessly surged in and out, washed up on the shores of justice.

There were more than a hundred and fifty cases heard each night. There were whores and transvestites, stinking, battered drunks and drug addicts. There were Puerto Ricans and Mexicans and Jews and Irish and Greeks and Italians, and they were accused of rape and theft and possession of guns or dope or assault or prostitution. And they all had one thing in common: They were poor. They were poor and defeated and lost. They were the dregs, the misfits whom the affluent society had passed by. A large proportion of them came from Central Harlem, and because there was no more room in the prison system, all but the most serious offenders were dismissed or fined. They returned home to St. Nicholas Avenue and Morningside and Manhattan Avenues, where in three and one-half square miles there lived two hundred and thirty-three thousand Blacks, eight thousand Puerto Ricans, and an estimated one million rats.

The majority of clients who came to Jennifer's office were people who had been ground down by poverty, the system, themselves. They were people who had long since surrendered. Jennifer found that their fears fed her self-confidence. She did not feel superior to them. She certainly could not hold herself up as a shining example of success, and yet she knew there was one big difference between her and her clients: She would never give up.

Ken Bailey introduced Jennifer to Father Francis Joseph Ryan. Father Ryan was in his late fifties, a radiant, vital man with crisp gray-and-black hair that curled about his ears. He was always in serious need of a haircut. Jennifer liked him at once.

From time to time, when one of his parishioners would disappear, Father Ryan would come to Ken and enlist his services. Invariably, Ken would find the errant husband, wife, daughter or son. There would never be a charge.

"It's a down payment on heaven," Ken would explain.

One afternoon when Jennifer was alone Father Ryan dropped by the office.

"Ken's out, Father Ryan. He won't be back today."

"It's really you I wanted to see, Jennifer," Father Ryan said. He sat down in the uncomfortable old wooden chair in front of Jennifer's desk. "I have a friend who has a bit of a problem."

That was the way he always started out with Ken.

"Yes, Father?"

"She's an elderly parishioner, and the poor dear's having trouble getting her Social Security payments. She moved into my neighborhood a few months ago and some damned computer lost all her records, may it rust in hell."

"I see."

"I knew you would," Father Ryan said, getting to his feet. "I'm afraid there won't be any money in it for you."

Jennifer smiled. "Don't worry about that. I'll try to straighten things out."

She had thought it would be a simple matter, but it had taken her almost three days to get the computer reprogrammed.

One morning a month later, Father Ryan walked into Jennifer's office and said, "I hate to bother you, my dear, but I have a friend who has a bit of a problem. I'm afraid he has no—" He hesitated.

"—Money," Jennifer guessed.

"Ah! That's it. Exactly. But the poor fellow needs help badly."

"All right. Tell me about him."

"His name is Abraham. Abraham Wilson. He's the son of one of my parishioners. Abraham is serving a life sentence in Sing Sing for killing a liquor store owner during a holdup."

"If he was convicted and is serving his sentence, I don't see how I can help, Father."

Father Ryan looked at Jennifer and sighed. "That's not his problem."

"It isn't?"

"No. A few weeks ago Abraham killed another man—a fellow prisoner named Raymond Thorpe. They're going to try him for murder, and go for the death penalty."

Jennifer had read something about the case. "If I remember correctly, he beat the man to death."

"So they say."

Jennifer picked up a pad and a pen. "Do you know if there were any witnesses?"

"I'm afraid so."

"How many?"

"Oh, a hundred or so. It happened in the prison yard, you see."

"Terrific. What is it you want me to do?"

Father Ryan said simply, "Help Abraham."

Jennifer put down her pen. "Father, it's going to take your Boss to help him." She sat back in her chair. "He's going in with three strikes against him. He's Black, he's a convicted murderer, and he killed another man in front of a hundred witnesses. Assuming he did it, there just aren't any grounds for defense. If another prisoner was threatening him, there were guards he could have asked to help him. Instead, he took the law into his own hands. There isn't a jury in the world that wouldn't convict him."

"He's still a fellow human being. Would you just talk to him?"

Jennifer sighed. "I'll talk to him if you want me to, but I won't make any commitment."

Father Ryan nodded. "I understand. It would probably mean a great deal of publicity."

They were both thinking the same thing. Abraham Wilson was not the only one who had strikes against him.

Sing Sing Prison is situated at the town of Ossining, thirty miles upstate of Manhattan on the east bank of the Hudson

River, overlooking the Tappan Zee and Haverstraw Bay.

Jennifer went up by bus. She had telephoned the assistant warden and he had made arrangements for her to see Abraham Wilson, who was being held in solitary confinement.

During the bus ride, Jennifer was filled with a sense of purpose she had not felt in a long time. She was on her way to Sing Sing to meet a possible client charged with murder. This was the kind of case she had studied for, prepared herself for. She felt like a lawyer for the first time in a year, and yet she knew she was being unrealistic. She was not on her way to see a client. She was on her way to tell a man she could not represent him. She could not afford to become involved in a highly publicized case that she had no chance of winning.

Abraham Wilson would have to find someone else to defend him.

A dilapidated taxi took Jennifer from the bus station to the penitentiary, situated on seventy acres of land near the river. Jennifer rang the bell at the side entrance and a guard opened the door, checked off her name against his list, and directed her to the assistant warden's office.

The assistant warden was a large, square man with an old-fashioned military haircut and an acne-pitted face. His name was Howard Patterson.

"I would appreciate anything you can tell me about Abraham Wilson," Jennifer began.

"If you're looking for comfort, you're not going to get it here." Patterson glanced at the dossier on the desk in front of him. "Wilson's been in and out of prisons all his life. He was caught stealing cars when he was eleven, arrested on a mugging charge when he was thirteen, picked up for rape when he was fifteen, became a pimp at eighteen, served a sentence for putting one of his girls in the hospital . . ."

He leafed through the dossier. "You name it—stabbings, armed robbery and finally the big time—murder."

It was a depressing recital.

Jennifer asked, "Is there any chance that Abraham Wilson *didn't* kill Raymond Thorpe?"

"Forget it. Wilson's the first to admit it, but it wouldn't make any difference even if he denied it. We've got a hundred and twenty witnesses."

"May I see Mr. Wilson?"

Howard Patterson rose to his feet. "Sure, but you're wasting your time."

Abraham Wilson was the ugliest human being Jennifer Parker had ever seen. He was coal-black, with a nose that had been broken in several places, missing front teeth and tiny, shifty eyes set in a knife-scarred face. He was about six feet four inches and powerfully built. He had huge flat feet which made him lumber. If Jennifer had searched for one word to describe Abraham Wilson, it would have been *menacing*. She could imagine the effect this man would have on a jury.

Abraham Wilson and Jennifer were seated in a high-security visiting room, a thick wire mesh between them, a guard standing at the door. Wilson had just been taken out of solitary confinement and his beady eyes kept blinking against the light. If Jennifer had come to this meeting feeling she would probably not want to handle this case, after seeing Abraham Wilson she was positive. Merely sitting opposite him she could feel the hatred spewing out of the man.

Jennifer opened the conversation by saying, "My name is Jennifer Parker. I'm an attorney. Father Ryan asked me to see you."

Abraham Wilson spat through the screen, spraying Jennifer with saliva. "That mothafuckin' do-gooder."

It's a wonderful beginning, Jennifer thought. She carefully refrained from wiping the saliva from her face. "Is there anything you need here, Mr. Wilson?"

He gave her a toothless smile. "A piece of ass, baby. You innersted?"

She ignored that. "Do you want to tell me what happened?"

"Hey, you lookin' for my life story, you gotta pay me for it. I gonna sell it for da movin' pitchurs. Maybe I'll star in it mysef."

The anger coming out of him was frightening. All Jennifer wanted was to get out of there. The assistant warden had been right. She was wasting her time.

"I'm afraid there's really nothing I can do to help you unless you help me, Mr. Wilson. I promised Father Ryan I would at least come and talk to you."

Abraham Wilson gave her a toothless grin again. "That's mighty white of ya, sweetheart. Ya sure ya don't wanna change your mind 'bout that piece of ass?"

Jennifer rose to her feet. She had had enough. "Do you hate everybody?"

"Tell ya what, doll, you crawl inta my skin and I'll crawl inta yours, and then you'n me'll rap 'bout hate."

Jennifer stood there, looking into that ugly black face, digesting what he had said, and then she slowly sat down. "Do you want to tell me your side of the story, Abraham?"

He stared into her eyes, saying nothing. Jennifer waited, watching him, wondering what it must be like to wear that scarred black skin. She wondered how many scars were hidden inside the man.

The two of them sat there in a long silence. Finally, Abraham Wilson said, "I killed the somabitch."

"Why did you kill him?"

He shrugged. "The motha' was comin' at me with this great big butcher knife, and—"

"Don't con me. Prisoners don't walk around carrying butcher knives."

Wilson's face tightened and he said, "Get the fuck outa here, lady. I din't sen' for ya." He rose to his feet. "An' don't come round heah botherin' me no more, you heah? I'm a busy man."

He turned and walked over to the guard. A moment later they were both gone. That was that. Jennifer could at least tell Father Ryan that she had talked to the man. There was nothing further she could do.

A guard let Jennifer out of the building. She started across the courtyard toward the main gate, thinking about Abraham Wilson and her reaction to him. She disliked the man and, because of that, she was doing something she had no right to do: She was judging him. She had already pronounced him guilty and he had not yet had a trial. Perhaps someone *had* attacked him, not with a knife, of course, but with a rock or a brick. Jennifer stopped and stood there indecisively. Every instinct told her to go back to Manhattan and forget about Abraham Wilson.

Jennifer turned and walked back to the assistant warden's office.

"He's a hard case," Howard Patterson said. "When we can, we try rehabilitation instead of punishment, but Abraham Wilson's too far gone. The only thing that will calm him down is the electric chair."

What a weird piece of logic, Jennifer thought. "He told me the man he killed attacked him with a butcher knife."

"I guess that's possible."

The answer startled her. "What do you mean, 'that's possible'? Are you saying a convict in here could get possession of a knife? A butcher knife?"

Howard Patterson shrugged. "Miss Parker, we have twelve

hundred and forty convicts in this place, and some of them are men of great ingenuity. Come on. I'll show you something."

Patterson led Jennifer down a long corridor to a locked door. He selected a key from a large key ring, opened the door and turned on the light. Jennifer followed him into a small, bare room with built-in shelves.

"This is where we keep the prisoners' box of goodies." He walked over to a large box and lifted the lid.

Jennifer stared down into the box unbelievingly.

She looked up at Howard Patterson and said, "I want to see my client again."

6

Jennifer prepared for Abraham Wilson's trial as she had never prepared for anything before in her life. She spent endless hours in the law library checking for procedures and defenses, and with her client, drawing from him every scrap of information she could. It was no easy task. From the beginning, Wilson was truculent and sarcastic.

"You wanna know about me, honey? I got my first fuck when I was ten. How ole was you?"

Jennifer forced herself to ignore his hatred and his contempt, for she was aware that they covered up a deep fear. And so Jennifer persisted, demanding to know what Wilson's early life was like, what his parents were like, what had shaped the boy into the man. Over a period of weeks, Abraham Wilson's reluctance gave way to interest, and his interest finally gave way to fascination. He had never before had reason to think of himself in terms of what kind of person he was, or why.

Jennifer's prodding questions began to arouse memories,

some merely unpleasant, others unbearably painful. Several times during the sessions when Jennifer was questioning Abraham Wilson about his father, who had regularly given him savage beatings, Wilson would order Jennifer to leave him alone. She left, but she always returned.

If Jennifer had had little personal life before, she now had none. When she was not with Abraham Wilson, she was at her office, seven days a week, from early morning until long after midnight, reading everything she could find about the crimes of murder and manslaughter, voluntary and involuntary. She studied hundreds of appellate court decisions, briefs, affidavits, exhibits, motions, transcripts. She pored over files on intent and premeditation, self-defense, double jeopardy, and temporary insanity.

She studied ways to get the charge reduced to manslaughter.

Abraham had not planned to kill the man. But would a jury believe that? Particularly a local jury. The townspeople hated the prisoners in their midst. Jennifer moved for a change of venue, and it was granted. The trial would be held in Manhattan.

Jennifer had an important decision to make: Should she allow Abraham Wilson to testify? He presented a forbidding figure, but if the jurors were able to hear his side of the story from his own lips, they might have some sympathy for him. The problem was that putting Abraham Wilson on the stand would allow the prosecution to reveal Wilson's background and past record, including the previous murder he had committed.

Jennifer wondered which one of the assistant district attorneys Di Silva would assign to be her adversary. There were half a dozen very good ones who prosecuted murder trials, and Jennifer familiarized herself with their techniques.

She spent as much time as possible at Sing Sing, looking over the scene of the killing in the recreation yard, talking to guards and Abraham, and she interviewed dozens of convicts who had witnessed the killing.

"Raymond Thorpe attacked Abraham Wilson with a knife," Jennifer said. "A large butcher knife. You must have seen it."

"Me? I didn't see no knife."

"You *must* have. You were right there."

"Lady, I didn't see nothin'."

Not one of them was willing to get involved.

Occasionally Jennifer would take time out to have a regular meal, but usually she grabbed a quick sandwich at the coffee shop on the main floor of the courthouse. She was beginning to lose weight and she had dizzy spells.

Ken Bailey was becoming concerned about her. He took her to Forlini's across from the courthouse, and ordered a large lunch for her.

"Are you trying to kill yourself?" he demanded.

"Of course not."

"Have you looked in a mirror lately?"

"No."

He studied her and said, "If you have any sense, you'll drop this case."

"Why?"

"Because you're setting yourself up as a clay pigeon. Jennifer, I hear things on the street. The press is peeing in its collective pants, they're so eager to start taking potshots at you again."

"I'm an attorney," Jennifer said stubbornly. "Abraham Wilson is entitled to a fair trial. I'm going to try to see that he gets one." She saw the look of concern on Ken Bailey's face. "Don't worry about it. The case isn't going to get *that* much publicity."

"It isn't, huh? Do you know who's prosecuting?"

"No."

"Robert Di Silva."

* * *

Jennifer arrived at the Leonard Street entrance of the Criminal Courts Building and pushed her way past the people churning through the lobby, past the uniformed policemen, the detectives dressed like hippies, the lawyers identified by the briefcases they carried. Jennifer walked toward the large circular information desk, where no attendant had ever been posted, and took the elevator to the sixth floor. She was on her way to see the District Attorney. It had been almost a year since her last encounter with Robert Di Silva, and Jennifer was not looking forward to this one. She was going to inform him that she was resigning from Abraham Wilson's defense.

It had taken Jennifer three sleepless nights to make her decision. What it came down to finally was that the primary consideration had to be the best interests of her client. The Wilson case was not important enough for Di Silva to handle himself. The only reason, therefore, for the District Attorney's giving it his personal attention was because of Jennifer's involvement. Di Silva wanted vengeance. He was planning to teach Jennifer a lesson. And so she had finally decided she had no choice but to withdraw from Wilson's defense. She could not let him be executed because of a mistake she had once made. With her off the case, Robert Di Silva would probably deal with Wilson more leniently. Jennifer was on her way to save Abraham Wilson's life.

There was an odd feeling of reliving the past as she got off at the sixth floor and walked toward the familiar door marked *District Attorney, County of New York.* Inside, the same secretary was seated at the same desk.

"I'm Jennifer Parker. I have an appointment with—"

"Go right in," the secretary said. "The District Attorney is expecting you."

Robert Di Silva was standing behind his desk, chewing

on a wet cigar, giving orders to two assistants. He stopped as Jennifer entered.

"I was betting you wouldn't show up."

"I'm here."

"I thought you would have turned tail and run out of town by now. What do you want?"

There were two chairs opposite Robert Di Silva's desk, but he did not invite Jennifer to sit.

"I came here to talk about my client, Abraham Wilson."

Robert Di Silva sat down, leaned back in his chair and pretended to think. "Abraham Wilson . . . oh, yes. That's the nigger murderer who beat a man to death in prison. You shouldn't have any trouble defending him." He glanced at his two assistants and they left the room.

"Well, counselor?"

"I'd like to talk about a plea."

Robert Di Silva looked at her with exaggerated surprise. "You mean you came in to make a deal? You amaze me. I would have thought that someone with your great legal talent would be able to get him off scot-free."

"Mr. Di Silva, I know this looks like an open-and-shut case," Jennifer began, "but there are extenuating circumstances. Abraham Wilson was——"

District Attorney Di Silva interrupted. "Let me put it in legal language you can understand, counselor. You can take your extenuating circumstances and shove them up your ass!" He got to his feet and when he spoke his voice was trembling with rage. "Make a deal with you, lady? You fucked up my life! There's a dead body and your boy's going to burn for it. Do you hear me? I'm making it my personal business to see that he's sent to the chair."

"I came up here to withdraw from the case. You could reduce this to a manslaughter charge. Wilson's already in for life. You could——"

"No way! He's guilty of murder plain and simple!"

Jennifer tried to control her anger. "I thought the jury was supposed to decide that."

Robert Di Silva smiled at her without mirth. "You don't know how heartwarming it is to have an expert like you walk into my office and explain the law to me."

"Can't we forget our personal problems? I——"

"Not as long as I live. Say hello to your pal Michael Moretti for me."

Half an hour later, Jennifer was having coffee with Ken Bailey.

"I don't know what to do," Jennifer confessed. "I thought if I got off the case Abraham Wilson would stand a better chance. But Di Silva won't make a deal. He's not after Wilson—he's after me."

Ken Bailey looked at her thoughtfully. "Maybe he's trying to psych you out. He wants you running scared."

"I *am* running scared." She took a sip of her coffee. It tasted bitter. "It's a bad case. You should see Abraham Wilson. All the jury will have to do is *look* at him and they'll vote to convict."

"When does the trial come up?"

"In four weeks."

"Anything I can do to help?"

"Uh-huh. Put out a contract on Di Silva."

"Do you think there's any chance you can get Wilson an acquittal?"

"Looking at it from the pessimist's point of view, I'm trying my first case against the smartest District Attorney in the country, who has a vendetta against me, and my client is a convicted Black killer who killed again in front of a hundred and twenty witnesses."

"Terrific. What's the optimist's point of view?"

"I could get hit by a truck this afternoon."

* * *

The trial date was only three weeks away now. Jennifer arranged for Abraham Wilson to be transferred to the prison at Riker's Island. He was put in the House of Detention for Men, the largest and oldest jail on the island. Ninety-five percent of his prison mates were there awaiting trial for felonies: murder, arson, rape, armed robbery and sodomy.

No private cars were allowed on the island, and Jennifer was transported in a small green bus to the gray brick control building where she showed her identification. There were two armed guards in a green booth to the left of the building, and beyond that a gate where all unauthorized visitors were stopped. From the control building, Jennifer was driven down Hazen Street, the little road that went through the prison grounds, to the Anna M. Kross Center Building, where Abraham Wilson was brought to see her in the counsel room, with its eight cubicles reserved for attorney-client meetings.

Walking down the long corridor on her way to meet with Abraham Wilson, Jennifer thought: *This must be like the waiting room to hell.* There was an incredible cacophony. The prison was made of brick and steel and stone and tile. Steel gates were constantly opening and clanging shut. There were more than one hundred men in each cellblock, talking and yelling at the same time, with two television sets tuned to different channels and a music system playing country rock. Three hundred guards were assigned to the building, and their bellowing could be heard over the prison symphony.

A guard had told Jennifer, "Prison society is the politest society in the world. If a prisoner ever brushes up against another one, he immediately says, 'Excuse me.' Prisoners have a lot on their minds and the least little thing . . ."

Jennifer sat across from Abraham Wilson and she thought:

This man's life is in my hands. If he dies, it will be because I failed him. She looked into his eyes and saw the despair there.

"I'm going to do everything I can," Jennifer promised.

Three days before the Abraham Wilson trial was to begin, Jennifer learned that the presiding judge was to be the Honorable Lawrence Waldman, who had presided over the Michael Moretti trial and had tried to get Jennifer disbarred.

7

At four o'clock on a Monday morning in late September of 1970, the day the trial of Abraham Wilson was to begin, Jennifer awakened feeling tired and heavy-eyed. She had slept badly, her mind filled with dreams of the trial. In one of the dreams, Robert Di Silva had put her in the witness box and asked her about Michael Moretti. Each time Jennifer tried to answer the questions, the jurors interrupted her with a chant: *Liar! Liar! Liar!*

Each dream was different, but they were all similar. In the last one, Abraham Wilson was strapped in the electric chair. As Jennifer leaned over to console him, he spit in her face. Jennifer awoke trembling, and it was impossible for her to go back to sleep. She sat up in a chair until dawn and watched the sun come up. She was too nervous to eat. She wished she could have slept the night before. She wished that she were not so tense. She wished that this day was over.

As she bathed and dressed she had a premonition of doom.

She felt like wearing black, but she chose a green Chanel copy she had bought on sale at Loehmann's.

At eight-thirty, Jennifer Parker arrived at the Criminal Courts Building to begin the defense in the case of The People of the State of New York against Abraham Wilson. There was a crowd outside the entrance and Jennifer's first thought was that there had been an accident. She saw a battery of television cameras and microphones, and before Jennifer realized what was happening, she was surrounded by reporters.

A reporter said, "Miss Parker, this is your first time in court, isn't it, since you fouled up the Michael Moretti case for the District Attorney?"

Ken Bailey had warned her. *She* was the central attraction, not her client. The reporters were not there as objective observers; they were there as birds of prey and she was to be their carrion.

A young woman in jeans pushed a microphone up to Jennifer's face. "Is it true that District Attorney Di Silva is out to get you?"

"No comment." Jennifer began to fight her way toward the entrance of the building.

"The District Attorney issued a statement last night that he thinks you shouldn't be allowed to practice law in the New York courts. Would you like to say anything about that?"

"No comment." Jennifer had almost reached the entrance.

"Last year Judge Waldman tried to get you disbarred. Are you going to ask him to disqualify himself from—?"

Jennifer was inside the courthouse.

The trial was scheduled to take place in Room 37. The corridor outside was crowded with people trying to get in, but the courtroom was already full. It was buzzing with noise and there was a carnival atmosphere in the air. There were extra rows reserved for members of the press. *Di Silva saw to that,* Jennifer thought.

Abraham Wilson was seated at the defense table, towering over everyone around him like an evil mountain. He was dressed in a dark blue suit that was too small for him, and a white shirt and blue tie that Jennifer had bought him. They did not help. Abraham Wilson looked like an ugly killer in a dark blue suit. *He might just as well have worn his prison clothes,* Jennifer thought, discouraged.

Wilson was staring defiantly around the courtroom, glowering at everyone who met his look. Jennifer knew her client well enough now to understand that his belligerence was a cover-up for his fright; but what would come over to everyone —including the judge and the jury—was an impression of hostility and hatred. The huge man was a threat. They would regard him as someone to be feared, to be destroyed.

There was not a trace in Abraham Wilson's personality that was loveable. There was nothing about his appearance that could evoke sympathy. There was only that ugly, scarred face with its broken nose and missing teeth, that enormous body that would inspire fear.

Jennifer walked over to the defense table where Abraham Wilson was sitting and took the seat next to him. "Good morning, Abraham."

He glanced over at her and said, "I didn't think you was comin'."

Jennifer remembered her dream. She looked into his small, slitted eyes. "You knew I'd be here."

He shrugged indifferently. "It don't matter one way or another. They's gonna get me, baby. They's gonna convict me of murder and then they's gonna pass a law makin' it legal to boil me in oil, then they's gonna boil me in oil. This ain't gonna be no trial. This is gonna be a show. I hope you brung your popcorn."

There was a stir around the prosecutor's table and Jennifer looked up to see District Attorney Di Silva taking his place at the table next to a battery of assistants. He looked at Jennifer and smiled. Jennifer felt a growing sense of panic.

A court officer said, "All rise," and Judge Lawrence Waldman entered from the judge's robing room.

"Hear ye, Hear ye. All people having business with Part Thirty-seven of this Court, draw near, give your attention and you shall be heard. The Honorable Justice Lawrence Waldman presiding."

The only one who refused to stand was Abraham Wilson. Jennifer whispered out of the corner of her mouth, "Stand up!"

"Fuck 'em, baby. They gonna have to come and drag me up."

Jennifer took his giant hand in hers. "On your feet, Abraham. We're going to beat them."

He looked at her for a long moment, then slowly got to his feet, towering over her.

Judge Waldman took his place on the bench. The spectators resumed their seats. The court clerk handed a court calendar to the judge.

"The People of the State of New York versus Abraham Wilson, charged with the murder of Raymond Thorpe."

Jennifer's instinct normally would have been to fill the jury box with Blacks, but because of Abraham Wilson she was not so sure. Wilson was not one of them. He was a renegade, a killer, "a disgrace to their race." They might convict him more readily than would whites. All Jennifer could do was try to keep the more obvious bigots off the jury. But bigots did not go around advertising. They would keep quiet about their prejudices, waiting to get their vengeance.

By late afternoon of the second day, Jennifer had used up her ten peremptory challenges. She felt that her *voir dire—*

the questioning of the jurors—was clumsy and awkward, while Di Silva's was smooth and skillful. He had the knack of putting the jurors at ease, drawing them into his confidence, making friends of them.

How could I have forgotten what a good actor Di Silva is? Jennifer wondered.

Di Silva did not exercise his peremptory challenges until Jennifer had exhausted hers, and she could not understand why. When she discovered the reason, it was too late. Di Silva had outsmarted her. Among the final prospective jurors questioned were a private detective, a bank manager and the mother of a doctor—all of them *Establishment*—and there was nothing now that Jennifer could do to keep them off the jury. The District Attorney had sandbagged her.

Robert Di Silva rose to his feet and began his opening statement.

"If it please the court"—he turned to the jury—"and you ladies and gentlemen of the jury, first of all I would like to thank you for giving up your valuable time to sit in this case." He smiled sympathetically. "I know what a disruption jury service can be. You all have jobs to get back to, families needing your attention."

It's as though he's one of them, Jennifer thought, *the thirteenth juror.*

"I promise to take up as little of your time as possible. This is really a very simple case. That's the defendant sitting over there—Abraham Wilson. The defendant is accused by the State of New York of murdering a fellow inmate at Sing Sing Prison, Raymond Thorpe. There's no doubt that he did. He's admitted it. Mr. Wilson's attorney is going to plead self-defense."

The District Attorney turned to look at the huge figure of Abraham Wilson, and the eyes of the jurors automatically followed him. Jennifer could see the reactions on their faces. She forced herself to concentrate on what District Attorney Di Silva was saying.

"A number of years ago twelve citizens, very much like yourselves, I am sure, voted to put Abraham Wilson away in a penitentiary. Because of certain legal technicalities, I am not permitted to discuss with you the crime that Abraham Wilson committed. I *can* tell you that that jury sincerely believed that locking Abraham Wilson up would prevent him from committing any further crimes. Tragically, they were wrong. For even locked away, Abraham Wilson was able to strike, to kill, to satisfy the blood lust in him. We know now, finally, that there is only one way to prevent Abraham Wilson from killing again. And that is to execute him. It won't bring back the life of Raymond Thorpe, but it can save the lives of other men who might otherwise become the defendant's next victims."

Di Silva walked along the jury box, looking each juror in the eye. "I told you that this case won't take up much of your time. I'll tell you why I said that. The defendant sitting over there—Abraham Wilson—murdered a man in cold blood. He has confessed to the killing. But even if he had not confessed, we have witnesses who saw Abraham Wilson commit that murder in cold blood. More than a hundred witnesses, in fact.

"Let us examine the phrase, 'in cold blood.' Murder for *any* reason is as distasteful to me as I know it is to you. But sometimes murders are committed for reasons we can at least understand. Let's say that someone with a weapon is threatening your loved one—a child, or a husband or a wife. Well, if you had a gun you might pull that trigger in order to save your loved one's life. You and I might not *condone* that kind of thing, but I'm sure we can at least understand it. Or, let's take another example. If you were suddenly awakened in the middle of the night by an intruder threatening your life and you had a chance to kill him to save yourself, and you killed him—well, I think we can all understand how *that* might happen. And that wouldn't make us desperate criminals or evil people, would it? It was something we did in the heat of the moment." Di Silva's voice hardened. "But *cold-blooded murder* is something else again. To take the life of another human being, without the excuse of any feelings or passions, to do it for money or drugs or the sheer pleasure of killing—"

He was deliberately prejudicing the jury, yet not overstepping the bounds, so that there could be no error calling for mistrial or reversal.

Jennifer watched the faces of the jurors, and there was no question but that Robert Di Silva had them. They were agreeing with every word he said. They shook their heads and nodded and frowned. They did everything but applaud him. He was an orchestra leader and the jury was his orchestra. Jennifer had never seen anything like it. Every time the District Attorney mentioned Abraham Wilson's name—and he mentioned it with almost every sentence—the jury automatically looked over at the defendant. Jennifer had cautioned Wilson not to look at the jury. She had drilled it into him over and over again that he was to look anywhere in the courtroom except at the jury box, because the air of defiance he exuded was enraging. To her horror now, Jennifer found that Abraham Wilson's eyes were fastened on the jury box, locking eyes with the jurors. Aggression seemed to be pouring out of him.

Jennifer said in a low voice, "Abraham . . ."

He did not turn.

The District Attorney was finishing his opening address. "The Bible says, 'An eye for an eye, a tooth for a tooth.' That is vengeance. The State is not asking for vengeance. It is asking for justice. Justice for the poor man whom Abraham Wilson cold-bloodedly—*cold-bloodedly*—murdered. Thank you."

The District Attorney took his seat.

As Jennifer rose to address the jury, she could feel their hostility and impatience. She had read books about how lawyers were able to read juries' minds, and she had been skeptical. But no longer. The message from the jury was coming at her loudly and clearly. They had already decided her client was guilty, and they were impatient because Jennifer was wasting their time, keeping them in court when they could be out doing more important things, as their friend the District Attorney had pointed out. Jennifer and Abraham Wilson were the enemy.

Jennifer took a deep breath and said, "If Your Honor please," and then she turned back to the jurors. "Ladies and gentlemen, the reason we have courtrooms, the reason we are all here today, is because the law, in its wisdom, knows that there are always two sides to every case. Listening to the District Attorney's attack on my client, listening to him pronounce my client guilty without benefit of a jury's verdict—*your* verdict—one would not think so."

She looked into their faces for a sign of sympathy or support. There was none. She forced herself to go on. "District Attorney Di Silva used the phrase over and over, '*Abraham Wilson is guilty.*' That is a lie. Judge Waldman will tell you that no defendant is guilty until a judge or jury declares that he is guilty. That is what we are all here to find out, isn't it? Abraham Wilson has been charged with murdering a fellow inmate at Sing Sing. But Abraham Wilson did not kill for money or for dope. He killed to save his own life. You remember those clever examples that the District Attorney gave you when he explained the difference between killing in cold blood and in hot blood. Killing in hot blood is when you're protecting someone you love, or when you're defending yourself. Abraham Wilson killed in self-defense, and I tell you now that any of us in this courtroom, under identical circumstances, would have done exactly the same thing.

"The District Attorney and I agree on one point: Every man has the right to protect his own life. If Abraham Wilson had not acted exactly as he did, he would be dead." Jennifer's voice was ringing with sincerity. She had forgotten her nervousness in the passion of her conviction. "I ask each of you to remember one thing: Under the law of this state, the prosecution must prove beyond any reasonable doubt that the act of killing was not committed in self-defense. And before this trial is over we will present solid evidence to show you that Raymond Thorpe was killed in order to prevent his murdering my client. Thank you."

The parade of witnesses for the State began. Robert Di Silva had not missed a single opportunity. His character witnesses for the deceased, Raymond Thorpe, included a minister, prison guards and fellow convicts. One by one they took the stand and testified to the sterling character and pacific disposition of the deceased.

Each time the District Attorney was finished with a witness, he turned to Jennifer and said, "Your witness."

And each time Jennifer replied, "No cross-examination."

She knew that there was no point in trying to discredit the character witnesses. By the time they were finished, one would have thought that Raymond Thorpe had been wrongfully deprived of sainthood. The guards, who had been carefully coached by Robert Di Silva, testified that Thorpe had been a model prisoner who went around Sing Sing doing good works, intent only on helping his fellow man. The fact that Raymond Thorpe was a convicted bank robber and rapist was a tiny flaw in an otherwise perfect character.

What badly damaged Jennifer's already weak defense was the physical description of Raymond Thorpe. He had been a slightly built man, only five feet nine inches tall. Robert Di Silva dwelt on that, and he never let the jurors forget it. He painted a graphic picture of how Abraham Wilson had viciously attacked the smaller man and had smashed Thorpe's head against a concrete building in the exercise yard, instantly killing him. As Di Silva spoke, the jurors' eyes were fastened on the giant figure of the defendant sitting at the table, dwarfing everyone near him.

The District Attorney was saying, "We'll probably never know what caused Abraham Wilson to attack this harmless, defenseless little man—"

And Jennifer's heart suddenly leaped. One word that Di Silva had said had given her the chance she needed.

"—We may never know the reason for the defendant's vicious attack, but one thing we *do* know, ladies and gentlemen —it wasn't because the murdered man was a threat to Abraham Wilson.

"Self-defense?" He turned to Judge Waldman. "Your Honor, would you please direct the defendant to rise?"

Judge Waldman looked at Jennifer. "Does counsel for the defense have any objection?"

Jennifer had an idea what was coming, but she knew that any objection on her part could only be damaging. "No, Your Honor."

Judge Waldman said, "Will the defendant rise, please?"

Abraham Wilson sat there a moment, his face defiant; then he slowly rose to his full height of six feet four inches.

Di Silva said, "There is a court clerk here, Mr. Galin, who is five feet nine inches tall, the exact height of the murdered man, Raymond Thorpe. Mr. Galin, would you please go over and stand next to the defendant?"

The court clerk walked over to Abraham Wilson and stood next to him. The contrast between the two men was ludicrous. Jennifer knew she had been outmaneuvered again, but there was nothing she could do about it. The visual impression could never be erased. The District Attorney stood there looking at the two men for a moment, and then said to the jury, his voice almost a whisper, *"Self-defense?"*

The trial was going worse than Jennifer had dreamed in

her wildest nightmares. She could feel the jury's eagerness to get the trial over with so they could deliver a verdict of guilty.

Ken Bailey was seated among the spectators and, during a recess, Jennifer had a chance to exchange a few words with him.

"It's not an easy case," Ken said sympathetically. "I wish you didn't have King Kong for a client. Christ, just looking at him is enough to scare the hell out of anybody."

"He can't help that."

"As the old joke goes, he could have stayed home. How are you and our esteemed District Attorney getting along?"

Jennifer gave him a mirthless smile. "Mr. Di Silva sent me a message this morning. He intends to remove me from the law business."

When the parade of prosecution witnesses was over and Di Silva had rested his case, Jennifer rose and said, "I would like to call Howard Patterson to the stand."

The assistant warden of Sing Sing Prison reluctantly rose and moved toward the witness box, all eyes fixed on him. Robert Di Silva watched intently as Patterson took the oath. Di Silva's mind was racing, computing all the probabilities. He knew he had won the case. He had his victory speech all prepared.

Jennifer was addressing the witness. "Would you fill the jury in on your background, please, Mr. Patterson?"

District Attorney Di Silva was on his feet. "The State will waive the witness's background in order to save time, and we will stipulate that Mr. Patterson is the assistant warden at Sing Sing Prison."

"Thank you," Jennifer said. "I think the jury should be informed that Mr. Patterson had to be subpoenaed to come here today. He is here as a hostile witness." Jennifer turned to Patterson. "When I asked you to come here voluntarily and testify on behalf of my client, you refused. Is that true?"

"Yes."

"Would you tell the jury *why* you had to be subpoenaed to get you here?"

"I'll be glad to. I've been dealing with men like Abraham Wilson all my life. They're born troublemakers."

Robert Di Silva was leaning forward in his chair, grinning, his eyes locked on the faces of the jurors. He whispered to an assistant, "Watch her hang herself."

Jennifer said, "Mr. Patterson, Abraham Wilson is not on trial here for being a troublemaker. He's on trial for his life. Wouldn't you be willing to help a fellow human being who was unjustly accused of a capital crime?"

"If he were unjustly accused, yes." The emphasis on *unjustly* brought a knowing look to the faces of the jurors.

"There have been killings in prison before this case, have there not?"

"When you lock up hundreds of violent men together in an artificial environment, they're bound to generate an enormous amount of hostility, and there's—"

"Just yes or no, please, Mr. Patterson."

"Yes."

"Of those killings that have occurred in your experience, would you say that there have been a variety of motives?"

"Well, I suppose so. Sometimes—"

"Yes or no, please."

"Yes."

"Has self-defense ever been a motive in any of those prison killings?"

"Well, sometimes—" He saw the expression on Jennifer's face. "Yes."

"So, based on your vast experience, it is entirely possible, is it not, that Abraham Wilson was actually defending his own life when he killed Raymond Thorpe?"

"I don't think it—"

"I asked if it is possible. Yes or no."

"It is highly unlikely," Patterson said stubbornly.

Jennifer turned to Judge Waldman. "Your Honor, would you please direct the witness to answer the question?"

Judge Waldman looked down at Howard Patterson. "The witness will answer the question."

"Yes."

But the fact that his whole attitude said *no* had registered on the jury.

Jennifer said, "If the court please, I have subpoenaed from the witness some material I would like to submit now in evidence."

District Attorney Di Silva rose. "What kind of material?"

"Evidence that will prove our contention of self-defense."

"Objection, Your Honor."

"What are you objecting to?" Jennifer asked. "You haven't seen it yet."

Judge Waldman said, "The court will withhold a ruling until it sees the evidence. A man's life is at stake here. The defendant is entitled to every possible consideration."

"Thank you, Your Honor." Jennifer turned to Howard Patterson. "Did you bring it with you?" she asked.

He nodded, tight-lipped. "Yes. But I'm doing this under protest."

"I think you've already made that very clear, Mr. Patterson. May we have it, please?"

Howard Patterson looked over to the spectator area where a man in a prison guard uniform was seated. Patterson nodded to him. The guard rose and came forward, carrying a covered wooden box.

Jennifer took it from him. "The defense would like to place this in evidence as Exhibit A, Your Honor."

"What is it?" District Attorney Di Silva demanded.

"It's called a *goodie box*."

There was a titter from the spectators.

Judge Waldman looked down at Jennifer and said slowly,

"Did you say a *goodie box*? What is in the box, Miss Parker?"

"Weapons. Weapons that were made in Sing Sing by the prisoners for the purpose of—"

"Objection!" The District Attorney was on his feet, his voice a roar. He hurried toward the bench. "I'm willing to make allowances for my colleague's inexperience, Your Honor, but if she intends to practice criminal law, then I would suggest she study the basic rules of evidence. There is no evidence linking anything in this so-called *goodie box* with the case that is being tried in this court."

"This box proves—"

"This box proves nothing." The District Attorney's voice was withering. He turned to Judge Waldman. "The State objects to the introduction of this exhibit as being immaterial and irrelevant."

"Objection sustained."

And Jennifer stood there, watching her case collapse. Everything was against her: the judge, the jury, Di Silva, the evidence. Her client was going to the electric chair unless . . .

Jennifer took a deep breath. "Your Honor, this exhibit is absolutely vital to our defense. I feel—"

Judge Waldman interrupted. "Miss Parker, this court does not have the time or the inclination to give you instructions in the law, but the District Attorney is quite right. Before coming into this courtroom you should have acquainted yourself with the basic rules of evidence. The first rule is that you cannot introduce evidence that has not been properly prepared for. Nothing has been put into the record about the deceased being armed or not armed. Therefore, the question of these weapons becomes extraneous. You are overruled."

Jennifer stood there, the blood rushing to her cheeks. "I'm sorry," she said stubbornly, "but it is *not* extraneous."

"That is enough! You may file an exception."

"I don't want to file an exception, Your Honor. You're denying my client his rights."

"Miss Parker, if you go any further I will hold you in contempt of court."

"I don't care what you do to me," Jennifer said. "The ground *has* been prepared for introducing this evidence. The District Attorney prepared it himself."

Di Silva said, "What? I never—"

Jennifer turned to the court stenographer. "Would you please read Mr. Di Silva's statement, beginning with the line, 'We'll probably never know what caused Abraham Wilson to attack . . .'?"

The District Attorney looked up at Judge Waldman. "Your Honor, are you going to allow—?"

Judge Waldman held up a hand. He turned to Jennifer. "This court does not need you to explain the law to it, Miss Parker. When this trial is ended, you will be held in contempt of court. Because this is a capital case, I am going to hear you out." He turned to the court stenographer. "You may proceed."

The court stenographer turned some pages and began reading. "We'll probably never know what caused Abraham Wilson to attack this harmless, defenseless little man—"

"That's enough," Jennifer interrupted. "Thank you." She looked at Robert Di Silva and said slowly, "Those are your words, Mr. Di Silva. *We'll probably never know what caused Abraham Wilson to attack this harmless, defenseless little man . . .*" She turned to Judge Waldman. "The key word, Your Honor, is *defenseless*. Since the District Attorney himself told this jury that the victim was defenseless, he left an open door for us to pursue the fact that the victim might *not* have been defenseless, that he might, in fact, have had a weapon. Whatever is brought up in the direct is admissible in the cross."

There was a long silence.

Judge Waldman turned to Robert Di Silva. "Miss Parker has a valid point. You did leave the door open."

Robert Di Silva was looking at him unbelievingly. "But I only—"

"The court will allow the evidence to be entered as Exhibit A."

Jennifer took a deep, grateful breath. "Thank you, Your Honor." She picked up the covered box, held it up in her hands and turned to face the jury. "Ladies and gentlemen, in his final summation the District Attorney is going to tell you that what you are about to see in this box is not direct evidence. He will be correct. He is going to tell you that there is nothing to link any of these weapons to the deceased. He will be correct. I am introducing this exhibit for another reason. For days now, you have been hearing how the ruthless, trouble-making defendant, who stands six feet four inches tall, wantonly attacked Raymond Thorpe, who stood only five feet nine inches tall. The picture that has been so carefully, and falsely, painted for you by the prosecution is that of a sadistic, murdering bully who killed another inmate for no reason. But ask yourselves this: Isn't there always *some* motive? Greed, hate, lust, *something*? I believe—and I'm staking my client's life on·that belief—that there *was* a motive for that killing. The *only* motive, as the District Attorney himself told you, that justifies killing someone: self-defense. A man fighting to protect his own life. You have heard Howard Patterson testify that in his experience murders *have* occurred in prison, that convicts *do* fashion deadly weapons. What that means is that it was possible that Raymond Thorpe was armed with such a weapon, that indeed it was *he* who was attacking the defendant, and the defendant, trying to protect himself, was forced to kill him—*in self-defense*. If you decide that Abraham Wilson ruthlessly—and without any motivation at all— killed Raymond Thorpe, then you must bring in a verdict of guilty as charged. If, however, after seeing this evidence, you have a reasonable doubt in your minds, then it is your duty to return a verdict of not guilty." The covered box was becoming heavy in her hands. "When I first looked into this box I could not believe what I saw. You, too, may find it hard to believe— but I ask you to remember that it was brought here under protest by the assistant warden of Sing Sing Prison. This, ladies and gentlemen, is a collection of confiscated weapons secretly made by the convicts at Sing Sing."

As Jennifer moved toward the jury box, she seemed to stumble and lose her balance. The box fell out of her grasp, the top flew off, and the contents spilled out over the courtroom floor. There was a gasp. The jurors began to get to their feet so they could have a better look. They were staring at the hideous collection of weapons that had tumbled from the box. There were almost one hundred of them, of every size, shape and description. Homemade hatchets and butcher knives, stilettos and deadly looking scissors with the ends honed, pellet guns, and a large, vicious-looking cleaver. There were thin wires with wooden handles, used for strangling, a leather sap, a sharpened ice pick, a machete.

Spectators and reporters were on their feet now, craning to get a better look at the arsenal that lay scattered on the floor. Judge Waldman was angrily pounding his gavel for order.

Judge Waldman looked at Jennifer with an expression she could not fathom. A bailiff hurried forward to pick up the spilled contents of the box. Jennifer waved him away.

"Thank you," she said, "I'll do it."

As the jurors and spectators watched, Jennifer got down on her knees and began picking up the weapons and putting them back in the box. She worked slowly, handling the weapons gingerly, looking at each one without expression before she replaced it. The jurors had taken their seats again, but they were watching every move she made. It took Jennifer a full five minutes to return the weapons to the box, while District Attorney Di Silva sat there, fuming.

When Jennifer had put the last weapon in the deadly arsenal back in the box, she rose, looked at Patterson, then turned and said to Di Silva, "Your witness."

It was too late to repair the damage that had been done. "No cross," the District Attorney said.

"Then I would like to call Abraham Wilson to the stand."

8

"Your name?"

"Abraham Wilson."

"Would you speak up, please?"

"Abraham Wilson."

"Mr. Wilson, did you kill Raymond Thorpe?"

"Yes, ma'am."

"Would you tell the court why?"

"He was gonna kill me."

"Raymond Thorpe was a much smaller man than you. Did you really believe that he would be able to kill you?"

"He was comin' at me with a knife that made him purty tall."

Jennifer had kept out two objects from the goodie box. One was a finely honed butcher knife; the other was a large pair of metal tongs. She held up the knife. "Was this the knife that Raymond Thorpe threatened you with?"

"Objection! The defendant has no way of knowing—"

"I'll rephrase the question. Was this similar to the knife that Raymond Thorpe threatened you with?"

"Yes, ma'am."

"And these tongs?"

"Yes, ma'am."

"Had you had trouble with Thorpe before?"

"Yes, ma'am."

"And when he came at you armed with these two weapons, you were forced to kill him in order to save your own life?"

"Yes, ma'am."

"Thank you."

Jennifer turned to Di Silva. "Your witness."

Robert Di Silva rose to his feet and moved slowly toward the witness box.

"Mr. Wilson, you've killed before, haven't you? I mean, this wasn't your first murder?"

"I made a mistake and I'm payin' for it. I—"

"Spare us your sermon. Just answer yes or no."

"Yes."

"So a human life doesn't have much value to you."

"That ain't true. I—"

"Do you call committing two murders valuing human life? How many people would you have killed if you *didn't* value human life? Five? Ten? Twenty?"

He was baiting Abraham Wilson and Wilson was falling for it. His jaw was clenched and his face was filling with anger. *Be careful!*

"I only kilt two people."

"Only! You *only* killed two people!" The District Attorney shook his head in mock dismay. He stepped close to the witness box and looked up at the defendant. "I'll bet it gives you a feeling of power to be so big. It must make you feel a little bit like God. Any time you want to, you can take a life here, take a life there . . ."

Abraham Wilson was on his feet, rising to his full height. "You somabitch!"

No! Jennifer prayed. *Don't!*

"Sit down!" Di Silva thundered. "Is that the way you lost your temper when you killed Raymond Thorpe?"

"Thorpe was tryin' ta kill me."

"With these?" Di Silva held up the butcher knife and the pair of tongs. "I'm sure you could have taken that knife away from him." He waved the tongs around. "And you were afraid of this?" He turned back to the jury and held up the tongs deprecatingly. "This doesn't look so terribly lethal. If the deceased had been able to hit you over the head with it, it might have caused a small bump. What exactly is this pair of tongs, Mr. Wilson?"

Abraham Wilson said softly, "They're testicle crushers."

The jury was out for eight hours.

Robert Di Silva and his assistants left the courtroom to take a break, but Jennifer stayed in her seat, unable to tear herself away.

When the jury filed out of the room, Ken Bailey came up to Jennifer. "How about a cup of coffee?"

"I couldn't swallow anything."

She sat in the courtroom, afraid to move, only dimly aware of the people around her. It was over. She had done her best. She closed her eyes and tried to pray, but the fear in her was too strong. She felt as though she, along with Abraham Wilson, was about to be sentenced to death.

The jury was filing back into the room, their faces grim and foreboding, and Jennifer's heart began to beat faster. She could see by their faces that they were going to convict. She thought she would faint. Because of her, a man was going to be executed. She should never have taken the case in the first place. What right had she to put a man's life in her hands? She must have been insane to think she could win over someone as experienced as Robert Di Silva. She wanted to run up to the jurors before they could give their verdict and say, *Wait! Abraham Wilson hasn't had a fair trial. Please let another attorney defend him. Someone better than I am.*

But it was too late. Jennifer stole a look at Abraham Wilson's face. He sat there as immobile as a statue. She could feel no hatred coming from him now, only a deep despair. She wanted to say something to comfort him, but there were no words.

Judge Waldman was speaking. "Has the jury reached a verdict?"

"It has, Your Honor."

The judge nodded and his clerk walked over to the foreman of the jury, took a slip of paper from him and handed it to the judge. Jennifer felt as though her heart were going to come out of her chest. She could not breathe. She wanted to hold back this moment, to freeze it forever before the verdict was read.

Judge Waldman studied the slip of paper in his hands; then he slowly looked around the courtroom. His eyes rested on the members of the jury, on Robert Di Silva, on Jennifer and finally on Abraham Wilson.

"The defendant will please rise."

Abraham Wilson got to his feet, his movements slow and tired, as though all the energy had been drained out of him.

Judge Waldman read from the slip of paper. "This jury finds the defendant, Abraham Wilson, not guilty as charged."

There was a momentary hush and the judge's further words were drowned out in a roar from the spectators. Jennifer stood there, stunned, unable to believe what she was hearing. She turned toward Abraham Wilson, speechless. He stared at her for an instant with those small, mean eyes. And then that ugly face broke into the broadest grin that Jennifer had ever seen.

He reached down and hugged her and Jennifer tried to fight back her tears.

The press was crowding around Jennifer, asking for a statement, barraging her with questions.

"How does it feel to beat the District Attorney?"

"Did you think you were going to win this case?"

"What would you have done if they had sent Wilson to the electric chair?"

Jennifer shook her head to all questions. She could not bring herself to talk to them. They had come here to watch a spectacle, to see a man being hounded to his death. If the verdict had gone the other way . . . she could not bear to think about it. Jennifer began to collect her papers and stuff them into a briefcase.

A bailiff approached her. "Judge Waldman wants to see you in his chambers, Miss Parker."

She had forgotten that there was a contempt of court citation waiting for her but it no longer seemed important. The only thing that mattered was that she had saved Abraham Wilson's life.

Jennifer glanced over at the prosecutor's table. District Attorney Silva was savagely stuffing papers into a briefcase, berating one of his assistants. He caught Jennifer's look. His eyes met hers and he needed no words.

Judge Lawrence Waldman was seated at his desk when Jennifer walked in. He said curtly, "Sit down, Miss Parker." Jennifer took a seat. "I will not allow you or anyone else to turn my courtroom into a sideshow."

Jennifer flushed. "I tripped. I couldn't help what—"

Judge Waldman raised a hand. "Please. Spare me." Jennifer clamped her lips tightly together.

Judge Waldman leaned forward in his chair. "Another thing I will not tolerate in my court is insolence." Jennifer watched him warily, saying nothing. "You overstepped the bounds this afternoon. I realize that your excessive zeal was in defense of a man's life. Because of that, I have decided not to cite you for contempt."

"Thank you, Your Honor." Jennifer had to force the words out.

The judge's face was unreadable as he continued: "Almost invariably, when a case is finished I have a sense of whether justice has been served or not. In this instance, quite frankly, I'm not sure." Jennifer waited for him to go on.

"That's all, Miss Parker."

In the evening editions of the newspapers and on the television news that night, Jennifer Parker was back in the headlines, but this time she was the heroine. She was the legal David who had slain Goliath. Pictures of her and Abraham Wilson and District Attorney Di Silva were plastered all over the front pages. Jennifer hungrily devoured every word of the stories, savoring them. It was such a sweet victory after all the disgrace she had suffered earlier.

Ken Bailey took her to dinner at Luchow's to celebrate, and Jennifer was recognized by the captain and several of the customers. Strangers called Jennifer by name and congratulated her. It was a heady experience.

"How does it feel to be a celebrity?" Ken grinned.

"I'm numb."

Someone sent a bottle of wine to the table.

"I don't need anything to drink," Jennifer said. "I feel as though I'm already drunk."

But she was thirsty and she drank three glasses of wine while she rehashed the trial with Ken.

"I was scared. Do you know what it's like to hold someone else's life in your hands? It's like playing God. Can you think of anything scarier than that? I mean, I come from *Kelso* . . . could we have another bottle of wine, Ken?"

"Anything you want."

Ken ordered a feast for them both, but Jennifer was too excited to eat.

"Do you know what Abraham Wilson said to me the first time I met him? He said, 'You crawl into my skin and I'll crawl into yours and then you and me will rap about hate.' Ken, I was *in* his skin today, and do you know something? I thought the jury was going to convict *me*. I felt as though I was going to be executed. I love Abraham Wilson. Could we have some more wine?"

"You haven't eaten a bite."

"I'm thirsty."

Ken watched, concerned, as Jennifer kept filling and emptying her glass. "Take it easy."

She waved a hand in airy dismissal. "It's California wine. It's like drinking water." She took another swallow. "You're my best friend. Do you know who's not my best friend? The great Robert Di Sliva. Di Sivla."

"Di Silva."

"Him, too. He hates me. D'ja see his face today? O-o-ooh, he was mad! He said he was gonna run me out of court. But he didn't, did he?"

"No, he—"

"You know what I think? You know what I *really* think?"

"I—"

"Di Sliva thinks I'm Ahab and he's the white whale."

"I think you have that backwards."

"Thank you, Ken. I can always count on you. Let's have 'nother bottle of wine."

"Don't you think you've had enough?"

"Whales get thirsty." Jennifer giggled. "Tha's me. The big old white whale. Did I tell you I love Abraham Wilson? He's the most beautiful man I ever met. I looked in his eyes, Ken, my frien', 'n' he's beautiful! Y'ever look in Di Sivla's eyes? O-o-ooh! They're cold! I mean, he's 'n iceberg. But he's not a bad man. Did I tell you 'bout Ahab 'n' the big white whale?"

"Yes."

"I love old Ahab. I love everybody. 'N' you know why, Ken? 'Cause Abraham Wilson is alive tonight. He's alive. Le's have 'nother bottle a wine to celebrate . . ."

It was two A.M. when Ken Bailey took Jennifer home. He helped her up the four flights of stairs and into her little apartment. He was breathing hard from the climb.

"You know," Ken said, "I can feel the effects of all that wine."

Jennifer looked at him pityingly. "People who can't handle it shoudn' drink."

And she passed out cold.

She was awakened by the shrill screaming of the telephone. She carefully reached for the instrument, and the slight movement sent rockets of pain through every nerve ending in her body.

" 'Lo . . ."

"Jennifer? This is Ken."

" 'Lo, Ken."

"You sound terrible. Are you all right?"

She thought about it. "I don't think so. What time is it?"

"It's almost noon. You'd better get down here. All hell is breaking loose."

"Ken—I think I'm dying."

"Listen to me. Get out of bed—slowly—take two aspirin and a cold shower, drink a cup of hot black coffee, and you'll probably live."

When Jennifer arrived at the office one hour later, she was feeling better. *Not good*, Jennifer thought, *but better*.

Both telephones were ringing when she walked into the office.

"They're for you." Ken grinned. "They haven't stopped! You need a switchboard."

There were calls from newspapers and national magazines and television and radio stations wanting to do in-depth stories on Jennifer. Overnight, she had become big news. There were other calls, the kind of which she had dreamed. Law firms that had snubbed her before were telephoning to ask when it would be convenient for her to meet with them.

In his office downtown, Robert Di Silva was screaming at his first assistant. "I want you to start a confidential file on Jennifer Parker. I want to be informed of every client she takes on. Got it?"

"Yes, sir."

"Move!"

9

"He ain't no button guy anymore'n I'm a fuckin' virgin. He's been workin' on the arm all his life."

"The asshole came suckin' up to me askin' me to put in the word with Mike. I said, 'Hey, paesano, I'm only a soldier, ya know?' If Mike needs another shooter he don't have to go lookin' in shit alley."

"He was tryin' to run a game on you, Sal."

"Well, I clocked him pretty good. He ain't connected and in this business, if you ain't connected, you're nothin'."

They were talking in the kitchen of a three-hundred-year-old Dutch farmhouse in upstate New Jersey.

There were three of them in the room: Nick Vito, Joseph Colella and Salvatore "Little Flower" Fiore.

Nick Vito was a cadaverous-looking man with thin lips that were almost invisible, and deep green eyes that were dead. He wore two hundred dollar shoes and white socks.

Joseph "Big Joe" Colella was a huge slab of a man, a granite monolith, and when he walked he looked like a building moving. Someone had once called him a vegetable garden. "Colella's got a potato nose, cauliflower ears and a pea brain."

Colella had a soft, high-pitched voice and a deceptively gentle manner. He owned a race horse and had an uncanny knack for picking winners. He was a family man with a wife and six children. His specialties were guns, acid and chains. Joe's wife, Carmelina, was a strict Catholic, and on Sundays when Colella was not working, he always took his family to church.

The third man, Salvatore Fiore, was almost a midget. He stood five feet three inches and weighed a hundred and fifteen pounds. He had the innocent face of a choirboy and was equally adept with a gun or a knife. Women were greatly attracted to the little man, and he boasted a wife, half a dozen girl friends, and a beautiful mistress. Fiore had once been a jockey, working the tracks from Pimlico to Tijuana. When the racing commissioner at Hollywood Park banned Fiore for doping a horse, the commissioner's body was found floating in Lake Tahoe a week later.

The three men were *soldati* in Antonio Granelli's Family, but it was Michael Moretti who had brought them in, and they belonged to him, body and soul.

In the dining room, a Family meeting was taking place. Seated at the head of the table was Antonio Granelli, *capo* of the most powerful Mafia Family on the east coast. Seventy-two years old, he was still a powerful-looking man with the shoulders and broad chest of a laborer, and a shock of white hair. Born in Palermo, Sicily, Antonio Granelli came to America when he was fifteen and went to work on the waterfront on the west side of lower Manhattan. By the time he was twenty-one, he was lieutenant to the dock boss. The two men had an argument, and when the boss mysteriously disappeared, Antonio Granelli had taken over. Anyone who wanted to work on the docks had to pay him. He had used the money to begin his climb to power, and had expanded rapidly, branching out into loan-sharking and the numbers racket, prostitution and gambling and drugs and murder. Over the years he had been indicted thirty-two times and had only been convicted once, on a minor assault charge. Granelli was a ruthless man with the down-to-earth cunning of a peasant, and a total amorality.

To Granelli's left sat Thomas Colfax, the Family *consigliere*. Twenty-five years earlier, Colfax had had a brilliant future as a corporation lawyer, but he had defended a small olive-oil company which turned out to be Mafia-controlled and, step by step, had been lured into handling other cases for the Mafia until finally, through the years, the Granelli Family had become his sole client. It was a very lucrative client and Thomas Colfax became a wealthy man, with extensive real estate holdings and bank accounts all over the world.

To the right of Antonio Granelli sat Michael Moretti, his son-in-law. Michael was ambitious, a trait that made Granelli nervous. Michael did not fit into the pattern of the Family. His father, Giovanni, a distant cousin of Antonio Granelli, had been born not in Sicily but in Florence. That alone made the Moretti family suspect—everybody knew that Florentines were not to be trusted.

Giovanni Moretti had come to America and opened a shop as a shoemaker, running it honestly, without even a back room for gambling or loan-sharking or girls. Which made him stupid.

Giovanni's son, Michael, was entirely different. He had put himself through Yale and the Wharton School of Business. When Michael had finished school, he had gone to his father with one request: He wanted to meet his distant relative, Antonio Granelli. The old shoemaker had gone to see his cousin and the meeting had been arranged. Granelli was sure that Michael was going to ask for a loan so that he could go into some kind of business, maybe open a shoe shop like his dumb father. But the meeting had been a surprise.

"I know how to make you rich," Michael Moretti had begun.

Antonio Granelli had looked at the impudent young man and had smiled tolerantly. "I am rich."

"No. You just *think* you're rich."

The smile had died away. "What the hell you talkin' about, kid?"

And Michael Moretti had told him.

Antonio Granelli had moved cautiously at first, testing each piece of Michael's advice. Everything had succeeded brilliantly. Where before, the Granelli Family had been involved in profitable illegal activities, under Michael Moretti's supervision it branched out. Within five years the Family was into dozens of legitimate businesses, including meat-packing, linen supplies, restaurants, trucking companies and pharmaceuticals. Michael found ailing companies that needed financing and the Family went in as a minor partner and gradually took over, stripping away whatever assets there were. Old companies with impeccable reputations suddenly found themselves bankrupt. The businesses that showed a satisfactory profit, Michael hung on to and he increased the profits tremendously, for the workers in those businesses were controlled by his unions, and the company took their insurance through one of the Family-owned insurance companies, and they bought their automobiles from one of the Family's automobile dealers. Michael created a symbiotic giant, a series of businesses through which the consumer was constantly being milked—and the milk flowed to the Family.

In spite of his successes, Michael Moretti was aware that he had a problem. Once he had shown Antonio Granelli the rich, ripe horizons of legitimate enterprise, Granelli no longer needed him. He was expensive, because in the beginning he had persuaded Antonio Granelli to give him a percentage of what everyone was sure would be a small pot. But as Michael's ideas began to bear fruit and the profits poured in, Granelli had second thoughts. By chance, Michael learned that Granelli had held a meeting to discuss what the Family should do with him.

"I don't like to see all this money goin' to the kid," Granelli had said. "We get rid of him."

Michael had circumvented that scheme by marrying into the Family. Rosa, Antonio Granelli's only daughter, was nineteen years old. Her mother had died giving birth to her, and Rosa had been brought up in a convent and was allowed to come home only during the holidays. Her father adored her, and he saw to it that she was protected and sheltered. It was on a school holiday, an Easter, that Rosa met Michael Moretti. By the time she returned to the convent, she was madly in love with him. The memory of his dark good looks drove her to do things when she was alone that the nuns told her were sins against God.

Antonio Granelli was under the delusion that his daughter thought he was merely a successful businessman, but over the years, Rosa's classmates had shown her newspaper and magazine articles about her father and his real business, and whenever the government made an attempt to indict and convict one of the Granelli Family, Rosa was always aware of it. She never discussed it with her father, and so he remained happy in his belief that his daughter was an innocent and that she was spared the shock of knowing the truth.

The truth, if he had know it, would have surprised Granelli for Rosa found her father's business terribly exciting. She hated the discipline of the nuns at the convent and that, in turn, led her to hate all authority. She daydreamed about her father as a kind of Robin Hood, challenging authority, defying the government. The fact that Michael Moretti was an important man in her father's organization made him that much more exciting to her.

From the beginning, Michael was very careful how he handled Rosa. When he managed to be alone with her they exchanged ardent kisses and embraces, but Michael never let it go too far. Rosa was a virgin and she was willing—eager—to give herself to the man she loved. It was Michael who held back.

"I respect you too much, Rosa, to go to bed with you before we're married."

In reality, it was Antonio Granelli he respected too much. *He'd chop my balls off*, Michael thought.

And so it happened that at the time Antonio Granelli was discussing the best way to get rid of Michael Moretti, Michael and Rosa came to him and announced that they were in love and intended to get married. The old man screamed and raged and gave a hundred reasons why it would happen only over someone's dead body. But in the end, true love prevailed and Michael and Rosa were married in an elaborate ceremony.

After the wedding the old man had called Michael aside. "Rosa's all I got, Michael. You take good care of her, huh?"

"I will, Tony."

"I'm gonna be watchin' you. You better make her happy. You know what I mean, Mike?"

"I know what you mean."

"No whores or chippies. Understand? Rosa likes to cook. You see that you're home for dinner every night. You're gonna be a son-in-law to be proud of."

"I'm going to try very hard, Tony."

Antonio Granelli had said casually, "Oh, by the way, Mike, now that you're a member of the Family, that royalty deal I gave you—maybe we oughta change it."

Michael had clapped him on the arm. "Thanks, Papa, but it's enough for us. I'll be able to buy Rosa everything she wants."

And he had walked away, leaving the old man staring after him.

That had been seven years earlier, and the years that followed had been wonderful for Michael. Rosa was pleasant and easy to live with and she adored him, but Michael knew that if she died or went away, he would get along without her. He would simply find someone else to do the things she did for him. He was not in love with Rosa. Michael did not think he was capable of loving another human being; it was as though something was missing in him.

He had no feelings for people, only for animals. Michael had been given a collie puppy for his tenth birthday. The two of them were inseparable. Six weeks later the dog had been killed in a hit-and-run accident, and when Michael's father offered to buy him another dog, Michael had refused. He had never owned another dog after that.

Michael had grown up watching his father slaving his life away for pennies, and Michael had resolved that would never happen to him. He had known what he wanted from the time he had first heard talk about his famous distant cousin Antonio Granelli. There were twenty-six Mafia Families in the United States, five of them in New York City, and his cousin Antonio's was the strongest. From his earliest childhood, Michael thrived on tales of the Mafia. His father told him about the night of the Sicilian Vespers, September 10, 1931, when the balance of power had changed hands. In that single night, the *Young Turks* in the Mafia staged a bloody coup that wiped out more than forty *Mustache Petes*, the old guard who had come over from Italy and Sicily.

Michael was of the new generation. He had gotten rid of the old thinking and had brought in fresh ideas. A nine-man national commission controlled all the Families now, and Michael knew that one day he would run that commission.

Michael turned now to study the two men seated at the dining room table of the New Jersey farmhouse. Antonio Granelli still had a few years left but, with luck, not too many.

Thomas Colfax was the enemy. The lawyer had been against Michael from the beginning. As Michael's influence with the old man had increased, Colfax's had decreased.

Michael had brought more and more of his own men into the Organization, men like Nick Vito and Salvatore Fiore and Joseph Colella, who were fiercely loyal to him. Thomas Colfax had not liked that.

When Michael had been indicted for the murders of the Ramos brothers, and Camillo Stela had agreed to testify against him in court, the old lawyer had believed that he was finally going to be rid of Michael, for the District Attorney had an airtight case.

Michael had thought of a way out in the middle of the night. At four in the morning, he had gone out to a telephone booth and called Joseph Colella.

"Next week some new lawyers are going to be sworn in on the District Attorney's staff. Can you get me their names?"

"Sure, Mike. Easy."

"One more thing. Call Detroit and have them fly in a cherry—one of their boys who's never been tagged." And Michael had hung up.

Two weeks later, Michael Moretti had sat in the courtroom studying the new assistant district attorneys. He had looked them over carefully, his eyes traveling from face to face, searching and judging. What he planned to do was dangerous, but its very daring could make it work. He was dealing with young beginners who would be too nervous to ask a lot of questions, and anxious to be helpful and make their mark. Well, someone was certainly going to make his mark.

Michael had finally selected Jennifer Parker. He liked the fact that she was inexperienced and that she was tense and trying to hide it. He liked the fact that she was female and would feel under more pressure than the men. When Michael was satisfied with his decision, he turned to a man in a gray suit sitting among the spectators and nodded toward Jennifer. That was all.

Michael had watched as the District Attorney had finished his examination of that son-of-a-bitch, Camillo Stela. He had turned to Thomas Colfax and said, *Your witness for cross.* Thomas Colfax had risen to his feet. *If it please Your Honor, it is now almost noon. I would prefer not to have my cross-examination interrupted. Might I request that the court recess for lunch now and I'll cross-examine this afternoon?*

And a recess had been declared. Now was the moment!

Michael saw his man casually drift up to join the men who were crowded around the District Attorney. The man made himself a part of the group. A few moments later, he walked over to Jennifer and handed her a large envelope. Michael sat there, holding his breath, willing Jennifer to take the envelope and move toward the witness room. She did. It was not until he saw her return without it that Michael Moretti relaxed.

That had been a year ago. The newspapers had crucified the girl, but that was *her* problem. Michael had not given any further thought to Jennifer Parker until the newspapers had begun recently to feature the Abraham Wilson trial. They had dragged up the old Michael Moretti case and Jennifer Parker's part in it. They had run her picture. She was a stunning-looking girl, but there was something more—there was a sense of independence about her that stirred something in him. He stared at the picture for a long time.

Michael began to follow the Abraham Wilson trial with increasing interest. When the boys had celebrated with a victory dinner after Michael's mistrial was declared, Salvatore Fiore had proposed a toast. "The world got rid of one more fuckin' lawyer."

But the world had not gotten rid of her, Michael thought.

Jennifer Parker had bounced back and was still in there, fighting. Michael liked that.

He had seen her on television the night before, discussing her victory over Robert Di Silva, and Michael had been oddly pleased.

Antonio Granelli had asked, "Ain't she the mouthpiece you set up, Mike?"

"Uh-huh. She's got a brain, Tony. Maybe we can use her one of these days."

10

The day after the Abraham Wilson verdict, Adam Warner telephoned. "I just called to congratulate you."

Jennifer recognized his voice instantly and it affected her more than she would have believed possible.

"This is—"

"I know." *Oh, God*, Jennifer thought. *Why did I say that?* There was no reason to let Adam know how often she had thought about him in the past few months.

"I wanted to tell you I thought you handled the Abraham Wilson case brilliantly. You deserved to win it."

"Thank you." *He's going to hang up*, Jennifer thought. *I'll never see him again. He's probably too busy with his harem.*

And Adam Warner was saying, "I was wondering if you'd care to have dinner with me one evening?"

Men hate overeager girls, "What about tonight?"

Jennifer heard the smile in his voice. "I'm afraid my first free night is Friday. Are you busy?"

"No." She had almost said, *Of course not.*

"Shall I pick you up at your place?"

Jennifer thought about her dreary little apartment with its lumpy sofa, the ironing board set up in a corner. "It might be easier if we met somewhere."

"Do you like the food at Lutèce?"

"May I tell you after I've eaten there?"

He laughed. "How's eight o'clock?"

"Eight o'clock is lovely."

Lovely. Jennifer replaced the receiver and sat there in a glow of euphoria. *This is ridiculous,* she thought. *He's probably married and has two dozen children.* Almost the first thing Jennifer had noticed about Adam when they had had dinner was that he was not wearing a wedding ring. *Inconclusive evidence,* she thought wryly. There definitely should be a law forcing all husbands to wear wedding rings.

Ken Bailey walked into the office. "How's the master attorney?" He looked at her more closely. "You look like you just swallowed a client."

Jennifer hesitated, then said, "Ken, would you run a check on someone for me?"

He walked over to her desk, picked up a pad and pencil. "Shoot. Who is it?"

She started to say Adam's name, then stopped, feeling like a fool. What business had she prying into Adam Warner's private life? *For God's sake,* she told herself, *all he did is ask you to have dinner with him, not marry him.* "Never mind."

Ken put the pencil down. "Whatever you say."

"Ken—"

"Yes?"

"Adam Warner. His name is Adam Warner."

Ken looked at her in surprise. "Hell, you don't need me to run a check on him. Just read the newspapers."

"What do you know about him?"

Ken Bailey flopped into a chair across from Jennifer and steepled his fingers together. "Let me see. He's a partner in Needham, Finch, Pierce and Warner; Harvard Law School; comes from a rich socialite family; in his middle thirties—"

Jennifer looked at him curiously. "How do you know so much about him?"

He winked. "I have friends in high places. There's a rumor they're going to run Mr. Warner for the United States Senate. There's even a little presidential ground swell going on. He's got what they call charisma."

He certainly has, Jennifer thought. She tried to make her next question sound casual. "What about his personal life?"

Ken Bailey looked at her oddly. "He's married to the daughter of an ex-Secretary of the Navy. She's the niece of Stewart Needham, Warner's law partner."

Jennifer's heart sank. So that was that.

Ken was watching her, puzzled. "Why this sudden interest in Adam Warner?"

"Just curious."

Long after Ken Bailey had left, Jennifer sat there thinking about Adam. *He asked me to dinner as a professional courtesy. He wants to congratulate me. But he's already done that over the telephone. Who cares why? I'm going to see him again. I wonder whether he'll remember to mention he has a wife. Of course not. Well, I'll have dinner with Adam on Friday night and that will be the end of that.*

Late that afternoon, Jennifer received a telephone call from Peabody & Peabody. It was from the senior partner himself.

"I've been meaning to get around to this for some time," he said. "I wondered if you and I might have lunch soon."

His casual tone did not deceive Jennifer. She was sure the idea of having lunch with her had not occurred to him until after he had read about the Abraham Wilson decision. He certainly did not want to meet with her to discuss serving subpoenas.

"What about tomorrow?" he suggested. "My club."

They met for lunch the following day. The senior Peabody was a pale, prissy man, an older version of his son. His vest failed to conceal a slight paunch. Jennifer liked the father just as little as she had liked the son.

"We have an opening for a bright young trial attorney in our firm, Miss Parker. We can offer you fifteen thousand dollars a year to start with."

Jennifer sat there listening to him, thinking how much that offer would have meant to her a year earlier when she had desperately needed a job, needed someone who believed in her.

He was saying, "I'm sure that within a few years there would be room for a partnership for you in our firm."

Fifteen thousand dollars a year and a partnership. Jennifer thought about the little office she shared with Ken, and her tiny, shabby four-flight walk-up apartment with its fake fireplace.

Mr. Peabody was taking her silence for acquiescence. "Good. We'd like you to begin as soon as possible. Perhaps you could start Monday. I—"

"No."

"Oh. Well, if Monday's not convenient for you—"

"I mean, no, I can't take your offer, Mr. Peabody," Jennifer said, and amazed herself.

"I see." There was a pause. "Perhaps we could start you at twenty thousand dollars a year." He saw the expression on her face. "Or twenty-five thousand. Why don't you think it over?"

"I've thought it over. I'm going to stay in business for myself."

The clients were beginning to come. Not a great many and

not very affluent, but they were clients. The office was becoming too small for her.

One morning after Jennifer had kept two clients waiting
outside in the hallway while she was dealing with a third,
Ken said, "This isn't going to work. You're going to have to
move out of here and get yourself a decent office uptown."

Jennifer nodded. "I know. I've been thinking about it."

Ken busied himself with some papers so that he did not
have to meet her eyes. "I'll miss you."

"What are you talking about? You have to go with me."

It took a moment for the words to sink in. He looked up
and a broad grin creased his freckled face.

"Go with you?" He glanced around the cramped, windowless room. "And give up all this?"

The following week, Jennifer and Ken Bailey moved into
larger offices in the five hundred block on Fifth Avenue. The
new quarters were simply furnished and consisted of three
small rooms: one for Jennifer, one for Ken and one for a
secretary.

The secretary they hired was a young girl named Cynthia
Ellman fresh out of New York University.

"There won't be a lot for you to do for a while," Jennifer
apologized, "but things will pick up."

"Oh, I know they will, Miss Parker." There was heroine
worship in the girl's voice.

She wants to be like me, Jennifer thought. *God forbid!*

Ken Bailey walked in and said, "Hey, I get lonely in that
big office all by myself. How about dinner and the theater
tonight?"

"I'm afraid I—" She was tired and had some briefs to
read, but Ken was her best friend and she could not refuse
him.

"I'd love to go."

* * *

They went to see *Applause*, and Jennifer enjoyed it tremendously. Lauren Bacall was totally captivating. Jennifer and Ken had supper afterward at Sardi's.

When they had ordered, Ken said, "I have two tickets for the ballet Friday night. I thought we might—"

Jennifer said, "I'm sorry, Ken. I'm busy Friday night."

"Oh." His voice was curiously flat.

From time to time, Jennifer would find Ken staring at her when he thought he was unobserved, and there was an expression on his face that Jennifer found hard to define. She knew Ken was lonely, although he never talked about any of his friends and never discussed his personal life. She could not forget what Otto had told her, and she wondered whether Ken himself knew what he wanted out of life. She wished that there were some way she could help him.

It seemed to Jennifer that Friday was never going to arrive. As her dinner date with Adam Warner drew closer, Jennifer found it more and more difficult to concentrate on business. She found herself thinking about Adam constantly. She knew she was being ridiculous. She had seen the man only once in her life, and yet she was unable to get him out of her mind. She tried to rationalize by telling herself that it was because he had saved her when she was facing disbarment proceedings, and then had sent her clients. That was true, but Jennifer knew it was more than that. It was something she could not explain, even to herself. It was a feeling she had never had before, an attraction she had never felt for any other man. She wondered what Adam Warner's wife was like. She was undoubtedly one of the chosen women who, every Wednesday, walked through the red door at Elizabeth Arden's for a day of head-to-toe pampering. She would be sleek and sophisticated, with the polished aura of the wealthy socialite.

* * *

On the magic Friday morning at ten o'clock, Jennifer made an appointment with a new Italian hairdresser Cynthia had told her all the models were going to. At ten-thirty, Jennifer called to cancel it. At eleven, she rescheduled the appointment.

Ken Bailey invited Jennifer to lunch, but she was too nervous to eat anything. Instead, she went shopping at Bendel's, where she bought a short, dark green chiffon dress that matched her eyes, a pair of slender brown pumps and a matching purse. She knew she was far over her budget, but she could not seem to stop herself.

She passed the perfume department on the way out, and on an insane impulse bought a bottle of Joy perfume. It was insane because the man was married.

Jennifer left the office at five o'clock and went home to change. She spent two hours bathing and dressing for Adam, and when she was finished she studied herself critically in the mirror. Then she defiantly combed out her carefully coiffured hair and tied it back with a green ribbon. *That's better*, she thought. *I'm a lawyer going to have dinner with another lawyer.* But when she closed the door she left behind a faint fragrance of rose and jasmine.

Lutèce was nothing like what Jennifer had expected. A French tricolor flew above the entrance of the small town house. Inside, a narrow hall led to a small bar and beyond was a sunroom, bright and gay, with porch wicker and plaid tablecloths. Jennifer was met at the door by the owner, André Soltner.

"May I help you?"

"I'm meeting Mr. Adam Warner. I think I'm a little early."

He waved Jennifer toward the small bar. "Would you care for a drink while you are waiting, Miss Parker?"

"That would be nice," Jennifer said. "Thank you."

"I'll send a waiter over."

Jennifer took a seat and amused herself watching the be-jeweled and mink-draped women arriving with their escorts. Jennifer had read and heard about Lutèce. It was reputed to be Jacqueline Kennedy's favorite restaurant and to have excellent food.

A distinguished-looking gray-haired man walked up to Jennifer and said, "Mind if I join you for a moment?"

Jennifer stiffened. "I'm waiting for someone," she began. "He should be here—"

He smiled and sat down. "This isn't a pickup, Miss Parker." Jennifer looked at him in surprise, unable to place him. "I'm Lee Browning, of Holland and Browning." It was one of the most prestigious law firms in New York. "I just wanted to congratulate you on the way you handled the Wilson trial."

"Thank you, Mr. Browning."

"You took a big chance. It was a no-win case." He studied her a moment. "The rule is, when you're on the wrong side of a no-win case, make sure it's one where there's no publicity involved. The trick is to spotlight the winners and kick the losers under the rug. You fooled a lot of us. Have you ordered a drink yet?"

"No—"

"May I—?" He beckoned to a waiter. "Victor, bring us a bottle of champagne, would you? Dom Perignon."

"Right away, Mr. Browning."

Jennifer smiled. "Are you trying to impress me?"

He laughed aloud. "I'm trying to hire you. I imagine you've been getting a lot of offers."

"A few."

"Our firm deals mostly in corporate work, Miss Parker, but some of our more affluent clients frequently get carried away and have need of a criminal defense attorney. I think we could make you a very attractive proposal. Would you care to stop by my office and discuss it?"

"Thank you, Mr. Browning. I'm really flattered, but I just moved into my own offices. I'm hoping it will work out."

He gave her a long look. "It will work out." He raised his eyes as someone approached and got to his feet and held out his hand. "Adam, how are you?"

Jennifer looked up and Adam Warner was standing there shaking hands with Lee Browning. Jennifer's heart began to beat faster and she could feel her face flush. *Idiot schoolgirl!*

Adam Warner looked at Jennifer and Browning and said, "You two know each other?"

"We were just beginning to get acquainted," Lee Browning said easily. "You arrived a little too soon."

"Or just in time." He took Jennifer's arm. "Better luck next time, Lee."

The captain came up to Adam. "Would you like your table now, Mr. Warner, or would you like to have a drink at the bar first?"

"We'll take a table, Henri."

When they had been seated, Jennifer looked around the room and recognized half a dozen celebrities.

"This place is like a *Who's Who*," she said.

Adam looked at her. "It is now."

Jennifer felt herself blush again. *Stop it, you fool.* She wondered how many other girls Adam Warner had brought here while his wife was sitting at home, waiting for him. She wondered if any of them ever learned that he was married, or whether he always managed to keep that a secret from them. Well, she had an advantage. *You're going to be in for a surprise, Mr. Warner,* Jennifer thought.

They ordered drinks and dinner and busied themselves making small talk. Jennifer let Adam do most of the talking.

He was witty and charming, but she was armored against his charm. It was not easy. She found herself smiling at his anecdotes, laughing at his stories.

It won't do him any good, Jennifer told herself. She was not looking for a fling. The specter of her mother haunted her. There was a deep passion within Jennifer that she was afraid to explore, afraid to release.

They were having dessert and Adam still had not said one word that could be misconstrued. Jennifer had been building up her defenses for nothing, fending off an attack that had never materialized, and she felt like a fool. She wondered what Adam would have said if he had known what she had been thinking all evening. Jennifer smiled at her own vanity.

"I never got a chance to thank you for the clients you sent me," Jennifer said. "I did telephone you a few times, but—"

"I know." Adam hesitated, then added awkwardly, "I didn't want to return your phone calls." Jennifer looked at him in surprise. "I was afraid to," he said simply.

And there it was. He had taken her by surprise, caught her off guard, but his meaning was unmistakable. Jennifer knew what was coming next. And she did not want him to say it. She did not want him to be like all the others, the married men who pretended they were single. She despised them and she did not want to despise this man.

Adam said quietly, "Jennifer, I want you to know I'm married." She sat there staring at him, her mouth open.

"I'm sorry. I should have told you sooner." He smiled wryly. "Well, there really was no sooner, was there?"

Jennifer was filled with a strange confusion. "Why—why did you ask me to dinner, Adam?"

"Because I had to see you again."

Everything began to seem unreal to Jennifer. It was as though she were being pulled under by some giant tidal wave. She sat there listening to Adam saying all the things he felt, and she knew that every word was true. She knew because she felt the same way. She wanted him to stop before he said too much. She wanted him to go on and say more.

"I hope I'm not offending you," Adam said.

There was a sudden shyness about him that shook Jennifer.

"Adam, I—I—"

He looked at her and even though they had not touched, it was as if she were in his arms.

Jennifer said shakily, "Tell me about your wife."

"Mary Beth and I have been married fifteen years. We have no children."

"I see."

"She—we decided not to have any. We were both very young when we got married. I had known her a long time. Our families were neighbors at a summer place we had in Maine. When she was eighteen, her parents were killed in a plane crash. Mary Beth was almost insane with grief. She was all alone. I—we got married."

He married her out of pity and he's too much of a gentleman to say so, Jennifer thought.

"She's a wonderful woman. We've always had a very good relationship."

He was telling Jennifer more than she wanted to know, more than she could handle. Every instinct in her warned her to get away, to flee. In the past she had easily been able to cope with the married men who had tried to become involved with her, but Jennifer knew instinctively that this was different. If she ever let herself fall in love with this man, there would be no way out. She would have to be insane ever to begin anything with him.

Jennifer spoke carefully. "Adam, I like you very much. I don't get involved with married men."

He smiled, and his eyes behind the glasses held honesty and warmth. "I'm not looking for a backstreet affair. I enjoy being with you. I'm very proud of you. I'd like us to see each other once in a while."

Jennifer started to say, *What good would that do?* but the words came out, "That would be good."

So we'll have lunch once a month, Jennifer thought. *It can't hurt anything.*

11

One of Jennifer's first visitors to her new office was Father Ryan. He wandered around the three small rooms and said, "Very nice, indeed. We're getting up in the world, Jennifer."

Jennifer laughed. "This isn't exactly getting up in the world, Father. I have a long way to go."

He eyed her keenly. "You'll make it. By the way, I went to visit Abraham Wilson last week."

"How is he getting along?"

"Fine. They have him working in the prison machine shop. He asked me to give you his regards."

"I'll have to visit him myself one day soon."

Father Ryan sat in his chair, staring at her, until Jennifer said, "Is there something I can do for you, Father?"

He brightened. "Ah, well, I know you must be busy, but now that you've brought it up, a friend of mine has a bit of a problem. She was in an accident. I think you're just the one to help her."

Automatically Jennifer replied, "Have her come in and see me, Father."

"I think you'll have to go to her. She's a quadruple amputee."

Connie Garrett lived in a small, neat apartment on Houston Street. The door was opened for Jennifer by an elderly white-haired woman wearing an apron.

"I'm Martha Steele, Connie's aunt. I live with Connie. Please come in. She's expecting you."

Jennifer walked into a meagerly furnished living room. Connie Garrett was propped up with pillows in a large arm-chair. Jennifer was shocked by her youth. For some reason, she had expected an older woman. Connie Garrett was about twenty-four, Jennifer's age. There was a wonderful radiance in her face, and Jennifer found it obscene that there was only a torso with no arms or legs attached to it. She repressed a shudder.

Connie Garrett gave her a warm smile and said, "Please sit down, Jennifer. May I call you Jennifer? Father Ryan has told me so much about you. And, of course, I've seen you on television. I'm so glad you could come."

Jennifer started to reply, "My pleasure," and realized how inane it would have sounded. She sat down in a soft com-fortable chair opposite the young woman.

"Father Ryan said you were in an accident a few years ago. Do you want to tell me what happened?"

"It was my fault, I'm afraid. I was crossing an intersection and I stepped off the sidewalk and slipped and fell in front of a truck."

"How long ago was this?"

"Three years ago last December. I was on my way to Bloomingdale's to do some Christmas shopping."

"What happened after the truck hit you?"

"I don't remember anything. I woke up in the hospital.

They told me that an ambulance brought me there. There was an injury to my spine. Then they found bone damage and it kept spreading until—" She stopped and tried to shrug. It was a pitiful gesture. "They tried to fit me with artificial limbs, but they don't work on me."

"Did you bring suit?"

She looked at Jennifer, puzzled. "Father Ryan didn't tell you?"

"Tell me what?"

"My lawyer sued the utility company whose truck hit me, and we lost the case. We appealed and lost the appeal."

Jennifer said, "He should have mentioned that. If the appellate court turned you down, I'm afraid there's nothing that can be done."

Connie Garrett nodded. "I didn't really believe there was. I just thought—well, Father Ryan said you could work miracles."

"That's *his* territory. I'm only a lawyer."

She was angry with Father Ryan for having given Connie Garrett false hope. Grimly, Jennifer decided she would have a talk with him.

The older woman was hovering in the background. "Can I offer you something, Miss Parker? Some tea and cake, perhaps?"

Jennifer suddenly realized she was hungry, for she had had no time for lunch. But she visualized sitting opposite Connie Garrett while she was being fed by hand, and she could not bear the thought.

"No, thanks," Jennifer lied. "I just had lunch."

All Jennifer wanted to do was get out of there as quickly as possible. She tried to think of some cheering note she could leave on, but there was nothing. *Damn Father Ryan!*

"I—I'm really sorry. I wish I—"

Connie Garrett smiled and said, "Please don't worry about it."

It was the smile that did it. Jennifer was sure if she had been in Connie Garrett's place she would never have been able to smile.

"Who was your lawyer?" Jennifer heard herself asking.

"Melvin Hutcherson. Do you know him?"

"No, but I'll look him up." She went on, without meaning to, "I'll have a talk with him."

"That would be so nice of you." There was warm appreciation in Connie Garrett's voice.

Jennifer thought of what the girl's life must be like, sitting there totally helpless, day after day, month after month, year after year, unable to do anything for herself.

"I can't promise anything, I'm afraid."

"Of course not. But do you know something, Jennifer? I feel better just because you came."

Jennifer rose to her feet. It was a moment to shake hands, but there was no hand to shake.

She said awkwardly, "It was nice meeting you, Connie. You'll hear from me."

On the way back to her office, Jennifer thought about Father Ryan and resolved that she would never succumb to his blandishments again. There was nothing anyone could do for that poor crippled girl, and to offer her any kind of hope was indecent. But she would keep her promise. She would talk to Melvin Hutcherson.

When Jennifer returned to her office there was a long list of messages for her. She looked through them quickly, looking for a message from Adam Warner. There was none.

12

Melvin Hutcherson was a short, balding man with a tiny button nose and washed-out pale blue eyes. He had a shabby suite of offices on the West Side that reeked of poverty. The receptionist's desk was empty.

"Gone to lunch," Melvin Hutcherson explained.

Jennifer wondered if he had a secretary. He ushered her into his private office, which was no larger than the reception office.

"You told me over the phone you wanted to talk about Connie Garrett."

"That's right."

He shrugged. "There's not that much to talk about. We sued and we lost. Believe me, I did a bang-up job for her."

"Did you handle the appeal?"

"Yep. We lost that, too. I'm afraid you're spinning your wheels." He regarded her a moment. "Why do you want to waste your time on something like this? You're hot. You could be working on big money cases."

"I'm doing a friend a favor. Would you mind if I looked at the transcripts?"

"Help yourself," Hutcherson shrugged. "They're public property."

Jennifer spent the evening going over the transcripts of Connie Garrett's lawsuit. To Jennifer's surprise, Melvin Hutcherson had told the truth: He had done a good job. He had named both the city and the Nationwide Motors Corporation as co-defendants, and had demanded a trial by jury. The jury had exonerated both defendants.

The Department of Sanitation had done its best to cope with the snowstorm that had swept the city that December; all its equipment had been in use. The city had argued that the storm was an act of God, and that if there was any negligence, it was on the part of Connie Garrett.

Jennifer turned to the charges against the truck company. Three eyewitnesses had testified that the driver had tried to stop the truck to avoid hitting the victim, but that he had been unable to brake in time, and the truck had gone into an unavoidable spin and had hit her. The verdict in favor of the defendant had been upheld by the Appellate Division and the case had been closed.

Jennifer finished reading the transcripts at three o'clock in the morning. She turned off the lights, unable to sleep. On paper, justice had been done. But the image of Connie Garrett kept coming into her mind. A girl in her twenties, without arms or legs. Jennifer visualized the truck hitting the young girl, the awful agony she must have suffered, the series of terrible operations that had been performed, each one cutting away parts of her limbs. Jennifer turned on the light and sat up in bed. She dialed Melvin Hutcherson's home number.

"There's nothing in the transcripts about the doctors," Jennifer said into the telephone. "Did you look into the possibility of malpractice?"

A groggy voice said, "Who the fuck is this?"

"Jennifer Parker. Did you—"

"For Christ's sake! It's—it's four o'clock in the morning! Don't you have a watch?"

"This is important. The hospital wasn't named in the suit. What about those operations that were performed on Connie Garrett? Did you check into them?"

There was a pause while Melvin Hutcherson tried to gather his thoughts. "I talked to the heads of neurology and orthopedics at the hospital that took care of her. The operations were necessary to save her life. They were performed by the top men there and were done properly. That's why the hospital wasn't named in the suit."

Jennifer felt a sharp sense of frustration. "I see."

"Look, I told you before, you're wasting your time on this one. Now why don't we both get some sleep?"

And the receiver clicked in Jennifer's ear. She turned out the light and lay back again. But sleep was farther away than ever. After a while, Jennifer gave up the struggle, arose and made herself a pot of coffee. She sat on her sofa drinking it, watching the rising sun paint the Manhattan skyline, the faint pink gradually turning into a bright, explosive red.

Jennifer was disturbed. For every injustice there was supposed to be a remedy at law. Had justice been done in Connie Garrett's case? She glanced at the clock on the wall. It was six-thirty. Jennifer picked up the telephone again and dialed Melvin Hutcherson's number.

"Did you check out the record of the truck driver?" Jennifer asked.

A sleepy voice said, "Jesus Christ! Are you some kind of crazy? When do you sleep?"

"The driver of the utility truck. Did you check out his record?"

"Lady, you're beginning to insult me."

"I'm sorry," Jennifer insisted, "but I have to know."

"The answer is yes. He had a perfect record. This was his first accident."

So that avenue was closed. "I see." Jennifer was thinking hard.

"Miss Parker," Melvin Hutcherson said, "do me a big favor, will you? If you have any more questions, call me during office hours."

"Sorry," Jennifer said absently. "Go back to sleep."

"Thanks a lot!"

Jennifer replaced the receiver. It was time to get dressed and go to work.

13

It had been three weeks since Jennifer had had dinner with Adam at Lutèce. She tried to put him out of her mind, but everything reminded her of Adam: A chance phrase, the back of a stranger's head, a tie similar to the one he had worn. There were many men who tried to date her. She was propositioned by clients, by attorneys she had opposed in court and by a night-court judge, but Jennifer wanted none of them. Lawyers invited her out for what was cynically referred to as "funch," but she was not interested. There was an independence about her that was a challenge to men.

Ken Bailey was always there, but that fact did nothing to assuage Jennifer's loneliness. There was only one person who could do that, damn him!

He telephoned on a Monday morning. "I thought I'd take a chance and see if you happened to be free for lunch today."

She was not. She said, "Of course I am."

Jennifer had sworn to herself that if Adam ever called her

again she would be friendly yet distant, and courteous but definitely not available.

The moment she heard Adam's voice she forgot all those things and said, *Of course I am.*

The last thing in the world she should have said.

They had lunch at a small restaurant in Chinatown, and they talked steadily for two hours that seemed like two minutes. They talked about law and politics and the theater, and solved all the complex problems of the world. Adam was brilliant and incisive and fascinating. He was genuinely interested in what Jennifer was doing, and took a joyous pride in her successes. *He has a right to*, Jennifer thought. *If not for him, I'd be back in Kelso, Washington.*

When Jennifer returned to the office, Ken Bailey was waiting for her.

"Have a good lunch?"

"Yes, thank you."

"Is Adam Warner going to become a client?" His tone was too casual.

"No, Ken. We're just friends."

And it was true.

The following week, Adam invited Jennifer to have lunch in the private dining room of his law firm. Jennifer was impressed with the huge, modern complex of offices. Adam introduced her to various members of the firm, and Jennifer felt like a minor celebrity, for they seemed to know all about her. She met Stewart Needham, the senior partner. He was distantly polite to Jennifer, and she remembered that Adam was married to his niece.

Adam and Jennifer had lunch in the walnut-paneled dining room run by a chef and two waiters.

"This is where the partners bring their problems."

Jennifer wondered whether he was referring to her.

It was hard for her to concentrate on the meal.

Jennifer thought about Adam all that afternoon. She knew she had to forget about him, had to stop seeing him. He belonged to another woman.

That night, Jennifer went with Ken Bailey to see *Two by Two*, the new Richard Rodgers show.

As they stepped into the lobby there was an excited buzz from the crowd, and Jennifer turned to see what was happening. A long, black limousine had pulled up to the curb and a man and woman were stepping out of the car.

"It's him!" a woman exclaimed, and people began to gather around the car. The burly chauffeur stepped aside and Jennifer saw Michael Moretti and his wife. It was Michael that the crowd focused on. He was a folk hero, handsome enough to be a movie star, daring enough to have captured everyone's imagination. Jennifer stood in the lobby watching as Michael Moretti and his wife made their way through the crowd. Michael passed within three feet of Jennifer, and for an instant their eyes met. Jennifer noticed that his eyes were so black that she could not see his pupils. A moment later he disappeared into the theater.

Jennifer was unable to enjoy the show. The sight of Michael Moretti had brought back a flood of fiercely humiliating memories. Jennifer asked Ken to take her home after the first act.

Adam telephoned Jennifer the next day and Jennifer steeled herself to refuse his invitation. *Thank you, Adam, but I'm really very busy.*

But all Adam said was, "I have to go out of the country for a while."

It was like a blow to the stomach. "How—how long will you be gone?"

"Just a few weeks. I'll give you a call when I get back."

"Fine," Jennifer said brightly. "Have a nice trip."

She felt as though someone had died. She visualized Adam on a beach in Rio, surrounded by half-naked girls, or in a penthouse in Mexico City, drinking margaritas with a nubile, dark-eyed beauty, or in a Swiss chalet making love to—*Stop it!* Jennifer told herself. She should have asked him where he was going. It was probably a business trip to some dreary place where he would have no time for women, perhaps the middle of some desert where he would be working twenty-four hours a day.

She should have broached the subject, very casually, of course. *Will you be taking a long plane trip? Do you speak any foreign languages? If you get to Paris, bring me back some Vervaine tea. I suppose the shots must be painful. Are you taking your wife with you? Am I losing my mind?*

Ken had come into her office and was staring at her. "You're talking to yourself. Are you okay?"

No! Jennifer wanted to shout. *I need a doctor. I need a cold shower. I need Adam Warner.*

She said, "I'm fine. Just a little tired."

"Why don't you get to bed early tonight?"

She wondered whether Adam would be going to bed early.

Father Ryan called. "I went to see Connie Garrett. She told me you've dropped by a few times."

"Yes." The visits were to assuage her feeling of guilt because she was unable to be of any help. It was frustrating.

Jennifer plunged herself into work, and still the weeks seemed to drag by. She was in court nearly every day and worked on briefs almost every night.

"Slow down. You're going to kill yourself," Ken advised her.

But Jennifer needed to exhaust herself physically and

mentally. She did not want to have time to think. *I'm a fool,* she thought. *An unadulterated fool.*

It was four weeks before Adam called.

"I just got back," he said. The sound of his voice thrilled her. "Can we meet for lunch somewhere?"

"Yes. I'd enjoy that, Adam." She thought she had carried that off well. A simple *Yes, I'd enjoy that, Adam.*

"The Oak Room in the Plaza?"

"Fine."

It was the most businesslike, unromantic dining room in the world, filled with affluent middle-aged wheelers and dealers, stockbrokers and bankers. It had long been one of the few remaining bastions of privacy for men, and its doors had only recently been opened to women.

Jennifer arrived early and was seated. A few minutes later, Adam appeared. Jennifer watched the tall, lean figure moving toward her and her mouth suddenly went dry. He looked tanned, and Jennifer wondered if her fantasies about Adam on some girl-ridden beach had been true. He smiled at her and took her hand, and Jennifer knew in that moment that it did not matter what logic she used about Adam Warner or married men. She had no control over herself. It was as though someone else were guiding her, telling her what she should do, telling her what she must do. She could not explain what was happening to her, for she had never experienced anything like it. *Call it chemistry,* she thought. *Call it karma, call it heaven.* All Jennifer knew was that she wanted to be in Adam Warner's arms more than she had ever wanted anything in her life. Looking at him, she visualized his making love to her, holding her, his hard body on top of her, inside her, and she felt her face becoming red.

Adam said apologetically, "Sorry about the short notice. A client canceled a luncheon date."

Jennifer silently blessed the client.

"I brought you something," Adam said. It was a lovely green and gold silk scarf. "It's from Milan."

So *that's* where he had been. *Italian girls.* "It's beautiful, Adam. Thank you."

"Have you ever been to Milan?"

"No. I've seen pictures of the cathedral there. It's lovely."

"I'm not much of a sightseer. My theory is that if you've seen one church, you've seen them all."

Later, when Jennifer thought about that luncheon, she tried to remember what they had talked about, what they had eaten, who had stopped by the table to say hello to Adam, but all she could remember was the nearness of Adam, his touch, his looks. It was as though he had her in some kind of spell and she was mesmerized, helpless to break it.

At one point Jennifer thought, *I know what to do. I'll make love with him. Once. It can't be as wonderful as my fantasies. Then I'll be able to get over him.*

When their hands touched accidentally, it was like an electric charge between them. They sat there talking of everything and nothing, and their words had no meaning. They sat at the table, locked in an invisible embrace, caressing each other, making fierce love, naked and wanton. Neither of them had any idea what they were eating or what they were saying. There was a different, more demanding hunger in them and it kept mounting and mounting, until neither of them could stand it any longer.

In the middle of their luncheon, Adam put his hand over Jennifer's and said huskily, "Jennifer——"

She whispered, "Yes. Let's get out of here."

Jennifer waited in the busy, crowded lobby while Adam registered at the desk. They were given a room in the old section of the Plaza Hotel, overlooking 58th Street. They used the back bank of elevators, and it seemed to Jennifer that it took forever to reach their floor.

If Jennifer was unable to remember anything about the

luncheon, she remembered everything about their room. Years later, she could recall the view, the color of the drapes and carpets, and each picture and piece of furniture. She could remember the sounds of the city, far below, that drifted into the room. The images of that afternoon were to stay with her the rest of her life. It was a magic, multicolored explosion in slow motion. It was having Adam undress her, it was Adam's strong, lean body in bed, his roughness and his gentleness. It was laughter and passion. Their hunger had built to a greed that had to be satisfied. The moment Adam began to make love to her, the words that flashed into Jennifer's mind were, *I'm lost.*

They made love again and again, and each time was an ecstasy that was almost unbearable.

Hours later, as they lay there quietly, Adam said, "I feel as though I'm alive for the first time in my life."

Jennifer gently stroked his chest and laughed aloud.

Adam looked at her quizzically. "What's so funny?"

"Do you know what I told myself? That if I went to bed with you once, I could get you out of my system."

He twisted around and looked down at her. "And—?"

"I was wrong. I feel as though you're a part of me. At least" —she hesitated—"*part* of you is a part of me."

He knew what she was thinking.

"We'll work something out," Adam said. "Mary Beth is leaving Monday for Europe with her aunt for a month."

14

Jennifer and Adam Warner were together almost every night.

He spent the first night at her uncomfortable little apartment and in the morning he declared, "We're taking the day off to find you a decent place to live."

They went apartment hunting together, and late that afternoon Jennifer signed a lease in a new high-rise building off Sutton Place, called The Belmont Towers. The sign in front of the building had read *Sold Out*.

"Why are we going in?" Jennifer asked.

"You'll see."

The apartment they looked at was a lovely five-room duplex, beautifully furnished. It was the most luxurious apartment Jennifer had ever seen. There was a master bedroom and bath upstairs, and downstairs a guest bedroom with its own bath and a living room that had a spectacular view of the East River and the city. There was a large terrace, a kitchen and a dining room.

"How do you like it?" Adam asked.

"Like it? I love it," Jennifer exclaimed, "but there are two problems, darling. First of all, I couldn't possibly afford it. And secondly, even if I could, it belongs to someone else."

"It belongs to our law firm. We leased it for visiting VIP's. I'll have them find another place."

"What about the rent?"

"I'll take care of that. I—"

"No."

"That's crazy, darling. I can easily afford it and—"

She shook her head. "You don't understand, Adam. I have nothing to give you except me. I want that to be a gift."

He took her in his arms and Jennifer snuggled against him and said, "I know what—I'll work nights."

Saturday they went on a shopping spree. Adam bought Jennifer a beautiful silk nightgown and robe at Bonwit Teller, and Jennifer bought Adam a Turnbull & Asser shirt. They purchased a chess game at Gimbel's and cheesecake in Junior's near Abraham & Straus. They bought a Fortnum & Mason plum pudding at Altman's, and books at Doubleday. They visited the Gammon Shop and Caswell-Massey, where Adam bought Jennifer enough potpourri to last for ten years. They had dinner around the corner from the apartment.

They would meet at the apartment in the evening after work and discuss the day's events, and Jennifer would cook dinner while Adam set the table. Afterward, they read or watched television or played gin rummy or chess. Jennifer prepared Adam's favorite dishes.

"I'm shameless," she told him. "I won't stop at anything."

He held her close. "Please don't."

It was strange, Jennifer thought. Before they began their affair they saw each other openly. But now that they were

lovers, they dared not appear in public together, so they went
to places where they were not apt to run into friends: small
family restaurants downtown, a chamber music concert at the
Third Street Music School Settlement. They went to see a new
play at the Omni Theatre Club on 18th Street and had dinner
at the Grotta Azzurra on Broome Street, and ate so much that
they swore off Italian food for a month. *Only we don't have a
month,* Jennifer thought. Mary Beth was returning in fourteen
days.

They went to The Half Note to hear avant-garde jazz in the
Village, and peeked into the windows of the small art gal-
leries.

Adam loved sports. He took Jennifer to watch the Knicks
play, and Jennifer got so caught up in the game she cheered
until she was hoarse.

On Sunday they lazed around, having breakfast in their
robes, trading sections of the *Times,* listening to the church
bells ring across Manhattan, each offering up its own prayer.

Jennifer looked over at Adam absorbed in the crossword
puzzle and thought: *Say a prayer for me.* She knew that what
she was doing was wrong. She knew that it could not last. And
yet, she had never known such happiness, such euphoria.
Lovers lived in a special world, where every sense was height-
ened, and the joy Jennifer felt now with Adam was worth any
price she would have to pay later. And she knew she was
going to have to pay.

Time took on a different dimension. Before, Jennifer's life
had been measured out in hours and meetings with clients.
Now her time was counted by the minutes she could spend
with Adam. She thought about him when she was with him,
and she thought about him when she was away from him.

Jennifer had read of men having heart attacks in the arms
of their mistresses, and so she put the number of Adam's personal physician in her private telephone book by her bedside

so that if anything ever happened it could be handled discreetly and Adam would not be embarrassed.

Jennifer was filled with emotions that she had not known existed in her. She had never thought of herself as being domestic, but she wanted to do everything for Adam. She wanted to cook for him, to clean for him, to lay out his clothes in the morning. To take care of him.

Adam kept a set of clothes at the apartment, and he would spend most nights with Jennifer. She would lie next to him, watching him fall asleep, and she would try to stay awake as long as possible, terrified of losing a moment of their precious time together. Finally, when Jennifer could keep her eyes open no longer, she would snuggle in Adam's arms and fall asleep, contented and safe. The insomnia that had plagued Jennifer for so long had vanished. Whatever night devils had tormented her had disappeared. When she curled up in Adam's arms, she was instantly at peace.

She enjoyed walking around the apartment in Adam's shirts, and at night she would wear his pajama top. If she was still in bed in the morning when he left, Jennifer would roll over to his side of the bed. She loved the warm smell of him.

It seemed that all the popular love songs she heard had been written for Adam and her, and Jennifer thought, *Noel Coward was right. It's amazing how potent cheap music can be.*

In the beginning, Jennifer had thought that the overwhelming physical feeling they had for each other would diminish in time, but instead it grew stronger.

She told Adam things about herself that she had never told another human being. With Adam, there were no masks. She was Jennifer Parker, stripped naked, and still he loved her. It was a miracle. And they shared another miracle together: laughter.

Impossibly, she loved Adam more each day. She wished that what they had would never end. But she knew it would.

For the first time in her life, she became superstitious. There was a special blend of Kenya coffee that Adam liked. Jennifer bought some every few days.

But she bought only one small can at a time.

One of Jennifer's terrors was that something would happen to Adam when he was away from her and that she would not know it until she read about it, or heard about it on a news program. She never told Adam of her fears.

Whenever Adam was going to be late he would leave notes for Jennifer around the apartment where she would come upon them unexpectedly. She would find them in the breadbox or in the refrigerator, or in her shoe; they delighted her, and she saved each one.

Their last remaining days together raced by in a blur of joyous activity. Finally, it was the night before Mary Beth was to return. Jennifer and Adam had dinner in the apartment, listened to music and made love. Jennifer lay awake all night, holding Adam in her arms. Her thoughts were of the happiness they had shared.

The pain would come later.

At breakfast, Adam said, "Whatever happens, I want you to know this—you're the only woman I've ever truly loved."

The pain came then.

15

The anodyne was work, and Jennifer immersed herself in it totally so that she had no time to think.

She had become the darling of the press, and her courtroom successes were highly publicized. More clients came to her than she could handle, and while Jennifer's chief interest was in criminal law, at Ken's urging she began to accept a variety of other cases.

Ken Bailey had become more important than ever to Jennifer. He handled the investigations on her cases, and he was brilliant. She was able to discuss other problems with him and she valued his advice.

Jennifer and Ken moved again, this time into a large suite of offices on Park Avenue. Jennifer hired two bright young attorneys, Dan Martin and Ted Harris, both from Robert Di Silva's staff, and two more secretaries.

Dan Martin was a former football player from Northwestern University and he had the appearance of an athlete and the mind of a scholar.

Ted Harris was a slight, diffident young man who wore thick, milk-bottle spectacles and was a genius.

Martin and Harris took care of the legwork and Jennifer handled the appearances at trials.

The sign on the door read: *JENNIFER PARKER & ASSOCIATES.*

The cases that came into the office ranged from defending a large industrial corporation on a pollution charge to representing a drunk who had suffered whiplash when he was bounced from a tavern. The drunk, of course, was a gift from Father Ryan.

"He has a bit of a problem," Father Ryan told Jennifer. "He's really a decent family man, but the poor fellow has such pressures that he sometimes takes a drop too much."

Jennifer could not help but smile. As far as Father Ryan was concerned, none of his parishioners was guilty and his only desire was to help them get out of the difficulty they had carelessly gotten themselves into. One reason Jennifer understood the priest so well was that basically she felt the same as he did. They were dealing with people in trouble who had no one to help them, with neither the money nor the power to fight the Establishment, and in the end they were crushed by it.

The word *justice* was honored mostly in the breach. In the courtroom, neither the prosecuting attorney nor the defense attorney sought justice: The name of the game was to win.

From time to time, Jennifer and Father Ryan talked about Connie Garrett, but the subject always left Jennifer depressed. There was an injustice there and it rankled her.

In his office in the back room of Tony's Place, Michael Moretti watched as Nick Vito carefully swept the office with an electronic device, looking for gypsy taps. Through his police connections, Michael knew that no electronic surveillance had been authorized by the authorities, but once in a while an overzealous tin hotdog, a young detective, would set up a gypsy—or illegal—tap, hoping to pick up information. Michael was a careful man. His office and home were swept every morning and every evening. He was aware that he was the number one target for half a dozen different law agencies, but he was not concerned. He knew what they were doing, but they did not know what he was doing; and if they did, they could not prove it.

Sometimes late at night Michael would look through the peephole of the restaurant's back door and watch the FBI agents pick up his garbage for analysis, and substitute other garbage for it.

One night Nick Vito said, "Jesus, boss, what if the jokers dig up something?"

Michael laughed. "I hope they do. Before they get here we switch our garbage with the restaurant next door."

No, the federal agents were not going to touch him. The Family's activities were expanding, and Michael had plans that he had not even revealed yet. The only stumbling block was Thomas Colfax. Michael knew he had to get rid of the old lawyer. He needed a fresh young mind. And again and again, his thoughts turned to Jennifer Parker.

Adam and Jennifer met for lunch once a week, and it was torture for both of them, for they had no time to be alone together, no privacy. They talked on the telephone every day, using code names. He was Mr. Adams and she was Mrs. Jay.

"I hate sneaking around like this," Adam said.

"I do too." But the thought of losing him terrified her.

The courtroom was where Jennifer escaped from her own

private pain. The courtroom was a stage, an area where she matched wits against the best that the opposition could offer. Her school was the courtroom and she learned well. A trial was a game played within certain rigid rules, where the better player won, and Jennifer was determined to be the better player.

Jennifer's cross-examinations became theatrical events, with a skilled speed and rhythm and timing. She learned to recognize the leader of a jury and to concentrate on him, knowing he could swing the others into line.

A man's shoes said something about his character. Jennifer looked for jurors who wore comfortable shoes, because they were inclined to be easygoing.

She learned about strategy, the overall plan of a trial, and about tactics, the day-by-day maneuvers. She became an expert at shopping for friendly judges.

Jennifer spent endless hours preparing each case, heeding the adage, *Most cases are won or lost before the trial begins.* She became adept at mnemonics so that she could remember jurors' names: Smith—a muscular man who could handle an anvil; Helm—a man steering a boat; Newman—a newborn baby.

The court usually recessed at four o'clock, and when Jennifer was cross-examining a witness in the late afternoon, she would stall until a few minutes before four and then hit the witness with a verbal blow that would leave a strong overnight impression on the jury.

She learned to read body language. When a witness on the stand was lying, there would be telltale gestures: stroking the chin, pressing the lips together, covering the mouth, pulling the earlobes or grooming the hair. Jennifer became an expert at reading those signs, and she would zero in for the kill.

Jennifer discovered that being a woman was a disadvantage when it came to practicing criminal law. She was in macho territory. There were still very few women criminal attorneys and some of the male lawyers resented Jennifer. On her brief-case one day Jennifer found a sticker that read: *Women Law-yers Make the Best Motions.* In retaliation, Cynthia put a sign on her desk that read: *A Woman's Place is in the House . . . and in the Senate.*

Most juries started out by being prejudiced against Jennifer, for many of the cases she handled were sordid, and there was a tendency to make an association between her and her client. She was expected to dress like Jane Eyre and she refused, but she was careful to dress in such a fashion that she would not arouse the envy of the women jurors, and at the same time appear feminine enough so as not to antagonize the men who might feel she was a lesbian. At one time, Jennifer would have laughed at any of these considerations. But in the courtroom she found them to be stern realities. Because she had entered a man's world she had to work twice as hard and be twice as good as the competition. Jennifer learned to prepare thor-oughly not only her own cases, but the cases of her opposi-tion as well. She would lie in bed at night or sit at the desk in her office and plot her opponent's strategy. What would she do if she were on the other side? What surprises would she try to pull? She was a general, planning both sides of a lethal battle.

Cynthia buzzed on the intercom. "There's a man on line three who wants to talk to you, but he won't give his name or tell me what it's about."

Six months earlier, Cynthia would simply have hung up on the man. Jennifer had taught her never to turn anyone away.

"Put him through," Jennifer said.

A moment later she heard a man's voice ask cautiously, "Is this Jennifer Parker?"

"Yes."

He hesitated. "Is this a safe line?"

"Yes. What can I do for you?"

"It's not for me. It's for—for a friend of mine."

"I see. What's your friend's problem?"

"This has to be in confidence, you understand."

"I understand."

Cynthia walked in and handed Jennifer the mail. "Wait," Jennifer mouthed.

"My friend's family locked her up in an insane asylum. She's sane. It's a conspiracy. The authorities are in on it."

Jennifer was only half-listening now. She braced the telephone against her shoulder while she went through the morning's mail.

The man was saying, "She's rich and her family's after her money."

Jennifer said, "Go on," and continued examining the mail.

"They'd probably have me put away, too, if they found I was trying to help her. It could be dangerous for me, Miss Parker."

A nut case, Jennifer decided. She said, "I'm afraid I can't do anything, but I'd suggest you get hold of a good psychiatrist to help your friend."

"You don't understand. They're all in on it."

"I do understand," Jennifer said soothingly. "I—"

"Will you help her?"

"There's nothing I can—I'll tell you what. Why don't you give me your friend's name and address and if I get a chance, I'll look into it."

There was a long silence. Finally the man spoke. "This is confidential, remember."

Jennifer wished he would get off the telephone. Her first appointment was waiting in the reception room. "I'll remember."

"Cooper. Helen Cooper. She had a big estate on Long Island, but they took it away from her."

Obediently, Jennifer made a note on a pad in front of her. "Fine. What sanatorium did you say she was in?" There was a click and the line went dead. Jennifer threw the note into the waste basket.

Jennifer and Cynthia exchanged a look. "It's a weird world out there," Cynthia said. "Miss Marshall is waiting to see you."

Jennifer had talked to Loretta Marshall on the telephone a week earlier. Miss Marshall had asked Jennifer to represent her in a paternity suit against Curtis Randall III, a wealthy socialite.

Jennifer had spoken to Ken Bailey. "We need information on Curtis Randall III. He lives in New York, but I understand he spends a lot of time in Palm Beach. I want to know what his background is, and if he's been sleeping with a girl named Loretta Marshall."

She had told Ken the names of the Palm Beach hotels that the woman had given her. Two days later, Ken Bailey had reported back.

"It checks out. They spent two weeks together at hotels in Palm Beach, Miami and Atlantic City. Loretta Marshall gave birth to a daughter eight months ago."

Jennifer sat back in her chair and looked at him thoughtfully. "It sounds as though we might have a case."

"I don't think so."

"What's the problem?"

"The problem is our client. She's slept with everybody including the Yankees."

"You're saying that the father of the baby could be any number of men."

"I'm saying it could be half the world."

"Are any of the others wealthy enough to give child support?"

"Well, the Yankees are pretty rich, but the big league moneyman is Curtis Randall III."

He handed her a long list of names.

Loretta Marshall walked into the office. Jennifer had not been sure what to expect. A pretty, empty-headed prostitute, in all probability. But Loretta Marshall was a complete surprise. Not only was she not pretty, she was almost homely. Her figure was ordinary. From the number of Miss Marshall's romantic conquests, Jennifer had expected nothing less than a sexy raving beauty. Loretta Marshall was the stereotype of an elementary grade schoolteacher. She was clad in a plaid wool skirt, a button-down-collar shirt, a dark blue cardigan and sensible shoes. At first, Jennifer had been sure that Loretta Marshall was planning to use her to force Curtis Randall to pay for the privilege of raising a baby that was not his. After an hour's conversation with the girl, Jennifer found that her opinion had changed. Loretta Marshall was transparently honest.

"Of course, I have no proof that Curtis is Melanie's father," she smiled shyly. "Curtis isn't the only man I've slept with."

"Then what makes you think he's the father of your child, Miss Marshall?"

"I don't *think*. I'm sure of it. It's hard to explain, but I even know the night Melanie was conceived. Sometimes a woman can feel those things."

Jennifer studied her, trying to find any sign of guile or deceit. There was none. The girl was totally without pretense. Perhaps, Jennifer thought, men found that part of her charm.

"Are you in love with Curtis Randall?"

"Oh, yes. And Curtis said he loved me. Of course, I'm not sure he still does, after what's happened."

If you loved him, Jennifer wondered, *how could you have slept with all those other men?* The answer might have lain in that sad, homely face and plain figure.

"Can you help me, Miss Parker?"

Jennifer said cautiously, "Paternity cases are always difficult. I have a list of more than a dozen men you've slept with in the past year. There are probably others. If *I* have such a list, you can be sure that Curtis Randall's attorney will have one."

Loretta Marshall frowned. "What about blood samples, that kind of thing . . . ?"

"Blood tests are admissible in evidence only if they prove that the defendant could not be the father. They're legally inconclusive."

"I don't really care about me. It's Melanie I want protected. It's only right that Curtis should take care of his daughter."

Jennifer hesitated, weighing her decision. She had told Loretta Marshall the truth. Paternity cases were difficult. To say nothing about being messy and unpleasant. The attorneys for the defense would have a field day when they got this woman on the stand. They would bring up a parade of her lovers and, before they were through, they would make her look like a whore. It was not the type of case that Jennifer wanted to become involved in. On the other hand, she believed Loretta Marshall. This was no ordinary gold digger out to gouge an ex-lover. The girl was convinced that Curtis Randall was the father of her child. Jennifer made her decision.

"All right," she said, "we'll take a crack at it."

Jennifer set up a meeting with Roger Davis, the lawyer representing Curtis Randall. Davis was a partner in a large Wall Street firm and the importance of his position was indicated by the spacious corner suite he occupied. He was pompous and arrogant, and Jennifer disliked him on sight.

"What can I do for you?" Roger Davis asked.

"As I explained on the telephone, I'm here on behalf of Loretta Marshall."

He looked at her and said impatiently, "So?"

"She's asked me to institute a paternity suit against Mr. Curtis Randall III. I would prefer not to do that."

"You'd be a damned fool if you did."

Jennifer held her temper in check. "We don't wish to drag your client's name through the courts. As I'm sure you know, this kind of case always gets nasty. Therefore, we're prepared to accept a reasonable out-of-court settlement."

Roger Davis gave Jennifer a wintry smile. "I'm sure you are. Because you have no case. None at all."

"I think we have."

"Miss Parker, I haven't time to mince words. Your client is a whore. She'll have intercourse with anything that moves. I have a list of men she's slept with. It's as long as my arm. You think *my* client is going to get hurt? Your client will be *destroyed*. She's a schoolteacher, I believe. Well, when I get through with her she'll never teach anywhere again as long as she lives. And I'll tell you something else. Randall believes he's the father of that baby. But you'll never prove it in a million years."

Jennifer sat back, listening, her face expressionless.

"Our position is that your client could have become impregnated by anyone in the Third Army. You want to make a deal? Fine. I'll tell you what we'll do. We'll buy your client birth-control pills so that it doesn't happen again."

Jennifer stood up, her cheeks burning. "Mr. Davis," she said, "that little speech of yours is going to cost your client half a million dollars."

And Jennifer was out the door.

Ken Bailey and three assistants could turn up nothing against Curtis Randall III. He was a widower, a pillar of society, and he had had very few sexual flings.

"The son of a bitch is a born-again puritan," Ken Bailey complained.

They were seated in the conference room at midnight, the night before the paternity trial was to begin. "I've talked to one of the attorneys in Davis's office, Jennifer. They're going to destroy our client. They're not bluffing."

"Why are you sticking your neck out for this girl?" Dan Martin asked.

"I'm not here to judge her sex life, Dan. She believes that Curtis Randall is the father of her baby. I mean, she really *believes* it. All she wants is money for her daughter—nothing for herself. I think she deserves her day in court."

"We're not thinking about her," Ken replied. "We're thinking about you. You're on a hot roll. Everybody's watching you. I think this is a no-win case. It's going to be a black mark against you."

"Let's all get some sleep," Jennifer said. "I'll see you in court."

The trial went even worse than Ken Bailey had predicted. Jennifer had had Loretta Marshall bring her baby into the courtroom, but now Jennifer wondered if she had not made a tactical error. She sat there, helpless, as Roger Davis brought witness after witness to the stand and forced each of them to admit they had slept with Loretta Marshall. Jennifer did not dare cross-examine them. They were victims, and they were testifying in public only because they had been forced to. All Jennifer could do was sit by while her client's name was besmirched. She watched the faces of the jurors, and she could read the growing hostility there. Roger Davis was too clever to characterize Loretta Marshall as a whore. He did not have to. The people on the stand did it for him.

Jennifer had brought in her own character witnesses to

testify to the good work that Loretta Marshall had done as a teacher, to the fact that she attended church regularly and was a good mother; but all this made no impression in the face of the horrifying array of Loretta Marshall's lovers. Jennifer had hoped to play on the sympathy of the jury by dramatizing the plight of a young woman who had been betrayed by a wealthy playboy and then abandoned when she had become pregnant. The trial was not working out that way.

Curtis Randall III was seated at the defendant's table. He could have been chosen by a casting director. He was an elegant-looking man in his late fifties, with striking gray hair and tanned, regular features. He came from a social background, belonged to all the right clubs and was wealthy and successful. Jennifer could feel the women on the jury mentally undressing him.

Sure, Jennifer thought. *They're thinking that they're worthy to go to bed with Mr. Charming, but not that what-does-he-see-in-her slut sitting in the courtroom with a ten-month old baby in her arms.*

Unfortunately for Loretta Marshall, the child looked nothing like its father. Or its mother, for that matter. It could have belonged to anybody.

As though reading Jennifer's thoughts, Roger Davis said to the jury, "There they sit, ladies and gentlemen, mother and child. Ah! But *whose* child? You've seen the defendant. I defy anyone in this courtroom to point out *one single point of resemblance* between the defendant and this infant. Surely, if my client were the father of this child, there would be *some* sign of it. Something in the eyes, the nose, the chin. Where is that resemblance? It doesn't exist, and for a very simple reason. The defendant is not the father of this child. No, I'm very much afraid that what we have here is the classic example of a loose woman who was careless, got pregnant, and then looked around to see which lover could best afford to pay the bills."

His voice softened. "Now, none of us is here to judge her. What Loretta Marshall chooses to do with her personal life is her own business. The fact that she is a teacher and can influence the minds of small children, well, that is not in my purview, either. I am not here to moralize; I'm simply here to protect the interests of an innocent man."

Jennifer studied the jury and she had the sinking feeling that every one of them was on the side of Curtis Randall. Jennifer still believed Loretta Marshall. If only the baby looked like its father! Roger Davis was right. There was no resemblance at all. And he had made sure the jury was aware of that.

Jennifer called Curtis Randall to the stand. She knew that this was her only chance to try to repair the damage that had been done, her final opportunity to turn the case around. She studied the man in the witness chair for a moment.

"Have you ever been married, Mr. Randall?"

"Yes. My wife died in a fire." There was an instinctive reaction of sympathy from the jury.

Damn! Jennifer moved on quickly. "You never remarried?"

"No. I loved my wife very much, and I—"

"Did you and your wife have any children?"

"No. Unfortunately, she was not able to."

Jennifer gestured toward the baby. "Then Melanie is your only—"

"Objection!"

"Sustained. Counsel for the plaintiff knows better than that."

"I'm sorry, Your Honor. It slipped out." Jennifer turned back to Curtis Randall. "Do you like children?"

"Yes, very much."

"You're the chairman of the board of your own corporation, are you not, Mr. Randall?"

"Yes."

"Haven't you ever wished for a son to carry on your name?"

"I suppose every man wants that."

"So if Melanie had been born a boy instead of—"

"Objection!"

"Sustained." The judge turned to Jennifer. "Miss Parker, I
will ask you again to stop doing that."

"Sorry, Your Honor." Jennifer turned back to Curtis
Randall. "Mr. Randall, are you in the habit of picking up
strange women and taking them to hotels?"

Curtis Randall ran his tongue nervously over his lower
lip. "No, I am not."

"Isn't it true that you first met Loretta Marshall in a bar
and took her to a hotel room?"

His tongue was working at his lips again. "Yes, ma'am,
but that was just—that was just sex."

Jennifer stared at him. "You say 'that was just sex' as
though you feel sex is something dirty."

"No, ma'am." His tongue flicked out again.

Jennifer was watching it, fascinated, as it moved across
his lips. She was filled with a sudden, wild sense of hope. She
knew now what she had to do. She had to keep pushing him.
And yet she could not push him so hard that the jury would
become antagonistic toward her.

"How many women have you picked up in bars?"

Roger Davis was on his feet. "Irrelevant, Your Honor. And
I object to this line of questioning. The only woman involved
in this case is Loretta Marshall. We have already stipulated
that the defendant had sexual intercourse with her. Aside
from that, his personal life has no relevance in this courtroom."

"I disagree, Your Honor. If the defendant is the kind of
man who—"

"Sustained. Please discontinue that line of questioning, Miss Parker."

Jennifer shrugged. "Yes, Your Honor." She turned back to Curtis Randall. "Let's get back to the night you picked up Loretta Marshall in a bar. What kind of bar was it?"

"I—I really don't know. I'd never been there before."

"It was a singles bar, wasn't it?"

"I have no idea."

"Well, for your information, the *Play Pen* was and is a singles bar. It has the reputation of being a pickup place, a rendezvous where men and women go to meet partners they can take to bed. Isn't that why you went there, Mr. Randall?"

Curtis Randall began to lick his lips again. "It—it may have been. I don't remember."

"You don't remember?" Jennifer's voice was weighted with sarcasm. "Do you happen to remember the date on which you first met Loretta Marshall in that bar?"

"No, I don't. Not exactly."

"Then let me refresh your memory."

Jennifer walked over to the plaintiff's table and began looking through some papers. She scribbled a note as though she were copying a date and handed it to Ken Bailey. He studied it, a puzzled expression on his face.

Jennifer moved back toward the witness box. "It was on January eighteenth, Mr. Randall."

Out of the corner of her eye, Jennifer saw Ken Bailey leaving the courtroom.

"It could have been, I suppose. As I said, I don't remember."

For the next fifteen minutes, Jennifer went on questioning Curtis Randall. It was a rambling, gentle cross-examination, and Roger Davis did not interrupt, because he saw that Jennifer was making no points with the jurors, who were beginning to look bored.

Jennifer kept talking, keeping an eye out for Ken Bailey.

In the middle of a question, Jennifer saw him hurry into the courtroom, carrying a small package.

Jennifer turned to the judge. "Your Honor, may I ask for a fifteen-minute recess?"

The judge looked at the clock on the wall. "Since it's almost time for lunch, the court will adjourn until one-thirty."

At one-thirty the court was in session again. Jennifer had moved Loretta Marshall to a seat closer to the jury box, with the baby on her lap.

The judge said, "Mr. Randall, you are still under oath. You will not have to be sworn in again. Take the stand, please."

Jennifer watched as Curtis Randall sat down in the witness box. She walked up to him and said, "Mr. Randall, how many illegitimate children have you sired?"

Roger Davis was on his feet. "Objection! This is outrageous, Your Honor. I will not have my client subjected to this kind of humiliation."

The judge said, "Objection sustained." He turned to Jennifer. "Miss Parker, I have warned you—"

Jennifer said contritely, "I'm sorry, Your Honor."

She looked at Curtis Randall and saw that she had accomplished what she had wanted. He was nervously licking his lips. Jennifer turned toward Loretta Marshall and her baby. The baby was busily licking its lips. Jennifer slowly walked over to the baby and stood in front of her a long moment, focusing the attention of the jury.

"Look at that child," Jennifer said softly.

They were all staring at little Melanie, her pink tongue licking her underlip.

Jennifer turned and walked back to the witness box. "And look at this man."

Twelve pairs of eyes turned to focus on Curtis Randall. He sat there nervously licking his underlip, and suddenly the resemblance was unmistakable. Forgotten was the fact that

Loretta Marshall had slept with dozens of other men. Forgotten was the fact that Curtis Randall was a pillar of the community.

"This is a man," Jennifer said mournfully, "of position and means. A man everyone looks up to. I want to ask you only one question: What kind of man is it who would deny his own child?"

The jury was out less than one hour, returning with a judgment for the plaintiff. Loretta Marshall would receive two hundred thousand dollars in cash and two thousand dollars a month for child support.

When the verdict came in, Roger Davis strode up to Jennifer, his face flushed with anger. "Did you do something with that baby?"

"What do you mean?"

Roger Davis hesitated, unsure of himself. "That lip thing. That's what won the jury over, the baby licking her lips like that. Can you explain it?"

"As a matter of fact," Jennifer said loftily, "I can. It's called heredity." And she walked away.

Jennifer and Ken Bailey disposed of the bottle of corn syrup on the way back to the office.

16

Adam Warner had known from almost the beginning that his marriage to Mary Beth had been a mistake. He had been impulsive and idealistic, trying to protect a young girl who seemed lost and vulnerable to the world.

He would give anything not to hurt Mary Beth, but Adam was deeply in love with Jennifer. He needed someone to talk to, and he decided on Stewart Needham. Stewart had always been sympathetic. He would understand Adam's position.

The meeting turned out to be quite different from what Adam had planned. As Adam walked into Stewart Needham's office, Needham said, "Perfect timing. I've just been on the phone with the election committee. They're formally asking you to run for the United States Senate. You'll have the full backing of the party."

"I—that's wonderful," Adam said.

"We have a lot to do, my boy. We have to start organizing things. I'll set up a fund-raising committee. Here's where I think we should begin . . ."

For the next two hours, they discussed plans for the campaign.

When they had finished, Adam said, "Stewart, there's something personal I'd like to talk to you about."

"I'm afraid I'm late for a client now, Adam."

And Adam had the sudden feeling that Stewart Needham had known what was on Adam's mind all the while.

Adam had a date to meet Jennifer for lunch at a dairy restaurant on the West Side. She was waiting for him in a rear booth.

Adam walked in, charged with energy, and from his expression Jennifer knew that something had happened.

"I have some news for you," Adam told her. "I've been asked to run for the United States Senate."

"Oh, Adam!" Jennifer was filled with a sudden excitement. "That's wonderful! You'll make such a great senator!"

"The competition's going to be fierce. New York's a tough state."

"It doesn't matter. No one can stop you." And Jennifer knew it was true. Adam was intelligent and courageous, willing to fight the battles he believed in. As he had once fought her battle.

Jennifer took his hand and said warmly, "I'm so proud of you, darling."

"Easy, I haven't been elected yet. You've heard about cups, lips and slips."

"That has nothing to do with my being proud of you. I love you so much, Adam."

"I love you, too."

Adam thought about telling Jennifer of the discussion he had almost had with Stewart Needham, but he decided not to. It could wait until he had straightened things out.

"When will you start campaigning?"

"They want me to announce that I'm running right away. I'll have unanimous party backing."

"That's wonderful!"

There was something that was *not* wonderful tugging at the back of Jennifer's mind. It was something she did not want to put into words, but she knew that sooner or later she was going to have to face it. She wanted Adam to win, but the Senate race would be a sword of Damocles hanging over her head. If Adam won, Jennifer would lose him. He would be running on a reform ticket and there would be no margin in his life for any scandal. He was a married man and if it was learned he had a mistress, it would be political suicide.

That night, for the first time since she had fallen in love with Adam, Jennifer had insomnia. She was awake until dawn battling the demons of the night.

Cynthia said, "There's a call waiting for you. It's the Martian again."

Jennifer looked at her blankly.

"You know, the one with the story about the insane asylum."

Jennifer had put the man completely out of her mind. He obviously was someone in need of psychiatric help.

"Tell him to—" She sighed. "Never mind. I'll tell him myself."

She picked up the telephone. "Jennifer Parker."

The familiar voice said, "Did you check the information I gave you?"

"I haven't had a chance." She remembered she had thrown away the notes she had made. "I'd like to help you. Will you give me your name?"

"I can't," he whispered. "They'll come after me, too. You just check it out. Helen Cooper. Long Island."

"I can recommend a doctor who—" The line went dead.

Jennifer sat there a moment, thinking, and then asked Ken Bailey to come into the office.

"What's up, Chief?"

"Nothing—I think. I've had a couple of crank calls from someone who won't leave his name. Would you please see if you can find out anything about a woman named Helen Cooper. She's supposed to have had a large estate on Long Island."

"Where is she now?"

"Either in some insane asylum or on Mars."

Two hours later, Ken Bailey walked in and surprised Jennifer by saying, "Your Martian has landed. There's a Helen Cooper committed at The Heathers Asylum in Westchester."

"Are you sure?" Ken Bailey looked hurt. "I didn't mean that," Jennifer said. Ken was the best investigator she had ever known. He never said anything unless he was positive of it, and he never got his facts wrong.

"What's our interest in the lady?" Ken asked.

"Someone thinks she's been framed into the asylum. I'd like you to check out her background. I want to know about her family."

The information was on Jennifer's desk the following morning. Helen Cooper was a dowager who had been left a fortune of four million dollars by her late husband. Her daughter had married the superintendent of the building where they lived and, six months after the marriage, the bride and groom had gone to court to ask that the mother be declared incompetent, and that the estate be put under their control. They had found three psychiatrists who had testified to Helen Cooper's incompetency and the court had committed her to the asylum.

Jennifer finished reading the report and looked up at Ken

Bailey. "The whole thing sounds a little fishy, doesn't it?"

"Fishy? You could wrap it up in a newspaper and serve it with chips. What are you going to do about it?"

It was a difficult question. Jennifer had no client. If Mrs. Cooper's family had had her locked away, they certainly would not welcome Jennifer's interference, and since the woman herself had been declared insane, she was not competent to hire Jennifer. It was an interesting problem. One thing Jennifer knew: Client or not, she was not going to stand by and see someone railroaded into an insane asylum.

"I'm going to pay a visit to Mrs. Cooper," Jennifer decided.

The Heathers Asylum was located in Westchester in a large, wooded area. The grounds were fenced in and the only access was through a guarded gate. Jennifer was not yet ready to let the family know what she was doing, so she had telephoned around until she had found an acquaintance with a connection to the sanatorium. He had made arrangements for her to pay a visit to Mrs. Cooper.

The head of the asylum, Mrs. Franklin, was a dour, hardfaced woman who reminded Jennifer of Mrs. Danvers in *Rebecca*.

"Strictly speaking," Mrs. Franklin sniffed, "I should not be letting you talk to Mrs. Cooper. However, we'll call this an unofficial visit. It won't go in the records."

"Thank you."

"I'll have her brought in."

Helen Cooper was a slim, attractive-looking woman in her late sixties. She had vivid blue eyes that blazed with intelligence, and she was as gracious as though she were receiving Jennifer in her own home.

"It was good of you to come and visit me," Mrs. Cooper said, "but I'm afraid I'm not quite sure why you're here."

"I'm an attorney, Mrs. Cooper. I received two anonymous telephone calls telling me you were in here and that you didn't belong here."

Mrs. Cooper smiled gently. "That must have been Albert."

"Albert?"

"He was my butler for twenty-five years. When my daughter, Dorothy, married, she fired him." She sighed. "Poor Albert. He really belongs to the past, to another world. I suppose, in a sense, I do too. You're very young, my dear, so perhaps you're not aware of how much things have changed. Do you know what's missing today? Graciousness. It's been replaced, I'm afraid, by greed."

Jennifer asked quietly, "Your daughter?"

Mrs. Cooper's eyes saddened. "I don't blame Dorothy. It's her husband. He's not a very attractive man, not morally, at least. I'm afraid my daughter is not very attractive physically. Herbert married Dorothy for her money and found out that the estate was entirely in my hands. He didn't like that."

"Did he say that to you?"

"Oh, yes indeed. My son-in-law was quite open about it. He thought I should give my daughter the estate then, instead of making her wait until I died. I would have, except that I didn't trust him. I knew what would happen if he ever got his hands on all that money."

"Have you ever had any history of mental illness, Mrs. Cooper?"

Helen Cooper looked at Jennifer and said wryly, "According to the doctors, I'm suffering from schizophrenia and paranoia."

Jennifer had the feeling that she had never spoken to a more sane person in her life.

"You are aware that three doctors testified that you were incompetent?"

"The Cooper estate is valued at four million dollars, Miss Parker. You can influence a lot of doctors for that kind of money. I'm afraid you're wasting your time. My son-in-law controls the estate now. He'll never let me leave here."

"I'd like to meet your son-in-law."

The Plaza Towers was on East 72nd Street, in one of the most beautiful residential areas of New York. Helen Cooper had her own penthouse there. Now the name plate on the door read *Mr. and Mrs. Herbert Hawthorne.*

Jennifer had telephoned ahead to the daughter, Dorothy, and when Jennifer arrived at the apartment, both Dorothy and her husband were waiting for her. Helen Cooper had been right about her daughter. She was not attractive. She was thin and mousy-looking, with no chin, and her right eye had a cast in it. Her husband, Herbert, looked like a clone of Archie Bunker. He was at least twenty years older than Dorothy.

"Come on in," he grunted.

He escorted Jennifer from the reception hall into an enormous living room, the walls of which were covered with paintings by French and Dutch masters.

Hawthorne said to Jennifer bluntly, "Now, suppose you tell me what the hell this is all about."

Jennifer turned to the girl. "It's about your mother."

"What about her?"

"When did she first start showing signs of insanity?"

"She—"

Herbert Hawthorne interrupted. "Right after Dorothy and me got married. The old lady couldn't stand me."

That's certainly one proof of sanity, Jennifer thought.

"I read the doctors' reports," Jennifer said. "They seemed biased."

"What do you mean, biased?" His tone was truculent.

"What I mean is that the reports indicated that they were dealing in gray areas where there were no clear-cut criteria for establishing what society calls sanity. Their decision was shaped, in part, by what you and your wife told them about Mrs. Cooper's behavior."

"What are you tryin' to say?"

"I'm saying that the evidence is not clear-cut. Three other doctors could have come up with an entirely different conclusion."

"Hey, look," Herbert Hawthorne said, "I dunno what you think you're tryin' to pull, but the old lady's a looney. The doctors said so and the court said so."

"I read the court transcript," Jennifer replied. "The court also suggested that her case be periodically reviewed."

There was consternation on Herbert Hawthorne's face. "You mean they might let her out?"

"They're *going* to let her out," Jennifer promised. "I'm going to see to it."

"Wait a minute! What the hell is goin' on here?"

"That's what I intend to find out." Jennifer turned to the girl. "I checked out your mother's previous medical history. There has never been anything wrong with her, mentally or emotionally. She—"

Herbert Hawthorne interrupted. "That don't mean a damn thing! These things can come on fast. She—"

"In addition," Jennifer continued to Dorothy, "I checked on your mother's social activities before you had her put away. She lived a completely normal life."

"I don't care what you or anybody else says. She's crazy!" Herbert Hawthorne shouted.

Jennifer turned to him and studied him a moment. "Did you ask Mrs. Cooper to give the estate to you?"

"That's none of your goddamned business!"

"I'm making it my business. I think that's all for now." Jennifer moved toward the door.

Herbert Hawthorne stepped in front of her, blocking her way. "Wait a minute. You're buttin' in where you're not wanted. You're lookin' to make a little cash for yourself, right? Okay, I understand that, honey. Tell you what I'll do. Why don't I give you a check right now for a thousand dollars for services rendered and you just drop this whole thing. Huh?"

"Sorry," Jennifer replied. "No deal."

"You think you're gonna get more from the old lady?"

"No," Jennifer said. She looked him in the eye. "Only one of us is in this for the money."

It took six weeks of hearings and psychiatric consultations and conferences with four different state agencies. Jennifer brought in her own psychiatrists and when they were finished with their examinations and Jennifer had laid out all the facts at her disposal, the judge reversed his earlier decision and Helen Cooper was released and her estate restored to her control.

The morning of Mrs. Cooper's release she telephoned Jennifer.

"I want to take you to lunch at Twenty-One."

Jennifer looked at her calendar. She had a crowded morning, a luncheon date and a busy afternoon in court, but she knew how much this meant to the elderly woman. "I'll be there," Jennifer said.

Helen Cooper's voice was pleased. "We'll have a little celebration."

The luncheon went beautifully. Mrs. Cooper was a thoughtful hostess, and obviously they knew her well at 21.

Jerry Berns escorted them to a table upstairs, where they were surrounded by beautiful antiques and Georgian silver. The food and service were superb.

Helen Cooper waited until they were having their coffee.

Then she said to Jennifer, "I'm very grateful to you, my dear. I don't know how large a fee you were planning to charge, but I want to give you something more."

"My fees are high enough."

Mrs. Cooper shook her head. "It doesn't matter." She leaned forward, took Jennifer's hands in hers and dropped her voice to a whisper.

"I'm going to give you Wyoming."

17

The front page of *The New York Times* carried two stories of interest, side by side. One was an announcement that Jennifer Parker had obtained an acquittal for a woman accused of slaying her husband. The other was an article about Adam Warner running for the United States Senate.

Jennifer read the story about Adam again and again. It gave his background, told about his service as a pilot in the Viet Nam War, and gave an account of his receiving the Distinguished Flying Cross for bravery. It was highly laudatory, and a number of prominent people were quoted as saying that Adam Warner would be a credit to the United States Senate and to the nation. At the end of the article, there was a strong hint that if Adam were successful in his campaign, it could easily be a stepping-stone to his running for the presidency of the United States.

In New Jersey, at Antonio Granelli's farmhouse, Michael Moretti and Antonio Granelli were finishing breakfast.

Michael was reading the article about Jennifer Parker.

He looked up at his father-in-law and said, "She's done it again, Tony."

Antonio Granelli spooned up a piece of poached egg. "Who done what again?"

"That lawyer. Jennifer Parker. She's a natural."

Antonio Granelli grunted. "I don' like the idea of no woman lawyer workin' for us. Women are weak. You never know what the hell they gonna do."

Michael said cautiously, "You're right, a lot of them are, Tony."

It would not pay for him to antagonize his father-in-law. As long as Antonio Granelli was alive, he was dangerous; but watching him now, Michael knew he would not have to wait much longer. The old man had had a series of small strokes and his hands trembled. It was difficult for him to talk, and he walked with a cane. His skin was like dry, yellowed parchment. All the juices had been sucked out of him. This man, who was at the head of the federal crime list, was a toothless tiger. His name had struck terror into the hearts of countless *mafiosi* and hatred in the hearts of their widows. Now, very few people got to see Antonio Granelli. He hid behind Michael, Thomas Colfax, and a few others he trusted.

Michael had not been *raised*—made the head of the Family—yet, but it was just a question of time. "Three-Finger Brown" Lucchese had been the strongest of the five eastern Mafia chieftains, then Antonio Granelli, and soon . . . Michael could afford to be patient. He had come a long, long way from the time when, as a cocky, fresh-faced kid, he had stood in front of the major dons in New York and held a flaming scrap of paper in his hand and sworn: "This is the way I will burn if I betray the secrets of Cosa Nostra."

Now, sitting at breakfast with the old man, Michael said, "Maybe we could use the Parker woman for small stuff. Just to see how she does."

Granelli shrugged. "Just be careful, Mike. I don' wan' no strangers in on Family secrets."

"Let me handle her."

Michael made the telephone call that afternoon.

When Cynthia announced that Michael Moretti was calling, it brought an instant spate of memories, all of them unpleasant. Jennifer could not imagine why Michael Moretti would be calling her.

Out of curiosity, she picked up the telephone. "What is it you want?"

The sharpness of her tone took Michael Moretti aback. "I want to see you. I think you and I should have a little talk."

"What about, Mr. Moretti?"

"It's nothing I'd care to discuss on the telephone. I can tell you this, Miss Parker—it's something that would be very much in your interest."

Jennifer said evenly, "I can tell you this, Mr. Moretti. Nothing you could ever do or say could be of the slightest interest to me," and she slammed down the receiver.

Michael Moretti sat at his desk staring at the dead phone in his hand. He felt a stirring within him, but it was not anger. He was not sure what it was, and he was not sure he liked it. He had used women all his life and his dark good looks and innate ruthlessness had gotten him more eager bed partners than he could remember.

Basically, Michael Moretti despised women. They were too soft. They had no spirit. *Rosa, for example. She's like a little pet dog who does everything she's told*, Michael thought. *She keeps my house, cooks for me, fucks me when I want to be fucked, shuts up when I tell her to shut up*.

Michael had never known a woman of spirit, a woman who had the courage to defy him. Jennifer Parker had had the nerve to hang up on him. What was it she had said? *Nothing you could ever do or say could be of the slightest interest to me.* Michael Moretti thought about that and smiled to himself. She was wrong. He was going to show her how wrong she was.

He sat back, remembering what she had looked like in court, remembering her face and her body. He suddenly wondered what she would be like in bed. A wildcat, probably. He started thinking about her nude body under his, fighting him. He picked up the telephone and dialed a number.

When a girl's voice answered he said, "Get naked. I'm on my way over."

On her way back to the office after lunch, as Jennifer was crossing Third Avenue she was almost run down by a truck. The driver slammed on his brakes and the rear end of the truck skidded sideways, barely missing her.

"Jesus Christ, lady!" the driver yelled. "Why don't you watch where the hell you're goin'!"

Jennifer was not listening to him. She was staring at the name on the back of the truck. It read *Nationwide Motors Corporation*. She stood there watching, long after the truck had disappeared from sight. Then she turned and hurried back to the office.

"Is Ken here?" she asked Cynthia.

"Yes. He's in his office."

She went in to see him. "Ken, can you check out Nationwide Motors Corporation? We need a list of all the accident cases their trucks have been involved in for the past five years."

"That's going to take a while."

"Use LEXIS." That was the national legal computer.

"You want to tell me what's going on?"

"I'm not sure yet, Ken. It's just a hunch. I'll let you know if anything comes of it."

She had overlooked something in the case of Connie Garrett, that lovely quadruple amputee who was destined to spend the rest of her life as a freak. The driver may have had a good record, but what about the *trucks*? Maybe somebody was liable, after all.

The next morning Ken Bailey laid a report in front of Jennifer. "Whatever the hell you're after, looks like you've hit the jackpot. Nationwide Motors Corporation has had fifteen accidents in the last five years, and some of their trucks have been recalled."

Jennifer felt an excitement begin to build in her. "What was the problem?"

"A deficiency in the braking system that causes the rear end of the truck to swing around when the brakes are hit hard."

It was the rear end of the truck that had hit Connie Garrett.

Jennifer called a staff meeting with Dan Martin, Ted Harris and Ken Bailey. "We're going into court on the Connie Garrett case," Jennifer announced.

Ted Harris stared at her through his milk-bottle glasses. "Wait a minute, Jennifer, I checked that out. She lost on appeal. We're going to get hit with *res judicata*."

"What's *res judicata*?" Ken Bailey asked.

Jennifer explained, "It means for civil cases what double jeopardy means for criminal cases. 'There must be an end to litigation.'"

Ted Harris added, "Once a final judgment has been made on the merits of a case, it can only be opened again under very special circumstances. We have no grounds to reopen."

"Yes, we have. We're going after them on *discovery*."

The principle of discovery read: *Mutual knowledge of all relevant facts gathered by both parties is essential to proper litigation.*

"The deep-pocket defendant is Nationwide Motors. They

held back information from Connie Garrett's attorney. There's a deficiency in the braking system of their trucks and they kept it out of the record."

She looked at the two lawyers. "Here's what I think we should do . . ."

Two hours later, Jennifer was seated in Connie Garrett's living room.

"I want to move for a new trial. I believe we have a case."

"No. I couldn't go through another trial."

"Connie—"

"Look at me, Jennifer. I'm a freak. Every time I look in the mirror I want to kill myself. Do you know why I don't?" Her voice sank to a whisper. "Because I can't. I *can't!*"

Jennifer sat there, shaken. How could she have been so insensitive?

"Suppose I try for an out-of-court settlement? I think that when they hear the evidence they'll be willing to settle without going to trial."

The offices of Maguire and Guthrie, the attorneys who represented the Nationwide Motors Corporation, were located on upper Fifth Avenue in a modern glass and chrome building with a splashing fountain in front. Jennifer announced herself at the reception desk. The receptionist asked her to be seated, and fifteen minutes later Jennifer was escorted into the offices of Patrick Maguire. He was the senior partner in the firm, a tough, hard-bitten Irishman with sharp eyes that missed nothing.

He motioned Jennifer to a chair. "It's nice to meet you, Miss Parker. You've gotten yourself quite a reputation around town."

"Not all bad, I hope."

"They say you're tough. You don't look it."

"I hope not."

"Coffee? Or some good Irish whiskey?"

"Coffee, please."

Patrick Maguire rang and a secretary brought in two cups of coffee on a sterling silver tray.

Maguire said, "Now what is it I can do for you?"

"It's about the Connie Garrett case."

"Ah, yes. As I recall, she lost the case and the appeal."

As I recall. Jennifer would have bet her life that Patrick Maguire could have recited every statistic in the case.

"I'm going to file for a new trial."

"Really? On what grounds?" Maguire asked politely.

Jennifer opened her attaché case and took out the brief she had prepared. She handed it to him.

"I'm requesting a reopening on failure to disclose."

Maguire leafed through the papers, unperturbed. "Oh, yes," he said. "That brake business."

"You knew about it?"

"Of course." He tapped the file with a stubby finger. "Miss Parker, this won't get you anywhere. You would have to prove that the same truck involved in the accident had a faulty brake system. It's probably been overhauled a dozen times since the accident, so there would be no way of proving what its condition was then." He pushed the file back toward her. "You have no case."

Jennifer took a sip of her coffee. "All I have to do is prove what a bad safety record those trucks have. Ordinary diligence should have made your client know that they were defective."

Maguire said casually, "What is it you're proposing?"

"I have a client in her early twenties who's sitting in a room she'll never leave for the rest of her life because she has no arms or legs. I'd like to get a settlement that would make up a little bit for the anguish she's going through."

Patrick Maguire took a sip of his coffee. "What kind of settlement did you have in mind?"

"Two million dollars."

He smiled. "That's a great deal of money for someone with no case."

"If I go to court, Mr. Maguire, I promise you I'll have a case. And I'll win a lot more than that. If you force us to sue, we're going to sue for five million dollars."

He smiled again. "You're scaring the bejeezus out of me. More coffee?"

"No, thanks." Jennifer arose.

"Wait a minute! Sit down, please. I haven't said no."

"You haven't said yes."

"Have some more coffee. We brew it ourselves."

Jennifer thought of Adam and the Kenya coffee.

"Two million dollars is a lot of money, Miss Parker."

Jennifer said nothing.

"Now, if we were talking about a lesser amount, I might be able to—" He waved his hands expressively.

Jennifer remained silent.

Finally Patrick Maguire said, "You really want two million, don't you?"

"I really want five million, Mr. Maguire."

"All right. I suppose we might be able to arrange something."

It had been easy!

"I have to leave for London in the morning, but I'll be back next week."

"I want to wrap this up. I'd appreciate it if you would talk to your client as soon as possible. I'd like to give my client a check next week."

Patrick Maguire nodded. "That can probably be worked out."

All the way back to the office, Jennifer was filled with a sense of unease. It had been too simple.

That night on her way home, Jennifer stopped at a drugstore. When she came out and started across the street, she saw Ken Bailey walking with a handsome young blond man. Jennifer hesitated, then turned into a side street so that she would not be seen. Ken's private life was his own business.

On the day that Jennifer was scheduled to meet with Patrick Maguire, she received a call from his secretary.

"Mr. Maguire asked me to give you his apologies, Miss Parker. He's going to be tied up in meetings all day. He'll be happy to meet with you at your convenience tomorrow."

"Fine," Jennifer said. "Thank you."

The call sounded an alarm in Jennifer's mind. Her instincts had been right. Patrick Maguire was up to something.

"Hold all my calls," she told Cynthia.

She locked herself in her office, pacing back and forth, trying to think of every possible angle. Patrick Maguire had first told Jennifer she had no case. With almost no persuasion, he had then agreed to pay Connie Garrett two million dollars. Jennifer remembered how uneasy she had been at the time. Since then, Patrick Maguire had been unavailable. First London—if he had really gone to London—and then the conferences that had kept him from returning Jennifer's telephone calls all week. And now another delay.

But why? The only reason would be if— Jennifer stopped pacing and picked up the interoffice telephone and called Dan Martin.

"Check on the date of Connie Garrett's accident, would you, Dan? I want to know when the statute of limitations is up."

Twenty minutes later, Dan Martin walked into Jennifer's office, his face white.

"We blew it," he said. "Your hunch was right. The statute of limitations ran out today."

She felt suddenly sick. "There's no chance of a mistake?"

"None. I'm sorry, Jennifer. One of us should have checked it out before. It—it just never occurred to me."

"Or me." Jennifer picked up the telephone and dialed a number. "Patrick Maguire, please. Jennifer Parker."

She waited for what seemed an eternity, and then she said brightly into the telephone, "Hello there, Mr. Maguire. How was London?" She listened. "No, I've never been there . . . Ah, well, one of these days . . . The reason I'm calling," she said casually, "is that I just talked to Connie Garrett. As I told you before, she really doesn't want to go to court unless she has to. So if we could settle this today—"

Patrick Maguire's laugh boomed through the receiver. "Nice try, Miss Parker. The statute of limitations is up today. No one is going to sue anybody. If you'd like to settle for a lunch sometime we can talk about the fickle finger of fate."

Jennifer tried to keep the anger out of her voice. "That's a pretty rotten trick, friend."

"It's a pretty rotten world, friend," Patrick Maguire chuckled.

"It's not how you play the game, it's whether you win or not, right?"

"You're pretty good, honey, but I've been at it a lot longer than you. Tell your client I said better luck next time."

And he rang off.

Jennifer sat there holding the telephone in her hand. She thought of Connie Garrett sitting at home, waiting for the news. Jennifer's head began to pound and a film of perspiration popped out on her forehead. She reached in her desk drawer for an aspirin and looked at the clock on the wall. It was four o'clock. They had until five o'clock to file with the Clerk of the Superior Court.

"How long would it take you to prepare the filing?" Jennifer asked Dan Martin, who stood there suffering with her.

He followed her glance. "At least three hours. Maybe four. There's no way."

There has to be a way, Jennifer thought.

Jennifer said, "Doesn't Nationwide have branches all over the United States?"

"Yes."

"It's only one o'clock in San Francisco. We'll file against them there and ask for a change of venue later."

Dan Martin shook his head. "Jennifer, all the papers are here. If we got a firm in San Francisco and briefed them on what we need and they drew up new papers, there's no way they could make the five o'clock deadline."

Something in her refused to give up. "What time is it in Hawaii?"

"Eleven in the morning."

Jennifer's headache disappeared as if by magic, and she leapt from her chair in excitement. "That's it, then! Find out if Nationwide does business there. They must have a factory, sales office, garage—anything. If they do, we file there."

Dan Martin stared at her for a moment and then his face lit up. "Gotcha!" He was already hurrying toward the door.

Jennifer could still hear Patrick Maguire's smug tone on the telephone. *Tell your client, better luck next time.* There would never be a next time for Connie Garrett. It had to be *now*.

Thirty minutes later Jennifer's intercom buzzed and Dan Martin said excitedly, "Nationwide Motors manufactures their drive shafts on the island of Oahu."

"We've got them! Get hold of a law firm there and have them file the papers immediately."

"Did you have any special firm in mind?"

"No. Pick someone out of Martindale-Hubbell. Just make sure they serve the papers on the local attorney for National. Have them call us back the minute those papers are filed. I'll be waiting here in the office."

"Anything else I can do?"

"Pray."

* * *

The call from Hawaii came at ten o'clock that evening. Jennifer grabbed the phone and a soft voice said, "Miss Jennifer Parker, please."

"Speaking."

"This is Miss Sung of the law firm of Gregg and Hoy in Oahu. We wanted to let you know that fifteen minutes ago we served the papers you requested on the attorney for Nationwide Motors Corporation."

Jennifer exhaled slowly. "Thank you. Thank you very much."

Cynthia sent in Joey La Guardia. Jennifer had never seen the man before. He had telephoned, asking her to represent him in an assault case. He was short, compactly built and wore an expensive suit that looked as though it had been carefully tailored for someone else. He had an enormous diamond ring on his little finger.

La Guardia smiled with yellowed teeth and said, "I come to you 'cause I need some help. Anybody can make a mistake, right, Miss Parker? The cops picked me up 'cause I did a little number on a coupla guys, but I thought they was out to get me, you know? The alley was dark and when I seen them comin' at me—well, it's a rough neighborhood down there. I jumped them before they could jump me."

There was something about his manner that Jennifer found distasteful and false. He was trying too hard to be ingratiating.

He pulled out a large wad of money.

"Here. A grand down an' another grand when we go to court. Okay?"

"My calendar is full for the next few months. I'll be glad to recommend some other attorneys to you."

His manner became insistent. "No. I don't want nobody else. You're the best."

"For a simple assault charge you don't need the best."

"Hey, listen," he said, "I'll give you more money." There

was a desperation in his voice. "*Two* grand down and—"

Jennifer pressed the buzzer under her desk and Cynthia walked in. "Mr. La Guardia's leaving, Cynthia."

Joey La Guardia glared at Jennifer for a long moment, scooped up his money and thrust it back in his pocket. He walked out of the office without a word. Jennifer pressed the intercom button.

"Ken, could you please come in here a minute?"

It took Ken Bailey less than thirty minutes to get a complete report on Joey La Guardia.

"He's got a rap sheet a mile long," he told Jennifer. "He's been in and out of the pen since he was sixteen." He glanced at the piece of paper in his hand. "He's out on bail. He was picked up last week for assault and battery. He beat up two old men who owed the Organization money."

Everything suddenly clicked into place. "Joey La Guardia works for the Organization?"

"He's one of Michael Moretti's enforcers."

Jennifer was filled with a cold fury. "Can you get me the telephone number of Michael Moretti?"

Five minutes later, Jennifer was speaking to Moretti.

"Well, this is an unexpected pleasure, Miss Parker. I—"

"Mr. Moretti, I don't like being set up."

"What are you talking about?"

"Listen to me. And listen well. I'm not for sale. Not now, not ever. I won't represent you or anyone who works for you. All I want is for you to leave me alone. Is that clear?"

"Can I ask you a question?"

"Go ahead."

"Will you have lunch with me?"

Jennifer hung up on him.

Cynthia's voice came over the intercom. "A Mr. Patrick Maguire is here to see you, Miss Parker. He has no appointment, but he said—"

Jennifer smiled to herself. "Have Mr. Maguire wait."

She remembered their conversation on the telephone. *It's not how you play the game, it's whether you win or not, right? You're pretty good, honey, but I've been at it a lot longer than you. Tell your client I said better luck next time.*

Jennifer kept Patrick Maguire waiting for forty-five minutes, and then buzzed Cynthia.

"Send Mr. Maguire in, please."

Patrick Maguire's genial manner was gone. He had been outwitted, and he was angry and did not bother to conceal it.

He walked over to Jennifer's desk and snapped, "You're causing me a lot of problems, friend."

"Am I, friend?"

He sat down, uninvited. "Let's stop playing games. I had a call from the general counsel of Nationwide Motors. I underestimated you. My client is willing to make a settlement." He reached into his pocket, pulled out an envelope and handed it to Jennifer. She opened it. Inside was a certified check made out to Connie Garrett. It was for one hundred thousand dollars.

Jennifer slipped the check back in the envelope and returned it to Patrick Maguire.

"It's not enough. We're suing for five million dollars."

Maguire grinned. "No, you're not. Because your client's not going into court. I just paid her a visit. There's no way you can ever get that girl into a courtroom. She's terrified and, without her, you haven't got a chance."

Jennifer said angrily, "You had no right to talk to Connie Garrett without my being present."

"I was only trying to do everybody a favor. Take the money and run, friend."

Jennifer got to her feet. "Get out of here. You turn my stomach."

Patrick Maguire rose. "I didn't know your stomach *could* be turned."

And he walked out, taking the check with him.

Watching him go, Jennifer wondered whether she had made a terrible mistake. She thought of what a hundred thousand dollars could do for Connie Garrett. But it was not enough. Not for what that girl would have to endure every day for the rest of her life.

Jennifer knew that Patrick Maguire was right about one thing. Without Connie Garrett in the courtroom, there was no chance that a jury would return a verdict for five million dollars. Words could never persuade them of the horror of her life. Jennifer needed the impact of Connie Garrett's presence in the courtroom, with the jury looking at her day after day; but there was no way Jennifer could persuade the young woman to go into court. She had to find another solution.

Adam telephoned.

"I'm sorry I couldn't call you before," he apologized. "I've been having meetings on the Senate race and—"

"It's all right, darling. I understand." *I've got to understand,* she thought.

"I miss you so much."

"I miss you, too, Adam." *You'll never know how much.*

"I want to see you."

Jennifer wanted to say, *When?* but she waited.

Adam went on. "I have to go to Albany this afternoon. I'll call you when I get back."

"All right." There was nothing else she could say. There was nothing she could do.

At four o'clock in the morning, Jennifer awakened from a terrible dream and knew how she was going to win five million dollars for Connie Garrett.

18

"We've set up a series of fund-raising dinners across the state. We'll hit the larger towns only. We'll get to the whistle-stops through a few national television shows like *Face The Nation*, the *Today* show and *Meet the Press*. We figure that we can pick up—Adam, are you listening?"

Adam turned to Stewart Needham and the other three men in the conference room—top media experts, Needham had assured him—and said, "Yes, of course, Stewart."

He had been thinking of something else entirely. Jennifer. He wanted her here at his side, sharing the excitement of the campaign, sharing this moment, sharing his life.

Adam had tried several times to discuss his situation with Stewart Needham, but each time his partner had managed to change the subject.

Adam sat there thinking about Jennifer and Mary Beth. He knew that it was unfair to compare them, but it was impossible not to.

Jennifer is stimulating to be with. She's interested in every-

thing and makes me feel alive. Mary Beth lives in her own private little world . . .

Jennifer and I have a thousand things in common. Mary Beth and I have nothing in common but our marriage . . .

I love Jennifer's sense of humor. She knows how to laugh at herself. Mary Beth takes everything seriously . . .

Jennifer makes me feel young. Mary Beth seems older than her years . . .

Jennifer is self-reliant. Mary Beth depends on me to tell her what to do . . .

Five important differences between the woman I'm in love with and my wife.

Five reasons why I can never leave Mary Beth.

19

On a Wednesday morning in early August the trial of *Connie Garrett* v. *Nationwide Motors Corporation* began. Ordinarily, the trial would only have been worth a paragraph or two in the newspapers, but because Jennifer Parker was representing the plaintiff, the media were out in full force.

Patrick Maguire sat at the defense table, surrounded by a battery of assistants dressed in conservative gray suits.

The process of selecting a jury began. Maguire was casual, almost to the point of indifference, for he knew that Connie Garrett was not going to appear in court. The sight of a beautiful young quadruple amputee would have been a powerful emotional lever with which to pry a large sum of money out of a jury—but there would be no girl and no lever.

This time, Maguire thought, *Jennifer Parker has outsmarted herself.*

The jury was impaneled and the trial got underway. Patrick Maguire made his opening statement and Jennifer had to admit to herself that he was very good indeed. He dwelt at length on the plight of poor young Connie Garrett, saying all the things that Jennifer had planned to say, stealing her emotional thunder. He spoke of the accident, stressing the fact that Connie Garrett had slipped on ice and that the truck driver had not been at fault.

"The plaintiff is asking you ladies and gentlemen to award her five million dollars." Maguire shook his head incredulously. "*Five million dollars!* Have you ever seen that much money? I haven't. My firm handles some affluent clients, but I want to tell you that in all my years of practicing law, I have never even seen *one* million dollars—or *half* a million dollars."

He could see by the looks on the faces of the jurors that neither had they.

"The defense is going to bring witnesses in here who will tell you how the accident happened. And it *was* an accident. Before we're through, we'll show you that Nationwide Motors had no culpability in this matter. You will have noticed that the person bringing the suit, Connie Garrett, is not in court today. Her attorney has informed Judge Silverman that she will not make an appearance at all. Connie Garrett is not in this courtroom today where she belongs, but I can tell you where she is. Right now, as I'm standing here talking to you, Connie Garrett is sitting at home counting the money she thinks you're going to give her. She's waiting for her telephone to ring and for her attorney to tell her how many millions of dollars she suckered out of you.

"You and I know that any time there's an accident where a big corporation is involved—no matter how indirectly—there are people who are immediately going to say, 'Why, that company is rich. It can afford it. Let's take it for all we can.'"

Patrick Maguire paused.

"Connie Garrett's not in this courtroom today because she couldn't face you. She knows that what she's trying to do is immoral. Well, we're going to send her away empty-handed as a lesson to other people who might be tempted to try the same thing in the future. A person has to take responsibility for his or her own actions. If you slip on a piece of ice on the street, you can't blame big brother for it. And you shouldn't try to swindle five million dollars out of him. Thank you."

He turned to bow to Jennifer, and then walked over to the defense table and sat down.

Jennifer rose to her feet and approached the jury. She studied their faces, trying to evaluate the impression that Patrick Maguire had made.

"My esteemed colleague has told you that Connie Garrett will not be in this courtroom during the trial. That is correct." Jennifer pointed to an empty space at the plaintiff's table. "That is where Connie Garrett would be sitting if she were here. Not in that chair. In a special wheelchair. The chair she lives in. Connie Garrett won't be in this courtroom, but before this trial is over you will all have an opportunity to meet her and get to know her as I have gotten to know her."

There was a puzzled frown on Patrick Maguire's face. He leaned over and whispered to one of his assistants.

Jennifer was going on. "I listened as Mr. Maguire spoke so eloquently, and I want to tell you I was touched. I found my heart bleeding for this multibillion-dollar corporation that's being mercilessly attacked by this twenty-four-year-old woman who has no arms or legs. This woman who, at this very moment is sitting at home, greedily awaiting that telephone call that will tell her she's rich." Jennifer's voice dropped.

"Rich to do what? Go out and buy diamonds for the hands she doesn't have? Buy dancing shoes for the feet she doesn't have? Buy beautiful dresses that she can never wear? A Rolls Royce to take her to parties she's not invited to? Just think of all the fun she's going to have with that money."

Jennifer spoke very quietly and sincerely as her eyes moved slowly across the faces of the jurors. "Mr. Maguire has never seen five million dollars at one time. Neither have I. But I'll tell you this. If I were to offer any one of you five million dollars in cash right now, and all I wanted in exchange was to cut off both your arms and both your legs, I don't think five million dollars would seem like very much money. . . .

"The law in this case is very clear," Jennifer explained. "In an earlier trial, which the plaintiff lost, the defendants were aware of a defect in the braking system in their trucks, and they withheld that knowledge from the defendant and from the court. In doing so, they acted illegally. That is the basis for this new trial. According to a recent government survey, the biggest contributors to truck accidents involve wheels and tires, brakes and steering systems. If you will just examine these figures for a moment . . ."

Patrick Maguire was appraising the jury and he was an expert at it. As Jennifer droned on about the statistics, Maguire could tell that the jurors were getting bored with this trial. It was becoming too technical. The trial was no longer about a crippled girl. It was about trucks and braking distances and faulty brake drums. The jurors were losing interest.

Maguire glanced over at Jennifer and thought, *She's not as clever as she's reputed to be.* Maguire knew that if he had been on the other side defending Connie Garrett, he would have ignored the statistics and mechanical problems and played on the jury's emotions. Jennifer Parker had done exactly the opposite.

Patrick Maguire leaned back in his chair now and relaxed.

Jennifer was approaching the bench. "Your Honor, with the court's permission, I have an exhibit I would like to introduce."

"What kind of exhibit?" Judge Silverman asked.

"When this trial began I promised the jury that they would get to know Connie Garrett. Since she is unable to be here in person, I would like permission to show some pictures of her."

Judge Silverman said, "I see no objection to that." He

turned to Patrick Maguire. "Does the attorney for the defense have any objection?"

Patrick Maguire got to his feet, moving slowly, thinking fast. "What kind of pictures?"

Jennifer said, "A few pictures taken of Connie Garrett at home."

Patrick Maguire would have preferred not to have the pictures, but on the other hand, photographs of a crippled girl sitting in a wheelchair were certainly a lot less dramatic than the actual appearance of the girl herself would have been. And there was another factor to consider: If he objected, it would make him look unsympathetic in the eyes of the jury.

He said generously, "By all means, show the pictures."

"Thank you."

Jennifer turned to Dan Martin and nodded. Two men in the back row moved forward with a portable screen and a motion picture projector and began to set them up.

Patrick Maguire stood up, surprised. "Wait a minute! What is this?"

Jennifer replied innocently, "The pictures you just agreed to let me show."

Patrick Maguire stood there, silently fuming. Jennifer had said nothing about motion pictures. But it was too late to object. He nodded curtly and sat down again.

Jennifer had the screen positioned so the jury and Judge Silverman could see it clearly.

"May we have the room darkened, Your Honor?"

The judge signaled the bailiff and the shades were lowered. Jennifer walked over to the 16mm projector and turned it on, and the screen came to life.

For the next thirty minutes there was not a sound to be heard in the courtroom. Jennifer had hired a professional cameraman and a young director of commercials to make the film. They had photographed a day in the life of Connie

Garrett, and it was a stark, realistic horror story. Nothing had been left to the imagination. The film showed the beautiful young amputee being taken out of bed in the morning, being carried to the toilet, being cleaned like a small, helpless baby . . . being bathed . . . being fed and dressed. . . . Jennifer had seen the film over and over and now, as she watched it again, she felt the same lump in her throat and her eyes filled with tears, and she knew that it must be having the same effect on the judge and the jury and the spectators in the courtroom.

When the film was ended, Jennifer turned to Judge Silverman. "The plaintiff rests."

The jury had been out for more than ten hours, and with each passing hour Jennifer's spirits sank lower. She had been sure of an immediate verdict. If they had been as affected by the film as she had been, a verdict should not have taken more than an hour or two.

When the jury had filed out, Patrick Maguire had been frantic, certain that he had lost his case, that he had underestimated Jennifer Parker once again. But as the hours passed and the jury still did not return, Maguire's hopes began to rise. It would not have taken the jury this long to make an emotional decision. "We're going to be all right. The longer they're in there arguing, the more their emotions are going to cool off."

A few minutes before midnight, the foreman sent a note to Judge Silverman for a legal ruling. The judge studied the request, then looked up. "Will both attorneys approach the bench, please?"

When Jennifer and Patrick Maguire were standing in front of him, Judge Silverman said, "I want to apprise you of a note I have just received from the foreman. The jury is asking whether they are legally permitted to award Connie Garrett more than the five million dollars her attorney is suing for."

Jennifer felt suddenly giddy. Her heart began to soar. She turned to look at Patrick Maguire. His face was drained of color.

"I'm informing them," Judge Silverman said, "that it is within their province to set any amount they feel is justified."

Thirty minutes later the jury filed back into the courtroom. The foreman announced they had found in favor of the plaintiff. The amount of damages she was entitled to was six million dollars.

It was the largest personal injury award in the history of the State of New York.

20

When Jennifer walked into her office the following morning she found an array of newspapers spread across her desk. She was on the front page of every one of them. There were four dozen beautiful red roses in a vase. Jennifer smiled. Adam had found time to send her flowers.

She opened the card. It read: *Congratulations. Michael Moretti.*

The intercom buzzed and Cynthia said, "Mr. Adams is on the line."

Jennifer grabbed the telephone. She tried to keep her voice calm. "Hello, darling."

"You've done it again."

"I got lucky."

"Your client got lucky. Lucky to have you as an attorney. You must be feeling wonderful."

Winning cases made her feel good. Being with Adam made her feel wonderful. "Yes."

"I have something important to tell you," Adam said. "Can you meet me for a drink this afternoon?"

Jennifer's heart sank. There was only one thing Adam could have to tell her: He was never going to see her again.

"Yes. Yes, of course . . ."

"Mario's? Six o'clock?"

"Fine."

She gave the roses to Cynthia.

Adam was waiting in the restaurant, seated at a back table. *So he won't be embarrassed if I get hysterical,* Jennifer thought. Well, she was determined not to cry. Not in front of Adam.

She could tell from his gaunt, haggard face what he had been going through, and she intended to make this as easy as possible for him. Jennifer sat down and Adam took her hand in his.

"Mary Beth is giving me a divorce," Adam said, and Jennifer stared at him, speechless.

It was Mary Beth who had begun the conversation. They had returned from a fund-raising dinner where Adam had been the main speaker. The evening had been an enormous success. Mary Beth had been quiet during the ride home, a curious tension about her.

Adam said, "I thought the evening went well, didn't you?"

"Yes, Adam."

Nothing more was said until they reached the house.

"Would you like a nightcap?" Adam asked.

"No, thank you. I think we should have a talk."

"Oh? About what?"

She looked at him and said, "About you and Jennifer Parker."

It was like a physical blow. Adam hesitated for a moment, wondering whether to deny it or—

"I've known it for some time. I haven't said anything because I wanted to make up my mind about what to do."

"Mary Beth, I—"

"Please let me finish. I know that our relationship hasn't been—well—all we hoped it would be. In some ways, perhaps I haven't been as good a wife as I should have been."

"Nothing that's happened is your fault. I—"

"Please, Adam. This is very difficult for me. I've made a decision. I'm not going to stand in your way."

He looked at her unbelievingly. "I don't—"

"I love you too much to hurt you. You have a brilliant political future ahead of you. I don't want anything to spoil that. Obviously, I'm not making you completely happy. If Jennifer Parker can make you happy, I want you to have her."

He had a feeling of unreality, as though the whole conversation were taking place underwater. "What will happen to you?"

Mary Beth smiled. "I'll be fine, Adam. Don't worry about me. I have my own plans."

"I—I don't know what to say."

"There's no need to say anything. I've said it all for both of us. If I held on to you and made you miserable, it wouldn't do either of us any good, would it? I'm sure Jennifer's lovely or you wouldn't feel about her the way you do." Mary Beth walked over to him and took him in her arms. "Don't look so stricken, Adam. What I'm doing is the best thing for everyone."

"You're remarkable."

"Thank you." She gently traced his face with her fingertips and smiled. "My dearest Adam. I'll always be your best friend. Always." Then she came closer and put her head on his shoulder. He could hardly hear her soft voice. "It's been such a long time since you held me in your arms, Adam. You wouldn't have to tell me you love me, but would you— would you like to—hold me in your arms once more and make love to me? Our last time together?"

* * *

Adam was thinking of this now as he said to Jennifer, "The divorce was Mary Beth's idea."

Adam went on talking, but Jennifer was no longer listening to the words; she was only hearing the music. She felt as though she were floating, soaring. She had steeled herself for Adam to tell her he could never see her again—and now this! It was too much to absorb. She knew how painful the scene with Mary Beth must have been for Adam, and Jennifer had never loved Adam more than she did at this moment. She felt as though a crushing load had been lifted from her chest, as though she could breathe again.

Adam was saying, "Mary Beth was wonderful about it. She's an incredible woman. She's genuinely happy for both of us."

"That's hard to believe."

"You don't understand. For some time now we've lived more like . . . brother and sister. I've never discussed it with you, but—" he hesitated and said carefully, "Mary Beth doesn't have strong . . . drives."

"I see."

"She'd like to meet you."

The thought of it disturbed Jennifer. "I don't think I could, Adam. I'd feel—uncomfortable."

"Trust me."

"If—if you want me to, Adam, of course."

"Good, darling. We'll go for tea. I'll drive you out."

Jennifer thought for a moment. "Wouldn't it be better if I went alone?"

The following morning, Jennifer drove out the Saw Mill River Parkway, headed upstate. It was a crisp, clear morning, a lovely day for a drive. Jennifer turned on the car radio and tried to forget her nervousness about the meeting facing her.

The Warner house was a magnificently preserved house of Dutch origin, overlooking the river at Croton-on-Hudson, set on a large estate of rolling green acres. Jennifer drove up the driveway to the imposing front entrance. She rang the bell and a moment later the door was opened by an attractive woman in her middle thirties. The last thing Jennifer had expected was this shy southern woman who took her hand, gave her a warm smile and said, "I'm Mary Beth. Adam didn't do you justice. Please come in."

Adam's wife was wearing a beige wool skirt that was softly full, and a silk blouse opened just enough to reveal a mature but still lovely breast. Her beige-blond hair was worn long and slightly curling about her face, and was flattering to her blue eyes. The pearls around her neck could never be mistaken as cultured. There was an air of old-world dignity about Mary Beth Warner.

The interior of the house was lovely, with wide, spacious rooms filled with antiques and beautiful paintings.

A butler served tea in the drawing room from a Georgian silver tea service.

When he had left the room, Mary Beth said, "I'm sure you must love Adam very much."

Jennifer said awkwardly, "I want you to know, Mrs. Warner, that neither of us planned—"

Mary Beth Warner put a hand on Jennifer's arm. "You don't have to tell me that. I don't know whether Adam told you, but our marriage has turned into a marriage of politeness. Adam and I have known each other since we were children. I think I fell in love with Adam the first time I saw him. We went to the same parties and had the same friends, and I suppose it was inevitable that one day we would get married. Don't misunderstand. I still adore Adam and I'm sure he adores me. But people do change, don't they?"

"Yes."

Jennifer looked at Mary Beth and she was filled with a deep feeling of gratitude. What could have been an ugly and sordid scene had turned into something friendly and wonderful.

Adam had been right. Mary Beth was a lovely lady.

"I'm very grateful to you," Jennifer said.

"And I'm grateful to you," Mary Beth confided. She smiled shyly and said, "You see, I'm very much in love, too. I was going to get the divorce immediately but I thought, for Adam's sake, we'd best wait until after the election."

Jennifer had been so busy with her own emotions that she had forgotten about the election.

Mary Beth went on: "Everyone seems sure that Adam is going to be our next senator, and a divorce now would gravely hurt his chances. It's only six months away, so I decided it would be better for him if I delayed it." She looked at Jennifer. "But forgive me—is that agreeable with you?"

"Of course it is," Jennifer said.

She would have to completely readjust her thinking. Her future would now be tied to Adam. If he became senator, she would live with him in Washington, D.C. It would mean giving up her law practice here, but that did not matter. Nothing mattered except that they could be together.

Jennifer said, "Adam will make a wonderful senator."

Mary Beth raised her head and smiled. "My dear, one day Adam Warner is going to make a wonderful *President*."

The telephone was ringing when Jennifer arrived back at the apartment. It was Adam. "How did you get along with Mary Beth?"

"Adam, she was wonderful!"

"She said the same thing about you."

"You read about old southern charm, but you don't come across it very often. Mary Beth has it. She's quite a lady."

"So are you, darling. Where would you like to be married?"

Jennifer said, "Times Square, for all I care. But I think we should wait, Adam."

"Wait for what?"

"Until after the election. Your career is important. A divorce could hurt you right now."

"My private life is—"

"—going to become your public life. We mustn't do anything that might spoil your chances. We can wait six months."

"I don't want to wait."

"I don't either, darling." Jennifer smiled. "We won't really be waiting, will we?"

21

Jennifer and Adam had lunch together almost every day, and once or twice a week Adam spent the night at their apartment. They had to be more discreet than ever, for Adam's campaign had actively begun, and he was becoming a nationally prominent figure. He gave speeches at political rallies and fund-raising dinners, and his opinions on national issues were quoted more and more frequently in the press.

Adam and Stewart Needham were having their ritual morning tea.

"Saw you on the *Today* show this morning," Needham said. "Fine job, Adam. You got every single point across. I understand they've invited you back again."

"Stewart, I hate doing those shows. I feel like some goddamned actor up there, performing."

Stewart nodded, unperturbed. "That's what politicians are, Adam—actors. Playing a part, being what the public wants them to be. Hell, if politicians acted like themselves in public

—what expression do the kids use?—letting it all hang out?—this country'd be a damned monarchy."

"I don't like the fact that running for public office has become a personality contest."

Stewart Needham smiled. "Be grateful you've got the personality, my boy. Your ratings in the polls keep going up every week." He stopped to pour more tea. "Believe me, this is only the beginning. First the Senate, then the number one target. Nothing can stop you." He paused to take a sip of his tea. "Unless you do something foolish, that is."

Adam looked up at him. "What do you mean?"

Stewart Needham delicately wiped his lips with a damask napkin.

"Your opponent is a gutter fighter. I'll bet you that right now he's examining your life under a microscope. He won't find any ammunition, will he?"

"No." The word came to Adam's lips automatically.

"Good," Stewart Needham said. "How's Mary Beth?"

Jennifer and Adam were spending a lazy weekend at a country house in Vermont that a friend of Adam's had loaned him. The air was crisp and fresh, hinting at the winter to come. It was a perfect weekend, comfortable and relaxed, with long hikes during the day and games and easy conversation before a blazing fire at night.

They had carefully gone through all the Sunday papers. Adam was moving up in every poll. With a few exceptions, the media were for Adam. They liked his style, his honesty, his intelligence and his frankness. They kept comparing him to John Kennedy.

Adam sprawled in front of the fireplace, watching flame shadows dancing across Jennifer's face. "How would you like to be the wife of the President?"

"Sorry. I'm already in love with a senator."

"Will you be disappointed if I don't win, Jennifer?"

"No. The only reason I want it is because you want it, darling."

"If I do win, it will mean living in Washington."

"If we're together, nothing else matters."

"What about your law practice?"

Jennifer smiled. "The last time I heard, they had lawyers in Washington."

"What if I asked you to give it up?"

"I'd give it up."

"I don't want you to. You're too damned good at it."

"All I care about is being with you. I love you so much, Adam."

He stroked her soft dark brown hair and said, "I love you, too. So much."

They went to bed, and later, they slept.

On Sunday night they drove back to New York. They picked up Jennifer's car at the garage where she had parked it, and Adam returned to his home. Jennifer went back to their apartment in New York.

Jennifer's days were unbelievably full. If she had thought she was busy before, now she was besieged. She was representing international corporations that had bent a few laws and been caught, senators with their fingers in the till, movie stars who had gotten into trouble. She represented bank presidents and bank robbers, politicians and heads of unions.

Money was pouring in, but that was not important to Jennifer. She gave large bonuses to the office staff, and lavish gifts.

Corporations that came up against Jennifer no longer sent in their second string of lawyers, so Jennifer found herself pitted against some of the top legal talent of the world.

She was admitted into the American College of Trial Lawyers, and even Ken Bailey was impressed.

"Jesus," he said, "you know, only one percent of the lawyers in this country can get in?"

"I'm their token woman," Jennifer laughed.

When Jennifer represented a defendant in Manhattan, she could be certain that Robert Di Silva would either prosecute the case personally or mastermind it. His hatred of Jennifer had grown with every victory she had.

During one trial in which Jennifer was pitted against the District Attorney, Di Silva put a dozen top experts on the stand as witnesses for the prosecution.

Jennifer called no experts. She said to the jury: "If we want a spaceship built or the distance of a star measured, we call in the experts. But when we want something really important done, we collect twelve ordinary folks to do it. As I recall, the founder of Christianity did the same thing."

Jennifer won the case.

One of the techniques Jennifer found effective with a jury was to say, "I know that the words 'law' and 'courtroom' sound a little frightening and remote from your lives, but when you stop to think about it, all we're doing here is dealing with the rights and wrongs done to human beings like ourselves. Let's forget we're in a courtroom, my friends. Let's just imagine we're sitting around in my living room, talking about what's happened to this poor defendant, this fellow human being."

And, in their minds, the jurors *were* sitting in Jennifer's living room, carried away by her spell.

This ploy worked beautifully for Jennifer until one day when she was defending a client against Robert Di Silva. The District Attorney rose to his feet and made the opening address to the jury.

"Ladies and gentlemen," Di Silva said, "I'd like for you to forget you're in a court of law. I want you to imagine that you're sitting at home in my living room and we're just sitting around informally chatting about the terrible things the defendant has done."

Ken Bailey leaned over and whispered to Jennifer, "Do you hear what that bastard's doing? He's stealing your stuff!"

"Don't worry about it," Jennifer replied coolly.

When Jennifer got up to address the jury, she said:

"Ladies and gentlemen, I've never heard anything as outrageous as the remarks of the District Attorney." Her voice rang with righteous indignation. "For a minute, I couldn't believe I had heard him correctly. How dare he tell you to *forget* you're sitting in a court of law! This courtroom is one of the most precious possessions our nation has! It is the foundation of our freedom. Yours and mine and the defendant's. And for the District Attorney to suggest that you forget where you are, that you forget your sworn duty, I find both shocking and contemptible. I'm asking you, ladies and gentlemen, to *remember* where you are, to remember that all of us are here to see that justice is done and that the defendant is vindicated."

The jurors were nodding approvingly.

Jennifer glanced toward the table where Robert Di Silva was sitting. He was staring straight ahead, a glazed look in his eyes.

Jennifer's client was acquitted.

After each court victory, there would be four dozen red roses on Jennifer's desk, with a card from Michael Moretti. Each time, Jennifer would tear up the cards and have Cynthia take away the flowers. Somehow they seemed obscene coming from him. Finally Jennifer sent Michael Moretti a note, asking him to stop sending her flowers.

When Jennifer returned from the courtroom after winning her next case, there were five dozen red roses waiting for her.

22

The Rainy Day Robber case brought Jennifer new head-lines. The accused man had been called to her attention by Father Ryan.

"A friend of mine has a bit of a problem—" he began, and they both burst out laughing.

The friend turned out to be Paul Richards, a transient, accused of robbing a bank of a hundred and fifty thousand dollars. A robber had walked into the bank wearing a long black raincoat, under which was hidden a sawed-off shotgun. The collar of the raincoat was raised so that his face was partially hidden. Once inside the bank, the man had brandished the shotgun and forced a teller to hand over all his available cash. The robber had then fled in a waiting automobile. Several witnesses had seen the getaway car, a green sedan, but the license number had been covered with mud.

Since bank robberies were a federal offense, the FBI had entered the case. They had put the *modus operandi* into a central computer and it had come up with the name of Paul Richards.

Jennifer went to visit him at Riker's Island.

"I swear to God I didn't do it," Paul Richards said. He was in his fifties, a red-faced man with cherubic blue eyes, too old to be running around pulling bank robberies.

"I don't care whether you're innocent or guilty," Jennifer explained, "but I have one rule. I won't represent a client who lies to me."

"I swear on my mother's life I didn't do it."

Oaths had ceased to impress Jennifer long ago. Clients had sworn their innocence to her on the lives of their mothers, wives, sweethearts and children. If God had taken those oaths seriously, there would have been a serious decline in the population.

Jennifer asked, "Why do you think the FBI arrested you?"

Paul Richards answered without hesitation. "Because about ten years ago I pulled a bank job and was dumb enough to get caught."

"You used a sawed-off shotgun under a raincoat?"

"That's right. I waited until it was raining, and then hit a bank."

"But you didn't do this last job?"

"No. Some smart bastard copied my act."

The preliminary hearing was before Judge Fred Stevens, a strict disciplinarian. It was rumored that he was in favor of shipping all criminals off to some inaccessible island where they would stay for the rest of their lives. Judge Stevens believed that anyone caught stealing for the first time should have his right hand chopped off, and if caught again, should have his left hand chopped off, in ancient Islamic tradition. He was the worst judge Jennifer could have asked for. She sent for Ken Bailey.

"Ken, I want you to dig up everything you can on Judge Stevens."

"Judge Stevens? He's as straight as an arrow. He—"

"I know he is. Do it, please."

The federal prosecutor who was handling the case was an old pro named Carter Gifford.

"How are you going to plead him?" Gifford asked.

Jennifer gave him a look of innocent surprise. "Not guilty, of course."

He laughed sardonically. "Judge Stevens will get a kick out of that. I suppose you're going to move for a jury trial."

"No."

Gifford studied Jennifer suspiciously. "You mean you're going to put your client in the hands of the hanging judge?"

"That's right."

Gifford grinned. "I knew you'd go around the bend one day, Jennifer. I can't wait to see this."

"The United States of America versus Paul Richards. Is the defendant present?"

The court clerk said, "Yes, Your Honor."

"Would the attorneys please approach the bench and identify themselves?"

Jennifer and Carter Gifford moved toward Judge Stevens.

"Jennifer Parker representing the defendant."

"Carter Gifford representing the United States Government."

Judge Stevens turned to Jennifer and said brusquely, "I'm aware of your reputation, Miss Parker. So I'm going to tell you right now that I do not intend to waste this court's time. I will brook no delays in this case. I want to get on with this preliminary hearing and get the arraignment over with. I intend to set a trial date as speedily as possible. I presume you will want a jury trial and—"

"No, Your Honor."

Judge Stevens looked at her in surprise. "You're not asking for a jury trial?"

"I am not. Because I don't think there's going to be an arraignment."

Carter Gifford was staring at her. *"What?"*

"In my opinion, you don't have enough evidence to bring my client to trial."

Carter Gifford snapped, "You need another opinion!" He turned to Judge Stevens. "Your Honor, the government has a very strong case. The defendant has already been convicted of committing exactly the same crime in exactly the same manner. Our computer picked him out of over two thousand possible suspects. We have the guilty man right here in this courtroom, and the prosecution has no intention of dropping the case against him."

Judge Stevens turned to Jennifer. "It seems to the court that there is enough *prima facie* evidence here to have an arraignment and a trial. Do you have anything more to say?"

"I do, Your Honor. There is not one single witness who can positively identify Paul Richards. The FBI has been unable to find any of the stolen money. In fact, the only thing that links the defendant to this crime is the imagination of the prosecutor."

The judge stared down at Jennifer and said with ominous softness, "What about the computer that picked him out?"

Jennifer sighed. "That brings us to a problem, Your Honor."

Judge Stevens said grimly, "I imagine it does. It is easy to confuse a live witness, but it is difficult to confuse a computer."

Carter Gifford nodded smugly, "Exactly, Your Honor."

Jennifer turned to face Gifford. "The FBI used the IBM 370/168, didn't it?"

"That's right. It's the most sophisticated equipment in the world."

Judge Stevens asked Jennifer, "Does the defense intend to challenge the efficiency of that computer?"

"On the contrary, Your Honor. I have a computer expert here in court today who works for the company that manufactures the 370/168. He programmed the information that turned up the name of my client."

"Where is he?"

Jennifer turned and motioned to a tall, thin man seated on a bench. He nervously came forward.

Jennifer said, "This is Mr. Edward Monroe."

"If you've been tampering with my witness," the prosecuting attorney exploded, "I'll—"

"All I did was to request Mr. Monroe to ask the computer if there were other possible suspects. I selected ten people who had certain general characteristics similar to my client. For purposes of identification, Mr. Monroe programmed in statistics on age, height, weight, color of eyes, birthplace—the same kind of data that produced the name of my client."

Judge Stevens asked impatiently, "What is the point of all this, Miss Parker?"

"The point is that the computer identified one of the ten people as a prime suspect in the bank robbery."

Judge Stevens turned to Edward Monroe. "Is this true?"

"Yes, Your Honor." Edward Monroe opened his briefcase and pulled out a computer readout.

The bailiff took it from Monroe and handed it to the judge. Judge Stevens glanced at it and his face became red.

He looked at Edward Monroe. "Is this some kind of joke?"

"No, sir."

"The computer picked *me* as a possible suspect?" Judge Stevens asked.

"Yes, sir, it did."

Jennifer explained, "The computer has no reasoning power, Your Honor. It can only respond to the information it is given. You and my client happen to be the same weight, height and age. You both drive green sedans, and you both come from the same state. That's really as much evidence as the prosecuting attorney has. The only other factor is the way in which the crime was done. When Paul Richards committed that bank robbery ten years ago, millions of people read about it. Any one of them could have imitated his *modus operandi*. Someone did." Jennifer indicated the piece of paper in Judge Stevens' hand. "That shows you how flimsy the State's case really is."

Carter Gifford sputtered, "Your Honor—" and stopped. He did not know what to say.

Judge Stevens looked again at the computer readout in his hand and then at Jennifer.

"What would you have done," he asked, "if the court had been a younger man, thinner than I, who drove a *blue* car?"

"The computer gave me ten other possible suspects," Jennifer said. "My next choice would have been New York District Attorney Robert Di Silva."

Jennifer was sitting in her office, reading the headlines, when Cynthia announced, "Mr. Paul Richards is here."

"Send him in, Cynthia."

He came into the office wearing a black raincoat and carrying a candy box tied with a red ribbon.

"I just wanted to tell you thanks."

"You see? Sometimes justice *does* triumph."

"I'm leaving town. I decided I need a little vacation." He handed Jennifer the candy box. "A little token of my appreciation."

"Thank you, Paul."

He looked at her admiringly. "I think you're terrific."

And he was gone.

Jennifer looked at the box of candy on her desk and smiled. She had received less for handling most of Father Ryan's friends. If she got fat, it would be Father Ryan's fault.

Jennifer untied the ribbon and opened the box. Inside was ten thousand dollars in used currency.

One afternoon as Jennifer was leaving the courthouse, she noticed a large, black, chauffeured Cadillac limousine at the curb. As she started to walk past it, Michael Moretti stepped out. "I've been waiting for you."

Close up, there was an electric vitality to the man that was almost overpowering.

"Get out of my way," Jennifer said. Her face was flushed and angry, and she was even more beautiful than Michael Moretti had remembered.

"Hey," he laughed, "cool down. All I want to do is talk to you. All you have to do is listen. I'll pay you for your time."

"You'll never have enough money."

She started to move past him. Michael Moretti put a conciliatory hand on her arm. Just touching her increased his excitement.

He turned on all of his charm. "Be reasonable. You won't know what you're turning down until you hear what I have to say. Ten minutes. That's all I want. I'll drop you off at your office. We can talk on the way."

Jennifer studied him a moment and said, "I'll go with you on one condition. I want the answer to a question."

Michael nodded. "Sure. Go ahead."

"Whose idea was it to frame me with the dead canary?"

He answered without hesitation. "Mine."

So now she knew. And she could have killed him. Grimly she stepped into the limousine and Michael Moretti moved in beside her. Jennifer noted that he gave the driver the address of her office building without asking.

As the limousine drove off, Michael Moretti said, "I'm glad

about all the great things that are happening to you."

Jennifer did not bother to reply.

"I really mean that."

"You haven't told me what it is you want."

"I want to make you rich."

"Thanks. I'm rich enough." Her voice was filled with the contempt she felt toward him. .

Michael Moretti's face flushed. "I'm trying to do you a favor and you keep fighting me."

Jennifer turned to look at him. "I don't want any favors from you."

He made his voice conciliatory. "Okay. Maybe I'm trying to make up a little for what I did to you. Look, I can send you a lot of clients. Important clients. Big money. You have no idea—"

Jennifer interrupted. "Mr. Moretti, do us both a favor. Don't say another word."

"But I can—"

"I don't want to represent you or any of your friends."

"Why not?"

"Because if I represented one of you, from then on you'd own me."

"You've got it all wrong," Michael protested. "My friends are in legitimate businesses. I mean banks, insurance companies—"

"Save your breath. My services aren't available to the Mafia."

"Who said anything about the Mafia?"

"Call it whatever you like. No one owns me but me. I intend to keep it that way."

The limousine stopped for a red light.

Jennifer said, "This is close enough. Thank you for the lift." She opened the door and stepped out.

Michael said, "When can I see you again?"

"Not ever, Mr. Moretti."

Michael watched her walk away.

My God, he thought, *that's a woman!* He suddenly became aware that he had an erection and smiled, because he knew that one way or another, he was going to have her.

23

It was the end of October, two weeks before the election, and the senatorial race was in full swing. Adam was running against the incumbent Senator John Trowbridge, a veteran politician, and the experts agreed it was going to be a close battle.

Jennifer sat at home one night, watching Adam and his opponent in a television debate. Mary Beth had been right. A divorce now could easily have wrecked Adam's growing chances for victory.

When Jennifer walked into the office after a long business lunch, there was an urgent message for her to call Rick Arlen.

"He's called three times in the last half-hour," Cynthia said.

Rick Arlen was a rock star who had, almost overnight, become the hottest singer in the world. Jennifer had heard about the enormous incomes of rock stars, but until she got involved with Rick Arlen's affairs, she had had no idea what that really meant. From records, personal appearances, merchandising and now motion pictures, Rick Arlen's income was more than fifteen million dollars a year. Rick was twenty-five years old, an Alabama farm boy who had been born with a gold mine in his throat.

"Get him for me," Jennifer said.

Five minutes later he was on the line. "Hey, man, I've been tryin' to reach you for hours."

"Sorry, Rick. I was in a meeting."

"Problem. Gotta see you."

"Can you come in to the office this afternoon?"

"I don't think so. I'm in Monte Carlo, doin' a benefit for Grace and the Prince. How soon can you get here?"

"I couldn't possibly get away now," Jennifer protested. "I have a desk piled up—"

"Baby, I *need* you. You've got to get on a bird this afternoon."

And he hung up.

Jennifer thought about the phone call. Rick Arlen had not wanted to discuss his problem over the telephone. It could be anything from drugs to girls to boys. She thought about sending Ted Harris or Dan Martin to solve whatever the problem was, but she liked Rick Arlen. In the end, Jennifer decided to go herself.

She tried to reach Adam before she left, but he was out of the office.

She said to Cynthia, "Get me reservations on an Air France flight to Nice. I'll want a car to meet me and drive me to Monte Carlo."

Twenty minutes later she had a reservation on a seven o'clock flight that evening.

"There's a helicopter service from Nice directly to Monte Carlo," Cynthia said. "I've booked you on that."

"Wonderful. Thank you."

* * *

When Ken Bailey heard why Jennifer was leaving, he said, "Who does that punk think he is?"

"He *knows* who he is, Ken. He's one of our biggest clients."

"When will you be back?"

"I shouldn't be gone more than three or four days."

"Things aren't the same when you're not here. I'll miss you."

Jennifer wondered whether he was still seeing the young blond man.

"Hold down the fort until I get back."

As a rule, Jennifer enjoyed flying. She regarded her time in the air as freedom from pressures, a temporary escape from all the problems that beset her on the ground, a quiet oasis in space away from her endlessly demanding clients. This flight across the Atlantic, however, was unpleasant. It seemed unusually bumpy, and Jennifer's stomach became queasy and upset.

She was feeling a bit better by the time the plane landed in Nice the next morning. There was a helicopter waiting to fly her to Monte Carlo. Jennifer had never ridden in a helicopter before and she had looked forward to it. But the sudden lift and the swooping motions made her ill again, and she was unable to enjoy the majestic sights of the Alps below and the Grande Corniche, with miniature automobiles winding up the steep mountainside.

The buildings of Monte Carlo appeared, and a few minutes later the helicopter was landing in front of the modern white summer casino on the beach.

Cynthia had telephoned ahead and Rick Arlen was there to meet Jennifer.

He gave her a big hug. "How was the trip?"

"A little rough."

He took a closer look at her and said, "You don't look so hot. I'll take you up to my pad and you can rest up for the big do tonight."

"What big do?"

"The gala. That's why you're here."

"What?"

"Yeah. Grace asked me to invite anyone I liked. I like you."

"Oh, Rick!"

Jennifer could cheerfully have strangled him. He had no idea how much he had disrupted her life. She was three thousand miles away from Adam, she had clients who needed her, court cases to try—and she had been lured to Monte Carlo to attend a party!

Jennifer said, "Rick, how could—?"

She looked at his beaming face and started to laugh.

Oh, well, she was here. Besides, the gala might turn out to be fun.

The gala was spectacular. It was a milk fund concert for orphans, sponsored by Their Serene Highnesses, Grace and Rainier Grimaldi, and it was held outdoors at the summer casino. It was a lovely evening. The night was balmy and the slight breeze coming off the Mediterranean stirred the tall palm trees. Jennifer wished Adam could have been here to share it with her. There were fifteen hundred seats occupied by a cheering audience.

Half a dozen international stars performed, but Rick Arlen was the headliner. He was backed up by a raucous three-piece band and flashing psychedelic lights that stained the velvet sky. When he finished, he received a standing ovation.

There was a private party afterward at the *piscine*, below the Hotel de Paris. Cocktails and a buffet supper were served around the enormous pool, in which dozens of lighted candles floated on lily pads.

Jennifer estimated that there were more than three hundred people there. Jennifer had not brought an evening gown, and just looking at the splendidly dressed women made her feel like the poor little match girl. Rick introduced her to dukes and duchesses and princesses. It seemed to Jennifer that half the royalty of Europe was there. She met heads of cartels and famous opera singers. There were fashion designers and heiresses and the great soccer player, Pele. Jennifer was in the midst of a conversation with two Swiss bankers when a wave of dizziness engulfed her.

"Excuse me," Jennifer said.

She went to find Rick Arlen. "Rick, I—"

He took one look at her and said, "You're white as a sheet, baby. Let's split."

Thirty minutes later, Jennifer was in bed in the villa that Rick Arlen had rented.

"A doctor's on his way," Rick told her.

"I don't need a doctor. It's just a virus or something."

"Right. It's the 'or something' he's gonna check out."

Dr. André Monteux was an elderly wisp of a man somewhere in his eighties. He wore a neatly trimmed full beard and carried a black medical case.

The doctor turned to Rick Arlen. "If you would leave us alone, please."

"Sure. I'll wait outside."

The doctor moved closer to the bed. "Alors. What have we here?"

"If I knew that," Jennifer said weakly, "I'd be making this house call and you'd be lying here."

He sat down on the edge of the bed. "How are you feeling?"

"Like I've come down with the bubonic plague."

"Put out your tongue, please."

Jennifer put out her tongue and began to gag. Dr. Monteux checked her pulse and took her temperature.

When he had finished, Jennifer asked, "What do you think it is, Doctor?"

"It could be any one of a number of things, beautiful lady. If you are feeling well enough tomorrow, I would like you to come to my office where I can do a thorough examination."

Jennifer felt too ill to argue. "All right," she said. "I'll be there."

In the morning Rick Arlen drove Jennifer into Monte Carlo where Dr. Monteux gave her a complete examination.

"It's a bug of some kind, isn't it?" Jennifer asked.

"If you wish a prediction," the elderly doctor replied, "I will send out for fortune cookies. If you wish to know what is wrong with you, we will have to be patient until the laboratory reports come back."

"When will that be?"

"It usually takes two or three days."

Jennifer knew there was no way she was going to stay there for two or three days. Adam might need her. She knew she needed him.

"In the meantime, I would like you to stay in bed and rest." He handed her a bottle of pills. "These will relax you."

"Thank you." Jennifer scribbled something on a piece of paper. "You can call me here."

It was not until Jennifer had gone that Dr. Monteux looked at the piece of paper. On it was written a New York telephone number.

At the Charles de Gaulle Airport in Paris, where she changed planes, Jennifer took two of the pills Dr. Monteaux had given her and a sleeping pill. She slept fitfully during most of the trip back to New York, but when she disembarked from the plane she was feeling no better. She had not arranged for anyone to meet her and she took a taxi to her apartment.

In the late afternoon, the telephone rang. It was Adam.

"Jennifer! Where have you—"

She tried to put energy into her voice. "I'm sorry, darling. I had to go to Monte Carlo to see a client and I couldn't reach you."

"I've been worried sick. Are you all right?"

"I'm fine. I—I've just been running around a lot."

"My God! I was imagining all kinds of terrible things."

"There's nothing to worry about," Jennifer assured him. "How's everything going with the campaign?"

"Fine. When am I going to see you? I was supposed to leave for Washington, but I can postpone—"

"No, you go ahead," Jennifer said. She did not want Adam to see her like this. "I'll be busy. We'll spend the weekend together."

"All right." His tone was reluctant. "If you're not doing anything at eleven, I'm on the CBS news."

"I'll watch, darling."

Jennifer was asleep five minutes after she had replaced the receiver.

In the morning Jennifer telephoned Cynthia to tell her she was not coming into the office. Jennifer had slept restlessly, and when she awakened she felt no better. She tried to eat breakfast but could not keep anything down. She felt weak and realized she had had nothing to eat for almost three days.

Her mind unwillingly went over the frightening litany of things that could be wrong with her. Cancer first, naturally. She felt for lumps in her breast, but she could not feel anything amiss. Of course, cancer could strike anywhere. It could be a virus of some kind, but the doctor surely would have known that immediately. The trouble was that it could be almost anything. Jennifer felt lost and helpless. She was not a hypochondriac, she had always been in wonderful health, and now she felt as though her body had somehow betrayed her. She could not bear it if anything happened to her. Not when everything was so wonderful.

She was going to be fine. Of course she was.

Another wave of nausea swept through her.

At eleven o'clock that morning, Dr. André Monteux called from Monte Carlo. A voice said, "Just a moment. I'll put the doctor on."

The moment stretched into a hundred years, and Jennifer clutched the telephone tightly, unable to bear the waiting.

Finally, Dr. Monteux's voice came on and he said, "How are you feeling?"

"About the same," Jennifer replied nervously. "Are the results of the tests in?"

"Good news," Dr. Monteux said. "It is not the bubonic plague."

Jennifer could stand no more. "What is it? What's the matter with me?"

"You are going to have a baby, Mrs. Parker."

Jennifer sat there numbly staring at the telephone. When she found her voice again she asked, "Are—are you sure?"

"Rabbits never lie. I take it this is your first baby."

"Yes."

"I would suggest you see an obstetrician as soon as possible. From the severity of the early symptoms, there may be some difficulties ahead for you."

"I will," Jennifer replied. "Thank you for calling, Dr. Monteux."

She replaced the receiver and sat there, her mind in a turmoil. She was not sure when it could have happened, or what her feelings were. She could not think straight.

She was going to have Adam's baby. And suddenly Jennifer knew how she felt. She felt *wonderful*; she felt as though she had been given some indescribably precious gift.

The timing was perfect, as though the gods were on their side. The election would soon be over and she and Adam would be married as quickly as possible. It would be a boy. Jennifer knew it. She could not wait to tell Adam.

She telephoned him at his office.

"Mr. Warner is not in," his secretary informed her. "You might try his home."

Jennifer was reluctant to call Adam at home, but she was bursting with her news. She dialed his number. Mary Beth answered.

"I'm sorry to bother you," Jennifer apologized. "There's something I have to talk to Adam about. This is Jennifer Parker."

"I'm pleased that you called," Mary Beth said. The warmth in her voice was reassuring. "Adam had some speaking engagements, but he's returning tonight. Why don't you come up to the house? We can all have dinner together. Say, seven o'clock?"

Jennifer hesitated for a moment. "That will be lovely."

It was a miracle that Jennifer did not have an accident driving to Croton-on-Hudson. Her mind was far away, dreaming of the future. She and Adam had often discussed having children. She could remember his words. *I want a couple that look exactly like you.*

As Jennifer drove along the highway, she thought she could feel a slight stirring in her womb, but she told herself that that was nonsense. It was much too early. But it would not be long now. Adam's baby was in her. It was alive and would soon be kicking. It was awesome, overwhelming. She—

Jennifer heard someone honking at her, and she looked up and saw that she had almost forced a truck driver off the road. She gave him an apologetic smile and drove on. Nothing could spoil this day.

It was dusk when Jennifer pulled up in front of the Warner house. A fine snow was beginning to fall, lightly powdering the trees. Mary Beth, wearing a long blue brocade gown, opened the front door to greet Jennifer, taking her arm and warmly welcoming her into the house, reminding Jennifer of the first time they had met.

Mary Beth looked radiantly happy. She was full of small talk, putting her visitor at ease. They went into the library where there was a cheerful fire crackling in the hearth.

"I haven't heard from Adam yet," Mary Beth said. "He's probably been detained. In the meantime, you and I can have a nice long chat. You sounded excited on the telephone." Mary Beth leaned forward conspiratorially. "What's your big news?"

Jennifer looked at the friendly woman across from her and blurted out, "I'm going to have Adam's baby."

Mary Beth leaned back in her chair and smiled. "Well! Now isn't that something! So am I!"

Jennifer stared at her. "I—I don't understand."

Mary Beth laughed. "It's really quite simple, my dear. Adam and I *are* married, you know."

Jennifer said slowly, "But—but you and Adam are getting a divorce."

"My dear girl, why on earth would I divorce Adam? I adore him."

Jennifer felt her head beginning to spin. The conversation was making no sense. "You're—you're in love with someone else. You said you—"

"I said that I'm in love. And I am. I'm in love with Adam. I told you, I've been in love with Adam since the first time I saw him."

She could not mean what she was saying. She was teasing Jennifer, playing some kind of silly game.

"Stop it!" Jennifer said. "You're like a brother and sister to each other. Adam doesn't make love to—"

Mary Beth's voice tinkled with laughter. "My poor dear! I'm surprised that someone as clever as you are could—" She leaned forward with concern. "You believed him! I'm so sorry. I am. I really am."

Jennifer was fighting to keep control of herself. "Adam is in love with me. We're getting married."

Mary Beth shook her head. Her blue eyes met Jennifer's and the naked hatred in them made Jennifer's heart stop for an instant.

"That would make Adam a bigamist. I'll never give him a divorce. If I had let Adam divorce me and marry you, he would lose the election. As it is, he's going to win it. Then we'll go on to the White House, Adam and I. There's no room in his life for anyone like you. There never was. He only thinks he's in love with you. But he'll get over that when he finds out I'm carrying his baby. Adam's always wanted a child."

Jennifer squeezed her eyes shut, trying to stop the terrible pain in her head.

"Can I get you something?" Mary Beth was asking solicitously.

Jennifer opened her eyes. "Have you told him you're having a baby?"

"Not yet." Mary Beth smiled. "I thought I'd tell him tonight when he gets home and we're in bed."

Jennifer was filled with loathing. "You're a monster . . ."

"It's all in the point of view, isn't it, honey? I'm Adam's wife. You're his whore."

Jennifer rose to her feet, feeling dizzy. Her headache had become an unbearable pounding. There was a roaring in her ears and she was afraid she was going to faint. She was moving toward the entrance, her legs unsteady.

Jennifer stopped at the door, pressing herself against it, trying to think. Adam had said he loved her, but he had slept with this woman, had made her pregnant.

Jennifer turned and walked out into the cold night air.

24

Adam was on a final campaign swing around the state. He telephoned Jennifer several times, but he was always surrounded by his entourage and it was impossible to talk, impossible for Jennifer to tell him her news.

Jennifer knew the explanation for Mary Beth's pregnancy: She had tricked Adam into sleeping with her. But Jennifer wanted to hear it from Adam.

"I'll be back in a few days and we'll talk then," Adam said.

The election was only five days away now. Adam deserved to win it; he was the better man. Jennifer felt that Mary Beth was right when she said it could be the stepping-stone to the presidency of the United States. She would force herself to wait and see what happened.

If Adam was elected senator, Jennifer would lose him. Adam would go to Washington with Mary Beth. There would be no way he could get a divorce. The scandal of a freshman senator divorcing a pregnant wife to marry his pregnant mistress would be too juicy a story for him ever to live down. But if Adam should lose the race, he would be free. Free to go back to his law practice, free to marry Jennifer and not worry or care about what anyone else thought. They would be able to live the rest of their lives together. Have their child.

Election Day dawned cold and rainy. Because of the interest in the senate race, a large voter turnout was expected at the polls despite the weather.

In the morning, Ken Bailey asked, "Are you going to vote today?"

"Yes."

"Looks like a close race, doesn't it?"

"Very close."

She went to the polls late that morning, and as she stepped into the voting booth she thought dully, *A vote for Adam Warner is a vote against Jennifer Parker.* She voted for Adam and left the booth. She could not bear to go back to her office. She walked the streets all afternoon, trying not to think, trying not to feel; thinking and feeling, knowing that the next few hours were going to determine the rest of her life.

25

"This is one of the closest elections we have had in years," the television announcer was saying.

Jennifer was at home alone watching the returns on NBC. She had made herself a light dinner of scrambled eggs and toast, and then was too nervous to eat anything. She sat in a robe huddled up on the couch, listening to her fate being broadcast to millions of people. Each viewer had his own reason for watching, for wanting one of the candidates to win or to lose, but Jennifer was sure that none of them was as deeply involved in the outcome of this election as she was. If Adam won, it would mean the end of their relationship . . . and the end of the baby in her womb.

There was a quick shot of Adam on the screen, and by his side, Mary Beth. Jennifer prided herself on being able to read people, to understand their motives, but she had been completely taken in by the moonlight-and-magnolias routine of the honey-voiced bitch. She kept pushing back the picture of Adam going to bed with that woman, making her pregnant.

Edwin Newman was saying, "Here are the latest returns in the senate race between the incumbent, John Trowbridge, and challenger Adam Warner. In Manhattan, John Trowbridge has a total of 221,375 votes. Adam Warner has a total of 214,895.

"In the Forty-fifth Election District of the Twenty-ninth Assembly District in Queens, John Trowbridge is two percentage points ahead."

Jennifer's life was being measured in percentage points.

"The totals from The Bronx, Brooklyn, Queens, Richmond and the counties of Nassau, Rockland, Suffolk and Westchester add up to 2,300,000 for John Trowbridge, and 2,120,000 for Adam Warner, with the votes from upstate New York just beginning to come in. Adam Warner has made a surprisingly strong showing against Senator Trowbridge, who is serving his third term. From the beginning, the polls have been almost evenly divided in this race. According to the latest returns, with sixty-two percent of the votes counted, Senator Trowbridge is beginning to pull ahead. When we read the last returns one hour ago, Senator Trowbridge was two percentage points ahead. The returns now indicate that he has increased his lead to two and a half percentage points. If this trend continues, the NBC computer will predict Senator Trowbridge to be the victor in the senatorial race for the United States Senate. Moving on to the contest between . . ."

Jennifer sat there, looking at the set, her heart pounding. It was as though millions of people were casting a vote to decide whether it would be Adam and Jennifer, or Adam and Mary Beth. Jennifer felt light-headed and giddy. She must remember to eat sometime. But not now. Nothing mattered now except what was happening on the screen in front of her. The suspense kept building, minute by minute, hour by hour.

At midnight, Senator John Trowbridge's lead was three percentage points. At two in the morning, with seventy-one percent of the votes counted, Senator Trowbridge was leading by a margin of three and a half percentage points. The computer declared that Senator John Trowbridge had won the election.

Jennifer sat there staring at the television set, drained of all emotion, of all feeling. Adam had lost. Jennifer had won. She had won Adam and their son. She was free to tell Adam now, to tell him about their baby, to plan for their future together.

Jennifer's heart ached for Adam, for she knew how much the election had meant to him. And yet in time, Adam would get over his defeat. One day he would try again, and she would help him. He was still young. The world lay before both of them. Before the three of them.

Jennifer fell asleep on the couch, dreaming about Adam and the election and the White House. She and Adam and their son were in the Oval Office. Adam was making his acceptance speech. Mary Beth walked in and began to interrupt. Adam started to yell at her and his voice got louder and louder. Jennifer woke up. The voice was the voice of Edwin Newman. The television set was still on. It was dawn.

Edwin Newman, looking exhausted, was reading the final election returns. Jennifer listened to him, her mind still half asleep.

As she started to rise from the couch she heard him say, "And here are the final results on the New York State senatorial election. In one of the most stunning upsets in years, Adam Warner has defeated the incumbent, Senator John Trowbridge, by a margin of less than one percent."

It was over. Jennifer had lost.

26

When Jennifer walked into the office late that morning, Cynthia said, "Mr. Adams is on the line, Miss Parker. He's been calling all morning."

Jennifer hesitated, then said, "All right, Cynthia, I'll take it." She went into her office and picked up the telephone. "Hello, Adam. Congratulations."

"Thanks. We have to talk. Are you free for lunch?"

Jennifer hesitated. "Yes."

It had to be faced sometime.

It was the first time Jennifer had seen Adam in three weeks. She studied his face. Adam looked haggard and drawn. He should have been flushed with victory, but instead he seemed oddly nervous and uncomfortable. They ordered a lunch which neither of them ate, and they talked about the election, their words a camouflage to hide their thoughts.

The charade had become almost unbearable when, finally, Adam said, "Jennifer . . ." He took a deep breath and plunged ahead. "Mary Beth is going to have a baby."

Hearing the words from him somehow made it an unbearable reality. "I'm sorry, darling. It—it just happened. It's difficult to explain."

"You don't have to explain." Jennifer could see the scene clearly. Mary Beth in a provocative negligee—or naked—and Adam—

"I feel like such a fool," Adam was saying. There was an uncomfortable silence and he went on. "I got a call this morning from the chairman of the National Committee. There's talk about grooming me as their next presidential candidate." He hesitated. "The problem is that with Mary Beth pregnant, this would be an awkward time for me to get a divorce. I don't know what the hell to do. I haven't slept in three nights." He looked at Jennifer and said, "I hate to ask this of you, but—do you think we could wait a little while until things sort themselves out?"

Jennifer looked across the table at Adam and felt such a deep ache, such an intolerable loss, that she did not think she could stand it.

"We'll see each other as often as possible in the meantime," Adam told her. "We—"

Jennifer forced herself to speak. "No, Adam. It's over."

He stared at her. "You don't mean that. I love you, darling. We'll find a way to—"

"There is no way. Your wife and baby aren't going to disappear. You and I are finished. I've loved it. Every moment of it."

She rose to her feet, knowing that if she did not get out of the restaurant she would start screaming. "We must never see each other again."

She could not bear to look at his pain-filled eyes.

"Oh, God, Jennifer! Don't do this. Please don't do this! We—"

She did not hear the rest. She was hurrying toward the door, running out of Adam's life.

27

Adam's telephone calls were neither accepted nor returned. His letters were sent back unopened. On the last letter Jennifer received, she wrote the word "deceased" on the envelope and dropped it in the mail slot. *It's true*, Jennifer thought. *I am dead.*

She had never known that such pain could exist. She had to be alone, and yet she was not alone. There was another human being inside her, a part of her and a part of Adam. And she was going to destroy it.

She forced herself to think about where she was going to have the abortion. A few years earlier an abortion would have meant some quack doctor in a dirty, sleazy back-alley room, but now that was no longer necessary. She could go to a hospital and have the operation performed by a reputable surgeon. Somewhere outside of New York City. Jennifer's photograph had been in the newspapers too many times, she had been on television too often. She needed anonymity, someplace where no one would ask questions. There must never,

never be a link between her and Adam Warner. *United States Senator* Adam Warner. Their baby must die anonymously.

Jennifer allowed herself to think of what the baby would have been like, and she began to weep so hard that it was difficult to breathe.

It had started to rain. Jennifer looked up at the sky and wondered whether God was crying for her.

Ken Bailey was the only person Jennifer could trust to help her.

"I need an abortion," Jennifer said without preamble. "Do you know of a good doctor?"

He tried to mask his surprise, but Jennifer could see the variety of emotions that flickered across his face.

"Somewhere out of town, Ken. Someplace where they won't know me."

"What about the Fiji Islands?" There was an anger in his voice.

"I'm serious."

"Sorry. I—you caught me off guard." The news had taken him completely by surprise. He worshipped Jennifer. He knew that he loved her, and there were times when he thought he was in love with her; but he could not be sure, and it was torture. He could never do to Jennifer what he had done to his wife. *God*, Ken thought, *why the hell couldn't You make up Your mind about me?*

He ran his hands through his red hair and said, "If you don't want to have it in New York, I'd suggest North Carolina. It's not too far away."

"Can you check it out for me?"

"Yeah. Fine. I—"

"Yes?"

He looked away from her. "Nothing."

*   *   *

Ken Bailey disappeared for the next three days. When he walked into Jennifer's office on the third day, he was unshaven and his eyes were hollow and red-rimmed.

Jennifer took one look at him and asked, "Are you all right?"

"I guess so."

"Is there anything I can do to help?"

"No." *If God can't help me, love, there's nothing you can do.*

He handed Jennifer a slip of paper. On it was written, *Dr. Eric Linden, Memorial Hospital, Charlotte, North Carolina.*

"Thank you, Ken."

"*De nada.* When are you going to do it?"

"I'll go down there this weekend."

He said awkwardly, "Would you like me to go with you?"

"No, thanks. I'll be fine."

"What about the return trip?"

"I'll be all right."

He stood there a moment, hesitating. "It's none of my business, but are you sure this is what you want to do?"

"I'm sure."

She had no choice. She wanted nothing more in the world than to keep Adam's baby, but she knew it would be insane to try to bring the baby up by herself.

She looked at Ken and said again, "I'm sure."

The hospital was a pleasant old two-story brick building on the outskirts of Charlotte.

The woman behind the registration desk was gray-haired, in her late sixties. "May I help you?"

"Yes," Jennifer said. "I'm Mrs. Parker. I have an appointment with Dr. Linden to—to—" She could not bring herself to say the words.

The receptionist nodded understandingly. "The doctor's expecting you, Mrs. Parker. I'll have someone show you the way."

An efficient young nurse led Jennifer to an examining room down the hall and said, "I'll tell Dr. Linden you're here. Would you like to get undressed? There's a hospital gown on the hanger."

Slowly, possessed by a feeling of unreality, Jennifer undressed and put on the white hospital gown. She felt as though she were putting on a butcher's apron. She was about to kill the life inside her. In her mind, the apron became spattered with blood, the blood of her baby. Jennifer found herself trembling.

A voice said, "Here, now. Relax."

Jennifer looked up to see a burly bald-headed man wearing horn-rimmed glasses that gave his face an owlish appearance.

"I'm Dr. Linden." He looked at the chart in his hand. "You're Mrs. Parker."

Jennifer nodded.

The doctor touched her arm and said soothingly, "Sit down." He went to the sink and filled a paper cup with water. "Drink this."

Jennifer obeyed. Dr. Linden sat in a chair, watching her until the trembling had subsided.

"So. You want to have an abortion."

"Yes."

"Have you discussed this with your husband, Mrs. Parker?"

"Yes. We—we both want it."

He studied her. "You appear to be in good health."

"I feel—I feel fine."

"Is it an economic problem?"

"No," Jennifer said sharply. Why was he bothering her with questions? "We—we just can't have the baby."

Dr. Linden took out a pipe. "This bother you?"

"No."

Dr. Linden lit the pipe and said, "Nasty habit." He leaned back and blew out a puff of smoke.

"Could we get this over with?" Jennifer asked.

Her nerves were stretched to the breaking point. She felt that at any moment she was going to scream.

Dr. Linden took another long, slow puff from his pipe. "I think we should talk for a few minutes."

By an enormous effort of will, Jennifer controlled her agitation. "All right."

"The thing about abortions," Dr. Linden said, "is that they're so final. You can change your mind now, but you can't change it after the baby's gone."

"I'm not going to change my mind."

He nodded and took another slow puff of the pipe. "That's good."

The sweet smell of the tobacco was making Jennifer nauseous. She wished he would put away his pipe. "Doctor Linden—"

He rose to his feet reluctantly and said, "All right, young lady, let's have a look at you."

Jennifer lay back on the examining table, her feet in the cold metal stirrups. She felt his fingers probing inside her body. They were gentle, and skilled, and she felt no embarrassment, only an ineffable sense of loss, a deep sorrow. Unbidden visions came into her mind of her young son, because she knew with certainty it would have been a boy, running and playing and laughing. Growing up in the image of his father.

Dr. Linden had finished his examination. "You can get dressed now, Mrs. Parker. You may stay here overnight, if you like, and we'll perform the operation in the morning."

"No!" Jennifer's voice was sharper than she had intended. "I'd like it done now, please."

Dr. Linden was studying her again, a quizzical expression on his face.

"I have two patients ahead of you. I'll have the nurse come in and get a lab work-up and then put you in your room. We'll go ahead with surgery in about four hours. All right?"

Jennifer whispered, "All right."

She lay on the narrow hospital bed, her eyes closed, waiting for Dr. Linden to return. There was an old-fashioned clock on the wall and its ticking seemed to fill the room. The tick-tock became words: *Young Adam, Young Adam, Young Adam, our son, our son, our son.*

Jennifer could not shut the vision of the baby out of her mind. At this moment it was inside her body, comfortable and warm and alive, protected against the world in its amniotic womb. She wondered whether it had any primeval fear of what was about to happen to it. She wondered whether it would feel pain when the knife killed it. She put her hands over her ears to shut out the ticking of the clock. She found she was beginning to breathe hard, and her body was covered with perspiration. She heard a sound and opened her eyes.

Dr. Linden was standing over her, a look of concern on his face. "Are you all right, Mrs. Parker?"

"Yes," Jennifer whispered. "I just want it finished."

Dr. Linden nodded. "That's what we're going to do." He took a syringe from the table next to her bed and moved toward her.

"What's in that?"

"Demerol and Phenergan to relax you. We'll be going into the operating room in a few minutes." He gave Jennifer the injection. "I take it that this is your first abortion?"

"Yes."

"Then let me explain the procedure to you. It's painless and relatively simple. In the operating room you'll be given nitrous oxide, a general anesthesia, and oxygen by mask. When you're unconscious, a speculum will be inserted into the vagina, so that we can see what we're doing. We will then begin dilating the cervix with a series of metal dilators, in increasing sizes, and scraping out the uterus with a curette. Any questions so far?"

"No."

A warm, sleepy feeling was stealing over her. She could feel her tension vanishing as though by magic, and the walls of the room began to blur. She wanted to ask the doctor something, but she could not remember what it was . . . something about the baby . . . it no longer seemed important. The important thing was that she was doing what she had to do. It would all be over in a few minutes, and she could start her life again.

She found herself drifting off into a wonderful, dreamy state . . . she was aware of people coming into the room, lifting her onto a metal table with wheels . . . she could feel the coldness of the metal on her back through her thin hospital gown. She was being rolled down the hallway and she started to count the lights overhead. It seemed important to get the number right, but she was not sure why. She was being wheeled into a white, antiseptic operating room and Jennifer thought, *This is where my baby is going to die. Don't worry, little Adam. I won't let them hurt you.* And without meaning to, she began to cry.

Dr. Linden patted her arm. "It's all right. This won't hurt."

Death without pain, Jennifer thought. *That was nice.* She loved her baby. She did not want him to be hurt.

Someone put a mask over her face and a voice said, "Breathe deeply."

Jennifer felt hands raise the hospital gown and spread her legs apart.

It was going to happen. It was going to happen now. Young Adam, Young Adam, Young Adam.

"I want you to relax," Dr. Linden said.

Jennifer nodded. *Good-bye, my baby.* She felt a cold, steel object begin to move between her thighs and slowly slide up inside her. It was the alien instrument of death that was going to murder Adam's baby.

She heard a strange voice scream out, "Stop it! Stop it! Stop it!"

And Jennifer looked up at the surprised faces staring down at her and realized that the screams were coming from her. The mask pressed down harder against her face. She tried to sit up, but there were straps holding her down. She was being sucked into a vortex that was moving faster and faster, drowning her.

The last thing she remembered was the huge white light in the ceiling whirling above her, spinning down and going deep inside her skull.

When Jennifer awakened, she was lying in the hospital bed in her room. Through the window she could see that it was dark outside. Her body felt sore and battered, and she wondered how long she had been unconscious. She was alive, but her baby—?

She reached for the bell pinned to her bed and pressed it. She kept pressing it, frantic, unable to stop herself.

A nurse appeared in the doorway, then quickly left. A few moments later Dr. Linden hurried in. He moved to the side of the bed and gently pried Jennifer's fingers away from the bell.

Jennifer grabbed his arm fiercely and said in a hoarse voice, "My baby—he's dead!"—!"

Dr. Linden said, "No, Mrs. Parker. He's alive. I hope it's a boy. You kept calling him Adam."

28

Christmas came and went, and it was a new year, 1973. The snows of February gave way to the brisk winds of March, and Jennifer knew that it was time to stop working.

She called a meeting of the office staff.

"I'm taking a leave of absence," Jennifer announced. "I'll be gone for the next five months."

There were murmurs of surprise.

Dan Martin asked, "We'll be able to reach you, won't we?"

"No, Dan. I'll be out of touch."

Ted Harris peered at her through his thick spectacles. "Jennifer, you can't just—"

"I'll be leaving at the end of this week."

There was a finality in her tone that brooked no further questions. The rest of the meeting was taken up with a discussion of pending cases.

When everyone else had left, Ken Bailey asked, "Have you really thought this thing through?"

"I have no choice, Ken."

He looked at her. "I don't know who the son of a bitch is, but I hate him."

Jennifer put her hand on his arm. "Thank you. I'll be all right."

"It's going to get rough, you know. Kids grow up. They ask questions. He'll want to know who his father is."

"I'll handle it."

"Okay." His tone softened. "If there's anything I can do—anything—I'll always be around."

She put her arms around him. "Thank you, Ken. I—thank you."

Jennifer stayed in her office long after everyone else had left, sitting alone in the dark, thinking. She would always love Adam. Nothing could ever change that, and she was sure that he still loved her. *Somehow,* Jennifer thought, *it would be easier if he did not.* It was an unbearable irony that they loved each other and could not be together, that their lives were going to move farther and farther apart. Adam's life would be in Washington now with Mary Beth and their child. Perhaps one day Adam would be in the White House. Jennifer thought of her own son growing up, wanting to know who his father was. She could never tell him, nor must Adam ever know that she had borne him a child, for it would destroy him.

And if anyone else ever learned about it, it would destroy Adam in a different way.

Jennifer had decided to buy a house in the country, somewhere outside of Manhattan, where she and her son could live together in their own little world.

She found the house by sheer accident. She had been on her way to see a client on Long Island and had turned off the Long Island Expressway at Exit 36, then had taken a wrong turn and found herself in Sands Point. The streets were quiet and shaded with tall, graceful trees, and the houses were set back from the road, each in its private little domain. There was a *For Sale* sign in front of a white colonial house on Sands Point Road. The grounds were fenced in and there was a lovely wrought-iron gate in front of a sweeping driveway, with lamp posts lighting the way, and a large front lawn with a row of yews sheltering the house. From the outside it looked enchanting. Jennifer wrote down the name of the realtor and made an appointment to see the house the following after-noon.

The real estate agent was a hearty, high-pressure type, the kind of salesman Jennifer hated. But she was not buying his personality, she was buying a house.

He was saying, "It's a real beauty. Yessir, a *real* beauty. About a hundred years old. It's in tip-top condition. Abso-lutely tip-top."

Tip-top was certainly an exaggeration. The rooms were airy and spacious, but in need of repair. *It would be fun,* Jennifer thought, *to fix up this house and decorate it.*

Upstairs, across from the master suite, was a room that could be converted into a nursery. She would do it in blue and—

"Like to walk around the grounds?"

It was the tree house that decided Jennifer. It was built on a platform high up in a sturdy oak tree. Her son's tree house. There were three acres, with the back lawn gently sloping down to the sound, where there was a dock. It would be a wonderful place for her son to grow up in, with plenty of room for him to run around. Later, he would have a small boat. There would be all the privacy here that they would need, for Jennifer was determined that this was going to be a world that belonged only to her and her child.

She bought the house the following day.

Jennifer had had no idea how painful it would be to leave

the Manhattan apartment she and Adam had shared. His bathrobe and pajamas were still there, and his slippers and shaving kit. Every room held hundreds of memories of Adam, memories of a lovely, dead past. Jennifer packed her things as quickly as possible and got out of there.

At the new house, Jennifer kept herself busy from early morning until late at night, so that there would be no time to think about Adam. She went into the shops in Sands Point and Port Washington to order furniture and drapes. She bought Porthault linens, and silver and china. She hired local workmen to come in and repair the faulty plumbing and leaky roof and worn-out electrical equipment. From early morning until dusk, the house was filled with painters, carpenters, electricians and wallpaper hangers. Jennifer was everywhere, supervising everything. She wore herself out during the day, hoping she would be able to sleep at night, but the demons had returned, torturing her with unspeakable nightmares.

She haunted antique shops, buying lamps and tables and objets d'art. She bought a fountain and statues for the garden, a Lipschitz, a Noguchi and a Miró.

Inside the house, everything was beginning to look beautiful.

Bob Clement was a California client of Jennifer's and the area rugs he had designed for the living room and the nursery made the rooms glow with subdued color.

Jennifer's abdomen was getting bigger, and she went into the village to buy maternity clothes. She had an unlisted telephone installed. It was there only for emergencies, and she gave no one the telephone number and expected no calls. The only person in the office who knew where she lived was Ken Bailey, and he was sworn to secrecy.

He drove out to see Jennifer one afternoon, and she showed him around the house and grounds and took enormous pleasure in his delight.

"It's beautiful, Jennifer. Really beautiful. You've done a hell of a job." He looked at her swollen abdomen. "How long is it going to be?"

"Another two months." She put his hand against her belly and said, "Feel this."

He felt a kick.

"He's getting stronger every day," Jennifer said proudly.

She cooked dinner for Ken. He waited until they were having dessert before he brought up the subject.

"I don't want to pry," he said, "but shouldn't whoever the proud papa is be doing something—?"

"Subject closed."

"Okay. Sorry. The office misses you like hell. We have a new client who—"

Jennifer held up a hand. "I don't want to hear about it."

They talked until it was time for Ken to leave, and Jennifer hated to see him go. He was a dear man and a good friend.

Jennifer shut herself off from the world in every possible way. She stopped reading the newspapers and would not watch television or listen to the radio. Her universe was here within these four walls. This was her nest, her womb, the place where she was going to bring her son into the world.

She read every book she could get her hands on about raising children, from Dr. Spock to Ames and Gesell and back again.

When Jennifer finished decorating the nursery, she filled it with toys. She visited a sporting goods shop and looked at footballs and baseball bats and a catcher's mitt. And she laughed at herself. *This is ridiculous. He hasn't even been born yet.* And she bought the baseball bat and the catcher's mitt. The football tempted her, but she thought, *That can wait.*

It was May, and then June.

The workmen finished and the house became quiet and serene. Twice a week Jennifer would drive into the village and shop at the supermarket, and every two weeks she would visit Dr. Harvey, her obstetrician. Jennifer obediently drank more milk than she wanted, took vitamins and ate all the proper, healthy foods. She was getting large now and clumsy, and it was becoming difficult for her to move about.

She had always been active, and she had thought she would loathe getting heavy and awkward, having to move slowly; but somehow, she did not mind it. There was no reason to hurry anymore. The days became long and dreamy and peaceful. Some diurnal clock within her had slowed its tempo. It was as though she were reserving her energy, pouring it into the other body living inside her.

One morning, Dr. Harvey examined her and said, "Another two weeks, Mrs. Parker."

It was so close now. Jennifer had thought she might be afraid. She had heard all the old wives' tales of the pain, the accidents, the malformed babies, but she felt no fear, only a longing to see her child, an impatience to get his birth over with so she could hold him in her arms.

Ken Bailey drove out to the house almost every day now, bringing with him *The Little Engine That Could, Little Red Hen, Pat the Bunny*, and a dozen Dr. Seuss books.

"He'll love these," Ken said.

And Jennifer smiled, because he had said "he." *An omen.*

They strolled through the grounds and had a picnic lunch at the water's edge and sat in the sun. Jennifer was self-conscious about her looks. She thought, *Why would he want to waste his time with the ugly fat lady from the circus?*

And Ken was looking at Jennifer and thinking: *She's the most beautiful woman I've ever seen.*

The first pains came at three o'clock in the morning. They

were so sharp that Jennifer was left breathless. A few moments later they were repeated and Jennifer thought exultantly, *It's happening*!

She began to count the time between the pains, and when they were ten minutes apart she telephoned her obstetrician. Jennifer drove to the hospital, pulling over to the side of the road every time a contraction came. An attendant was standing outside waiting for her when she arrived, and a few minutes later Dr. Harvey was examining her.

When he finished, he said reassuringly, "Well, this is going to be an easy delivery, Mrs. Parker. Just relax and we'll let nature take its course."

It was not easy, but neither was it unbearable. Jennifer could stand the pain because out of it something wonderful was happening. She was in labor for almost eight hours, and at the end of that time, when her body was wracked and contorted with spasms and she thought that it was never going to stop, she felt a quick easing and then a rushing emptiness, and a sudden blessed peace.

She heard a thin squeal and Dr. Harvey was holding up her baby, saying, "Would you like to take a look at your son, Mrs. Parker?"

Jennifer's smile lit the room.

29

His name was Joshua Adam Parker and he weighed in at eight pounds, six ounces, a perfectly formed baby. Jennifer knew that babies were supposed to be ugly at birth, wrinkled and red and resembling little apes. Not Joshua Adam. He was beautiful. The nurses at the hospital kept telling Jennifer what a handsome boy Joshua was, and Jennifer could not hear it often enough. The resemblance to Adam was striking. Joshua Adam had his father's gray-blue eyes and beautifully shaped head. When Jennifer looked at him, she was looking at Adam. It was a strange feeling, a poignant mixture of joy and sadness. How Adam would have loved to see his handsome son!

When Joshua was two days old he smiled up at Jennifer and she excitedly rang for the nurse.

"Look! He's smiling!"

"It's gas, Mrs. Parker."

"With other babies it might be gas," Jennifer said stubbornly. "My son is smiling."

Jennifer had wondered how she would feel about her baby, had worried whether she would be a good mother. Babies were surely boring to be around. They messed their diapers, demanded to be fed constantly, cried and slept. There was no communication with them.

I won't really feel anything about him until he's four or five years old, Jennifer had thought. How wrong, how wrong. From the moment of Joshua's birth, Jennifer loved her son with a love she had never known existed in her. It was a fiercely protective love. Joshua was so small, and the world so large.

When Jennifer brought Joshua home from the hospital, she was given a long list of instructions, but they only served to panic her. For the first two weeks a practical nurse stayed at the house. After that, Jennifer was on her own, and she was terrified she might do something wrong that would kill the baby. She was afraid he might stop breathing at any moment.

The first time Jennifer made Joshua's formula, she realized she had forgotten to sterilize the nipple. She threw the formula in the sink and started all over again. When she had finished she remembered she had forgotten to sterilize the bottle. She began again. By the time Joshua's meal was ready, he was screaming with rage.

There were times when Jennifer did not think she would be able to cope. At unexpected moments she was overwhelmed with feelings of unexplained depression. She told herself that it was the normal postpartum blues, but the explanation did not make her feel any better. She was constantly exhausted. It seemed to her that she was up all night giving Joshua his feedings and when she did finally manage to drop off to sleep, Joshua's cries would awaken her and Jennifer would stumble back into the nursery.

* * *

She called the doctor constantly, at all hours of the day and night.

"Joshua's breathing too fast" . . . "He's breathing too slowly" . . . "Joshua's coughing" . . . "He didn't eat his dinner" . . . "Joshua vomited."

In self-defense, the doctor finally drove to the house and gave Jennifer a lecture.

"Mrs. Parker, I've never seen a healthier baby than your son. He may *look* fragile, but he's as strong as an ox. Stop worrying about him and enjoy him. Just remember one thing —he's going to outlive both of us!"

And so Jennifer began to relax. She had decorated Joshua's bedroom with print curtains and a bedspread with a blue background sprigged with white flowers and yellow butter- flies. There was a crib, a play pen, a miniature matching chest and desk and chair, a rocking horse, and the chest full of toys.

Jennifer loved holding Joshua, bathing and diapering him, taking him for airings in his shiny new perambulator. She talked to him constantly, and when Joshua was four weeks old he rewarded her with a smile. *Not gas*, Jennifer thought hap- pily. *A smile!*

The first time Ken Bailey saw the baby, he stared at it for a long time. With a feeling of sudden panic, Jennifer thought, *He's going to recognize it. He's going to know it's Adam's baby.*

But all Ken said was, "He's a real beauty. He takes after his mother."

She let Ken hold Joshua in his arms and she laughed at Ken's awkwardness. But she could not help thinking, *Joshua will never have a father to hold him.*

Six weeks had passed and it was time to go back to work.

Jennifer hated the idea of being away from her son, even for a few hours a day, but the thought of returning to the office filled her with excitement. She had completely cut herself off from everything for so long. It was time to re-enter her other world.

She looked in the mirror and decided the first thing she had to do was get her body back in shape. She had been dieting and exercising since shortly after Joshua's birth, but now she went at it even more strenuously, and soon she began to look like her old self.

Jennifer started to interview housekeepers. She examined them as though each one was a juror: she probed, looking for weaknesses, lies, incompetence. She interviewed more than twenty potential candidates before she found one she liked and trusted, a middle-aged Scotswoman named Mrs. Mackey, who had worked for one family for fifteen years and had left when the children had grown up and gone away to school.

Jennifer had Ken check her out, and when Ken assured her that Mrs. Mackey was legitimate, Jennifer hired her.

A week later Jennifer returned to the office.

30

Jennifer Parker's sudden disappearance had created a spate of rumors around Manhattan law offices.

When word got out on the grapevine that Jennifer was back, the interest was enormous. The reception that Jennifer received on the morning she returned kept swelling, as attorneys from other offices dropped by to visit her.

Cynthia, Dan and Ted had hung streamers across the room and a huge *Welcome Back* sign. There was champagne and cake.

"At nine o'clock in the morning?" Jennifer protested.

But they insisted.

"It's been a madhouse here without you," Dan Martin told her. "You're not planning to do this again, are you?"

Jennifer looked at him and said, "No. I'm not planning to do this again."

Unexpected visitors kept dropping in to make sure Jennifer was all right and to wish her well.

She parried questions about where she had been with a smile and "We're not allowed to tell."

She held conferences all day with the members of her staff. Hundreds of telephone messages had accumulated.

When Ken Bailey was in Jennifer's office alone with her, he said, "You know who's been driving us nuts trying to reach you?"

Jennifer's heart leaped. "Who?"

"Michael Moretti."

"Oh."

"He's weird. When we wouldn't tell him where you were, he made us swear you were all right."

"Forget about Michael Moretti."

Jennifer went over all the cases that were being handled by the office. Business was excellent. They had acquired a lot of important new clients. Some of the older clients refused to deal with anyone but Jennifer, and were waiting for her return.

"I'll call them as soon as I can," Jennifer promised.

She went through the rest of the telephone messages. There were a dozen calls from Mr. Adams. Perhaps she should have let Adam know that she was all right, that nothing had happened to her. But she knew she could not bear hearing his voice, knowing he was close and that she would not be able to see him, touch him, hold him. Tell him about Joshua.

Cynthia had clipped news stories she thought would be of interest to Jennifer. There was a syndicated series on Michael Moretti, calling him the most important Mafia leader in the country. There was a photograph of him and under it the caption, *I'm just an insurance salesman.*

It took Jennifer three months to catch up on her backlog of cases. She could have handled it more rapidly, but she insisted on leaving the office at four o'clock every day, no matter what she was involved in. Joshua was waiting.

Mornings, before Jennifer went to the office, she made Joshua's breakfast herself and spent as much time as possible playing with him before she left.

When Jennifer came home in the afternoon, she devoted all of her time to Joshua. She forced herself to leave her business problems at the office, and turned down any cases that would take her away from her son. She stopped working weekends. She would let nothing intrude on her private world.

She loved reading aloud to Joshua.

Mrs. Mackey protested, "He's an infant, Mrs. Parker. He doesn't understand a word you're saying."

Jennifer would reply confidently, "Joshua understands."

And she would go on reading.

Joshua was a series of unending miracles. When he was three months old he began cooing and trying to talk to Jennifer. He amused himself in his crib with a large, tinkling ball and a toy bunny that Ken had brought him. When he was six months old, he was already trying to climb out of his crib, restless to explore the world. Jennifer held him in her arms and he grabbed her fingers with his tiny hands and they carried on long and serious conversations.

Jennifer's days at the office were full. One morning she received a call from Philip Redding, president of a large oil corporation.

"I wonder if we could meet," he said. "I have a problem."

Jennifer did not have to ask him what it was. His company had been accused of paying bribes in order to do business in the Middle East. There would be a large fee for handling the case, but Jennifer simply did not have the time.

"I'm sorry," she said. "I'm not available, but I can recommend someone who's very good."

"I was told not to take no for an answer," Philip Redding replied.

"By whom?"

"A friend of mine. Judge Lawrence Waldman."

Jennifer heard the name with disbelief. "Judge Waldman asked you to call me?"

"He said you're the best there is, but I already knew that."

Jennifer held the receiver in her hand, thinking of her previous experiences with Judge Waldman, how sure she had been that he hated her and was out to destroy her.

"All right. Let's have breakfast tomorrow morning," Jennifer said.

When she had hung up, she placed a call to Judge Waldman.

The familiar voice came on the telephone. "Well. I haven't talked to you in some time, young lady."

"I wanted to thank you for having Philip Redding call me."

"I wanted to make certain he was in good hands."

"I appreciate that, Your Honor."

"How would you like to have dinner with an old man one evening?"

Jennifer was taken by surprise. "I'd love having dinner with you."

"Fine. I'll take you to my club. They're a bunch of old fogies and they're not used to beautiful young women. It'll shake them up a bit."

Judge Lawrence Waldman belonged to the Century Association on West 43rd Street, and when he and Jennifer met there for dinner she saw that he had been teasing about old fogies. The dining room was filled with authors, artists, lawyers and actors.

"It is the custom not to make introductions here," Judge Waldman explained to Jennifer. "It's assumed that every person is immediately recognizable."

Seated at various tables, Jennifer recognized Louis Auchincloss, George Plimpton and John Lindsay, among others.

Socially, Lawrence Waldman was totally different from what Jennifer had expected. Over cocktails he said to Jennifer, "I once wanted to see you disbarred because I thought you had disgraced our profession. I'm convinced that I was wrong. I've been watching you closely. I think you're a credit to the profession."

Jennifer was pleased. She had encountered judges who were venal, stupid or incompetent. She respected Lawrence Waldman. He was both a brilliant jurist and a man of integrity.

"Thank you, Your Honor."

"Off the bench, why don't we make it Lawrence and Jennie?"

Her father was the only one who had ever called her Jennie.

"I'd like that, Lawrence."

The food was excellent and that dinner was the beginning of a monthly ritual they both enjoyed tremendously.

31

It was the summer of 1974. Incredibly, a year had flown by since Joshua Adam Parker had been born. He had taken his first tottering steps and he understood the words for nose and mouth and head.

"He's a genius," Jennifer flatly informed Mrs. Mackey.

Jennifer planned Joshua's first birthday party as though it were being given at the White House. On Saturday she shopped for gifts. She bought Joshua clothes and books and toys, and a tricycle he would not be able to use for another year or two. She bought favors for the neighbors' children she had invited to the party, and she spent the afternoon putting up streamers and balloons. She baked the birthday cake herself and left it on the kitchen table. Somehow, Joshua got hold of the cake and grabbed handfuls of it and crammed it into his mouth, ruining it before the other guests arrived.

Jennifer had invited a dozen children from the neighborhood, and their mothers. The only adult male guest was Ken

Bailey. He brought Joshua a tricycle, a duplicate of the one Jennifer had bought.

Jennifer laughed and said, "That's ridiculous, Ken. Joshua's not old enough for that."

The party only lasted two hours, but it was splendid. The children ate too much and were sick on the rug, and fought over the toys and cried when their balloons burst, but all in all, Jennifer decided, it was a triumph. Joshua had been a perfect host, handling himself, with the exception of a few minor incidents, with dignity and aplomb.

That night, after all the guests had left and Joshua had been put to bed, Jennifer sat at his bedside watching her sleeping son, marveling at this wonderful creature that had come from her body and the loins of Adam Warner. Adam would have been so proud to have seen how Joshua had behaved. Somehow, the joy was diminished because it was hers alone.

Jennifer thought of all the birthdays to come. Joshua would be two years old, then five, then ten and twenty. And he would be a man and he would leave her. He would make his own life for himself.

Stop it! Jennifer scolded herself. *You're feeling sorry for yourself*. She lay in bed that night, wide awake, reliving every detail of the party, remembering it all.

One day, perhaps, she could tell Adam about it.

32

In the months that followed, Senator Adam Warner was becoming a household word. His background, ability and charisma had made him a presence in the Senate from the beginning. He won a place on several important committees and he sponsored a piece of major labor legislation that passed quickly and easily. Adam Warner had powerful friends in Congress. Many had known and respected his father. The consensus was that Adam was going to be a presidential contender one day. Jennifer felt a bittersweet pride.

Jennifer received constant invitations from clients, associates and friends to dinner and the theater and various charity affairs, but she refused almost all of them. From time to time she would spend an evening with Ken. She enjoyed his company immensely. He was funny and self-deprecating, but beneath the facade of lightness, Jennifer knew, there was a sensitive, tormented man. He would sometimes come to the house for lunch or dinner on weekends, and he would play with Joshua for hours. They loved each other.

Once, when Joshua had been put to bed and Jennifer and Ken were having dinner in the kitchen, Ken kept staring at Jennifer until she asked, "Is anything wrong?"

"Christ, yes," Ken groaned. "I'm sorry. What a bitch of a world this is."

And he would say nothing further.

Adam had not tried to get in touch with Jennifer in almost nine months now, but she avidly read every newspaper and magazine article about him, and watched him whenever he appeared on television. She thought about him constantly. How could she not? Her son was a living reminder of Adam's presence. Joshua was two years old now and incredibly like his father. He had the same serious blue eyes and the identical mannerisms. Joshua was a tiny, dear replica, warm and loving and full of eager questions.

To Jennifer's surprise, Joshua's first words had been *car-car*, when she took him for a drive one day.

He was speaking in sentences now and he said *please* and *thank you*. Once, when Jennifer was trying to feed him in his high chair, he said impatiently, "Mama, go play with your toys."

Ken had bought Joshua a paint set, and Joshua industriously set about painting the walls of the living room.

When Mrs. Mackey wanted to spank him, Jennifer said, "Don't. It will wash off. Joshua's just expressing himself."

"That's all *I* wanted to do," Mrs. Mackey sniffed. "Express myself. You'll spoil that boy rotten."

But Joshua was not spoiled. He was mischievous and demanding, but that was normal for a two-year-old. He was afraid of the vacuum cleaner, wild animals, trains and the dark.

Joshua was a natural athlete. Once, watching him at play

with some of his friends, Jennifer turned to Mrs. Mackey and said, "Even though I'm Joshua's mother, I'm able to look at him objectively, Mrs. Mackey. I think he may be the Second Coming."

Jennifer had made it a policy to avoid any cases that would take her out of town and away from Joshua, but one morning she received an urgent call from Peter Fenton, a client who owned a large manufacturing firm.

"I'm buying a factory in Las Vegas and I'd like you to fly down there and meet with their lawyers."

"Let me send Dan Martin," Jennifer suggested. "You know I don't like to go out of town, Peter."

"Jennifer, you can wrap the whole thing up in twenty-four hours. I'll fly you down in the company plane and you'll be back the next day."

Jennifer hesitated. "All right."

She had been to Las Vegas and was indifferent to it. It was impossible to hate Las Vegas or to like it. One had to look upon it as a phenomenon, an alien civilization with its own language, laws and morals. It was like no other city in the world. Huge neon lights blazed all night long, proclaiming the glories of the magnificent palaces that had been built to deplete the purses of tourists who flocked in like lemmings and lined up to have their carefully hoarded savings taken away from them.

Jennifer gave Mrs. Mackey a long and detailed list of instructions about taking care of Joshua.

"How long are you going to be away, Mrs. Parker?"

"I'll be back tomorrow."

"Mothers!"

Peter Fenton's Lear jet picked Jennifer up early the next morning and flew her to Las Vegas. Jennifer spent the afternoon and evening working out the details of the contract.

When they finished, Peter Fenton asked Jennifer to have dinner with him.

"Thank you, Peter, but I think I'll stay in my room and get to bed early. I'm returning to New York in the morning."

Jennifer had talked to Mrs. Mackey three times during the day and had been reassured each time that little Joshua was fine. He had eaten his meals, he had no fever and he seemed happy.

"Does he miss me?" Jennifer asked.

"He didn't say," Mrs. Mackey sighed.

Jennifer knew that Mrs. Mackey thought she was a fool, but Jennifer did not care.

"Tell him I'll be home tomorrow."

"I'll give him the message, Mrs. Parker."

Jennifer had intended to have a quiet dinner in her suite, but for some reason, the rooms suddenly became oppressive, the walls seemed to be closing in on her. She could not stop thinking about Adam.

How could he have made love to Mary Beth and made her pregnant when . . .

The game Jennifer always played, that her Adam was just away on a business trip and would soon return to her, did not work this time. Jennifer's mind kept returning to a picture of Mary Beth in her lace negligee and Adam . . .

She had to get out, to be somewhere where there were noisy crowds of people. *Perhaps*, Jennifer thought, *I might even see a show.* She quickly showered, dressed and went downstairs.

Marty Allen was starring in the main show room. There was a long line at the entrance to the room for the late show, and Jennifer regretted that she had not asked Peter Fenton to make a reservation for her.

She went up to the captain at the head of the line and said, "How long a wait will there be for a table?"

"How many in your party?"

"I'm alone."

"I'm sorry, miss, but I'm afraid—"

A voice beside her said, "My booth, Abe."

The captain beamed and said, "Certainly, Mr. Moretti. This way, please."

Jennifer turned and found herself looking into the deep black eyes of Michael Moretti.

"No, thank you," Jennifer said. "I'm afraid I—"

"You have to eat." Michael Moretti took Jennifer's arm and she found herself walking beside him, following the captain to a choice banquette in the center of the large room. Jennifer loathed the idea of dining with Michael Moretti, but she did not know how to get out of it now without creating a scene. She wished fervently that she had agreed to have dinner with Peter Fenton.

They were seated at a banquette facing the stage and the captain said, "Enjoy your dinner, Mr. Moretti, miss."

Jennifer could feel Michael Moretti's eyes on her and it made her uncomfortable. He sat there, saying nothing. Michael Moretti was a man of deep silences, a man who distrusted words, as though they were a trap rather than a form of communication. There was something riveting about his silence. Michael Moretti used silence the way other men used speech.

When he finally spoke, Jennifer was caught off guard.

"I hate dogs," Michael Moretti said. "They die."

And it was as though he was revealing a private part of himself that came from some deep wellspring. Jennifer did not know what to reply.

Their drinks arrived and they sat there drinking quietly, and Jennifer listened to the conversation they were not having.

She thought about what he had said: *I hate dogs. They die.*

She wondered what Michael Moretti's early life had been like. She found herself studying him. He was attractive in a dangerous, exciting way. There was a feeling of violence about him, ready to explode.

Jennifer could not say why, but being with this man made her feel like a woman. Perhaps it was the way his ebony black eyes looked at her, then looked away from her, as though fearful of revealing too much. Jennifer realized it had been a long time since she had thought of herself as a woman. From the day she had lost Adam. *It takes a man to make a woman feel female*, Jennifer thought, *to make her feel beautiful, to make her feel wanted.*

Jennifer was grateful he could not read her mind.

Various people approached their booth to pay their respects to Michael Moretti: business executives, actors, a judge, a United States senator. It was power paying tribute to power, and Jennifer began to feel a sense of how much influence he wielded.

"I'll order for us," Michael Moretti said. "They prepare this menu for eight hundred people. It's like eating on an airline."

He raised his hand and the captain was at his side instantly. "Yes, Mr. Moretti. What would you like tonight, sir?"

"We'll have a *Chateaubriand*, pink and charred."

"Of course, Mr. Moretti."

"*Pommes soufflées* and an endive salad."

"Certainly, Mr. Moretti."

"We'll order dessert later."

A bottle of champagne was sent to the table, compliments of the management.

Jennifer found herself beginning to relax, enjoying herself almost against her will. It had been a long while since she had spent an evening with an attractive man. And even as the phrase came into Jennifer's mind, she thought, *How can*

I think of Michael Moretti as attractive? He's a killer, an amoral animal with no feelings.

Jennifer had known and defended dozens of men who had committed terrible crimes, but she had the feeling that none of them was as dangerous as this man. He had risen to the top of the Syndicate and it had taken more than a marriage to Antonio Granelli's daughter to accomplish that.

"I telephoned you once or twice while you were away," Michael said. According to Ken Bailey, he had called almost every day. "Where were you?" He made the question sound casual.

"Away."

A long silence. "Remember that offer I made you?"

Jennifer took a sip of her champagne. "Don't start that again, please."

"You can have any—"

"I told you, I'm not interested. There's no such thing as an offer you can't refuse. That's only in books, Mr. Moretti. I'm refusing."

Michael Moretti thought of the scene that had taken place in his father-in-law's home a few weeks earlier. There had been a meeting of the Family and it had not gone well. Thomas Colfax had argued against everything that Michael had proposed.

When Colfax had left, Michael had said to his father-in-law, "Colfax is turning into an old woman. I think it's time to put him out to pasture, Papa."

"Tommy's a good man. He's saved us a lot of trouble over the years."

"That's history. He doesn't have it anymore."

"Who would we get to take his place?"

"Jennifer Parker."

Antonio Granelli had shaken his head. "I told you, Michael.

It ain't good to have a woman know our business."

"This isn't just a woman. She's the best lawyer around."

"We'll see," Antonio Granelli had said. "We'll see."

Michael Moretti was a man who was used to getting what he wanted, and the more Jennifer stood up to him, the more he was determined to have her. Now, sitting next to her, Michael looked at Jennifer and thought, *One day you're going to belong to me, baby—all the way.*

"What are you thinking about?"

Michael Moretti gave Jennifer a slow, easy smile, and she instantly regretted the question. It was time to leave.

"Thank you for a wonderful dinner, Mr. Moretti. I have to get up early, so—"

The lights began to dim and the orchestra started an overture.

"You can't leave now. The show is starting. You'll love Marty Allen."

It was the kind of entertainment that only Las Vegas could afford to put on, and Jennifer thoroughly enjoyed it. She told herself she would leave immediately after the show, but when it was over and Michael Moretti asked Jennifer to dance, she decided it would be ungracious to refuse. Besides, she had to admit to herself that she was having a good time. Michael Moretti was a skillful dancer, and Jennifer found herself relaxing in his arms. Once, when another couple collided with them, Michael was pushed against Jennifer and for an instant she felt his male hardness, and then he immediately pulled away, careful to hold her at a discreet distance.

Afterward, they walked into the casino, a vast terrain of bright lights and noise, packed with gamblers engrossed in various games of chance, playing as though their lives depended on their winning. Michael took Jennifer to one of the dice tables and handed her a dozen chips.

"For luck," he said.

The pit boss and dealers treated Michael with deference, calling him *Mr. M.* and giving him large piles of hundred-dollar chips, taking his markers instead of cash. Michael played for large stakes and lost heavily, but he seemed unperturbed. Using Michael's chips, Jennifer won three hundred dollars, which she insisted on giving to Michael. She had no intention of being under any obligation to him.

From time to time during the course of the evening, various women came up to greet Michael. All of them were young and attractive, Jennifer noticed. Michael was polite to them, but it was obvious that he was only interested in Jennifer. In spite of herself, she could not help feeling flattered.

Jennifer had been tired and depressed at the beginning of the evening, but there was such a vitality about Michael Moretti that it seemed to spill over, charging the air, enveloping Jennifer.

Michael took her to a small bar where a jazz group was playing, and afterward they went on to the lounge of another hotel to hear a new singing group. Everywhere they went Michael was treated like royalty. Everyone tried to get his attention, to say hello to him, to touch him, to let him know they were there.

During the time they were together, Michael did not say one word at which Jennifer could take offense. And yet, Jennifer felt such a strong sexuality coming from him that it was like a series of waves beating at her. Her body felt bruised, violated. She had never experienced anything like it. It was a disquieting feeling and, at the same time, exhilarating. There was a wild, animal vitality about him that Jennifer had never encountered before.

It was four o'clock in the morning when Michael finally

walked Jennifer back to her suite. When they reached Jennifer's door, Michael took her hand and said, "Good night. I just want you to know this has been the greatest night of my life."

His words frightened Jennifer.

33

In Washington, Adam Warner's popularity was growing. He was written up in the newspapers and magazines with increasing frequency. Adam started an investigation of ghetto schools, and headed a Senate committee that went to Moscow to meet with dissidents. There were newspaper photographs of his arrival at Sheremetyevo Airport, being greeted by unsmiling Russian officials. When Adam returned ten days later, the newspapers gave warm praise to the results of his trip.

The coverage kept expanding. The public wanted to read about Adam Warner and the media fed their appetite. Adam became the spearhead for reform in the Senate. He headed a committee to investigate conditions in federal penitentiaries, and he visited prisons around the country. He talked to the inmates and guards and wardens, and when his committee's report was turned in, extensive reforms were begun.

In addition to the news magazines, women's magazines ran articles about him. In *Cosmopolitan*, Jennifer saw a picture of Adam, Mary Beth and their little daughter, Samantha. Jen-

nifer sat by the fireplace in her bedroom and looked at the
picture for a long, long time. Mary Beth was smiling into the
camera, exuding sweet, warm southern charm. The daughter
was a miniature of her mother. Jennifer turned to the picture
of Adam. He looked tired. There were small lines around his
eyes that had not been there before, and his sideburns were
beginning to be tinged with gray. For a moment, Jennifer had
the illusion that she was seeing the face of Joshua, grown up.
The resemblance was uncanny. The photographer had had
Adam turn directly into the camera, and it seemed to Jennifer
that he was looking at her. She tried to read the expression in
his eyes, and she wondered whether he ever thought about her.

Jennifer turned to look again at the photograph of Mary
Beth and her daughter. Then she threw the magazine into the
fireplace and watched it burn.

Adam Warner sat at the head of his dinner table, entertaining Stewart Needham and half a dozen other guests. Mary
Beth sat at the other end of the table, making small talk with a
senator from Oklahoma and his bejeweled wife. Washington
had been like a stimulant to Mary Beth. She was in her element here. Because of Adam's increasing importance, Mary
Beth had become one of Washington's top hostesses and she
reveled in that position. The social side of Washington bored
Adam, and he was glad to leave it to Mary Beth. She handled
it well and he was grateful to her.

"In Washington," Stewart Needham was saying, "more deals
get made over dinner tables than in the hallowed halls of Congress."

Adam looked around the table and wished that this evening
were over. On the surface, everything was wonderful. Inside,
everything was wrong. He was married to one woman and in
love with another. He was locked into a marriage from which
there was no escape. If Mary Beth had not become pregnant,
Adam knew he would have gone ahead with the divorce. It

was too late now; he was committed. Mary Beth had given him a beautiful little daughter and he loved her, but it was impossible to get Jennifer out of his mind.

The wife of the governor was speaking to him.

"You're so lucky, Adam. You have everything in the world a man could want, don't you?"

Adam could not bring himself to answer.

34

The seasons came and went and they revolved around Joshua. He was the center of Jennifer's world. She watched him grow and develop, day by day, and it was a never-ending wonder as he began to walk and talk and reason. His moods changed constantly and he was, in turn, wild and aggressive and shy and loving. He became upset when Jennifer had to leave him at night, and he was still afraid of the dark, so Jennifer always left a night light on for him.

When Joshua was two years old he was impossible, a typical "Terrible Two." He was destructive and stubborn and violent. He loved to "fix" things. He broke Mrs. Mackey's sewing machine, ruined the two television sets in the house and took Jennifer's wristwatch apart. He mixed the salt with the sugar and fondled himself when he thought he was alone. Ken Bailey brought Jennifer a German shepherd puppy, Max, and Joshua bit it.

When Ken came to the house to visit, Joshua greeted him with, "Hi! Do you have a ding-dong? Can I see it?"

That year, Jennifer would gladly have given Joshua away to the first passing stranger.

At three, Joshua suddenly became an angel, gentle, affectionate and loving. He had the physical coordination of his father, and he loved doing things with his hands. He no longer broke things. He enjoyed playing outdoors, climbing and running and riding his tricycle.

Jennifer took him to the Bronx Zoo and to marionette plays. They walked along the beach and saw a festival of Marx Brothers movies in Manhattan, and had ice cream sodas afterward at Old Fashioned Mr. Jennings on the ninth floor of Bonwit Teller.

Joshua had become a companion. As a Mother's Day gift, Joshua learned a favorite song of Jennifer's father—*Shine On, Harvest Moon*—and sang it to Jennifer. It was the most touching moment of her life.

It's true, Jennifer thought, *that we do not inherit the world from our parents; we borrow it from our children.*

Joshua had started nursery school and was enjoying it. At night when Jennifer came home, they would sit in front of the fireplace and read together. Jennifer would read *Trial Magazine* and *The Barrister* and Joshua would read his picture books. Jennifer would watch Joshua as he sprawled out on the floor, his brow knit in concentration, and she would suddenly be reminded of Adam. It was still like an open wound. She wondered where Adam was and what he was doing.

What he and Mary Beth and Samantha were doing.

Jennifer managed to keep her private and professional life separate, and the only link between the two was Ken Bailey.

He brought Joshua toys and books and played games with him and was, in a sense, a surrogate father.

One Sunday afternoon Jennifer and Ken stood near the tree house, watching Joshua climb up to it.

"Do you know what he needs?" Ken asked.

"No."

"A father." He turned to Jennifer. "His real father must be one prize shit."

"Please don't, Ken."

"Sorry. It's none of my business. That's the past. It's the future I'm concerned about. It isn't natural for you to be living alone like—"

"I'm not alone. I have Joshua."

"That's not what I'm talking about." He took Jennifer in his arms and kissed her gently. "Oh, God damn it, Jennifer. I'm sorry . . ."

Michael Moretti had telephoned Jennifer a dozen times. She returned none of his calls. Once she thought she caught a glimpse of him sitting in the back of a courtroom where she was defending a case, but when she looked again he was gone.

35

Late one afternoon as Jennifer was getting ready to leave the office, Cynthia said, "There's a Mr. Clark Holman on the phone."

Jennifer hesitated, then said, "I'll take it."

Clark Holman was an attorney with the Legal Aid Society.

"Sorry to bother you, Jennifer," he said, "but we have a case downtown that no one wants to touch, and I'd really appreciate it if you could help us out. I know how busy you are, but—"

"Who's the defendant?"

"Jack Scanlon."

The name registered instantly. It had been on the front pages of the newspapers for the past two days. Jack Scanlon had been arrested for kidnapping a four-year-old girl and holding her for ransom. He had been identified from a composite drawing the police had obtained from witnesses to the abduction.

"Why me, Clark?"

"Scanlon asked for you."

Jennifer looked at the clock on the wall. She was going to be late for Joshua. "Where is he now?"

"At the Metropolitan Correctional Center."

Jennifer made a quick decision. "I'll go down and talk to him. Make the arrangements, will you?"

"Right. Thanks a million. I owe you one."

Jennifer telephoned Mrs. Mackey. "I'm going to be a little late. Give Joshua his dinner and tell him to wait up for me."

Ten minutes later, Jennifer was on her way downtown.

To Jennifer, kidnapping was the most vicious of all crimes, particularly the kidnapping of a helpless young child; but every accused person was entitled to a hearing no matter how terrible the crime. That was the foundation of the law: justice for the lowliest as well as the highest.

Jennifer identified herself to the guard at the reception desk and was taken to the Lawyers' Visiting Room.

The guard said, "I'll get Scanlon for you."

A few minutes later a thin, aesthetic-looking man in his late thirties, with a blond beard and light blond hair was brought into the room. He looked almost Christlike.

He said, "Thank you for coming, Miss Parker." His voice was soft and gentle. "Thank you for caring."

"Sit down."

He took a chair opposite Jennifer.

"You asked to see me?"

"Yes. Even though I think only God can help me. I've done a very foolish thing."

She regarded him distastefully. "You call kidnapping a helpless little girl for ransom a 'foolish thing'?"

"I didn't kidnap Tammy for ransom."

"Oh? Why did you kidnap her?"

There was a long silence before Jack Scanlon spoke. "My

wife, Evelyn, died in childbirth. I loved her more than anything in the world. If ever there was a saint on earth, it was that woman. Evelyn wasn't a strong person. Our doctor advised her not to have a baby, but she didn't listen." He looked down at the floor in embarrassment. "It—it may be hard for you to understand, but she said she wanted it anyway, because it would be like having another part of me."

How well Jennifer understood that.

Jack Scanlon had stopped speaking, his thoughts far away. "So she had the baby?"

Jack Scanlon nodded. "They both died." It was difficult for him to go on. "For a while, I—I thought I would . . . I didn't want to go on living without her. I kept wondering what our child would have been like. I kept dreaming about how it would have been if they had lived. I kept trying to turn the clock back to the moment before Evelyn—" He stopped, his voice choked with pain. "I turned to the Bible and it saved my sanity. *Behold, I have set before you an open door which no one is able to shut.* Then, a few days ago, I saw a little girl playing on the street, and it was as though Evelyn had been reincarnated. She had her eyes, her hair. She looked up at me and smiled and I—I know it sounds crazy, but it was Evelyn smiling at me. I must have been out of my head. I thought to myself, *This is the daughter Evelyn would have had. This is our child.*"

Jennifer could see his fingernails digging into his flesh.

"I know it was wrong, but I took her." He looked up into Jennifer's eyes. "I wouldn't have harmed that child for anything in the world."

Jennifer was studying him closely, listening for a false note. There was none. He was a man in agony.

"What about the ransom note?" Jennifer asked.

"I didn't send a ransom note. The last thing in the world I cared about was money. I just wanted little Tammy."

"*Someone* sent the family a ransom note."

"The police keep saying I sent it, but I didn't."

Jennifer sat there, trying to fit the pieces together. "Did the story of the kidnapping appear in the newspapers before or after you were picked up by the police?"

"Before. I remember wishing they'd stop writing about it. I wanted to go away with Tammy and I was afraid someone would stop us."

"So anyone could have read about the kidnapping and tried to collect a ransom?"

Jack Scanlon twisted his hands helplessly. "I don't know. All I know is I want to die."

His pain was so obvious that Jennifer found herself moved by it. If he was telling the truth—and it was naked in his face—then he did not deserve to die for what he had done. He should be punished, yes, but not executed.

Jennifer made her decision. "I'm going to try to help you."

He said quietly, "Thank you. I really don't care anymore what happens to me."

"I do."

Jack Scanlon said, "I'm afraid I—I have no money to give you."

"Don't worry about it. I want you to tell me about yourself."

"What do you want to know?"

"Start from the beginning. Where were you born?"

"In North Dakota, thirty-five years ago. I was born on a farm. I guess you could call it a farm. It was a poor piece of land that nothing much wanted to grow on. We were poor. I left home when I was fifteen. I loved my mother, but I hated my father. I know the Bible says it's wrong to speak evil of your parents, but he was a wicked man. He enjoyed whipping me."

Jennifer could see his body tighten as he went on.

"I mean, he really enjoyed it. If I did the smallest thing he thought was wrong, he would whip me with a leather belt that had a big brass buckle on it. Then he'd make me get down on my knees and pray to God for forgiveness. For a long time I hated God as much as I hated my father." He stopped, too filled with memories to speak.

"So you ran away from home?"

"Yes. I hitchhiked to Chicago. I didn't have much schooling, but at home I used to read a lot. Whenever my father caught me, that was an excuse for another whipping. In Chicago, I got a job working in a factory. That's where I met Evelyn. I cut my hand on a milling machine and they took me to the dispensary, and there she was. She was a practical nurse." He smiled at Jennifer. "She was the most beautiful woman I'd ever seen. It took about two weeks before my hand was healed, and I went to her for a treatment every day. After that, we just kind of started going together. We talked about getting married, but the company lost a big order and I was laid off with the rest of the people in my department. That didn't matter to Evelyn. We got married and she took care of me. That was the only thing we ever argued about. I was brought up to believe that a man should take care of a woman. I got a job driving a truck and the money was good. The only part I hated was that we were separated, sometimes for a week at a time. Outside of that, I was awfully happy. We were both happy. And then Evelyn got pregnant."

A shudder ran through him. His hands began to tremble.

"Evelyn and our baby girl died." Tears were running down his cheeks. "I don't know why God did that. He must have had a reason, but I don't know why." He was rocking back and forth in his chair, unaware of what he was doing, his arms clasped in front of his chest, holding in his grief. *"I will instruct you and teach you the way you should go; I will counsel you."*

Jennifer thought, *This one the electric chair is not going to get!*

"I'll be back to see you tomorrow," Jennifer promised him.

Bail had been set at two hundred thousand dollars. Jack Scanlon did not have the bond money and Jennifer had it put up for him. Scanlon was released from the Correctional Center and Jennifer found a small motel on the West Side for him to move into. She gave him a hundred dollars to tide him over.

"I don't know how," Jack Scanlon said, "but I'll pay you back every cent. I'll start looking for a job. I don't care what it is. I'll do anything."

When Jennifer left him, he was searching through the want ads.

The federal prosecutor, Earl Osborne, was a large, heavyset man with a smooth round face and a deceptively bland manner. To Jennifer's surprise, Robert Di Silva was in Osborne's office.

"I heard you were taking on this case," Di Silva said. "Nothing's too dirty for you to handle, is it?"

Jennifer turned to Earl Osborne. "What's he doing here? This is a federal case."

Osborne replied, "Jack Scanlon took the girl away in her family's car."

"Auto theft, grand larceny," Di Silva said.

Jennifer wondered if Di Silva would have been there if she were not involved. She turned back to Earl Osborne.

"I'd like to make a deal," Jennifer said. "My client—"

Earl Osborne held up a hand. "Not a chance. We're going all the way on this one."

"There are circumstances—"

"You can tell us all about it at the preliminary."

Di Silva was grinning at her.

"All right," Jennifer said. "I'll see you in court."

Jack Scanlon found a job working at a service station on the West Side near his motel, and Jennifer stopped by to see him.

"The preliminary hearing is the day after tomorrow," Jennifer informed him. "I'm going to try to get the government to agree to a plea bargain and plead you guilty to a lesser charge. You'll have to serve some time, Jack, but I'll try to see that it's as short as possible."

The gratitude in his face was reward enough.

At Jennifer's suggestion, Jack Scanlon had bought a respectable suit to wear at the preliminary hearing. He had had his hair cut and his beard trimmed, and Jennifer was pleased with his appearance.

They went through the court formalities. District Attorney Di Silva was present. When Earl Osborne had presented his evidence and asked for an indictment, Judge Barnard turned to Jennifer.

"Is there anything you would like to say, Miss Parker?"

"There is, Your Honor. I'd like to save the government the cost of a trial. There are mitigating circumstances here that have not been brought out. I would like to plead my client guilty to a lesser charge."

"No way," Earl Osborne said. "The government will not agree to it."

Jennifer turned to Judge Barnard. "Could we discuss this in Your Honor's chambers?"

"Very well. I'll set a date for the trial after I've heard what counsel has to say."

Jennifer turned to Jack Scanlon, who was standing there, bewildered.

"You can go back to work," Jennifer told him. "I'll drop by and let you know what happened."

He nodded and said quietly, "Thank you, Miss Parker."

Jennifer watched him turn and leave the courtroom.

Jennifer, Earl Osborne, Robert Di Silva and Judge Barnard were seated in the judge's chambers.

Osborne was saying to Jennifer, "I don't know how you could even ask me to plea-bargain. Kidnapping for ransom is a capital offense. Your client is guilty and he's going to pay for what he did."

"Don't believe everything you read in the newspapers, Earl. Jack Scanlon had nothing to do with that ransom note."

"Who you trying to kid? If it wasn't for ransom, what the hell *was* it for?"

"I'll tell you," Jennifer said.

And she told them. She told them about the farm and the beatings and about Jack Scanlon falling in love with Evelyn and marrying her, and losing his wife and daughter in childbirth.

They listened in silence, and when Jennifer was finished, Robert Di Silva said, "So Jack Scanlon kidnapped the girl because it reminded him of the kid he would have had? And Jack Scanlon's wife died in childbirth?"

"That's right." Jennifer turned to Judge Barnard. "Your Honor, I don't think that's the kind of man you execute."

Di Silva said unexpectedly, "I agree with you."

Jennifer looked at him in surprise.

Di Silva was pulling some papers out of a briefcase. "Let me ask you something," he said. "How would you feel about executing *this* kind of man?" He began to read from a dossier. "Frank Jackson, age thirty-eight. Born in Nob Hill, San Francisco. Father was a doctor, mother a prominent socialite. At fourteen, Jackson got into drugs, ran away from home, picked up in Haight-Ashbury and returned to his parents. Three months later Jackson broke into his father's dispensary, stole all the drugs he could get his hands on and ran away. Picked up in Seattle for possession and selling, sent to a reformatory, released when he was eighteen, picked up one month later on a charge of armed robbery with intent to kill . . ."

Jennifer could feel her stomach tightening. "What does this have to do with Jack Scanlon?"

Earl Osborne gave her a frosty smile. "Jack Scanlon is Frank Jackson."

"I don't believe it!"

Di Silva said, "This yellow sheet came in from the FBI an hour ago. Jackson's a con artist and a psychopathic liar. Over the last ten years he's been arrested on charges ranging from pimping to arson to armed robbery. He did a stretch in Joliet. He's never held a steady job and he's never been married. Five years ago he was picked up by the FBI on a kidnapping charge. He kidnapped a three-year-old girl and sent a ransom note. The body of the little girl was found in a wooded area two months later. According to the coroner's report, the body was partially decomposed, but there were visible signs of small knife cuts all over her body. She had been raped and sodomized."

Jennifer felt suddenly ill.

"Jackson was acquitted on a technicality that some hotshot lawyer cooked up." When Di Silva spoke again his voice was filled with contempt. "That the man you want walking around the streets?"

"May I see that dossier, please?"

Silently, Di Silva handed it to Jennifer and she began reading it. It was Jack Scanlon. There was no question about it. There was a police mug shot of him stapled to the yellow sheet. He had looked younger then and he had no beard, but there was no mistaking him. Jack Scanlon—Frank Jackson—had lied to her about everything. He had made up his life story and Jennifer had believed every word. He had been so convincing that she had not even taken the trouble to have Ken Bailey check him out.

Judge Barnard said, "May I see that?"

Jennifer handed the dossier to him. The judge glanced through it and then looked at Jennifer. "Well?"

"I won't represent him."

Di Silva raised his eyebrows in mock surprise. "You shock me, Miss Parker. You're always saying that everyone is entitled to a lawyer."

"Everyone is," Jennifer replied evenly, "but I have a hard and fast rule: I won't represent anyone who lies to me. Mr. Jackson will have to get himself another lawyer."

Judge Barnard nodded. "The court will arrange that."

Osborne said, "I'd like his bail revoked immediately, Your Honor. I think he's too dangerous to be walking the streets."

Judge Barnard turned to Jennifer. "As of this moment you're still the attorney of record, Miss Parker. Do you have any objection to that?"

"No," Jennifer said tightly. "None."

Judge Barnard said, "I'll order his bail revoked."

Judge Lawrence Waldman had invited Jennifer to a charity dinner that evening. She had felt drained after the events of the afternoon and would have preferred to go home and have a quiet evening with Joshua, but she did not want to disappoint the judge. She changed clothes at the office and met Judge Waldman at the Waldorf-Astoria, where the party was taking place.

It was a gala event, with half a dozen Hollywood stars entertaining, but Jennifer was unable to enjoy it. Her mind was elsewhere. Judge Waldman had been watching her.

"Is anything wrong, Jennie?"

She managed a smile. "No, just a business problem, Lawrence."

And what kind of business am I really in, Jennifer wondered, *dealing with the dregs of humanity, the rapists and killers and kidnappers?* She decided it would be a wonderful night to get drunk.

The captain came over to the table and whispered in Jennifer's ear. "Excuse me, Miss Parker, there's a telephone call for you."

Jennifer felt an instant sense of alarm. The only one who knew where to reach her was Mrs. Mackey. She could only be calling because something was wrong.

"Excuse me," Jennifer said.

She followed the captain to a small office off the lobby.

Jennifer picked up the receiver and a man's voice whispered, "You bitch! You double-crossed me."

Jennifer felt her body begin to tremble. "Who is this?" she asked.

But she knew.

"You told the cops to come and get me."

"That's not true! I—"

"You promised to help me."

"I will help you. Where are—?"

"You lying cunt!" His voice dropped so low she could hardly make out his words. "You're going to pay for this. Oh, you're going to pay for this!"

"Wait a min—"

The telephone was dead. Jennifer stood there, chilled. Something had gone terribly wrong. Frank Jackson, alias Jack Scanlon, had somehow escaped and he was blaming Jennifer for what had happened. How had he known where she was? He must have followed her here. He could be waiting outside for her now.

Jennifer was trying to control the trembling of her body, trying to think, to reason out what had happened. He had seen the police coming to arrest him, or perhaps they had picked him up and he had gotten away from them. *How* did not matter. The important thing was that he was blaming her for what had happened.

Frank Jackson had killed before and he could kill again. Jennifer went into the ladies' room and stayed there until she was calm again. When she had regained control of herself, she returned to the table.

Judge Waldman took one look at her face. "What on earth's happened?"

Jennifer told him briefly. He was aghast.

"Good God! Would you like me to drive you home?"

"I'll be all right, Lawrence. If you could just make sure I get to my car safely, I'll be fine."

They quietly slipped out of the large ballroom and Judge Waldman stayed with Jennifer until the attendant brought her car.

"You're certain you don't want me to come with you?"

"Thanks. I'm sure the police will pick him up before morning. There aren't many people walking around who look like him. Good night."

Jennifer drove off, making sure no one was following her. When she was certain she was alone, she turned onto the Long Island Expressway and headed for home.

She kept looking in her rearview mirror, checking the cars behind her. Once she pulled off the road to let all the traffic pass her, and when the road behind her was clear, she drove on. She felt safer now. It could not be many hours before the police picked up Frank Jackson. There would be a general alert out for him by this time.

Jennifer turned into her driveway. The grounds and the house, which should have been brightly lighted, were dark. She sat in the car staring at the house unbelievingly, her mind beginning to shriek with alarm. Frantically, she tore the car door open and raced to the front door. It was ajar. Jennifer stood there for an instant, filled with terror, then stepped into the reception hall. Her foot kicked something warm and soft and she let out an involuntary gasp. She turned on the lights. Max lay on the blood-soaked rug. The dog's throat had been cut from ear to ear.

"Joshua!" It was a scream. "Mrs. Mackey!"

Jennifer ran from room to room, switching on all the lights and calling out their names, her heart pounding so hard that it was difficult for her to breathe. She raced up the stairs to Joshua's bedroom. His bed had been slept in, but it was empty.

Jennifer searched every room in the house, then raced downstairs, her mind numb. Frank Jackson must have known all along where she lived. He had followed her home one night from her office or after she left the service station. He had taken Joshua and he was going to kill him to punish her.

She was passing the laundry room when she heard a faint scrabbling sound coming from the closet. Jennifer moved toward the closed door slowly and pulled it open. It was black inside.

A voice whimpered, "Please don't hurt me any more."

Jennifer turned on the light. Mrs. Mackey was lying on the floor, her hands and feet tightly bound with wire. She was only half-conscious.

Jennifer quickly knelt beside her. "Mrs. Mackey!"

The older woman looked up at Jennifer and her eyes began to focus.

"He took Joshua." She began to sob.

As gently as she could, Jennifer untwisted the wire that was cutting into Mrs. Mackey's arms and legs. They were raw and bleeding. Jennifer helped the housekeeper to her feet.

Mrs. Mackey cried hysterically. "I c-couldn't stop him. I t-tried. I—"

The sound of the telephone cut into the room. The two

women were instantly silenced. The telephone rang again and again, and somehow it had an evil sound. Jennifer walked over to it and picked it up.

The voice said, "I just wanted to make sure you got home all right."

"Where is my son?"

"He is a beautiful boy, isn't he?" the voice asked.

"Please! I'll do anything. Anything you like!"

"You've already done everything, Mrs. Parker."

"No, please!" She was sobbing helplessly.

"I like to hear you cry," the voice whispered. "You'll get your son back, Mrs. Parker. Read tomorrow's papers."

And the line went dead.

Jennifer stood there, fighting against the faintness, trying to think. Frank Jackson had said, "He *is* a beautiful boy, isn't he?" That could mean Joshua was still alive. Otherwise, wouldn't he have said *was* beautiful? She knew she was simply playing games with words, trying to keep her sanity. She had to do something quickly.

Her first impulse was to telephone Adam, ask him to help. It was his son who had been kidnapped, his son who was going to be killed. But she knew there was nothing Adam could do. He was two hundred and thirty-five miles away. She had only two choices: One was to call Robert Di Silva, tell him what had happened and ask him to throw out a dragnet to try to catch Frank Jackson. *Oh, God, that will take too long!*

The second choice was the FBI. They were trained to handle kidnappings. The problem was that this was not like other kidnapping. There would be no ransom note for them to trace, no chance to try to trap Frank Jackson and save Joshua's life. The FBI moved according to its own strict ritual. It would not be of any help in this instance. She had to decide quickly . . . while Joshua was still alive. Robert Di Silva or the FBI. It was difficult to think.

She took a deep breath and made her decision. She looked up a telephone number. Her fingers were trembling so badly she had to dial the number three times before she got it right.

When a man answered, Jennifer said, "I want to speak to Michael Moretti."

36

"Sorry, lady. This is Tony's Place. I don't know no Mike Moretti."

"Wait!" Jennifer screamed. "Don't hang up!" She forced a calmness into her voice. "This is urgent. I'm a—a friend of his. My name is Jennifer Parker. I need to talk to him right away."

"Look, lady, I said—"

"Give him my name and this telephone number."

She gave him the number. Jennifer was beginning to stutter so badly she could hardly speak. "T-t-tell him—"

The line went dead.

Numbly, Jennifer replaced the receiver. She was back to one of her first two choices. Or both of them. There was no reason why Robert Di Silva and the FBI could not join forces to try to find Joshua. The thing that was driving her mad was that she knew how little chance they would have of finding Frank Jackson. There was no time. *Read tomorrow's papers.* There was a finality about his last words that made Jennifer certain he would not telephone her again, would not give anyone a chance to trace him. But she had to do *something*. She would try Di Silva. She reached for the telephone again. It rang as she touched it, startling her.

"This is Michael Moretti."

"Michael! Oh, Michael, help me, please! I—" She began to sob uncontrollably. She dropped the telephone, then picked it up again quickly, terrified he had hung up. "*Michael?*"

"I'm here." His voice was calm. "Get hold of yourself and tell me what's wrong."

"I— I'll—" She took in quick, deep breaths, trying to stop the trembling. "It's my son, Joshua. He's—he's been kidnapped. They're going to—kill him."

"Do you know who took him?"

"Y-yes. His name is F-Frank Jackson." Her heart was pounding.

"Tell me what happened." His voice was quiet and confident.

Jennifer forced herself to talk slowly, recounting the sequence of events.

"Can you describe what Jackson looks like?"

Jennifer conjured up a picture of him in her mind. She put the picture into words, and Michael said, "You're doing fine. Do you know where he served time?"

"At Joliet. He told me he's going to kill—"

"Where was the gas station he worked at?"

She gave Michael the address.

"Do you know the name of the motel he was staying at?"

"Yes. No." She could not remember. She dug her fingernails into her forehead until it began to bleed, forcing herself to think. He waited patiently.

It came to her suddenly. "It's the Travel Well Motel. It's on Tenth Avenue. But I'm sure he isn't there now."

"We'll see."

"I want my son back alive."

Michael Moretti did not reply and Jennifer understood why.

"If we find Jackson—?"

Jennifer took a deep, shuddering breath. *"Kill him!"*

"Stay by your telephone."

The connection was broken. Jennifer replaced the receiver. She felt strangely calmer, as though something had been accomplished. There was no reason to feel the confidence she did in Michael Moretti. From a logical point of view, it was a wild, insane thing to have done; but logic had nothing to do with this. Her son's life was at stake. She had deliberately sent a killer to catch a killer. If it did not work . . . She thought of the little girl whose body had been raped and sodomized.

Jennifer went to tend to Mrs. Mackey. She took care of her cuts and bruises and put her to bed. Jennifer offered her a sedative, but Mrs. Mackey pushed it away.

"I couldn't sleep," she cried. "Oh, Mrs. Parker! He gave that baby sleeping pills."

Jennifer stared at her in horror.

Michael Moretti sat at his desk, facing the seven men he had summoned. He had already given instructions to the first three.

He turned to Thomas Colfax. "Tom, I want you to use your connections. Go down and see Captain Notaras and have him pull the package on Frank Jackson. I want everything they've got on him."

"We're wasting a good connection, Mike. I don't think—"

"Don't argue! Just do it."

Colfax said stiffly, "Very well."

Michael turned to Nick Vito. "Check out the gas station where Jackson worked. Find out if he hung around any of the bars there, if he had any friends."

To Salvatore Fiore and Joseph Colella: "Get over to Jackson's motel. He's probably gone by now, but find out if he palled around with anyone. I want to know who his buddies were." He looked at his watch. "It's midnight. I'm giving you eight hours to find Jackson."

The men started out the door.

Michael called after them, "I don't want anything to happen to the kid. Keep calling in. I'll be waiting."

Michael Moretti watched them leave, then picked up one of the telephones on his desk and began to dial.

1:00 A.M.

The motel room was not large, but it was very neat. Frank Jackson liked things neat. He felt it was part of being brought up properly. The venetian blinds were rolled down and slanted so that no one could see into the room. The door was locked and chained, and he had pressed a chair against it. He walked over to the bed where Joshua lay. Frank Jackson had forced three sleeping pills down the boy's throat, and he was still sleeping soundly. Still, Jackson prided himself on being a man who took no chances, so Joshua's hands and feet were tightly bound together with the same kind of wire that had been used to tie up the old lady in the house. Jackson looked down at the sleeping boy and he was filled with a sense of sadness.

Why in God's name did people keep forcing him to do these terrible things? He was a gentle, peaceful man, but when everyone was against you, when everyone attacked you, you had to defend yourself. The trouble with everybody was that they always underestimated him. They failed to realize until too late that he was smarter than all of them.

He had known the police were coming for him half an hour before they arrived. He had been filling the tank of a Chevrolet Camaro and had seen his boss go inside the office to answer the telephone. Jackson had not been able to hear the conversation, but it was not necessary. He saw the covert looks his boss gave him as he whispered into the telephone. Frank Jackson knew immediately what was happening. The police were coming for him. The Parker bitch had double-crossed him, had told the police to lock him up. She was like all the rest of them. His boss was still talking on the telephone when Frank Jackson grabbed his jacket and disappeared. It had taken him less than three minutes to find an unlocked car on the street and hot-wire it, and moments later he was headed for Jennifer Parker's house.

Jackson really had to admire his own intelligence. Who else would have thought of following her to find out where she lived? He had done that the day she had gotten him out on bail. He had parked across the street from her house and had been surprised when Jennifer had been met at the gate by a little boy. He had watched them together and sensed even then that the kid might come in handy. He was an unexpected bonus, what the poets called a hostage to fate.

Jackson smiled to himself at how terrified the old bitch of a housekeeper had been. He had enjoyed twisting the wire into her wrists and ankles. No, not enjoyed, really. He was being too hard on himself. It had been *necessary*. The housekeeper had thought he was going to rape her. She disgusted him. All women did, except for his sainted mother. Women were dirty, unclean, even his whore of a sister. It was only the children who were pure. He thought of the last little girl he had taken. She had been beautiful, with long blond curls, but she had had to pay for her mother's sins. Her mother had had Jackson fired from his job. People tried to keep you from earning an honest living and then punished you when you broke their stupid laws. The men were bad enough, but the women were worse. Pigs who wanted to soil the temple of your body. Like the waitress, Clara, he was going to take to Canada. She was in love with him. She thought he was such a gentleman because he had never touched her. If she only knew! The idea of making love to her sickened him. But he was going to take her out of the country with him because the police would be looking for a man alone. He would shave off his beard and trim his hair, and when he crossed the border he would get rid of Clara. That would give him great pleasure.

Frank Jackson walked over to a battered cardboard suit-case on a luggage rack, opened it and took out a tool kit. From it he removed nails and a hammer. He laid them on the bed-side table next to the sleeping boy. Then he went into the bathroom and lifted a two-gallon gasoline can from the bath-tub. He carried it into the bedroom and set the can on the floor. Joshua was going to go up in flames. But that would be *after* the crucifixion.

2:00 A.M.

Throughout New York and around the country, the word was spreading. It started in bars and flophouses. A cautious word here and there, dropped into a willing ear. It began as a trickle and spread to cheap restaurants and noisy discotheques and all-night newsstands. It was picked up by taxi drivers and truckers and girls working the midnight streets. It was like a pebble dropped into a deep, dark lake, with the ripples begin-ning to widen and spread. Within a couple of hours everyone on the street knew that Michael Moretti wanted some infor-mation and wanted it fast. Not many people were given a chance to do a favor for Michael Moretti. This was a golden opportunity for somebody, because Moretti was a man who knew how to show his appreciation. The word was that he was looking for a thin blond guy who looked like Jesus. Peo-ple began searching their memories.

2:15 A.M.

Joshua Adam Parker stirred in his sleep and Frank Jackson moved to his side. He had not yet removed the boy's pajamas. Jackson checked to make sure that the hammer and nails were in place and ready. It was important to be meticulous about these things. He was going to nail the boy's hands and feet to the floor before he set the room on fire. He could have done it while the boy was asleep, but that would have been wrong. It was important that the boy be awake to see what was happening, to know he was being punished for the sins of his mother. Frank Jackson looked at his watch. Clara was coming to the motel to pick him up at seven-thirty. Five hours and fifteen minutes left. Plenty of time.

Frank Jackson sat down and studied Joshua, and once he tenderly fondled an errant lock of the small boy's hair.

3:00 A.M.

The first of the telephone calls began coming in.

There were two telephones on Michael Moretti's desk and it seemed that the moment he picked up one, the other started ringing.

"I got a line on the guy, Mike. A couple years ago he was workin' a scam in Kansas City with Big Joe Ziegler and Mel Cohen."

"Fuck what he was doing a couple of years ago. Where is he *now*?"

"Big Joe says he ain't heard from him in about six months. I'm tryin' to get hold of Mel Cohen."

"Do it!"

The next phone call was no more productive.

"I went over to Jackson's motel room. He checked out. He was carryin' a brown suitcase and a two-gallon can that coulda had gasoline in it. The clerk has no idea where he went."

"What about the neighborhood bars?"

"One of the bartenders recognized his description, but he says he wasn't a regular. He went in two or three times after work."

"Alone?"

"Accordin' to the bartender, yeah. He didn't seem interested in the girls there."

"Check out the gay bars."

The telephone rang again almost as soon as Michael had hung up. It was Salvatore Fiore.

"Colfax talked to Captain Notaras. The police property clerk got a record of a pawn ticket in Frank Jackson's personal effects. I got the number of the ticket and the name of the pawn shop. It's owned by a Greek, Gus Stavros, who fences hot rocks."

"Did you check it out?"

"We can't check it out until mornin', Mike. The place is closed. I—"

Michael Moretti exploded. "We can't *wait* until morning! Get your ass down there!"

There was a telephone call from Joliet. It was hard for Michael to follow the conversation because his caller had had a laryngectomy and his voice sounded as if it was coming from the bottom of a box.

"Jackson's cellmate was a man named Mickey Nicola. They were pretty tight."

"Any idea where Nicola is now?"

"Last I heard he was back east somewhere. He's a friend of Jackson's sister. We have no address on her."

"What was Nicola sent up for?"

"They nailed him on a jewelry heist."

3:30 A.M.

The pawnshop was located in Spanish Harlem at Second Avenue and 124th Street. It was in an unloved two-story building, with the shop downstairs and living quarters upstairs.

Gus Stavros was awakened by a flashlight shining in his face. He instinctively started to reach for the alarm button at the side of his bed.

"I wouldn't," a voice said.

The flashlight moved away and Gus Stavros sat up in bed. He looked at the two men standing on either side of him and knew he had been given good advice. A giant and a midget. Stavros could feel an asthma attack coming on.

"Go downstairs and take whatever you want," he wheezed. "I won't make a move."

The giant, Joseph Colella said, "Get up. Slow."

Gus Stavros rose from his bed, cautious not to make any sudden movements.

The small man, Salvatore Fiore, shoved a piece of paper under his nose. "This is the number of a pawn ticket. We want to see the merchandise."

"Yes, sir."

Gus Stavros walked downstairs, followed by the two men. Stavros had installed an elaborate alarm system only six months earlier. There were bells he could have pushed and secret places on the floor he could have stepped on and help would be on its way. He did none of those things because his instincts told him he would be dead before anyone could reach him. He knew that his only chance lay in giving the two men what they wanted. He only prayed he would not die from a goddamned asthma attack before he got rid of them.

He turned on the downstairs lights and they all moved toward the front of the shop. Gus Stavros had no idea what was going on, but he knew it could have been a great deal worse. If these men had come merely to rob him, they could have cleaned out the pawn shop and been gone by now. It seemed they were only interested in one piece of merchandise. He wondered how they had circumvented the elaborate new alarms on the doors and windows, but he decided not to ask.

"Move your ass," Joseph Colella said.

Gus looked at the pawn ticket number again and began to sort through his files. He found what he was looking for, nodded in satisfaction, and went to the large walk-in strong room and opened it, the two men close behind him. Stavros searched along a shelf until he found a small envelope. Turning to the two men, he opened the envelope and took out a large diamond ring that sparkled in the overhead lights.

"This is it," Gus Stavros said. "I gave him five hundred for it." The ring was worth at least twenty thousand dollars.

"You gave five hundred to who?" little Salvatore Fiore asked.

Gus Stavros shrugged. "A hundred customers a day come in here. The name on the envelope is John Doe."

Fiore pulled a piece of lead pipe out of nowhere and smashed it savagely against Gus Stavros' nose. He fell to the floor screaming with pain, drowning in his own blood.

Fiore asked quietly, "Who did you say brought it in?"

Fighting for breath, Gus Stavros gasped, "I don't know his name. He didn't tell me. I swear to God!"

"What did he look like?"

The blood was flowing into Gus Stavros' throat so fast he could hardly speak. He was beginning to faint, but he knew if he passed out before he talked he would never wake up.

"Let me think," he pleaded.

Stavros tried to focus, but he was so dizzy from the pain that it was difficult. He forced himself to remember the customer walking in, taking the ring out of a box and showing it to him. It was coming back to him.

"He—he was kind of blond and skinny—" He choked on some blood. "Help me up."

Salvatore Fiore kicked him in the ribs. "Keep talkin'."

"He had a beard, a blond beard . . ."

"Tell us about the rock. Where did it come from?"

Even in his extreme pain, Gus Stavros hesitated. If he talked, he would be a dead man later. If he did not, he would die now. He decided to postpone his death as long as possible.

"It came from the Tiffany job."

"Who was in on the job with the blond guy?"

Gus Stavros was finding it harder to breathe. "Mickey Nicola."

"Where can we find Nicola?"

"I don't know. He—he shacks up with some girl in Brooklyn."

Fiore lifted a foot and nudged Stavros' nose. Gus Stavros screamed with pain.

Joseph Colella asked, "What's the broad's name?"

"Jackson. Blanche Jackson."

4:30 A.M.

The house was set back from the street, surrounded by a small white picket fence with a carefully tended garden in front. Salvatore Fiore and Joseph Colella tramped through the flowers and made their way to the back door. It took them less than five seconds to open it. They stepped inside and moved toward the stairs. From a bedroom above they could hear the sounds of a bed creaking and the voices of a man and a woman. The two men pulled out their guns and started to move quietly up the stairs.

The woman's voice was saying, "Oh, Christ! You're wonderful, Mickey! Give it to me harder, baby."

"It's all for you, honey, every bit of it. Don't come yet."

"Oh, I won't," the woman moaned. "Let's come to—"

She looked up and screamed. The man whirled around. He started to reach under the pillow but decided against it.

"Okay," he said. "My wallet's in my pants on the chair. Take it and get the hell out of here. I'm busy."

Salvatore Fiore said, "We don't want your wallet, Mickey."

The anger on Mickey Nicola's face turned to something else. He sat up in bed, moving cautiously, trying to figure out the situation. The woman had pulled the sheets up over her breasts, her face a combination of anger and fright.

Nicola carefully swung his feet over the side of the bed, sitting on the edge, ready to spring. His penis had gone limp. He was watching both men, waiting for an opportunity.

"What do you want?"

"Do you work with Frank Jackson?"

"Go fuck yourselves."

Joseph Colella turned to his companion. "Shoot his balls off."

Salvatore Fiore raised his gun and aimed.

Mickey Nicola screamed, "Wait a minute! You guys must be crazy!" He looked into the little man's eyes and said quickly, "Yeah. I've worked with Jackson."

The woman cried out angrily, "Mickey!"

He turned on her savagely. "Shut up! You think I want to be a fuckin' eunuch?"

Salvatore Fiore turned to the woman and said, "You're Jackson's sister, ain't you?"

Her face was filled with fury. "I never heard of him."

Fiore raised his gun and moved closer to the bed. "You got two seconds to talk to me or you two are gonna be splashed all over the wall."

There was something in his voice that chilled her. He raised his gun and the blood began to drain from the woman's face.

"Tell them what they want to know," Mickey Nicola cried.

The gun moved up to press against the woman's breast.

"Don't! Yes! Frank Jackson's my brother."

"Where can we find him?"

"I don't know. I don't see him. I swear to God I don't know! I—"

His hand tightened on the trigger.

She screamed, "*Clara*! Clara would know! Ask Clara!"

Joseph Colella said, "Who's Clara?"

"She's—she's a waitress Frank knows."

"Where can we find her?"

This time there was no hesitation. The words spilled out. "She works at a bar called The Shakers in Queens." Her body began to tremble.

Salvatore Fiore looked at the two of them and said politely, "You can go back to your fuckin' now. Have a nice day."

And the two men departed.

5:30 A.M.

Clara Thomas (nee Thomachevsky) was about to fulfill her lifelong dream. She hummed happily to herself as she packed her cardboard suitcase with the clothes she would need in Canada. She had taken trips with gentlemen friends before, but this was different. This was going to be her honeymoon trip. Frank Jackson was like no other man she had known. The men who came into the bar, pawing her and pinching her buttocks, were nothing but animals. Frank Jackson was different. He was a real gentleman. Clara paused in her packing to think about that word: *gentle man*. She had never thought of it that way before, but that was Frank Jackson. She had seen him only four times in her life, but she knew she was in love with him. She could tell he had been attracted to her from the very beginning, because he always sat at her booth. And after the second time he had walked her home when the bar had closed.

I must still have it, Clara thought smugly, *if I can get a handsome young guy like that.* She stopped her packing to walk over to the closet mirror to study herself. Maybe she was a little too heavy and her hair was a couple of shades too red, but dieting would take care of the extra pounds and she would be more careful the next time she dyed her hair. All in all, she wasn't too dissatisfied with what she saw. *The old broad's still pretty good-lookin'*, she told herself. She knew that Frank

Jackson wanted to take her to bed, even though he had never touched her. He was really special. There was an almost— Clara furrowed her forehead, trying to think of the word— *spiritual* quality about him. Clara had been brought up a good Catholic and she knew it was sacrilegious to even think such a thought, but Frank Jackson reminded her a little bit of Jesus. She wondered what Frank would be like in bed. Well, if he was shy, she would show him a trick or two. He had talked about their getting married as soon as they got to Canada. Her dream come true. Clara looked at her watch and decided she had better hurry. She had promised to pick Frank up at his motel at seven-thirty.

She saw them in the mirror as they walked into her bedroom. They had come out of nowhere. A giant and a little fellow. Clara watched as the two of them moved toward her.

The small man looked at the suitcase. "Where you goin', Clara?"

"None of your business. Just take what you want and get out of here. If there's anything in this joint worth more than ten bucks, I'll eat it."

"I got something you can eat," the big man Colella said.

"Up yours, buster," Clara snapped. "If this is gonna be a rape job, I want you to know the doctor's treatin' me for gonorrhea."

Salvatore Fiore said, "We ain't gonna hurt you. We just wanna know where Frank Jackson is."

They could see the change that came over her. Her body suddenly stiffened and her face became a mask.

"Frank Jackson?" There was a note of deep puzzlement in her voice. "I don't know any Frank Jackson."

Salvatore Fiore pulled a lead pipe out of his pocket and took a step toward her.

"You don't scare me," Clara said, "I—"

His arm lashed out across her face, and in the midst of the blinding pain she could feel her teeth crumbling inside her mouth like tiny pieces of grit. She opened her mouth to speak and blood began pouring out. The big man raised his pipe again.

"No, please don't!" She gagged.

Joseph Colella said politely, "Where can we find this Frank Jackson?"

"Frank is—is—"

Clara thought of her sweet, gentle man in the hands of these two monsters. They were going to hurt him and, instinctively, she knew that Frank would not be able to stand the pain. He was too sensitive. If she could only find a way to save him, he would be grateful to her forever.

"I don't know."

Salvatore Fiore moved forward and Clara heard the sound of her leg breaking at the same instant she felt the excruciating pain. She fell to the floor, unable to scream because of all the blood in her mouth.

Joseph Colella stood over her and said pleasantly, "Maybe you don't unnerstand. We ain't gonna kill you. We're just gonna keep breakin' things. When we're through with you, you'll look like a piece of garbage the cat threw away. Do you believe me?"

Clara believed him. Frank Jackson would never want to look at her again. She had lost him to these two bastards. No dream come true, no marriage. The little man was moving forward with the lead pipe again.

Clara moaned, "Don't. Please don't. Frank's at the—the Brookside Motel on Prospect Avenue. He—"

She fainted.

Joseph Colella walked over to the telephone and dialed a number.

Michael Moretti answered. "Yes?"

"Brookside Motel on Prospect Avenue. Want us to take him?"

"No. I'll meet you there. Make sure he doesn't leave."

"He won't go anywhere."

6:30 A.M.

The boy was beginning to stir again. The man watched as Joshua opened his eyes. The boy looked down at the wire on his wrists and legs, and then looked up and saw Frank Jackson, and the memories came flooding back.

This was the man who had pushed those pills down his throat and kidnapped him. Joshua knew all about kidnappings from television. The police would come and save him and put the man in jail. Joshua was determined not to show his fear, because he wanted to be able to tell his mother how brave he had been.

"My mother will be here with the money," Joshua assured the man, "so you don't have to hurt me."

Frank Jackson walked over to the bed and smiled down at the boy. He really was a beautiful child. He wished he could take the boy to Canada instead of Clara. Reluctantly, Frank Jackson looked at his watch. It was time to get things ready.

The boy held up his bound wrists. The blood had caked dry.

"Would you mind taking this off, please?" he asked politely. "I won't run away."

Frank Jackson liked it that the boy had said "please." It showed good manners. These days, most kids had no manners at all. They ran around the streets like wild animals.

Frank Jackson went into the bathroom where he had put the can of gasoline back in the tub so that it would not stain the rug in the living room. He prided himself on details like that. He carried the can into the bedroom and set it down. He moved to the boy's side, lifted up the bound figure and placed him on the floor. Then he picked up the hammer and two large nails and knelt next to the boy.

Joshua Parker was watching him, wide-eyed. "What are you going to do with that?"

"Something that will make you very happy. Have you ever heard of Jesus Christ?" Joshua nodded. "Do you know how he died?"

"On the cross."

"That's very good. You're a bright boy. We don't have a cross here, so we'll have to do the best we can."

The boy's eyes were beginning to fill with fear.

Frank Jackson said, "There's nothing to be afraid of. Jesus wasn't afraid. You mustn't be afraid."

"I don't want to be Jesus," Joshua whispered. "I want to go home."

"I'm going to send you home," Frank Jackson promised. "I'm going to send you home to Jesus."

Frank Jackson took a handkerchief out of his back pocket and moved it toward the boy's mouth. Joshua gritted his teeth together.

"Don't make me angry."

Frank Jackson pressed his thumb and forefinger against Joshua's cheeks and forced his mouth open. He shoved the handkerchief into Joshua's mouth and slapped a piece of tape across it to hold the handkerchief in place. Joshua was straining against the wires that bound his wrists and hands, and they began to bleed again. Frank Jackson ran his hands over the fresh cuts.

"The blood of Christ," he said softly.

He picked up one of the boy's hands, turned it over and held it down against the floor. Then he picked up a nail. Holding it against Joshua's palm with one hand, Frank Jackson picked up the hammer with his other. He drove the nail through the boy's hand into the floor.

* * *

7:15 A.M.

Michael Moretti's black limousine was stalled on the Brooklyn-Queens Expressway in early morning traffic, held up by a vegetable truck that had overturned and spilled its cargo across the road. Traffic had come to a standstill.

"Pull over to the other side of the road and get past him," Michael Moretti ordered Nick Vito.

"There's a police car up ahead, Mike."

"Go up and tell whoever's in charge that I want to talk to him."

"Right, boss."

Nick Vito got out of the car and hurried toward the squad car. A few moments later he returned with a police sergeant. Michael Moretti opened the window of the car and held out his hand. There were five one hundred dollar bills in it.

"I'm in a hurry, officer."

Two minutes later the police car, red light flashing, was guiding the limousine past the wreckage on the road. When they were clear of the traffic, the sergeant got out of the police car and walked back to the limousine.

"Can I give you an escort somewhere, Mr. Moretti?"

"No, thank you," Michael said. "Come and see me Monday." To Nick Vito: "Move it!"

7:30 A.M.

The neon sign in front read:

BROOKSIDE MOTEL

SINGLES—DOUBLES

DAILY AND WEEKLY RATES

INDIVIDUALES–DOBLES

PRECIOS ESPECIALES

Joseph Colella and Salvatore Fiore sat in their car across from Bungalow 7. A few minutes earlier they had heard a thump from inside, so they knew that Frank Jackson was still there.

We oughta jump in and cool him, Fiore thought. But Michael Moretti had given instructions.

They settled back to wait.

7:45 A.M.

Inside Bungalow 7, Frank Jackson was making his final preparations. The boy was a disappointment. He had fainted. Jackson had wanted to wait until Joshua regained consciousness before the other nails were driven in, but it was getting late. He picked up the can of gasoline and sprinkled it across the boy's body, careful not to let it touch that beautiful face. He visualized the body under the pajamas and wished that he had time to—but, no, that would be foolish. Clara would be here any moment. He must be ready to leave when she arrived. He reached in his pockets, pulled out a box of matches, and set them neatly beside the can of gasoline, the hammer and the nails. People simply did not appreciate how important neatness was.

Frank Jackson looked at his watch again and wondered what was keeping Clara.

7:50 A.M.

Outside Bungalow 7, the limousine skidded to a stop and Michael Moretti jumped out of the car. The two men in the sedan hurried over to join him.

Joseph Colella pointed to Bungalow 7. "He's in there."

"What about the kid?"

The big man shrugged. "Dunno. Jackson's got the curtains drawn."

"Should we go in now and take him?" Salvatore Fiore asked.

"Stay here."

The two men looked at him in surprise. He was a *capo-regime*. He had soldiers to make hits for him while he sat back in safety. And yet he was going in himself. It was not right.

Joseph Colella said, "Boss, Sal and I can—"

But Michael Moretti was already moving to the door of Bungalow 7, a gun fitted with a silencer in his hand. He paused for a second to listen, then stepped back and smashed the door open with one powerful kick.

Moretti took in the scene in a single frozen moment: the bearded man kneeling on the floor beside the small boy; the boy's hand nailed to the floor, the room reeking of gasoline.

The bearded man had turned toward the door and was staring at Michael. The last sounds he ever uttered were, "You're not Cl—"

Michael's first bullet took him in the center of his forehead. The second bullet shattered his pharynx, and the third bullet took him in the heart. But by that time he no longer felt anything.

Michael Moretti stepped to the door and waved to the two men outside. They hurried into the cabin. Michael Moretti knelt beside the boy and felt his pulse. It was thin and thready, but he was still alive. He turned to Joseph Colella.

"Call Doc Petrone. Tell him we're on our way over."

9:30 A.M.

The instant the telephone rang, Jennifer snatched it up, squeezing it tightly. "Hello!"

Michael Moretti's voice said, "I'm bringing your son home."

Joshua was whimpering in his sleep. Jennifer leaned over and put her arms around him, holding him gently. He had been asleep when Michael had carried him into the house. When Jennifer had seen Joshua's unconscious body, his wrists and ankles heavily bandaged, his body swathed in gauze, she had nearly gone out of her mind. Michael had brought the doctor with him and it had taken him half an hour to reassure Jennifer that Joshua was going to be all right.

"His hand will heal," the doctor assured her. "There will be a small scar there, but fortunately no nerves or tendons were damaged. The gasoline burns are superficial. I bathed his body in mineral oil. I'll look in on him for the next few days. Believe me, he's going to be fine."

Before the doctor left, Jennifer had him attend to Mrs. Mackey.

Joshua had been put to bed and Jennifer stayed at his side, waiting to reassure him when he awakened. He stirred now and his eyes opened.

When he saw his mother, he said tiredly, "I knew you'd come, Mom. Did you give the man the ransom money?"

Jennifer nodded, not trusting her voice.

Joshua smiled. "I hope he buys too much candy with the money and gets a stomachache. Wouldn't that be funny?"

She whispered, "Very funny, darling. Do you know what you and I are going to do next week? I'm going to take you to—"

Joshua was asleep again.

It was hours later when Jennifer walked back into the living room. She was surprised to see that Michael Moretti was still there. Somehow it reminded her of the first time she had met Adam Warner, when he had waited for her in her little apartment.

"Michael—" It was impossible to find the words. "I—I can't tell you how—how grateful I am."

He looked at her and nodded.

She forced herself to ask the question. "And—and Frank Jackson?"

"He won't bother anyone again."

So it was over. Joshua was safe. Nothing else mattered.

Jennifer looked at Michael Moretti and thought, *I owe him so much. How can I ever repay him?*

Michael was watching her, wrapped in silence.

BOOK
II

37

Jennifer Parker stood naked, staring out of the large picture window that overlooked the Bay of Tangier. It was a beautiful, crisp autumn day and the bay was filled with skimming white sails and deep-throated power boats. Half a dozen large yachts bobbed at anchor in the harbor. Jennifer felt his presence and turned.

"Like the view?"

"Love it."

He looked at her naked body. "So do I." His hands were on her breasts, caressing them. "Let's go back to bed."

His touch made Jennifer shiver. He demanded things that no man had ever dared ask of her, and he did things to her that had never been done to her before.

"Yes, Michael."

They walked back into the bedroom and there, for one fleeting moment, Jennifer thought of Adam Warner, and then she forgot everything except what was happening to her.

Jennifer had never known anyone like Michael Moretti. He was insatiable. His body was athletic, lean and hard, and it became a part of Jennifer's body, catching her up in its own frenzy, carrying her along on a rising wave of pounding excitement that went on and on until she wanted to scream with a wild joy. When they had finished making love and Jennifer lay there, spent, Michael began once more, and Jennifer was caught up with him again and again in an ecstasy that became almost too much to bear.

Now he lay on top of her, staring into her flushed, happy face. "You love it, don't you, baby?"

"Yes."

There was a shame in it, a shame at how much she needed him, needed his lovemaking.

Jennifer remembered the first time.

It was the morning Michael Moretti had brought Joshua safely back home. Jennifer had known that Frank Jackson was dead and that Michael Moretti had killed him. The man standing in front of her had saved her son for her, had killed for her. It filled Jennifer with some deep, primordial feeling.

"How can I thank you?" Jennifer had asked.

And Michael Moretti had walked over to her, taken her in his arms and kissed her. Out of some old loyalty to Adam, Jennifer had pretended to herself that it would end with that kiss; but instead, it became a beginning. She knew what Michael Moretti was, and yet all that counted as nothing against what he had done. She stopped thinking and let her emotions take over.

They went upstairs to her bedroom, and Jennifer told herself that she was repaying Michael for what he had done for her, and then they were in bed and it was an experience beyond anything that Jennifer had ever dreamed.

Adam Warner had made love to her, but Michael Moretti possessed her. He filled every inch of her body with exquisite sensations. It was as though he were making love in bright, flashing colors, and the colors kept changing from one moment to the next, like some wonderful kaleidoscope. One moment he made love gently and sensitively, and the next moment he was cruel and pounding and demanding, and the changes made Jennifer frantic. He withdrew from her, teasing her, making her want more, and when she was on the verge of fulfillment he pulled away.

When she could stand it no longer, she begged, "Please take me! Take me!"

And his hard organ began to pound into her again until she screamed with pleasure. She was no longer a woman paying back a debt. She was a slave to something she had never known before. Michael stayed with her for four hours, and when he left, Jennifer knew that her life had changed.

She lay in her bed thinking about what had happened, trying to understand it. How could she be so much in love with Adam and still have been so overwhelmed by Michael Moretti? Thomas Aquinas had said that when you got to the heart of evil, there was nothing there. Jennifer wondered if it was also true of love. She was aware that part of what she had done was out of a deep loneliness. She had lived too long with a phantom, a man she could neither see nor have, yet she knew she would always love Adam. Or was it just a memory of that love?

Jennifer was not sure what she felt about Michael. Gratitude, yes. But that was a small part of it. It was more. Much more. She knew who and what Michael Moretti was. He had killed for her, but he had killed for others, too. He had murdered men for money, for power, for vengeance. How could she feel as she did about a man like that? How could she have let him make love to her and have been so excited by him? She was filled with a sense of shame and she thought, *What kind of person am I?*

She had no answer.

The afternoon newspapers reported the story of a fire in a Queens motel. The remains of an unidentified man were found in the ruins. Arson was suspected.

*   *. *

After Joshua's return, Jennifer had tried to make everything as normal for him as possible, fearful of the trauma the preceding night might have inflicted upon him. When Joshua woke up, Jennifer prepared a meal and brought it to him in bed. It was a ridiculous meal, consisting of all the junk foods he loved: a hot dog and a peanut butter sandwich and Fritos and Hostess Twinkies and root beer.

"You should have seen him, Mom," Joshua said between bites. "He was crazy!" He held up his bandaged hand. "Do you think he really thought I was Jesus Christ?"

Jennifer repressed a shudder. "I—I don't know, darling."

"Why do people want to kill other people?"

"Well—" and Jennifer's thoughts suddenly went back to Michael Moretti. Did she have the right to judge him? She did not know the terrible forces that had shaped his life, that had turned him into what he had become. She had to learn more about him, to get to know and understand him.

Joshua was saying, "Do I have to go to school tomorrow?"

Jennifer put her arms around him. "No, darling. We're both going to stay home and play hooky all week. We—"

The telephone rang.

It was Michael. "How's Joshua?"

"He's wonderful—thank you."

"And how are you feeling?"

Jennifer felt her throat thickening with embarrassment. "I'm—I—I feel fine."

He chuckled. "Good. I'll see you for lunch tomorrow. Donato's on Mulberry Street. Twelve-thirty."

"All right, Michael. Twelve-thirty."

Jennifer spoke those words and there was no turning back.

The captain at Donato's knew Michael, and the best table in the restaurant had been reserved for him. People kept stopping by to say hello, and Jennifer was again amazed at the way everyone kowtowed to him. It was strange how much Michael Moretti reminded her of Adam Warner, for each, in his own way, was a man of power.

Jennifer started to question Michael about his background, wanting to learn how and why he had gotten trapped into the life he led.

He interrupted her. "You think I'm in this because of my family or because someone put pressure on me?"

"Well—yes, Michael. Of course."

He laughed. "I worked my butt off to get where I am. I love it. I love the money. I love the power. I'm a king, baby, and I love being king."

Jennifer looked at him, trying to understand. "But you can't enjoy—"

"Listen!" His silence had suddenly turned into words and sentences and confidences, pouring out as though they had been stored inside him for years, waiting for someone to come along to share them with. "My old man was a Coca-Cola bottle."

"A Coca-Cola bottle?"

"Right. There are billions of them in the world and you can't tell one from another. He was a shoemaker. He worked his fingers to the bone, trying to put food on the table. We had nothing. Being poor is only romantic in books. In real life, it's smelly rooms with rats and cockroaches and bad food that you can never get enough of. When I was a young punk, I did anything I could to make a buck. I ran errands for the big shots, I brought them coffee and cigars, I found them girls— anything to stay alive. Well, one summer I went down to Mexico City. I had no money, nothing. My ass was hanging out. One night a girl I met invited me to a large dinner party at a fancy restaurant. For dessert they served a special Mexican cake with a little clay doll baked inside it. Someone at the table explained that the custom was that whoever got the clay doll had to pay for the dinner. I got the clay doll." He paused. "I swallowed it."

Jennifer put her hand over his. "Michael, other people have grown up poor and—"

"Don't confuse me with other people." His tone was hard and uncompromising. "I'm me. I know who I am, baby. I wonder if you know who you are."

"I think I do."

"Why did you go to bed with me?"

Jennifer hesitated. "Well, I—I was grateful and—"

"Bullshit! You wanted me."

"Michael, I—"

"I don't have to buy my women. Not with money and not with gratitude."

Jennifer admitted to herself that he was right. She *had* wanted him, just as he had wanted her. *And yet*, Jennifer thought, *this man deliberately tried to destroy me once. How can I forget that?*

Michael leaned forward and took Jennifer's hand, palm up. Slowly, he caressed each finger, each mound, never taking his eyes from her.

"Don't play games with me. Not ever, Jennifer."

She felt powerless. Whatever there was between them transcended the past.

It was when they were having dessert that Michael said, "By the way, I have a case for you."

It was as though he had slapped her in the face.

Jennifer stared at him. "What kind of case?"

"One of my boys, Vasco Gambutti, has been arrested for killing a cop. I want you to defend him."

Jennifer sat there filled with hurt and anger that he was still trying to use her.

She said evenly, "I'm sorry, Michael. I told you before. I can't get involved with—with your . . . friends."

He gave her a lazy grin. "Did you ever hear the story about the little lion cub in Africa? He leaves his mother for the first time to go down to the river to get a drink, and a gorilla knocks him down. While he's picking himself up, a big leopard shoves him out of the way. A herd of elephants comes along and almost tramples him to death. The little cub returns home all shaken up and he says, 'You know something, Ma—it's a jungle out there!' "

There was a long silence between them. It *was* a jungle out there, Jennifer thought, but she had always stood at the edge of it, outside it, free to flee whenever she wanted to. She had made the rules and her clients had had to live by them. But now, Michael Moretti had changed all that. This was *his* jungle. Jennifer was afraid of it, afraid to get caught up in it. Yet, when she thought about what Michael had done for her, she decided it was a small thing he was asking.

She would do Michael this one favor.

38

"We're going to handle the Vasco Gambutti case," Jennifer informed Ken Bailey.

Ken looked at Jennifer in disbelief. "He's Mafia! One of Michael Moretti's hit men. That's not the kind of client we take."

"We're taking this one."

"Jennifer, we can't afford to get mixed up with the mob."

"Gambutti's entitled to a fair trial, just like anyone else." The words sounded hollow, even to her.

"I can't let you—"

"As long as this is my office, I'll make the decisions." She could see the surprise and hurt that came into his eyes.

Ken nodded, turned and walked out of the office. Jennifer was tempted to call him back and try to explain. But how could she? She was not sure she could even explain it to herself.

When Jennifer had her first meeting with Vasco Gambutti, she tried to regard him as just another client. She had handled clients before who were accused of murder, but somehow, this was different. This man was a member of a vast network of organized crime, a group that bled the country of untold billions of dollars, an arcane cabal that would kill when necessary to protect itself.

The evidence against Gambutti was overwhelming. He had been caught during the holdup of a fur shop and had killed an off-duty policeman who had tried to stop him. The morning newspapers announced that Jennifer Parker was going to be the defense attorney.

Judge Lawrence Waldman telephoned. "Is it true, Jennie?"

Jennifer knew instantly what he meant. "Yes, Lawrence."

A pause. "I'm surprised. You know who he is, of course."

"Yes, I know."

"You're getting into dangerous territory."

"Not really. I'm just doing a friend a favor."

"I see. Be careful."

"I will," Jennifer promised.

It was only afterward that Jennifer realized he had said nothing about their having dinner together.

After looking over the material her staff had assembled, Jennifer decided that she had no case at all.

Vasco Gambutti had been caught red-handed in a robbery-murder, and there were no extenuating circumstances. Furthermore, there was always a strong emotional pull in the minds of the jurors when the victim was a policeman.

She called Ken Bailey in and gave him his instructions.

He said nothing, but Jennifer could feel his disapproval and was saddened. She promised herself that this was the last time she would work for Michael.

Her private phone rang and she picked it up. Michael said, "Hello, baby. I'm hungry for you. Meet me in half an hour."

She sat there, listening, already feeling his arms around her, his body pressing against hers.

"I'll be there," Jennifer said.

The promise to herself was forgotten.

The Gambutti trial lasted ten days. The press was there in full force, eager to watch District Attorney Di Silva and Jennifer Parker in open combat again. Di Silva had done his homework thoroughly, and he deliberately understated his case, letting the jurors take the suggestions he dropped and build on them, creating horrors in their minds even greater than the ones he depicted.

Jennifer sat quietly through the testimony, seldom bothering to raise objections.

On the last day of the trial, she made her move.

There is an adage in law that when you have a weak defense, you put your opponent on trial. Because Jennifer had no defense for Vasco Gambutti, she had made a decision to put Scott Norman, the slain policeman, on trial. Ken Bailey had dug up everything there was to know about Scott Norman. His record was not good, but before Jennifer was through she made it seem ten times worse than it was. Norman had been on the police force for twenty years, and in that period had been suspended three times on charges of unnecessary violence. He had shot and almost killed an unarmed suspect, he had beaten up a drunk in a bar and he had sent to the hospital a man involved in a domestic quarrel. Although these incidents had taken place over a period of twenty years, Jennifer made it seem as though the deceased had committed an unbroken series of despicable acts. Jennifer had a parade of witnesses on the stand giving testimony against the dead police officer, and there was not one thing Robert Di Silva could do about it.

In his summation, Di Silva said, "Remember, ladies and gentlemen of the jury, that Officer Scott Norman is not the one on trial here. Officer Scott Norman was the victim. He was killed by"—pointing—"the defendant, Vasco Gambutti."

But even as the District Attorney spoke, he knew it was no use. Jennifer had made Officer Scott Norman appear to be as worthless a human being as Vasco Gambutti. He was no longer the noble policeman who had given his life to apprehend a criminal. Jennifer Parker had distorted the picture so that the victim was no better than the accused slayer.

The jury returned a verdict of not guilty on the charge of murder in the first degree and convicted Vasco Gambutti of manslaughter. It was a stunning defeat for District Attorney Di Silva, and the media were quick to announce another victory for Jennifer Parker.

"Wear your chiffon. It's a celebration," Michael told her.

They had dinner at a seafood restaurant in the Village. The restaurant owner sent over a bottle of rare champagne and Michael and Jennifer drank a toast.

"I'm very pleased."

Coming from Michael, it was an accolade.

He placed a small red-and-white-wrapped box in her hands. "Open it."

He watched as she untied the gold thread and removed the lid. In the box lay a large, square-cut emerald, surrounded by diamonds.

Jennifer stared at it. She started to protest. "Oh, Michael!" And she saw the look of pride and pleasure on his face.

"Michael—what am I going to do with you?"

And she thought: *Oh, Jennifer, what am I going to do with you?*

"You need it for that dress." He placed the ring on the third finger of her left hand.

"I—I don't know what to say. I—thank you. It's really a celebration, isn't it!"

Michael grinned. "The celebration hasn't started yet. This is only the foreplay."

* * *

They were riding in the limousine on their way to an apartment that Michael kept uptown. Michael pressed a button and raised the glass that separated the rear of the car from the driver.

We're locked away in our own little world, Jennifer thought. Michael's nearness excited her.

She turned to look into his black eyes and he moved toward her and slid his hand along her thighs, and Jennifer's body was instantly on fire.

Michael's lips found hers and their bodies were pressed together. Jennifer felt the hard maleness of him and she slid down to the floor of the car. She began to make love to him, caressing him and kissing him until Michael began to moan, and Jennifer moaned with him, moving faster and faster until she felt the spasms of his body.

The celebration had begun.

Jennifer was thinking of the past now as she lay in bed in the hotel room in Tangier, listening to the sounds of Michael in the shower. She felt satisfied and happy. The only thing missing was her young son. She had thought of taking Joshua with her on some of her trips, but instinctively she wanted to keep him and Michael Moretti far away from each other. Joshua must never be touched by that part of her life. It seemed to Jennifer that her life was a series of compartments: There was Adam, there was her son and there was Michael Moretti. And each had to be kept separate from the others.

Michael walked out of the bathroom wearing only a towel. The hair on his body glistened from the dampness of the shower. He was a beautiful, exciting animal.

"Get dressed. We have work to do."

39

It happened so gradually that it did not seem to be happening at all. It had begun with Vasco Gambutti, and shortly afterward Michael asked Jennifer to handle another case, then another, until soon it became a steady flow of cases.

Michael would call Jennifer and say, "I need your help, baby. One of my boys is having a problem."

And Jennifer was reminded of Father Ryan's words, *A friend of mine has a bit of a problem*. Was there really any difference? America had come to accept the Godfather syndrome. Jennifer told herself that what she was doing now was the same as what she had been doing all along. The truth was that there was a difference—a big difference.

She was at the center of one of the most powerful organizations in the world.

Michael invited Jennifer to the farmhouse in New Jersey,

where she met Antonio Granelli for the first time, and some of the other men in the Organization.

At a large table in the old-fashioned kitchen were Nick Vito, Arthur "Fat Artie" Scotto, Salvatore Fiore and Joseph Colella.

As Jennifer and Michael came in and stood in the doorway, listening, Nick Vito was saying, ". . . like the time I did a pound in Atlanta. I had a heavy H book goin'. This popcorn pimp comes up and tries to fuck me over 'cause he wants a piece of the action."

"Did you know the guy?" Fat Artie Scotto asked.

"What's to know? He wants to get his lights turned on. He tried to put the arm on me."

"On *you?*"

"Yeah. His head wasn't wrapped too tight."

"What'd you do?"

"Eddie Fratelli and me got him over in the ghinny corner of the yard and burned him. What the hell, he was doin' bad time, anyway."

"Hey, whatever happened to Little Eddie?"

"He's doin' a dime at Lewisburg."

"What about his bandit? She was some class act."

"Oh, yeah. I'd love to make her drawers."

"She's still got the hots for Eddie. Only the Pope knows why."

"I liked Eddie. He used to be an up-front guy."

"He went ape-shit. Speakin' of that, do you know who turned into a candy man . . . ?"

Shop talk.

Michael grinned at Jennifer's puzzled reaction to the conversation and said, "Come on—I'll introduce you to Papa."

Antonio Granelli was a shock to Jennifer. He was in a wheelchair, a feeble skeleton of a man, and it was hard to imagine him as he once must have been.

An attractive brunette with a full figure walked into the room, and Michael said to Jennifer, "This is Rosa, my wife."

Jennifer had dreaded this moment. Some nights after Michael had left her—fulfilled in every way a woman could be —she had fought with a guilt that almost overpowered her. *I don't want to hurt another woman. I'm stealing. I've got to stop this! I must!* And, always, she lost the battle.

Rosa looked at Jennifer with eyes that were wise. *She knows,* Jennifer thought.

There was a small awkwardness, and then Rosa said softly, "I'm pleased to meet you, Mrs. Parker. Michael tells me you're very intelligent."

Antonio Granelli grunted. "It's not good for a woman to be too smart. It's better to leave the brains to the men."

Michael said with a straight face, "I think of Mrs. Parker as a man, Papa."

They had dinner in the large, old-fashioned dining room. "You sit next to me," Antonio Granelli commanded Jennifer.

Michael sat next to Rosa. Thomas Colfax, the *consigliere,* sat opposite Jennifer and she could feel his animosity.

The dinner was superb. An enormous antipasto was served, and then *pasta fagioli.* There was a salad with garbanzo beans, stuffed mushrooms, veal *piccata,* linguini and baked chicken. It seemed that the dishes never stopped coming.

There were no visible servants in the house, and Rosa was constantly jumping up and clearing the table to bring in new dishes from the kitchen.

"My Rosa's a great cook," Antonio Granelli told Jennifer. "She's almost as good as her mother was. Hey, Mike?"

"Yes," Michael said politely.

"His Rosa's a wonderful wife," Antonio Granelli went on, and Jennifer wondered whether it was a casual remark or a warning.

Michael said, "You're not finishing your veal."

"I've never eaten so much in my life," Jennifer protested.

And it was not over yet.

There was a bowl of fresh fruit and a platter of cheese, and ice cream with a hot fudge sauce, and candy and mints.

Jennifer marveled at how Michael managed to keep his figure.

The conversation was easy and pleasant and could have been taking place in any one of a thousand Italian homes, and it was hard for Jennifer to believe that this family was different from any other family.

Until Antonio Granelli said, "You know anythin' about the *Unione Siciliana?*"

"No," Jennifer said.

"Let me tell you about it, lady."

"Pop—her name is Jennifer."

"That's not no Italian name, Mike. It's too hard for me to remember. I'll call you lady, lady. Okay?"

"Okay," Jennifer replied.

"The *Unione Siciliana* started in Sicily to protect the poor against injustices. See, the people in power, they robbed the poor. The poor had nothin'—no money, no jobs, no justice. So the *Unione* was formed. When there was injustice, people came to the members of the secret brotherhood and they got vengeance. Pretty soon the *Unione* became stronger than the law, because it was the *people's* law. We believe in what the Bible says, lady." He looked Jennifer in the eye. "If anyone betrays us, we get vengeance."

The message was unmistakable.

Jennifer had always known instinctively that if she ever worked for the Organization she would be taking a giant step, but like most outsiders, she had a misconception of what the Organization was like. The Mafia was generally depicted as a bunch of mobsters sitting around ordering people murdered and counting the money from loan-sharking and whorehouses. That was only a part of the picture. The meetings Jennifer attended taught her the rest of it: These were businessmen operating on a scale that was staggering. They owned hotels and banks, restaurants and casinos, insurance companies and factories, building companies and chains of hospitals. They controlled unions and shipping. They were in the record business and sold vending machines. They owned funeral parlors, bakeries and construction companies. Their yearly income was in the billions. How they had acquired those interests was none of Jennifer's concern. It was her job to defend those of them who got into trouble with the law.

Robert Di Silva had three of Michael Moretti's men indicted for shaking down a group of lunch wagons. They were charged with conspiracy to interfere with commerce by extortion and seven counts of interference with commerce. The only witness willing to testify against the men was a woman who owned one of the stands.

"She's going to blow us away," Michael told Jennifer. "She's got to be handled."

"You own a piece of a magazine publishing company, don't you?" Jennifer asked.

"Yes. What does that have to do with lunch wagons?"

"You'll see."

Jennifer quietly arranged for the magazine to offer a large sum of money for the witness's story. The woman accepted. In court, Jennifer used that to discredit the woman's motives, and the charges were dismissed.

Jennifer's relationship with her associates had changed. When the office had begun to take a succession of Mafia cases, Ken Bailey had come into Jennifer's office and said, "What's going on? You can't keep representing these hoodlums. They'll ruin us."

"Don't worry about it, Ken. They'll pay."

"You can't be that naïve, Jennifer. You're the one who's going to pay. They'll have you hooked."

Because she had known he was right, Jennifer said angrily, "Drop it, Ken."

He had looked at her for a long moment, then said, "Right. You're the boss."

The Criminal Courts was a small world, and news traveled swiftly. When word got out that Jennifer Parker was defending members of the Organization, well-meaning friends went to her and reiterated the same things that Judge Lawrence Waldman and Ken Bailey had told her.

"If you get involved with these hoodlums, you'll be tarred with the same brush."

Jennifer told them all: "Everyone is entitled to be defended."

She appreciated their warnings, but she felt that they did not apply to her. She was not a part of the Organization; she merely represented some of its members. She was a lawyer, like her father, and she would never do anything that would have made him ashamed of her. The jungle was there, but she was still outside it.

Father Ryan had come to see her. This time it was not to ask her to help out a friend.

"I'm concerned about you, Jennifer. I hear reports that you're handling—well—the wrong people."

"Who are the wrong people? Do you judge the people who come to you for help? Do you turn people away from God because they've sinned?"

Father Ryan shook his head. "Of course not. But it's one thing when an individual makes a mistake. It's something else when corruption is organized. If you help those people, you're condoning what they do. You become a part of it."

"No. I'm a lawyer, Father. I help people in trouble."

Jennifer came to know Michael Moretti better than anyone had ever known him. He exposed feelings to her that he had never revealed to anyone else. He was basically a lonely, solitary man, and Jennifer was the first person who had ever been able to penetrate his shell.

Jennifer felt that Michael *needed* her. She had never felt that with Adam. And Michael had forced her to admit how much she needed him. He had brought out feelings in her that she had kept suppressed—wild, atavistic passions that she had been afraid to let loose. There were no inhibitions with Michael. When they were in bed together, there were no limits, no barriers. Only pleasure, a pleasure Jennifer had never dreamed possible.

Michael confided to Jennifer that he did not love Rosa, but it was obvious that Rosa worshiped Michael. She was always at his service, waiting to take care of his needs.

Jennifer met other Mafia wives, and she found their lives fascinating. Their husbands went out to restaurants and bars and racetracks with their mistresses while their wives stayed home and waited for them.

A Mafia wife always had a generous allowance, but she had to be careful how she spent it, lest she attract the attention of the Internal Revenue Service.

There was a pecking order ranging from the lowly *soldato* to the *capo di tutti capi*, and the wife never owned a more expensive coat or car than the wife of her husband's immediate superior.

The wives gave dinner parties for their husbands' associates, but they were careful not to be more lavish than their position permitted in relation to the others.

At ceremonies such as weddings or baptisms, where gifts

were called for, a wife was never allowed to spend more than the wife above her station in the hierarchy.

The protocol was as stringent as that at U.S. Steel, or any other large business corporation.

The Mafia was an incredible moneymaking machine, but Jennifer became aware that there was another element in it that was equally important: power.

"The Organization is bigger than the government of most of the countries of the world," Michael told Jennifer. "We gross more than a half a dozen of the largest companies in America, put together."

"There's a difference," Jennifer pointed out. "They're legitimate and—"

Michael laughed. "You mean the ones that haven't been caught. Dozens of the country's biggest companies have been indicted for violating one law or another. Don't kid yourself about heroes, Jennifer. The average American today can't name two astronauts who have been up in space, but they know the names of Al Capone and Lucky Luciano."

Jennifer realized that in his own way, Michael was equally as dedicated as Adam was. The difference was that their lives had gone in opposite directions.

When it came to business, Michael had a total lack of empathy. It was his strong point. He made decisions based solely on what was expedient for the Organization.

In the past, Michael had been completely dedicated to fulfilling his ambitions. There had been no emotional room for a woman in his life. Neither Rosa nor Michael's girl friends had ever been a part of his real needs.

Jennifer was different. He needed her as he had needed no other woman. He had never known anyone like her. She excited him physically, but so had dozens of others. What made Jennifer special was her intelligence, her independence. Rosa obeyed him; other women feared him; Jennifer challenged him. She was his equal. He could talk to her, discuss things with her. She was more than intelligent. She was smart.

He knew that he was never going to let her go.

Occasionally Jennifer took business trips with Michael, but she tried to avoid traveling whenever she could because she wanted to spend as much time as possible with Joshua. He was six years old now and growing unbelievably fast. Jennifer had enrolled him in a private school nearby, and Joshua loved it.

He rode a two-wheel bicycle and had a fleet of toy racing cars and carried on long and earnest conversations with Jennifer and Mrs. Mackey.

Because Jennifer wanted Joshua to grow up to be strong and independent, she tried to walk a carefully balanced line, letting Joshua know how much she loved him, making him aware that she was always there when he needed her and yet giving him a sense of his own independence.

She taught him to love good books and to enjoy music. She took him to the theater, avoiding opening nights because there would be too many people there who might know her and ask questions. On weekends she and Joshua would have a movie binge. On Saturday they would see a movie in the afternoon, have dinner at a restaurant and then see a second movie. On Sunday they would go sailing or bicycling together. Jennifer gave her son all the love that was stored in her, but she was careful to try not to spoil him. She planned her strategy with Joshua more carefully than she had planned any court case, determined not to fall into the traps of a one-parent home.

Jennifer felt no sacrifice in spending so much time with Joshua; he was great fun. They played word games and Impressions and Twenty Questions, and Jennifer was delighted by the quickness of her son's mind. He was at the head of his class and an outstanding athlete, but he did not take himself seriously. He had a marvelous sense of humor.

When it did not interfere with his schoolwork, Jennifer would take Joshua on trips. During Joshua's winter vacation, Jennifer took time off to go skiing with him in the Poconos. In the summer she took him to London on a business trip with her, and they spent two weeks exploring the countryside. Joshua adored England.

"Could I go to school here?" he asked.

Jennifer felt a pang. It would not be long before he left her to go away to school, to seek his fortune, to get married and have his own home and family. Was that not what she wanted for him? Of course it was. When Joshua was ready, she would let him go with open arms, and yet she knew how difficult it was going to be.

Joshua was looking at her, waiting for an answer. "Can I, Mom?" he asked. "Maybe Oxford?"

Jennifer held him close. "Of course. They'll be lucky to get you."

On a Sunday morning when Mrs. Mackey was off, Jennifer had to go into Manhattan to pick up a transcript of a deposition. Joshua was visiting some friends. When Jennifer returned home, she started to prepare dinner for the two of them. She opened the refrigerator—and stopped dead in her tracks. There was a note inside, propped up between two bottles of milk. Adam had left her notes like that. Jennifer stared at it, mesmerized, afraid to touch it. Slowly, she reached for the note and unfolded it. It said, *Surprise! Is it okay if Alan has dinner with us?*

It took half an hour for Jennifer's pulse to return to normal.

From time to time, Joshua asked Jennifer about his father.

"He was killed in Viet Nam, Joshua. He was a very brave man."

"Don't we have a picture of him anywhere?"

"No, I'm sorry, darling. We—we weren't married very long before he died."

She hated the lie, but she had no choice.

Michael Moretti had only asked once about Joshua's father.

"I don't care what happened before you belonged to me— I'm just curious."

Jennifer thought about the power that Michael would have over Senator Adam Warner if Michael ever learned the truth.

"He was killed in Viet Nam. His name's not important."

40

In Washington, D.C., a Senate investigating committee headed by Adam Warner was in its final day of an intensive inquiry into the new XK-1 bomber that the Air Force was trying to get the Senate to approve. For weeks, expert witnesses had paraded up to Capitol Hill, half of them testifying that the new bomber would be an expensive albatross that would destroy the defense budget and ruin the country, and the other half testifying that unless the Air Force could get the bomber approved, America's defenses would be so weakened that the Russians would invade the United States the following Sunday.

Adam had volunteered to test-fly a prototype of the new bomber, and his colleagues had eagerly seized on his offer. Adam was one of them, a member of the club, and he would give them the truth.

Adam had taken the bomber up early on a Sunday morning with a skeleton crew and had put the plane through a series of rigorous tests. The flight had been an unqualified success, and he had reported back to the Senate committee that the new XK-1 bomber was an important advance in aviation. He recommended that the airplane go into production immediately. The Senate approved the funds.

The press enthusiastically played up the story. They described Adam as one of the new breed of investigative senators, a lawmaker who went out into the field to study the facts for himself instead of taking the word of lobbyists and others who were concerned with protecting their own interests.

Newsweek and *Time* both did cover stories on Adam, and the *Newsweek* story ended with:

> The Senate has found an honest and capable new guardian to investigate some of the vital problems that plague this country, and to bring to them light instead of heat. There is a growing feeling among the kingmakers that Adam Warner has the qualities that would grace the presidency.

Jennifer devoured the stories about Adam and she was filled with pride. And pain. She still loved Adam and she loved Michael Moretti, and she did not understand how it was possible, or what kind of woman she had become. Adam had created the loneliness in her life. Michael had erased it.

The smuggling of drugs from Mexico had increased enormously, and it was obvious that organized crime was behind it. Adam was asked to head an investigating committee. He coordinated the efforts of half a dozen United States law enforcement agencies, and flew to Mexico and obtained the cooperation of the Mexican government. Within three months, the drug traffic had slowed to a trickle.

In the farmhouse in New Jersey, Michael Moretti was saying, "We've got a problem."

They were seated in the large, comfortable study. In the room were Jennifer, Antonio Granelli and Thomas Colfax. Antonio Granelli had suffered a stroke and it had aged him twenty years overnight. He looked like a shrunken caricature of a man. The paralysis had affected the right side of his face so that when he spoke, saliva drooled from the corners of his mouth. He was old and almost senile, and he leaned more and more on Michael's judgment. He had even reluctantly come to accept Jennifer.

Not so Thomas Colfax. The conflict between Michael and Colfax had grown stronger. Colfax knew it was Michael's intention to replace him with this woman. Colfax admitted to himself that Jennifer Parker was a clever lawyer, but what could she possibly know of the traditions of the *borgata*? Of what had made the brotherhood work so smoothly all these years? How could Michael bring in a stranger—worse, a woman!—and trust her with their life-and-death secrets? It was an untenable situation. Colfax had talked to the *capo-regimi*—the squad lieutenants—and the *soldati*—the soldiers —one by one, voicing his fears, trying to win them over to his side, but they were afraid to go against Michael. If he trusted this woman, then they felt they must trust her also.

Thomas Colfax decided he would have to bide his time. But he would find a way to get rid of her.

Jennifer was well aware of his feelings. She had replaced him, and his pride would never let him forgive her for that. His loyalty to the Syndicate would keep him in line and protect her, but if his hatred for her should become stronger than that loyalty . . .

Michael turned to Jennifer. "Have you ever heard of Adam Warner?"

Jennifer's heart stopped for an instant. It was suddenly hard for her to breathe. Michael was watching her, waiting for an answer.

"You—you mean the senator?" Jennifer managed to say.

"Uh-huh. We're going to have to cool the son of a bitch."

Jennifer could feel the blood drain from her face. "Why, Michael?"

"He's hurting our operation. Because of him, the Mexican government is closing down factories belonging to friends of ours. Everything's starting to come apart. I want the bastard out of our hair. He's got to go."

Jennifer's mind was racing. "If you touch Senator Warner," she said, choosing her words carefully, "you'll destroy yourself."

"I'm not going to let—"

"Listen to me, Michael. Get rid of him, and they'll send ten men to take his place. A hundred. Every newspaper in the country will be after you. The investigation that's going on now will be nothing compared to what will happen if Senator Warner is harmed."

Michael said angrily, "I'm telling you we're *hurting!*"

Jennifer changed her tone. "Michael, use your head. You've seen these investigations before. How long do they last? Five minutes after the senator is finished, he'll be investigating something else and all this will be over. The factories that are closed down will open up again and you'll be back in business. That way there won't be any repercussions. You try to do it your way and you'll never hear the end of it."

"I disagree," Thomas Colfax said. "In my opinion—"

Michael Moretti growled, "No one asked for your opinion."

Thomas Colfax jerked as though he had been slapped. Michael paid no attention. Colfax turned to Antonio Granelli for support. The old man was asleep.

Michael said to Jennifer, "Okay, counselor, we'll leave Warner alone for now."

Jennifer realized she had been holding her breath. She exhaled slowly. "Is there anything else?"

"Yeah." Michael picked up a heavy gold lighter and lit a cigarette. "A friend of ours, Marco Lorenzo, has been convicted of extortion and robbery."

Jennifer had read about the case. According to the newspapers, Lorenzo was a congenital criminal with a long string of arrests for crimes of violence.

"Do you want me to file an appeal?"

"No, I want you to see that he goes to jail."

Jennifer looked at him in surprise.

Michael put the cigarette lighter back on his desk. "I got word that Di Silva wants to ship him back to Sicily. Marco's got enemies there. If they send him back he won't live twenty-four hours. The safest place for him is Sing Sing. When the heat's off in a year or two we'll get him out. Can you swing it?"

Jennifer hesitated. "If we were in another jurisdiction I could probably do it. But Di Silva won't plea-bargain with me."

Thomas Colfax said quickly, "Perhaps we should let someone else take care of this."

"If I had wanted someone else to take care of it," Michael snapped, "I would have said so." He turned back to Jennifer. "I want you to handle it."

Michael Moretti and Nick Vito watched from the window as Thomas Colfax climbed into his sedan and drove off.

Michael said, "Nick, I want you to get rid of him."

"*Colfax?*"

"I can't trust him anymore. He's living in the past with the old man."

"Whatever you say, Mike. When do you want me to do it?"

"Soon. I'll let you know."

Jennifer was seated in Judge Lawrence Waldman's chambers. It was the first time she had seen him in more than a year. The friendly telephone calls and dinner invitations had stopped. Well, that could not be helped, Jennifer thought. She liked Lawrence Waldman and she regretted losing his friendship, but she had made her choice.

They were waiting for Robert Di Silva and they sat there in an uncomfortable silence, neither bothering to make small talk. When the District Attorney walked in and took a seat, the meeting began.

Judge Waldman said to Jennifer, "Bobby says that you want to discuss a plea bargain before I pass sentence on Lorenzo."

"That's right." Jennifer turned to District Attorney Di Silva. "I think it would be a mistake to send Marco Lorenzo to Sing Sing. He doesn't belong here. He's an illegal alien. I feel he should be shipped back to Sicily where he came from."

Di Silva looked at her in surprise. He had been going to recommend deportation, but if that was what Jennifer Parker wanted, then he would have to reevaluate his decision.

"Why do you recommend that?" Di Silva asked.

"For several reasons. First of all, it will keep him from committing any more crimes here, and—"

"So will being in a cell in Sing Sing."

"Lorenzo is an old man. He can't stand being confined. He'll go crazy if you put him in jail. All his friends are in Sicily. He can live there in the sun and die in peace with his family."

Di Silva's mouth tightened with anger. "We're talking about a hoodlum who's spent his life robbing and raping and killing, and you're worried about whether he's with his friends in the sun?" He turned to Judge Waldman. "She's unreal!"

"Marco Lorenzo has a right to—"

Di Silva pounded his fist on the desk. "He has no rights at all! He's been convicted of extortion and armed robbery."

"In Sicily, when a man—"

"He's not in Sicily, goddamn it!" Di Silva yelled. "He's

here! He committed the crimes here and he's going to pay for them here." He stood up. "Your Honor, we're wasting your time. The state refuses any plea bargaining in this case. We're asking that Marco Lorenzo be sentenced to Sing Sing."

Judge Waldman turned to Jennifer. "Do you have anything more to say?"

She looked at Robert Di Silva angrily. "No, Your Honor."

Judge Waldman said, "Sentencing will be tomorrow morning. You are both excused."

Di Silva and Jennifer rose and left the office.

In the corridor outside, the District Attorney turned to Jennifer and smiled. "You've lost your touch, counselor."

Jennifer shrugged. "You can't win them all."

Five minutes later, Jennifer was in a telephone booth talking to Michael Moretti.

"You can stop worrying. Marco Lorenzo will be going to Sing Sing."

41

Time was a swiftly flowing river that had no shores, no boundaries. Its seasons were not winter, spring, fall or summer, but birthdays and joys and troubles and pain. They were court battles won, and cases lost; the reality of Michael, the memories of Adam. But mainly, it was Joshua who was time's calendar, a reminder of how quickly the years were passing.

He was, incredibly, seven years old. Overnight, it seemed, he had gone from crayons and picture books to airplane models and sports. Joshua had grown tall and he resembled his father more every day, and not merely in his physical appearance. He was sensitive and polite, and he had a strong sense of fair play. When Jennifer punished him for something he had done, Joshua said stubbornly, "I'm only four feet tall, but I've got my rights."

He was a miniature Adam. Joshua was athletic, as Adam was. His heroes were the Bebble brothers and Carl Stotz.

"I never heard of them," Jennifer said.

"Where have you *been*, Mom? They invented Little League."

"Oh. *That* Bebble brothers and Carl Stotz."

On weekends, Joshua watched every sports event on television—football, baseball, basketball—it did not matter. In the beginning, Jennifer had let Joshua watch the games alone, but when he tried to discuss the plays with her afterward and Jennifer was completely at sea, she decided she had better watch with him. And so the two of them would sit in front of the television set, munching popcorn and cheering the players.

One day Joshua came in from playing ball, a worried expression on his face, and said, "Mom, can we have a man-to-man talk?"

"Certainly, Joshua."

They sat down at the kitchen table and Jennifer made him a peanut butter sandwich and poured a glass of milk.

"What's the problem?"

His voice was sober and filled with concern. "Well, I heard the guys talkin' and I was just wonderin'—do you think there'll still be sex when I grow up?"

Jennifer had bought a small Newport sailboat, and on weekends she and Joshua would go out on the sound for a sail. Jennifer liked to watch his face when he was at the helm. He wore an excited little smile, which she called his "Eric the Red" smile. Joshua was a natural sailor, like his father. The thought brought Jennifer up sharply. She wondered whether she was trying to live her life with Adam vicariously through Joshua. All the things she was doing with her son—the sailing, the sporting events—were things she had done with his father. Jennifer told herself she was doing them because Joshua liked doing them, but she was not sure she was being completely honest. She watched Joshua sheet in the jib, his cheeks tanned from the wind and the sun, his face beaming, and Jennifer realized that the reasons did not matter. The important thing was that her son loved his life with her. He was not a surrogate for his father. He was his own person and Jennifer loved him more than anyone on earth.

42

Antonio Granelli died and Michael took over full control of his empire. The funeral was lavish, as befitted a man of the Godfather's stature. The heads and members of Families from all over the country came to pay their respects to their departed friend, and to assure the new *capo* of their loyalty and support. The FBI was there, taking photographs, as well as half a dozen other government agencies.

Rosa was heartbroken, because she had loved her father very much, but she took consolation and pride in the fact that her husband was taking her father's place as head of the Family.

Jennifer was proving more valuable to Michael every day. When there was a problem, it was Jennifer whom Michael consulted. Thomas Colfax was becoming an increasingly bothersome appendage.

"Don't worry about him," Michael told Jennifer. "He's going to retire soon."

* * *

The soft chimes of the telephone awakened Jennifer. She lay in bed, listening a moment, then sat up and looked at the digital clock on the nightstand. It was three o'clock in the morning.

She lifted the receiver. "Hello."

It was Michael. "Can you get dressed right away?"

Jennifer sat up straighter and tried to blink the sleep from her eyes. "What's happened?"

"Eddie Santini was just picked up on an armed robbery charge. He's a two-time loser. If they convict him, they'll throw the key away."

"Were there any witnesses?"

"Three, and they all got a good look at him."

"Where is he now?"

"The Seventeenth Precinct."

"I'm on my way, Michael."

Jennifer put on a robe and went down to the kitchen and made herself a steaming pot of coffee. She sat drinking it in the breakfast room, staring out at the night, thinking. *Three witnesses. And they all got a good look at him.*

She picked up the telephone and dialed. "Give me the City Desk."

Jennifer spoke rapidly. "I got some information for you. A guy named Eddie Santini's just been picked up on an armed robbery charge. His attorney's Jennifer Parker. She's gonna try to spring him."

She hung up and repeated the call to two other newspapers and a television station. When Jennifer was through telephoning, she looked at her watch and had another leisurely cup of coffee. She wanted to make certain the photographers had time to get to the precinct on 51st Street. She went upstairs and got dressed.

Before Jennifer left, she went into Joshua's bedroom. His night-light was on. He was sound asleep, the blankets twisted around his restless body. Jennifer gently straightened the blankets, kissed him on the forehead and started to tiptoe out of the room.

"Where you goin'?"

She turned and said, "I'm going to work. Go back to sleep."

"What time is it?"

"It's four o'clock in the morning."

Joshua giggled. "You sure work funny hours for a lady."

She came back to his bedside. "And you sure sleep funny hours for a man."

"Are we going to watch the Mets game tonight?"

"You bet we are. Back to Dreamland."

"Okay, Mom. Have a good case."

"Thanks, pal."

A few minutes later, Jennifer was in her car, on her way into Manhattan.

When Jennifer arrived, a lone photographer from the *Daily News* was waiting. He stared at Jennifer and said, "It's true! You really handling the Santini case?"

"How did you know that?" Jennifer demanded.

"A little birdie, counselor."

"You're wasting your time. No pictures."

She went inside and arranged for Eddie Santini's bail, stalling the proceedings until she was sure the television cameraman and a reporter and photographer had arrived from *The New York Times*. She decided she could not wait for the *Post*.

The police captain on duty said, "There're some reporters and television people out front, Miss Parker. You can go out the back way if you want."

"It's all right," Jennifer said. "I'll handle them."

She led Eddie Santini to the front corridor where the

photographers and reporters were waiting.

She said, "Look, gentlemen, no pictures, please."

And Jennifer stepped aside while the photographer and television cameraman took pictures.

A reporter asked, "What makes this case big enough for you to handle?"

"You'll find out tomorrow. Meanwhile, I would advise you not to use those pictures."

One of the reporters called out, "Come on, Jennifer! Haven't you heard of freedom of the press?"

At noon Jennifer got a call from Michael Moretti. His voice was angry. "Have you seen the newspapers?"

"No."

"Well, Eddie Santini's picture is all over the front pages and on the television news. I didn't tell you to turn this goddamned thing into a circus!"

"I know you didn't. It was my own idea."

"Jesus! What's the point?"

"The point, Michael, is those three witnesses."

"What about them?"

"You said they got a good look at Eddie Santini. Well, when they get up in court to identify him, they're going to have to prove they didn't identify him because they saw his picture all over the newspapers and television."

There was a long silence, and then Michael's voice said admiringly, "I'm a son of a bitch!"

Jennifer had to laugh.

Ken Bailey was waiting in her office that afternoon when Jennifer walked in, and she knew instantly from the look on his face that something was wrong.

"Why didn't you tell me?" Ken demanded.

"Tell you what?"

"About you and Mike Moretti."

Jennifer checked the retort that rose to her lips. Saying *It's none of your business* was too easy. Ken was her friend; he cared. In a way, it was his business. Jennifer remembered it all, the tiny office they had shared, how he had helped her. *I've got a lawyer friend who's been bugging me to serve some subpoenas for him. I haven't got time. He pays twelve-fifty for each subpoena plus mileage. Would you help me out?*

"Ken, let's not discuss this."

His tone was filled with cold fury. "Why not? Everybody else is discussing it. The word is that you're Moretti's girl." His face was pale. "Jesus!"

"My personal life—"

"He lives in a sewer and you brought that sewer into the office! You've got us all working for Moretti and his hoodlums."

"Stop it!"

"I am. That's what I came to tell you. I'm leaving."

His words were a shock. "You can't leave. You're wrong about what you think of Michael. If you'll just meet him, you'll see—"

The moment the words were out, Jennifer knew she had made a mistake.

He looked at her sadly and said, "He's really wrapped you up, hasn't he? I remember you when you knew who you were. That's the girl I want to remember. Say good-bye to Joshua for me."

And Ken Bailey was gone.

Jennifer felt the tears begin to come, and her throat constricted so tightly that she could hardly breathe. She put her head down on the desk and closed her eyes, trying to shut out the hurt.

When she opened her eyes, night had fallen. The office

was in darkness except for the eerie red glow cast by the city lights. She walked over to the window and stared out at the city below. It looked like a jungle at night, with only a dying campfire to keep away the encroaching terrors.

It was Michael's jungle. There was no way out of it.

43

The Cow Palace in San Francisco was a madhouse, filled with noisy, chanting delegates from all over the country. There were three candidates vying for the presidential nomination, and each had done well in the primaries. But the star, the one who outshone them all, was Adam Warner. The nomination was his on the fifth ballot, and it was made unanimous. His party finally had a candidate they could put forward with pride. The incumbent President, the leader of the opposition party, had a low credibility rating and was considered by the majority of people to be inept.

"Unless you take your cock out and pee in front of a camera on the six o'clock news," Stewart Needham told Adam, "you're going to be the next President of the United States."

After his nomination, Adam flew to New York for a meeting at the Regency Hotel with Needham and several influential members of the party. Present in the room was Blair

Roman, head of the second largest advertising agency in the country.

Stewart Needham said, "Blair will be in charge of running the publicity end of your campaign, Adam."

"Can't tell you how glad I am to be aboard." Blair Roman grinned. "You're going to be my third President."

"Really?" Adam was not impressed with the man.

"Let me fill you in on some of the game plan." Blair Roman started pacing the room, swinging an imaginary golf club as he walked. "We're going to saturate the country with television commercials, build an image of you as the man who can solve America's problems. Big Daddy—only a young, good-looking Big Daddy. You get it, Mr. President?"

"Mr. Roman . . ."

"Yes?"

"Would you mind not calling me 'Mr. President'?"

Blair Roman laughed. "Sorry. Slip of the tongue, A.W. In my mind you're already in the White House. Believe me, I know you're the man for the job or I wouldn't be undertaking this campaign. I'm too rich to have to work for money."

Beware of people who say they're too rich to have to work for money, Adam thought.

"*We* know you're the man for the job—now we have to let the *people* know it. If you'll just take a look at these charts I've prepared, I've broken down different sections of the country into various ethnic groups. We're going to send you to key places where you can press the flesh."

He leaned forward into Adam's face and said earnestly, "Your wife is going to be a big asset. Women's magazines will go crazy for stuff on your family life. We're going to *merchandise* you, A.W."

Adam found himself beginning to get irritated. "Just how do you plan to do that?"

"It's simple. You're a product, A.W. We're going to sell you just like we'd sell any other product. We—"

Adam turned to Stewart Needham. "Stewart, could I see you alone?"

"Certainly." Needham turned to the others and said, "Let's break for dinner and meet back here at nine o'clock. We'll continue the discussion then."

When the two men were alone, Adam said, "Jesus, Stewart! He's planning to turn this thing into a circus! 'You're a product, A.W. We're going to sell you just like we'd sell any other product.' He's disgusting!"

"I know how you feel, Adam," Stewart Needham said soothingly, "but Blair gets results. When he said you're his third President, he wasn't kidding. Every President since Eisenhower has had an advertising agency masterminding his campaign. Whether you like it or not, a campaign needs salesmanship. Blair Roman knows the psychology of the public. As distasteful as it may be, the reality is that if you want to be elected to any public office, you have to be sold—you have to be merchandised."

"I hate it."

"That's part of the price you're going to have to pay." He walked over to Adam and put an arm across his shoulder. "All you have to do is keep the objective in mind. You want the White House? All right. We're going to do everything we can to get you there. But you have to do your part. If being the ringmaster in a three-ring circus is part of it, bear with it."

"Do we really need Blair Roman?"

"We need *a* Blair Roman. Blair's as good as there is. Let me handle him. I'll keep him away from you as much as possible."

"I'd appreciate that."

The campaign began. It started with a few television spots and personal appearances and gradually grew bigger and bigger until it spanned the nation. Wherever one went, there was Senator Adam Warner in living color. In every part of the country he could be watched on television, heard on radio, seen on billboards. Law and order was one of the key issues of the campaign, and Adam's crime investigation committee was heavily stressed.

Adam taped one-minute television spots, three-minute television spots and five-minute spots, geared for different sections of the country. The television spots that went to West Virginia dealt with unemployment and the vast supply of underground coal that could make the area prosperous; the television segments for Detroit talked about urban blight; in New York City, the subject was the rising crime rate.

Blair Roman confided to Adam, "All you have to do is hit the highlights, A.W. You don't have to discuss key issues in depth. We're selling the product, and that's *you*."

Adam said, "Mr. Roman, I don't care what your goddamned statistics say. I'm not a breakfast food and I don't intend to be sold like one. I *will* talk about issues in depth because I think the American people are intelligent enough to want to know about them."

"I only—"

"I want you to try to set up a debate between me and the President, to discuss the basic issues."

Blair Roman said, "Right. I'll take a meeting with the President's boys right away, A.W."

"One more thing," Adam said.

"Yes? What's that?"

"Stop calling me A.W."

44

In the mail was a notice from the American Bar Association announcing its annual convention in Acapulco. Jennifer was in the midst of handling half a dozen cases, and ordinarily she would have ignored the invitation, but the convention was going to take place during Joshua's school vacation and Jennifer thought about how much Joshua would enjoy Acapulco.

She said to Cynthia, "Accept. I'll want three reservations." She would take Mrs. Mackey along.

At dinner that evening, Jennifer broke the news to Joshua. "How would you like to go to Acapulco?"

"That's in Mexico," he announced. "On the west coast."

"That's right."

"Can we go to a topless beach?"

"Joshua!"

"Well, they have them there. Being naked is only natural."

"I'll think about it."

"And can we go deep-sea fishing?"

Jennifer visualized Joshua trying to pull in a large marlin and she contained her smile. "We'll see. Some of those fish get pretty big."

"That's what makes it exciting," Joshua explained seriously. "If it's easy, it's no fun. There's no sport to it."

It could have been Adam talking.

"I agree."

"What else can we do there?"

"Well, there's horseback riding, hiking, sightseeing—"

"Let's not go to a bunch of old churches, okay? They all look alike."

Adam saying, *If you've seen one church, you've seen them all.*

The convention began on a Monday. Jennifer, Joshua and Mrs. Mackey flew to Acapulco on Friday morning on a Braniff jet. Joshua had flown many times before, but he was still excited by the idea of airplanes. Mrs. Mackey was petrified with fear.

Joshua consoled her. "Look at it this way. Even if we crash, it'll only hurt for a second."

Mrs. Mackey turned pale.

The plane landed at Benito Juarez Airport at four o'clock in the afternoon, and an hour later the three of them arrived at Las Brisas. The hotel was eight miles outside of Acapulco, and consisted of a series of beautiful pink bungalows built on a hill, each with its private patio. Jennifer's bungalow, like several of the others, had its own swimming pool. Reservations had been difficult to get, for there were half a dozen other conventions and Acapulco was overcrowded, but Jennifer had made a telephone call to one of her corporate clients, and an hour later she had been informed that Las Brisas was eagerly expecting her.

* * *

When they had unpacked, Joshua said, "Can we go into town and hear them talk? I've never been to a country where nobody speaks English." He thought a moment and added, "Unless you count England."

They went into the city and wandered along the Zocalo, the frenetic center of downtown, but to Joshua's disappointment the only language to be heard was English. Acapulco was crowded with American tourists.

They strolled along the colorful market on the main pier opposite Sanborn's in the old part of town, where there were hundreds of stalls selling a bewildering variety of merchandise.

In the late afternoon, they took a *calandria*, a horse-drawn carriage, to Pie de la Cuesta, the sunset beach, and then returned to town.

They had dinner at Armando's Le Club, and it was excellent.

"I *love* Mexican food," Joshua declared.

"I'm glad," Jennifer said. "Only this is French."

"Well, it has a Mexican flavor."

Saturday was a full day. They went shopping in the morning at the Quebrada, where the nicer stores were, and then stopped for a Mexican lunch at Coyuca 22. Joshua said "I suppose you're going to tell me this is French, too."

"No, this is the real thing, gringo."

"What's a gringo?"

"You are, amigo."

They walked by the *fronton* building near the Plaza Caleta, and Joshua saw the billboards advertising jai alai inside.

He stood there, wide-eyed, and Jennifer asked, "Would you like to see the jai alai games?"

Joshua nodded. "If it's not too expensive. If we run out of money we won't be able to get home."

"I think we can manage."

They went inside and watched the furious play of the teams. Jennifer placed a bet for Joshua and his team won.

When Jennifer suggested returning to the hotel, Joshua said, "Gosh, Mom, can't we see the divers first?"

The hotel manager had mentioned them that morning.

"Are you sure you wouldn't like to rest, Joshua?"

"Oh, if you're too tired, sure. I keep forgettin' about your age."

That did it. "Never mind my age." Jennifer turned to Mrs. Mackey. "Are you up to it?"

"Certainly," Mrs. Mackey groaned.

The diving act was at La Quebrada cliffs. Jennifer, Joshua and Mrs. Mackey stood on a public viewing platform while divers carrying lighted torches plunged one hundred and fifty feet into a narrow, rock-lined cove, timing their descent to coincide with the arrival of incoming breakers. The slightest miscalculation would have meant instant death.

When the exhibition was over, a boy came around to collect a donation for the divers.

"Uno peso, por favor."

Jennifer gave him five pesos.

She dreamed about the divers that night.

Las Brisas had its own beach, La Concha, and early Sunday morning Jennifer, Joshua and Mrs. Mackey drove down in one of the pink canopied jeeps that the hotel supplied to its guests. The weather was perfect. The harbor was a sparkling blue canvas dotted with speedboats and sailboats.

Joshua stood at the edge of the terrace, watching the water skiers race by.

"Did you know water skiing was invented in Acapulco, Mom?"

"No. Where did you hear that?"

"I either read it in a book or I made it up."

"I vote for 'made it up.'"

"Does that mean I can't go water skiing?"

"Those speedboats are pretty fast. Aren't you afraid?"

Joshua looked out at the skiers skimming over the water. "That man said, 'I'm going to send you home to Jesus.' And then he put a nail in my hand."

It was the first reference he had made to the terrible ordeal he had gone through.

Jennifer knelt and put her arms around her son. "What made you think of that, Joshua?"

He shrugged. "I don't know. I guess because Jesus walked on water and everyone out there is walking on water." He saw the stricken look on his mother's face. "I'm sorry, Mom. I don't think about it much, honest."

She hugged him tightly and said, "It's all right, darling. Of course you can go water skiing. Let's have lunch first."

The outdoor restaurant at La Concha had wrought-iron tables set with pink linen, shaded by pink-and-white-striped umbrellas. Lunch was a buffet and the long serving table was crowded with an incredible assortment of dishes. There were fresh lobster and crab and salmon, selections of cold and hot meats, salads, a variety of raw and cooked vegetables, cheeses and fruits. There was a separate table for an array of freshly baked desserts. The two women watched Joshua fill and empty his plate three times before he sat back, satisfied.

"It's a very good restaurant," he pronounced. "I don't care *what* kind of food it is." He stood up. "I'll go check on the water skiing."

Mrs. Mackey had barely picked at her food.

"Are you feeling all right?" Jennifer asked. "You haven't eaten anything since we arrived."

Mrs. Mackey leaned forward and whispered darkly, "I don't want Montezuma's Revenge!"

"I don't think you have to worry about that in a place like this."

"I don't hold with foreign food," Mrs. Mackey sniffed.

Joshua ran back to the table and said, "I got a boat. Is it okay if I go now, Mom?"

"Don't you want to wait a while?"

"What for?"

"Joshua, you'll sink with all you've eaten."

"Test me!" he begged.

While Mrs. Mackey watched on shore, Jennifer and Joshua got into the speedboat and Joshua had his first water-skiing lesson. He spent the first five minutes falling down, and after that, performed as though born to water skiing. Before the afternoon was over, Joshua was doing tricks on one ski, and finally skiing on his heels with no skis.

They spent the rest of the afternoon lazing on the sand and swimming.

On the way back to Las Brisas in the jeep, Joshua snuggled up against Jennifer and said, "You know something, Mom? I think this was probably the best day of my whole life."

Michael's words flashed through her mind: *I just want you to know this has been the greatest night of my life.*

Early Monday morning Jennifer arose and got dressed to attend the convention. She put on a full-flowing dark green skirt and an off-the-shoulder blouse embroidered in giant red roses, that revealed her patina of suntan. She studied herself in the mirror and was pleased. Despite the fact that her son thought she was over the hill, Jennifer was aware that she looked like Joshua's beautiful thirty-four-year-old sister. She laughed to herself and thought that this vacation was one of her better ideas.

Jennifer said to Mrs. Mackey, "I have to go to work now. Take good care of Joshua. Don't let him get too much sun."

* * *

The huge convention center was a cluster of five buildings joined by roofed circulation terraces, sprawled over thirty-five acres of lush greenery. The carefully tended lawns were studded with pre-Columbian statues.

The Bar Association Convention was being held in Teotihuacan, the main hall, holding an audience of seventy-five hundred people.

Jennifer went to the registration desk, signed in and entered the large hall. It was packed. In the crowd she spotted dozens of friends and acquaintances. Nearly all of them had changed from conservative business suits and dresses to brightly colored sport shirts and pants. It was as though everyone was on vacation. *There is a good reason*, Jennifer thought, *for holding the convention in a place like Acapulco instead of in Chicago or Detroit.* They could take off their stiff collars and somber ties and let themselves go under a tropical sun.

Jennifer had been given a program at the door but, deep in conversation with some friends, had paid no attention to it.

A deep voice boomed over the loudspeaker, "Attention, please! Would you all please take your seats? Attention, please! We would like to get the meeting started. Would you sit down, please!"

Reluctantly the small groups began to break up as people started to find seats. Jennifer looked up to see that half a dozen men had mounted the dais.

In the center was Adam Warner.

Jennifer stood there, frozen, as Adam walked to the chair next to the microphone and took a seat. She felt her heart begin to pound. The last time she had seen Adam had been when they had had lunch at the little Italian restaurant, the day he had told her that Mary Beth was pregnant.

Jennifer's immediate impulse was to flee. She had had no

idea Adam would be there and she could not bear the thought of facing him. Adam and his son being in the same city filled her with panic. Jennifer knew she had to get out of there quickly.

She turned to leave as the chairman announced over the loudspeaker, "If the rest of you ladies and gentlemen will take your seats, we will begin."

As people around her began sitting down, Jennifer found herself conspicuous by standing. Jennifer slid into a seat, determined to slip away at the first opportunity.

The chairman said, "We are honored this morning to have as our guest speaker a nominee for the presidency of the United States. He is a member of the New York Bar Association and one of the most distinguished members of the United States Senate. It is with great pride that I introduce *Senator Adam Warner.*"

Jennifer watched as Adam rose, accepting the warm applause. He stepped to the microphone and looked out across the room. "Thank you, Mr. Chairman, ladies and gentlemen."

Adam's voice was rich and resonant, and he had an air of authority that was mesmerizing. The silence in the room was total.

"There are many reasons why we are gathered here today." He paused. "Some of us like to swim and some of us like to snorkel. . . ." There was a swell of appreciative laughter. "But the main reason we are here is to exchange ideas and knowledge and discuss new concepts. Today, lawyers are under greater attack than at any time in my memory. Even the Chief Justice of the Supreme Court has been sharply critical of our profession."

Jennifer loved the way he used *our*, making him one with the rest of them. She let his words wash over her, content just to look at him, to watch the way he moved, to hear his voice. At one point he stopped to run his fingers through his hair, and it gave Jennifer a sharp pang. It was a gesture of Joshua's. Adam's son was only a few miles away and Adam would never know.

Adam's voice grew stronger, more forceful. "Some of you in this room are criminal lawyers. I must admit I have always considered that to be the most exciting branch of our profession. Criminal lawyers often deal in life and death. It is a very honorable profession and one of which we can all be proud. However"—his voice grew hard—"there are some of them"—and now Jennifer noticed that Adam was disassociating himself by his choice of the pronoun—"who are a disgrace to the oath they have taken. The American system of jurisprudence is based on the inalienable right of every citizen to have a fair trial. But when the law is made a mockery of, when lawyers spend their time and energy, imagination and skill, finding ways to defy that law, finding ways to subvert justice, then I think it is time something must be done." Every eye in the room was fastened on Adam as he stood there, eyes blazing. "I am speaking, ladies and gentlemen, out of personal experience and a deep anger for some of the things I see happening. I am currently heading a Senate committee conducting an investigation of organized crime in the United States. My committee has found itself thwarted and frustrated time after time by men who hold themselves to be more powerful than the highest enforcement agencies of our nation. I have seen judges suborned, the families of witnesses threatened, key witnesses disappear. Organized crime in our country is like a deadly python that is squeezing our economy, swallowing up our courts, threatening our very lives. The great majority of lawyers are honorable men and women doing honorable jobs, but I want to give warning to that small minority who think their law is above our law: You're making a grave mistake and you're going to pay for that mistake. Thank you."

Adam sat down to a tumultuous burst of applause that became a standing ovation. Jennifer found herself on her feet applauding with the others, but her thoughts were on Adam's last words. It was as though he had been speaking directly to her. Jennifer turned and headed toward the exit, pushing her way through the crowd.

As Jennifer approached the door she was hailed by a Mexican lawyer with whom she had worked a year earlier.

He kissed her hand gallantly and said, "What an honor to have you in our country again, Jennifer. I insist you have dinner with me this evening."

Jennifer and Joshua had planned to go to The Maria Elena that night to watch the native dancers. "I'm sorry, Luis. I have an engagement."

His large, liquid eyes showed his disappointment. "Tomorrow then?"

Before Jennifer could answer, an assistant district attorney from New York was at her side.

"Hello, there," he said. "What are you doing slumming with the common folk? How about having dinner with me tonight? There's a Mexican disco called Nepentha, where they have a glass floor lit from underneath and a mirror overhead."

"It sounds fascinating, thanks, but I'm busy tonight."

A few moments later Jennifer found herself surrounded by lawyers she had worked for and against all over the country. She was a celebrity and they all wanted to talk to her. It was half an hour before Jennifer could break free. She hurried toward the lobby, and as she moved to the exit, Adam was walking toward her, surrounded by the press and secret service men. Jennifer tried to retreat, but it was too late. Adam had seen her.

"Jennifer!"

For an instant she thought of pretending she had not heard him, but she could not embarrass him in front of the others. She would say hello quickly and be on her way.

She watched as Adam moved toward her, saying to the press, "I have no more statements to make now, ladies and gentlemen."

A moment later Adam was touching her hand, looking into her eyes, and it was as though they had never been apart. They stood there in the lobby, surrounded by people, and yet they might have been completely alone. Jennifer had no idea how long they stood there looking at each other.

Finally, Adam said, "I—I think we'd better have a drink."

"It would be wiser if we didn't." She had to get out of this place.

Adam shook his head. "Overruled."

He took her arm and led her into the crowded bar. They found a table at the rear of the room.

"I've called you and I've written to you," Adam said. "You never called me back and my letters were returned."

He was watching her, his eyes filled with questions. "There isn't a day that's gone by that I haven't thought about you. Why did you disappear?"

"It's part of my magic act," Jennifer said lightly.

A waiter came to take their order. Adam turned to Jennifer. "What would you like?"

"Nothing. I really have to leave, Adam."

"You can't go now. This is a celebration. The anniversary of the revolution."

"Theirs or ours?"

"What's the difference?" He turned to the waiter. "Two margaritas."

"No. I—" *All right*, she thought, *one drink*. "Make mine a double," Jennifer said recklessly.

The waiter nodded and left.

"I read about you all the time," Jennifer said. "I'm very proud of you, Adam."

"Thank you." Adam hesitated. "I've been reading about you, too."

She responded to the tone in his voice. "But you're not proud of me."

"You seem to have a lot of Syndicate clients."

Jennifer found her defenses going up. "I thought your lecture was over."

"This isn't a lecture, Jennifer. I'm concerned about you. My committee is after Mike Moretti, and we're going to get him."

Jennifer looked around the bar filled with lawyers. "For God's sake, Adam, we shouldn't be having this discussion, especially in here."

"Where, then?"

"Nowhere. Michael Moretti is my client. I can't discuss him with you."

"I want to talk to you. Where?"

She shook her head. "I told you I——"

"I have to talk about us."

"There is no us." Jennifer started to rise.

Adam put his hand on her arm. "Please, don't go. I can't let you go. Not yet."

Reluctantly, Jennifer sat down.

Adam's eyes were fastened on her face. "Do you ever think of me?"

Jennifer looked up at him and did not know whether to laugh or cry. Did she ever think of him! He lived in her house. She kissed him good morning every day, made his breakfast, went sailing with him, loved him. "Yes," Jennifer said finally, "I think of you."

"I'm glad. Are you happy?"

"Of course." She knew she had said it too quickly. She made her voice more casual. "I have a successful practice, I'm well off financially, I travel a great deal, I see a lot of attractive men. How is your wife?"

"She's fine." His voice was low.

"And your daughter?"

He nodded, and there was pride in his face. "Samantha's wonderful. She's just growing up too fast."

She would be Joshua's age.

"You've never married?"

"No."

There was a long moment, and then Jennifer tried to continue, but she had hesitated too long. It was too late. Adam had looked into her eyes and he had known instantly.

He clasped her hand in his. "Oh, Jennifer. Oh, my darling!"

Jennifer could feel the blood rushing to her face. She had known all along that this would be a terrible mistake.

"I have to go, Adam. I have an appointment."

"Break it," he urged.

"I'm sorry. I can't." All she wanted to do was get out of there, to get her son away from there, to flee back home.

Adam was saying, "I'm supposed to fly back to Washington on an afternoon plane. I can arrange to stay over if you'll see me tonight."

"No. No!"

"Jennifer, I can't let you go again. Not like this. We have to talk. Just have dinner with me."

He was pressing her hand tighter. She looked at him and fought with all her strength and found herself weakening.

"Please, Adam," she begged. "We shouldn't be seen together. If you're after Michael Moretti—"

"This has nothing to do with Moretti. A friend of mine has offered me the use of his boat. It's called the *Paloma Blanca.* It's docked at the Yacht Club. Eight o'clock."

"I won't be there."

"I will. I'll be waiting for you."

Across the room, at the crowded bar, Nick Vito was sitting with two Mexican *puttanas* a friend had delivered to him. Both were pretty and coarse and underage, the way Nick

Vito liked them. His friend had promised they would be special, and he had been right. They were rubbing up against him, whispering exciting promises in his ear, but Nick Vito was not listening. He was staring across the room at the booth where Jennifer Parker and Adam Warner were seated.

"Why don't we go up to your room now, *querido*?" one of the girls suggested to Nick.

Nick Vito was tempted to walk over to Jennifer and the stranger she was with and say hello, but both girls had their hands between his legs and were stroking him. He was going to make one hell of a sandwich.

"Yeah, let's go upstairs," Nick Vito said.

45

The *Paloma Blanca* was a motor sailer and it shone proud and white and gleaming in the moonlight. Jennifer approached it slowly, looking around to make sure that no one had observed her. Adam had told her he would elude the secret service men and apparently he had succeeded. After Jennifer had seated Joshua and Mrs. Mackey at Maria Elena, she had taken a taxi and had had the driver drop her off two blocks before the pier.

Jennifer had picked up the phone half a dozen times to call Adam to say she would not meet him. She had started to write a note, then had torn it up. From the moment she had left Adam at the bar, Jennifer had been in an agony of indecision. She thought of all the reasons why she should not see Adam. Nothing good could possibly come of it, and it could lead to a tremendous amount of harm. Adam's career could be at stake. He was riding on a crest of public popularity, an idealist in a time of cynicism, the country's hope for the future. He was the darling of the media, but the same press that had helped to create him would be out there waiting to push him into the abyss if he betrayed their image of him.

And so Jennifer had made up her mind not to see him. She was another woman, living a different life, and she belonged to Michael now. . . .

Adam was waiting for her at the top of the gangplank.

"I was so afraid you weren't coming," he said.

And she was in his arms and they were kissing.

"What about the crew, Adam?" Jennifer finally asked.

"I sent them away. Do you still remember how to sail?"

"I still remember."

They hoisted the sail and sheeted in for a starboard tack, and ten minutes later the *Paloma Blanca* was heading through the harbor toward the open sea. For the first half hour they were busy navigating, but there was not a moment when they were not acutely aware of each other. The tension kept mounting, and they both knew that what was going to happen was inevitable.

When they finally cleared the harbor and were sailing into the moonlit Pacific, Adam moved to Jennifer's side and put his arms around her.

They made love on the deck under the stars, with the soft, fragrant breeze cooling their naked bodies.

The past and the future were swept away and there was only the present holding the two of them together in its swiftly fleeting moments. For Jennifer knew that this night in Adam's arms was not a beginning; it was an ending. There was no way to bridge the worlds that separated them. They had traveled too far from each other and there was no road back. Not now, not ever. She would always have a part of Adam in Joshua, and that would be enough for her, would have to be enough for her.

This night would have to last her the rest of her life.

They lay there together, listening to the gentle susurration of the sea against the boat.

Adam said, "Tomorrow—"

"Don't talk," Jennifer whispered. "Just love me, Adam."

She covered his lips with small kisses and fluttered her fingers delicately along the strong, lean lines of his body. She moved her hands down in slow circles until she found him, and her fingers began to stroke him.

"Oh God, Jennifer," Adam whispered, and his mouth began to move slowly down her naked body.

46

"The cocksucker kept givin' me the *malocchio*," little Salvator Fiore was complaining, "so I finally hadda burn 'im."

Nick Vito laughed, for anyone who was stupid enough to fool around with the Little Flower had to be out to lunch. Nick Vito was enjoying himself in the farmhouse kitchen with Salvatore Fiore and Joseph Colella, talking over old times, waiting for the conference in the living room to end. The midget and the giant were his best friends. They had gone through the fire together. Nick Vito looked at the two men and thought happily, *They're like my brothers*.

"How's your cousin Pete?" Nick asked the giant Colella.

"He did cancer and he's under the hammer, but he's gonna be okay."

"He's beautiful."

"Yeah. Pete's good people; he's just had a little bad luck. He was back-up man on a bank job, but it wasn't his stick, and the fuckin' cops tagged him and put him away. He did hard time. The hacks tried to turn him around but they was spinnin' their wheels."

"Hell, yes. Pete's got class."

"Yeah. He always went for big bucks, big broads and big cars."

From the living room there came the sound of raised, angry voices. They listened a moment.

"Sounds like Colfax has a bug up his ass."

Thomas Colfax and Michael Moretti were alone in the room, discussing a large gambling operation that the Family was about to start in the Bahamas. Michael had put Jennifer in charge of making the business arrangements.

"You can't do it, Mike," Colfax protested. "I know all the boys down there. She doesn't. You must let me handle it." He knew he was talking too loudly, but he was unable to control himself.

"Too late," Michael said.

"I don't trust the girl. Neither did Tony."

"Tony's not with us anymore." Michael's voice was dangerously quiet.

Thomas Colfax knew that this was the moment to back down. "Sure, Mike. All I'm saying is that I think the girl's a mistake. I grant you she's smart, but I'm warning you, before she's through she could send us all away."

It was Thomas Colfax whom Michael was concerned about. The Warner Crime Commission investigation was in full swing. When they reached Colfax, how long would the old man stand up to them before he cracked? He knew more about the Family than Jennifer Parker could ever know. Colfax was the one who could destroy them all, and Michael did not trust him.

Thomas Colfax was saying, "Send her away for awhile. Just until this investigation cools down. She's a woman. If they start putting pressure on her, she'll talk."

Michael studied him and made his decision. "All right, Tom. Maybe you've got a point there. Jennifer may not be dangerous, but on the other hand, if she's not with us a hundred percent, why take unnecessary chances?"

"That's all I'm suggesting, Mike." Thomas Colfax rose from his chair, relieved. "You're doing the wise thing."

"I know." Michael turned toward the kitchen and yelled out, "Nick!"

A moment later Nick Vito appeared.

"Drive the *consigliere* back to New York, will you, Nick?"

"Sure thing, boss."

"Oh. On the way I want you to stop and deliver a package for me." He turned to Thomas Colfax. "You don't mind?"

"Of course not, Mike." He was flushed with his victory.

Michael Moretti said to Nick Vito, "Come on. It's upstairs."

Nick followed Michael up to his bedroom. When they were inside, Michael closed the door.

"I'd like you to make a stop before you get out of New Jersey."

"Sure, boss."

"I want you to drop off some garbage." Nick Vito looked puzzled. "The *consigliere*," Michael explained.

"Oh. Okay. Whatever you say."

"Take him out to the dump. There won't be anyone around at this time of night."

Fifteen minutes later the limousine was headed for New York. Nick Vito was at the wheel, with Thomas Colfax in the passenger seat beside him.

"I'm glad Mike decided to sideline that bitch," Thomas Colfax said.

Nick glanced sideways at the unsuspecting lawyer seated beside him. "Uh-huh."

Thomas Colfax looked at the gold Baume & Mercier watch

on his wrist. It was three o'clock in the morning, long past his bedtime. It had been a long day and he was tired. *I'm getting too old for these battles*, he thought.

"How far out are we driving?"

"Not far," Nick mumbled.

Nick Vito's mind was in a turmoil. Killing was a part of his job and it was a part he enjoyed, because of the sense of power it gave him. Nick felt like a god when he killed; he was omnipotent. But tonight, he was bothered. He could not understand why he had been ordered to blow away Thomas Colfax. Colfax was the *consigliere*, the man everyone turned to when they were in trouble. Next to the Godfather, the *consigliere* was the most important man in the Organization. He had kept Nick out of the slammer a dozen times.

Shit! Nick thought. *Colfax was right. Mike should never have let a woman come into the business. Men thought with their brains. Women thought with their pussies. Oh, how he'd love to get his hands on Jennifer Parker! He'd fuck her until she cried 'Uncle' and then—*

"Watch it! You're going off the road!"

"Sorry." Nick quickly steered the car back into his lane.

The dump was a short distance ahead. Nick could feel the perspiration popping out under his arms. He glanced over again at Thomas Colfax.

Snuffing him out would be a cinch. It would be like putting a baby to sleep but, goddamn it! it was the wrong baby! Someone was giving Mike a hand job. This was a sin. It was like murdering his old man.

He wished he could have talked it over with Salvatore and Joe. They could have told him what to do.

Nick could see the dump ahead to the right of the highway. His nerves began to tighten, just as they always did before a hit. He pressed his left arm against his side and felt the reassuring bulk of the short-barreled .38 Smith & Wesson nestling there.

"I could use a good night's sleep," Thomas Colfax yawned.

"Yeah." He was going to get a long, long sleep.

The car was nearing the dump now. Nick checked the rear-view mirror and scanned the road ahead. There were no cars in sight.

He put his foot on the brake suddenly and said, "Goddamn it, it feels like I'm getting a flat."

He brought the car to a stop, opened the door and stepped out onto the road. He slipped the gun out of its holster and held it at his side. Then he moved around to the passenger side of the car and said, "Could you give me a hand?"

Thomas Colfax opened the door and stepped out. "I'm not very good at—" He saw the raised gun in Nick's hand and stopped. He tried to swallow. "W-What's the matter, Nick?" His voice cracked. "What have I done?"

That was the question that had been burning inside Nick Vito's mind all evening. Someone was running a game on Mike. Colfax was on *their* side, he was one of them. When Nick's younger brother had gotten in trouble with the Feds, it had been Colfax who had stepped in and saved the boy. He had even gotten him a job. *I owe him, goddamn it*, Nick thought.

He let his gun hand drop. "Honest to God, I don't know, Mr. Colfax. It ain't right."

Thomas Colfax looked at him a moment and sighed. "Do what you have to do, Nick."

"Jesus, I can't do this. You're my *consigliere*."

"Mike will kill you if you let me go."

Nick knew that Colfax was telling the truth. Michael Moretti was not a man to tolerate disobedience. Nick thought of Tommy Angelo. Angelo had been the wheel man on a fur heist. Michael had ordered him to take the car they had used and have it crushed in a compactor in a New Jersey junkyard the Family owned. Tommy Angelo had been in a hurry to keep a date, so he had dumped the car on an East Side street, where investigators had found it. Angelo had disappeared the next day, and the story was that his body had been put in the trunk of an old Chevy and compacted. No one crossed Michael Moretti and lived. *But there is a way*, Nick thought.

"Mike don't have to know it," Nick said. His usually slow brain was working rapidly, with an unnatural clarity. "Look," he said, "all you gotta do is blow the country. I'll tell Mike I buried you under the garbage so they'll never find you. You can hide out in South America or somewhere. You must have a little dough stashed away."

Thomas Colfax tried to keep the sudden hope out of his voice. "I have plenty, Nick. I'll give you whatever—"

Nick shook his head fiercely. "I ain't doin' this for money. I'm doin' it because"—*How could he put it into words?*—"I got *respect* for you. The only thing is, you gotta protect me. Can you catch a mornin' plane to South America?"

Thomas Colfax said, "No problem, Nick. Just drop me off at my house. My passport's there."

Two hours later, Thomas Colfax was on an Eastern Airlines jet. It was bound for Washington, D.C.

47

It was their last day in Acapulco, a perfect morning with warm, soft breezes playing melodies through the palm trees. The beach at La Concha was crowded with tourists greedily soaking up the sun before returning to the routine of their everyday lives.

Joshua came running up to the breakfast table wearing a bathing suit, his athletic little body fit and tan. Mrs. Mackey lumbered along behind him.

Joshua said, "I've had plenty of sufficient time to digest my food, Mom. Can I go water skiing now?"

"Joshua, you just finished eating."

"I have a very high metabolism rate," he explained earnestly. "I digest food fast."

Jennifer laughed. "All right. Have a good time."

"I will. Watch me, huh?"

Jennifer watched as Joshua raced along the pier to a waiting speedboat. She saw him engage the driver in earnest conversation, and then they both turned to look at Jennifer. She signaled an okay, and the driver nodded and Joshua began to put on water skis.

The motor boat roared into life and Jennifer looked up to see Joshua beginning to rise on his water skis.

Mrs. Mackey said proudly, "He's a natural athlete, isn't he?"

At that moment, Joshua turned to wave at Jennifer and lost his balance, falling against the pilings. Jennifer leaped to her feet and began racing toward the pier. An instant later, she saw Joshua's head appear above the surface of the water and he looked at her, grinning.

Jennifer stood there, her heart beating fast, and watched as Joshua put the water skis back on. As the boat circled and began to move forward again, it gained enough momentum to pull Joshua to his feet. He turned once to wave at Jennifer and then was racing away on top of the waves. She stood there watching, her heart still pounding from fright. If anything happened to him . . . She wondered whether other mothers loved their children as much as she loved her son, but it did not seem possible. She would have died for Joshua, killed for him. *I have killed for him*, she thought, *with the hand of Michael Moretti.*

Mrs. Mackey was saying, "That could have been a nasty fall."

"Thank God it wasn't."

Joshua was out on the water for an hour. When the boat pulled back into the slip, he let go of the tow rope and gracefully skied up onto the sand.

He ran over to Jennifer, filled with excitement. "You should have seen the accident, Mom. It was incredible! A big sailboat tipped over and we stopped and saved their lives."

"That's wonderful, son. How many lives did you save?"

"There were six of them."

"And you pulled them out of the water?"

Joshua hesitated. "Well, we didn't exactly pull them out of the water. They were kinda sittin' on the side of their boat. But they probably would have starved to death if we hadn't come along."

Jennifer bit her lip to keep from smiling, "I see. They were very lucky you came along, weren't they?"

"I'll say."

"Did you hurt yourself when you fell, darling?"

"Course not." He felt the back of his head. "I got a little bump."

"Let me feel it."

"What for? You know what a bump feels like."

Jennifer reached down and gently ran her hand along the back of Joshua's head.

Her fingers found a large lump. "It's as big as an egg, Joshua."

"It's nothing."

Jennifer rose to her feet. "I think we'd better get started back to the hotel."

"Can't we stay a little while longer?"

"I'm afraid not. We have to pack. You don't want to miss your ball game Saturday, do you?"

He sighed. "No. Old Terry Waters is just waitin' to take my place."

"No chance. He pitches like a girl."

Joshua nodded smugly. "He does, doesn't he?"

When they returned to Las Brisas, Jennifer telephoned the manager and asked him to send a doctor to the room. The doctor arrived thirty minutes later, a portly, middle-aged Mexican dressed in an old-fashioned white suit. Jennifer admitted him into the bungalow.

"How may I serve you?" Dr. Raul Mendoza asked.

"My son had a fall this morning. He has a nasty bump on his head. I want to make sure he's all right."

Jennifer led him into Joshua's bedroom, where he was packing a suitcase.

"Joshua, this is Doctor Mendoza."

Joshua looked up and asked, "Is somebody sick?"

"No. No one's sick, my lad. I just wanted the doctor to take a look at your head."

"Oh, for Pete's sake, Mom! What's the matter with my head?"

"Nothing. I would just feel better if Doctor Mendoza checked it over. Humor me, will you?"

"Women!" Joshua said. He looked at the doctor suspiciously. "You're not going to stick any needles in me or anything, are you?"

"No, senor, I am a very painless doctor."

"That's the kind I like."

"Please sit down."

Joshua sat on the edge of the bed and Dr. Mendoza ran his fingers over the back of Joshua's head. Joshua winced with pain but he did not cry out. The doctor opened his medical bag and took out an ophthalmoscope. "Open your eyes wide, please."

Joshua obeyed. Dr. Mendoza stared through the instrument.

"You see any naked dancin' girls in there?"

"Joshua!"

"I was just askin'."

Dr. Mendoza examined Joshua's other eye. "You are fit as a fiddle. That is the American slang expression, no?" He rose to his feet and closed his medical bag. "I would put some ice on that," he told Jennifer. "Tomorrow the boy will be fine."

It was as though a heavy load had been lifted from Jennifer's heart. "Thank you," she said.

"I will arrange the bill with the hotel cashier, senora. Goodbye, young man."

"Good-bye, Doctor Mendoza."

When the doctor had gone, Joshua turned to his mother. "You sure like to throw your money away, Mom."

"I know. I like to waste it on things like food, your health—"

"I'm the healthiest man on the whole team."

"Stay that way."

He grinned. "I promise."

They boarded the six o'clock plane to New York and were back in Sands Point late that night. Joshua slept all the way home.

48

The room was crowded with ghosts. Adam Warner was in his study, preparing a major television campaign speech, but it was impossible to concentrate. His mind was filled with Jennifer. He had been able to think of nothing else since he had returned from Acapulco. Seeing her had only confirmed what Adam had known from the beginning. He had made the wrong choice. He should never have given up Jennifer. Being with her again was a reminder of all that he had had, and thrown away, and he could not bear the thought of it.

He was in an impossible situation. A *no-win* situation, Blair Roman would have called it.

There was a knock on the door and Chuck Morrison, Adam's chief assistant, came in carrying a cassette. "Can I talk to you a minute, Adam?"

"Can it wait, Chuck? I'm in the middle of—"

"I don't think so." There was excitement in Chuck Morrison's voice.

"All right. What's so urgent?"

Chuck Morrison moved closer to the desk. "I just got a telephone call. It could be some crazy, but if it's not, then Christmas came early this year. Listen to this."

He placed a cassette in the machine on Adam's desk, pressed a switch and the tape began to play.

What did you say your name was?

It doesn't matter. I won't talk to anyone except Senator Warner.

The Senator is busy just now. Why don't you drop him a note and I'll see to—

No! Listen to me. This is very important. Tell Senator Warner I can deliver Michael Moretti to him. I'm taking my life in my hands making this phone call. Just give Senator Warner the message.

All right. Where are you?

I'm at the Capitol Motel on Thirty-second Street. Room Fourteen. Tell him not to come until after dark and to make sure he's not followed. I know you're taping this. If you play the tape for anyone but him, I'm a dead man.

There was a click and the tape ended.

Chuck Morrison said, "What do you think?"

Adam frowned. "The town is full of cranks. On the other hand, our boy sure knows what bait to use, doesn't he? Michael—by God—Moretti!"

At ten o'clock that night, Adam Warner, accompanied by four secret service men, cautiously knocked at the door of Room 14 of the Capitol Motel. The door was opened a crack.

The moment Adam saw the face of the man inside, he turned to the men with him and said, "Stay outside. Don't let anyone near this place."

The door opened wider and Adam stepped into the room.

"Good evening, Senator Warner."

"Good evening, Mr. Colfax."

The two men stood there appraising each other.

Thomas Colfax looked older than when Adam had last seen him, but there was another difference, almost indefinable. And then Adam realized what it was. Fear. Thomas Colfax was frightened. He had always been a self-assured, almost arrogant man, and now that self-assurance had disappeared.

"Thank you for coming, Senator." Colfax's voice sounded strained and nervous.

"I understand you want to talk to me about Michael Moretti."

"I can lay him in your lap."

"You're Moretti's attorney. Why would you want to do that?"

"I have my reasons."

"Let's say I decided to go along with you. What would you expect in return?"

"First, complete immunity. Second, I want to get out of the country. I'll need a passport and papers—a new identity."

So Michael Moretti had put out a contract on Thomas Colfax. It was the only explanation for what was happening. Adam could hardly believe his good fortune. It was the best possible break he could have had.

"If I get immunity for you," Adam said, "—and I'm not promising you anything yet—you understand that I would expect you to go into court and testify fully. I would want everything you've got."

"You'll have it."

"Does Moretti know where you are now?"

"He thinks I'm dead." Thomas Colfax smiled nervously. "If he finds me, I will be."

"He won't find you. Not if we make a deal."

"I'm putting my life in your hands, Senator."

"Frankly," Adam informed him, "I don't give a damn about you. I want Moretti. Let's lay down the ground rules.

If we come to an agreement, you'll get all the protection the government can give you. If I'm satisfied with your testimony, we'll provide you with enough money to live in any country you choose under an assumed identity. In return for that, you'll have to agree to the following: I'll want full testimony from you regarding Moretti's activities. You'll have to testify before a grand jury, and when we bring Moretti to trial, I'll expect you to be a witness for the government. Agreed?"

Thomas Colfax looked away. Finally he said, "Tony Granelli must be turning over in his grave. What happens to people? Whatever happened to honor?"

Adam had no answer. This was a man who had cheated the law a hundred times, who had gotten paid killers off scot-free, who had helped mastermind the activities of the most vicious crime organization the civilized world had ever known. And he was asking what had happened to honor.

Thomas Colfax turned to Adam. "We have a deal. I want it in writing, and I want it signed by the Attorney General."

"You'll have it." Adam looked around the shabby motel room. "Let's get out of this place."

"I won't go to a hotel. Moretti's got ears everywhere."

"Not where you're going."

At ten minutes past midnight a military truck and two jeeps, manned by armed marines, rolled up in front of Room 14. Four military police went into the room and came out a few moments later, closely escorting Thomas Colfax into the back of the truck. The procession pulled away from the motel with one jeep in front of the truck and the second jeep following in the rear, headed for Quantico, Virginia, thirty-five miles south of Washington. The three-car caravan proceeded at high speed, and forty minutes later arrived at the United States Marine Corps base at Quantico.

The commandant of the base, Major General Roy Wallace, and a detail of armed marines were waiting at the gate. As the caravan came to a stop, General Wallace said to the captain in charge of the detail, "The prisoner is to be taken directly to the stockade. There is to be no conversation with him."

Major General Wallace watched as the procession entered the compound. He would have given a month's pay to know the identity of the man in the truck. The general's command consisted of a 310-acre Marine Corps air station and part of the FBI's Academy, and was the principal center for training officers of the United States Marine Corps. He had never before been asked to house a civilian prisoner. It was totally outside regulations.

Two hours earlier, he had received a telephone call from the commandant of the Marine Corps himself. "There's a man on his way to your base, Roy. I want you to clear out the stockade and keep him in there until further orders."

General Wallace thought he had heard wrong. "Did you say *clear out the stockade*, sir?"

"That's right. I want this man in there by himself. No one is to be allowed near him. I want you to double the stockade guard. Understood?"

"Yes, General."

"One more thing, Roy. If anything happens to that man while he's in your custody, I'm going to have roasted ass for breakfast."

And the commandant had hung up.

General Wallace watched the truck lumber toward the stockade, then returned to his office and rang for his aide, Captain Alvin Giles.

"About the man we're putting in the stockade—" General Wallace said.

"Yes, General?"

"Our primary objective is his safety. I want you to hand-pick the guards yourself. No one else is to go near him. No visitors, no mail, no packages. Understood?"

"Yes, sir."

"I want you personally to be in the kitchen when his food is being prepared."

"Yes, General."

"If anyone shows any undue curiosity about him, I want that reported to me immediately. Any questions?"

"No, sir."

"Very good, Al. Stay on top of it. If anything goes wrong, I'll have roasted ass for breakfast."

49

Jennifer was awakened by the soft drumming of the early morning rain, and she lay in bed listening to it gently hammering against the house.

She glanced at the alarm clock. It was time to begin her day.

Half an hour later, Jennifer walked downstairs into the dining room to join Joshua for breakfast. He was not there.

Mrs. Mackey came in from the kitchen. "Good morning, Mrs. Parker."

"Good morning. Where's Joshua?"

"He seemed so tired that I thought I'd let him sleep a little longer. He doesn't have to start back to school until tomorrow."

Jennifer nodded. "Good idea."

She ate her breakfast and went upstairs to say good-bye to Joshua. He was lying in his bed, sound asleep.

Jennifer sat on the edge of the bed and said softly, "Hey, sleepyhead, do you want to say good-bye?"

He slowly opened one eye. "Sure, friend. 'Bye." His voice

was heavy with sleep. "Do I have to get up?"

"No. Tell you what. Why don't you laze around today? You can stay inside and have fun. It's raining too hard to go outdoors."

He nodded drowsily. "Okay, Mom."

His eyes closed again and he was asleep.

Jennifer spent the afternoon in court, and by the time she finished and arrived home it was after seven o'clock. The rain, which had been a drizzle all day, was coming down in torrents, and as Jennifer drove up the driveway, the house looked like a besieged castle surrounded by a gray, churning moat.

Mrs. Mackey opened the front door and helped Jennifer out of her dripping raincoat.

Jennifer shook the damp out of her hair and said, "Where's Joshua?"

"He's asleep."

Jennifer looked at Mrs. Mackey with concern. "Has he been sleeping all day?"

"Heavens, no. He's been up and around. I fixed his dinner, but when I went upstairs to get him he had dozed off again, so I just thought I'd let him be."

"I see."

Jennifer went upstairs into Joshua's room and quietly entered. Joshua was asleep. Jennifer leaned over and touched his forehead. He had no fever; his color was normal. She felt his pulse. There was nothing wrong except her imagination. She was letting it run away with her. Joshua had probably been playing too hard all day and it was natural that he was tired. Jennifer slipped out of the room and returned downstairs.

"Why don't you make some sandwiches for him, Mrs. Mackey? Leave them at the side of the bed. He can have them when he wakes up."

Jennifer had dinner at her desk, working on briefs, preparing a trial deposition for the next day. She thought about calling Michael to tell him she was back, but she was hesitant about speaking to him so soon after the night with Adam . . . He was too perceptive. It was after midnight when she finished reading. She stood up and stretched, trying to relieve the tension in her back and neck. She put her papers in her attaché case, turned out the lights and went upstairs. She passed by Joshua's room and looked in. He was still asleep.

The sandwiches on the stand beside the bed were untouched.

The following morning when Jennifer went down to breakfast, Joshua was there, dressed and ready for school.

"Morning, Mom."

"Good morning, darling. How are you feeling?"

"Great. I was really tired. Must have been that Mexican sun."

"Must have been."

"Acapulco's really neat. Can we go back there on my next vacation?"

"I don't know why not. You glad to be getting back to school?"

"I refuse to answer on the grounds that it might incriminate me."

In the middle of the afternoon, Jennifer was taking a deposition when Cynthia buzzed.

"I'm sorry to disturb you, but there's a Mrs. Stout on the line and—"

Joshua's homeroom teacher. "I'll take it."

Jennifer picked up the telephone. "Hello, Mrs. Stout. Is anything wrong?"

"Oh no, everything's fine, Mrs. Parker. I didn't mean to

alarm you. I just thought I might suggest to you that it would be a good idea if Joshua got more sleep."

"What do you mean?"

"He slept through most of his classes today. Miss Williams and Mrs. Toboco both mentioned it. Perhaps you could see to it that he gets to bed a bit earlier."

Jennifer stared at the telephone. "I—yes, I'll do that."

Slowly, she replaced the receiver and turned to the people in the room watching her.

"I—I'm sorry," she said. "Excuse me."

She hurried out to the reception room. "Cynthia, find Dan. Ask him to finish the deposition for me. Something has come up."

"All—" Jennifer was already out the door.

She drove home like a madwoman, exceeding the speed limit, going through red lights, her mind filled with visions of something terrible having happened to Joshua. The drive seemed interminable and when her house appeared in the distance, Jennifer half expected to see the driveway filled with ambulances and police cars. The driveway was deserted. Jennifer pulled up beside the front door and hurried into the house.

"Joshua!"

He was in the den watching a baseball game on television.

"Hi, Mom. You're home early. Did you get fired?"

Jennifer stood in the doorway staring at him, her body flooding with relief. She felt like an idiot.

"You should have seen the last inning. Craig Swan was fantastic!"

"How do you feel, son?"

"Great."

Jennifer put her hand on his forehead. He had no fever.

"You sure you're all right?"

"Of course I am. Why do you look so funny? You worried about something? You want to have a man-to-man talk?"

She smiled. "No, darling, I just—does anything hurt you?"

He groaned. "I'll say. The Mets are losing six to five. You know what happened in the first inning?"

He began an excited replay of his favorite team's exploits. Jennifer stood there looking at him, adoring him, thinking, *Damn my imagination! Of course he's all right.*

"You go on and watch the rest of the game. I'll see about dinner."

Jennifer went into the kitchen, lighthearted. She decided to make a banana cake, one of Joshua's favorite desserts.

Thirty minutes later, when Jennifer returned to the study, Joshua was lying on the floor, unconscious.

The ride to Blinderman Memorial Hospital seemed to take forever. Jennifer sat in the back of the ambulance clutching Joshua's hand. An attendant was holding an oxygen mask over Joshua's face. He had not regained consciousness. The ambulance's siren was keening, but the traffic was heavy and the ambulance went slowly while curious people gaped through the windows, staring at the white-faced woman and the unconscious boy. It seemed to Jennifer a sickening violation of privacy.

"Why can't they use one-way glass in ambulances?" Jennifer demanded.

The attendant looked up, startled. "Ma'am?"

"Nothing . . . nothing."

After what seemed an eternity, the ambulance pulled up at the emergency entrance at the back of the hospital. Two interns were waiting at the door. Jennifer stood there helpless, watching as Joshua was removed from the ambulance and transferred to a gurney.

An attendant asked, "Are you the boy's mother?"

"Yes."

"This way, please."

What followed was a blurred kaleidoscope of sound and

light and movement. Jennifer watched Joshua being wheeled down a long, white corridor to an X-ray room.

She started to follow, but the attendant said, "You'll have to check him in first."

A thin woman at the front desk was saying to Jennifer, "How do you plan to pay for this? Do you have Blue Cross or some other form of insurance?"

Jennifer wanted to scream at the woman, wanted to get back to Joshua's side, but she forced herself to answer the questions, and when they were over and Jennifer had filled out several forms, the woman allowed Jennifer to leave.

She hurried down to the X-ray room and went inside. The room was empty. Joshua was gone. Jennifer ran back to the hallway, looking around frantically. A nurse passed by.

Jennifer clutched her arm. "Where's my son?"

The nurse said, "I don't know. What's his name?"

"Joshua. Joshua Parker."

"Where did you leave him?"

"He—he was having X rays—he—" Jennifer was beginning to be incoherent. "What have they done with him! Tell me!"

The nurse took a closer look at Jennifer and said, "Wait here, Mrs. Parker. I'll see if I can find out."

She came back a few minutes later. "Dr. Morris would like to see you. Come this way, please."

Jennifer found that her legs were trembling. It was difficult to walk.

"Are you all right?" The nurse was staring at her.

Her mouth was dry with fear. "I want my son."

They came to a room filled with strange-looking equipment. "Wait here, please."

Dr. Morris came in a few moments later. He was a very fat man with a red face and nicotine stains on his fingers. "Mrs. Parker?"

"Where's Joshua?"

"Step in here a moment, please." He led Jennifer into a

small office across from the room with the strange-looking equipment. "Please sit down."

Jennifer took a seat. "Joshua is—it's—it's nothing serious, is it, Doctor?"

"We don't know yet." His voice was surprisingly soft for a man of his size. "I need some information. How old is your son?"

"He's only seven."

The *only* had slipped out, a reprimand to God.

"Was he in an accident recently?"

A vision flashed through Jennifer's mind of Joshua turning to wave and losing his balance and hitting the pilings. "He—he had a water skiing accident. He bumped his head."

The doctor was making notes. "How long ago was that?"

"I—a few—a few days ago. In Acapulco." It was difficult to think straight.

"Did he seem all right after the accident?"

"Yes. He had a lump on the back of his head, but otherwise he—he seemed fine."

"Did you notice any lapse of memory?"

"No."

"Any personality changes?"

"No."

"No convulsions or stiff neck or headache?"

"No."

The doctor stopped writing and looked up at Jennifer. "I've had an X ray done, but it's not enough. I want to do a CAT scan."

"A—?"

"It's a new computerized machine from England that takes pictures of the inside of the brain. I may want to make some additional tests afterward. Is that all right with you?"

"If-if-if"—she was stammering—"it's necessary. It-it won't hurt him, will it?"

"No. I may also need to do a spinal puncture."

He was frightening her.

She forced the question out of her mouth. "What do you think it is? What's the matter with my son?" She did not recognize the sound of her own voice.

"I'd prefer not to make any guesses, Mrs. Parker. We'll know in an hour or two. He's awake now, if you'd like to see him."

"Oh, please!"

A nurse led her to Joshua's room. He was lying in bed, a pale small figure. He looked up as Jennifer entered.

"Hi, Mom."

"Hi there." She sat at the edge of his bed. "How do you feel?"

"Kind of funny. It's like I'm not here."

Jennifer reached out and took his hand. "You're here, darling. And I'm with you."

"I can see two of everything."

"Did—did you tell the doctor that?"

"Uh-huh. I saw two of him. I hope he doesn't send you two bills."

Jennifer gently put her arms around Joshua and hugged him. His body seemed frail and shrunken.

"Mom?"

"Yes, darling?"

"You won't let me die, will you?"

Her eyes were suddenly stinging. "No, Joshua, I won't let you die. The doctors are going to make you well and then I'm going to take you home."

"Okay. And you promised we can go back to Acapulco sometime."

"Yes. As soon as—"

He was asleep.

* * *

Dr. Morris came into the room with two men wearing white jackets.

"We'd like to begin the tests now, Mrs. Parker. They won't take long. Why don't you wait in here and make yourself comfortable?"

Jennifer watched them take Joshua out of the room. She sat on the edge of the bed, feeling as though she had been physically beaten. All the energy had drained out of her. She sat there, staring at the white wall, in a trance.

A moment later a voice said, "Mrs. Parker—"

Jennifer looked up and Dr. Morris was there.

"Please go ahead and do the tests," Jennifer said.

He looked at her oddly. "We've finished."

Jennifer looked at the clock on the wall. She had been sitting there for two hours. Where had the time gone? She looked into the doctor's face, reading it, searching for the small, telltale signs that would reveal whether he had good news or bad news for her. How many times had she done this before, reading the faces of jurors, knowing in advance from their expressions what the verdict would be? A hundred times? Five hundred? Now, because of the panic raging within her, Jennifer could tell nothing. Her body began to shake uncontrollably.

Dr. Morris said, "Your son is suffering from a subdural hematoma. In layman's terms, there has been a massive trauma to his brain."

Her throat was suddenly so dry that no words could come out.

"Wh—" She swallowed and tried again. "What does that—?" She could not finish the sentence.

"I want to operate immediately. I'll need your permission."

He was playing some kind of cruel prank on her. In a moment he was going to smile and tell her that Joshua was fine. I. was just punishing you, Mrs. Parker, for wasting my time. There's nothing wrong with your son except that he needs sleep. He's a growing boy. You mustn't take up our time when we have patients to look after who are really ill. He was going to smile at her and say, "You can take your son home now."

Dr. Morris was going on. "He's young and his body seems strong. There's every reason to hope the operation will be a success."

He was going to cut open her baby's brain, tear into it with his sharp instruments, perhaps destroy whatever it was that made Joshua, Joshua. Perhaps—kill him.

"No!" It was an angry cry.

"You won't give us permission to operate?"

"I—" Her mind was so confused she could not think. "Wh—what will happen if you don't operate?"

Dr. Morris said simply, "Your son will die. Is the boy's father here?"

Adam! Oh, how she wanted Adam, how she wanted to feel his arms around her, comforting her. She wanted him to tell her that everything was going to be all right, that Joshua was going to be fine.

"No," Jennifer replied finally, "he's not. I—I give you my permission. Go ahead with the operation."

Dr. Morris filled out a form and handed it to her. "Would you sign this, please?"

Jennifer signed the paper without looking at it. "How long will it take?"

"I won't know until I open—" He saw the look on her face. "Until I begin the operation. Would you like to wait here?"

"No!" The walls were closing in on her, choking her. She could not breathe. "Is there a place where I can pray?"

It was a small chapel with a painting of Jesus over the altar. The room was deserted except for Jennifer. She knelt, but she was unable to pray. She was not a religious person;

why would God listen to her now? She tried to quiet her mind
so that she could talk to God, but her fear was too strong; it
had taken complete possession of her. She kept berating herself mercilessly. *If I only hadn't taken Joshua to Acapulco,*
she thought . . . *If I hadn't let him go water skiing . . .
If I hadn't trusted that Mexican doctor . . . If. If. If.* She
made bargains with God. *Make him well again and I'll do
anything you ask of me.*

She denied God. *If there was a God, would he do this to a
child who had never harmed anyone? What kind of God lets
innocent children die?*

Finally, out of sheer exhaustion, Jennifer's thoughts slowed
and she remembered what Dr. Morris had said. *He's young
and his body seems strong. There's every reason to hope the
operation will be a success.*

*Everything was going to be all right. Of course it was.
When this was over, she would take Joshua away someplace
where he could rest. Acapulco, if he liked. They would read
and play games and talk . . .*

When finally Jennifer was too exhausted to think any
longer, she slumped into a seat, her mind a dazed blank,
empty. Someone was touching her arm and she looked up
and Dr. Morris was standing over her. Jennifer looked into
his face and had no need to ask any questions.

She lost consciousness.

50

Joshua lay on a narrow metal table, his body eternally still. He looked as though he were peacefully asleep, his handsome young face filled with secret, far-off dreams. Jennifer had seen that expression a thousand times as Joshua had snuggled into his warm bed while Jennifer had sat at his side, studying the face of her young son, filled with a love that was so strong it choked her. And how many times had she gently tucked his blanket around him to protect him from the cold of the night?

Now the cold was deep inside Joshua's body. He would never be warm again. Those bright eyes would never open again and look at her, and she would never see the smile on his lips, or hear his voice, or feel his small, strong arms around her. He was naked beneath the sheet.

Jennifer said to the doctor, "I want you to cover him with a blanket. He'll be cold."

"He can't—" and Dr. Morris looked into Jennifer's eyes and what he saw there made him say, "Yes, of course, Mrs. Parker," and he turned to the nurse and said, "Get a blanket."

There were half a dozen people in the room, most of them in white uniforms and they all seemed to be talking to Jennifer, but she could not hear what they were saying. It was as though she were in a bell jar, shut off from the rest of them. She could see their lips moving, but there was no sound. She wanted to yell at them to go away, but she was afraid of frightening Joshua. Someone was shaking her arm and the spell was broken and the room was suddenly filled with a roar of sound, and everyone seemed to be talking at once.

Dr. Morris was saying, ". . . necessary to perform an autopsy."

Jennifer said quietly, "If you touch my son again, I'll kill you."

And she smiled at everyone around her because she did not want them to become angry with Joshua.

A nurse was trying to persuade Jennifer to leave the room, but she shook her head. "I can't leave him alone. Someone might turn out the lights. Joshua is afraid of the dark."

Someone squeezed her arm and Jennifer felt the prick of a needle, and a moment later a feeling of great warmth and peace engulfed her, and she slept.

When Jennifer awakened, it was late afternoon. She was in a small room in the hospital and someone had undressed her and clothed her in a hospital gown. She rose to her feet and dressed and went looking for Dr. Morris. She was supernaturally calm.

Dr. Morris said, "We'll make all the funeral arrangements for you, Mrs. Parker. You won't have to—"

"I'll take care of it."

"Very well." He hesitated, embarrassed. "About the autopsy, I know you didn't mean what you said this morning. I—"

"You're wrong."

During the next two days, Jennifer went through all the

rituals of death. She went to a local undertaker and made the funeral arrangements. She selected a white casket with a satin lining. She was self-possessed and dry-eyed and, later, when she tried to think about it, she had no recollection of any of it. It was as though someone else had taken over her body and mind and was acting for her. She was in a state of deep shock, hiding behind its protective shell to keep from going insane.

As Jennifer was leaving the undertaker's office, he said, "If there are any special clothes you would like your son buried in, Mrs. Parker, you can have them brought in and we'll dress him."

"I'll dress Joshua myself."

He looked at her in surprise. "If you wish, of course, but—" He watched her leave, wondering if she knew what it was like to dress a corpse.

Jennifer drove home, pulled the car into the driveway and entered the house.

Mrs. Mackey was in the kitchen, her eyes red, her face twisted with grief. "Oh, Mrs. Parker! I can't believe—"

Jennifer neither saw nor heard her. She moved past Mrs. Mackey and walked upstairs into Joshua's room. It was exactly the same. Nothing had changed, except that the room was empty. Joshua's books and games and baseball and skiing equipment were all there, waiting for him. Jennifer stood in the doorway, staring at the room, trying to remember why she had come there. *Oh, yes. Clothes for Joshua.* She walked over to the closet. There was a dark blue suit she had bought for him on his last birthday. Joshua had worn it the evening she had taken him to dinner at Lutèce. She remembered that evening vividly. Joshua had looked so grown up and Jennifer had thought with a pang, *One day he'll be sitting here with the girl he's going to marry.* That day would never come now. There would be no growing up. No girl. No life.

Next to the blue suit were several pairs of blue jeans and slacks and tee shirts, one with the name of Joshua's baseball team on it. Jennifer stood there running her hands aimlessly over the clothes, losing all track of time.

Mrs. Mackey appeared at her side. "Are you all right, Mrs. Parker?"

Jennifer said politely, "I'm fine, thank you, Mrs. Mackey."

"Can I help you with something?"

"No, thank you. I'm going to dress Joshua. What do you think he would like to wear?" Her voice was bright and cheerful, but her eyes were dead.

Mrs. Mackey looked into them and was frightened. "Why don't you lie down a bit, dear? I'm going to call the doctor."

Jennifer's hands moved across the clothes hanging in the closet. She pulled the baseball uniform from the hanger. "I think Joshua would like this. Now, what else will he need?"

Mrs. Mackey watched helplessly as Jennifer went over to the dresser and took out underwear, socks and a shirt. *Joshua needed these things because he was going away on a holiday. A long holiday.*

"Do you think he'll be warm enough in this?"

Mrs. Mackey burst into tears. "Please, don't," she begged. "Leave those things. I'll take care of it."

But Jennifer was already on her way downstairs with them.

The body was in the mortuary's slumber room. They had placed Joshua on a long table that dwarfed the small figure.

When Jennifer returned with Joshua's clothes, the mortician tried once again. "I spoke to Doctor Morris. We both agree that it would be much better, Mrs. Parker, if you would let us handle this. We're quite used to it and—"

Jennifer smiled at him. "Get out."

He swallowed and said, "Yes, Mrs. Parker."

Jennifer waited until he had left the room and then she turned to her son.

She looked into his sleeping face and said, "Your mother is going to take care of you, my darling. You're going to wear your baseball uniform. You'll like that, won't you?"

She pulled the sheet away and looked at his naked, shrunken body, and then she began to dress him. She started to slip his shorts on him and she recoiled from the icy cold of his flesh. It was as hard and stiff as marble. Jennifer tried to tell herself that this piece of chill, lifeless flesh was not her son, that Joshua was away somewhere, warm and happy, but she was unable to make herself believe it. It was Joshua on this table. Jennifer's body began to shake. It was as though the cold inside Joshua had gotten inside her, chilling her to the marrow. She said fiercely to herself, *Stop it! Stop it! Stop it! Stop it! Stop it!*

She took deep, shuddering breaths, and when she was finally calmer she resumed dressing her son, talking to him all the while. She pulled his shorts on, then his trousers, and when she lifted him up to put his shirt on, his head slipped and fell against the table and Jennifer cried out, "I'm sorry, Joshua, forgive me!" and she began to weep.

It took Jennifer almost three hours to dress Joshua. He was wearing his baseball uniform and favorite tee shirt, white socks and sneakers. The baseball cap shadowed his face, so Jennifer finally laid it on his chest. "You can carry it with you, my darling."

When the undertaker came and looked into the room, Jennifer was standing over the dressed body, holding Joshua's hand and talking to him.

The man walked over and said gently, "We'll take care of him now."

Jennifer took one last look at her son. "Please be careful with him. He hurt his head, you know."

The funeral was simple. Jennifer and Mrs. Mackey were

the only ones there to watch the small white coffin being lowered into the freshly dug grave. Jennifer had thought of telling Ken Bailey, for Ken and Joshua had loved each other, but Ken was no longer in their lives.

When the first shovelful of dirt had been thrown on the coffin, Mrs. Mackey said, "Come along, dear. I'll take you home."

Jennifer said politely, "I'm fine. Joshua and I won't be needing you any more, Mrs. Mackey. I'll see that you get a year's wages and I'll give you a reference. Joshua and I thank you for everything."

Mrs. Mackey stood there staring as Jennifer turned and walked away. She walked carefully, standing very straight, as though she were going down an eternal corridor wide enough for only one person.

The house was still and peaceful. She went up to Joshua's room and closed the door behind her and lay on his bed, looking at all the things that belonged to him, all the things he had loved. Her whole world was in this room. There was nothing for her to do now, nowhere for her to go. There was only Joshua. Jennifer started with the day he was born and relived all her memories of him.

Joshua taking his first steps . . . Joshua saying *car-car* and *Mama, go play with your toys* . . . Joshua going off to school alone for the first time, a tiny, brave figure . . . Joshua lying in bed with the measles, his body racked with misery . . . Joshua hitting a home run and winning the game for his team . . . Joshua sailing . . . Joshua feeding an elephant at the zoo . . . Joshua singing *Shine On, Harvest Moon* on Mother's Day . . . The memories flowed on, home movies in her mind. They stopped on the day Jennifer and Joshua were to leave for Acapulco.

Acapulco . . . where she had seen Adam and made love with him. She was being punished because she had thought only of herself. *Of course*, Jennifer thought. *This is my punishment. This is my hell.*

And she started all over again, beginning with the day Joshua was born . . . Joshua taking his first steps . . . Joshua saying *car-car*, and *Mama, go play with your toys* . . .

Time slipped away. Sometimes Jennifer would hear a telephone ring in some distant recess of the house, and once she heard someone knocking at the front door, but those sounds had no meaning for her. She would not allow anything to interrupt her being with her son. She stayed in the room, eating nothing and drinking nothing, lost in her own private world with Joshua. She had no sense of time, no idea how long she lay there.

It was five days later that Jennifer heard the front door bell again and the sound of someone pounding on the door, but she paid no attention. Whoever it was would go away and leave her alone. Dimly she heard the sound of glass breaking, and a few moments later the door to Joshua's room burst open and Michael Moretti loomed in the doorway.

He took one look at the gaunt, hollow-eyed figure staring up at him from the bed and he said, "Jesus Christ!"

It took all of Michael Moretti's strength to get Jennifer out of the room. She fought him hysterically, punching him and clawing at his eyes. Nick Vito was waiting downstairs and it took the two of them to force Jennifer into the car. Jennifer had no idea who they were or why they were there. She only knew that they were taking her away from her son. She tried to tell them that she would die if they did this to her, but she was finally too exhausted to fight any longer. She fell asleep.

When Jennifer awakened, she was in a bright, clean room with a picture window with a view of a mountain and a blue lake in the distance. A uniformed nurse was seated in a chair next to the bed, reading a magazine. She looked up as Jennifer opened her eyes.

"Where am I?" It hurt her throat to speak.

"You're with friends, Miss Parker. Mr. Moretti brought you here. He's been very concerned about you. He'll be so pleased to know you're awake."

The nurse hurried out of the room. Jennifer lay there, her mind blank, willing herself not to think. But the memories began to return, unbidden, and there was nowhere to hide from them, nowhere to escape to. Jennifer realized that she had been trying to commit suicide without actually having the courage to do it. She simply had wanted to die and was willing it to happen. Michael had saved her. It was ironic. Not Adam, but Michael. She supposed it was unfair to blame Adam. She had kept the truth from him, had kept him ignorant of the son who had been born and who was now dead. Joshua was dead. Jennifer could face that now. The pain was deep and agonizing, and she knew it was a pain that would be with her for as long as she lived. But she could bear it. She would have to. It was justice, demanding its payment.

Jennifer heard footsteps and looked up. Michael had come into the room. He stood there, looking at her with wonder. He had been like a wild man when Jennifer had disappeared. He had nearly been out of his mind for fear that something had happened to her.

He walked over to her bed and looked down at her. "Why didn't you tell me?" Michael sat down on the side of the bed. "I'm sorry."

She took his hand. "Thank you for bringing me here. I—think I was a little crazy."

"A little."

"How long have I been here?"

"Four days. The doctor's been feeding you intravenously."

Jennifer nodded, and even that small movement caused great effort. She felt inordinately weary.

"Breakfast is on the way. He gave me orders to fatten you up."

"I'm not hungry. I don't think I ever want to eat again."

"You'll eat."

And to Jennifer's surprise, Michael was right. When the nurse brought her soft-boiled eggs and toast and tea on a tray, Jennifer found she was famished.

Michael stayed there and watched her, and when Jennifer was finished Michael said, "I've got to go back to New York to take care of a few things. I'll return in a couple of days."

He leaned over and kissed her gently. "See you Friday." He slowly traced his fingers across her face. "I want you well, quick. You hear?"

Jennifer looked at him and said, "I hear."

51

The large conference room at the United States Marine Corps base was filled to overflowing. Outside the room, a squad of armed guards was on the alert. Inside was an extraordinary gathering. A special grand jury was seated in chairs against the wall. On one side of a long table sat Adam Warner, Robert Di Silva and the assistant director of the FBI. Across from them sat Thomas Colfax.

Bringing the grand jury to the base had been Adam's idea.

"It's the only way we can be sure of protecting Colfax."

The grand jury had agreed to Adam's suggestions, and the secret session was about to begin.

Adam said to Thomas Colfax, "Would you identify yourself, please?"

"My name is Thomas Colfax."

"What is your occupation, Mr. Colfax?"

"I'm an attorney, licensed to practice in the State of New York, as well as in many other states in this country."

"How long have you been practicing law?"

"For more than thirty-five years."

"Do you have a general practice?"

"No, sir. I have one client."

"Who is your client?"

"For most of those thirty-five years it was Antonio Granelli, now deceased. His place was taken by Michael Moretti. I represent Michael Moretti and his Organization."

"Are you referring to organized crime?"

"I am, sir."

"Because of the position you held for so many years, is it a fair assumption to say that you are in a unique position to know the inner workings of what we shall call the Organization?"

"Very little went on there that I did not know about."

"And criminal activities were involved?"

"Yes, Senator."

"Would you describe the nature of some of those activities?"

For the next two hours, Thomas Colfax spoke. His voice was steady and sure. He named names, places and dates, and at times his recital was so fascinating that the people in the room forgot where they were, caught up in the horror stories Colfax was telling.

He talked of murder contracts given out, of witnesses killed so they could not testify; of arson, mayhem, white slavery— it was a catalogue out of Hieronymus Bosch. For the first time, the innermost operation of the largest crime syndicate in the world was being exposed, laid bare for everyone to see.

Occasionally, Adam or Robert Di Silva would ask a question, prompting Thomas Colfax, having him fill in gaps wherever necessary.

The session was going far better than Adam could have wished when suddenly, near the end, with only a few minutes left, the catastrophe occurred.

One of the men on the grand jury had asked a question about a money-laundering operation.

"That happened about two years ago. Michael kept me away from some of the later stuff. Jennifer Parker handled that."

Adam froze.

Robert Di Silva said, "Jennifer Parker?" There was a bursting eagerness in his question.

"Yes, sir." A vindictive note crept into Thomas Colfax's voice. "She's the Organization's house counsel now."

Adam wanted desperately to quiet him, to keep what he was saying off the record, but it was too late. Di Silva was going for the jugular vein and nothing would stop him.

"Tell us about her," Di Silva said tightly.

Thomas Colfax went on. "Jennifer Parker's involved in setting up dummy corporations, laundering money . . ."

Adam tried to break in. "I don't—"

". . . murder."

The word hung in the room.

Adam broke the silence. "We—we have to stick to the facts, Mr. Colfax. You're not trying to tell us that Jennifer Parker was involved in a killing?"

"That's exactly what I'm telling you. She ordered a hit on a man who kidnapped her son. The man's name was Frank Jackson. She told Moretti to kill him and he did."

There was an excited murmur of voices.

Her son! Adam was thinking: *There has to be some mistake.*

He stammered, "I think—I think we have enough evidence without hearsay. We—"

"It's not hearsay," Thomas Colfax assured him. "I was in the room with Moretti when she called."

Adam's hands under the table were pressing together so hard that they were drained of blood. "The witness looks tired. I think that's enough for this session."

Robert Di Silva said to the special grand jury, "I'd like to make a suggestion about procedure . . ."

Adam was not listening. He was wondering where Jennifer was. She had disappeared again. Adam had repeatedly tried to find her. But now he was desperate. He had to reach her, and quickly.

52

The largest undercover operation in law enforcement in the United States began to move ahead.

The Federal Strike Force Against Organized Crime and Racketeering worked side by side with the FBI, the Postal and Customs Services, the Internal Revenue Service, the Federal Bureau of Narcotics, and half a dozen other agencies.

The scope of the investigation included murder, conspiracy to commit murder, racketeering, extortion, income tax evasion, union frauds, arson, loan-sharking and drugs.

Thomas Colfax had given them the key to a Pandora's box of crime and corruption that was going to help wipe out a major part of organized crime.

Michael Moretti's Family would be hardest hit, but the evidence touched dozens of other Families around the country.

Across the United States and abroad, government agents were quietly questioning friends and business associates of the men on their lists. Agents in Turkey, Mexico, San Salvador, Marseilles and Honduras were liaising with their counterparts, giving them information on illegal activities taking place in those countries. Small-time crooks were pulled into the net, and when they talked they were given their freedom in exchange for evidence against the top crime figures. It was all being handled discreetly, so that the main quarry would have no warning of the storm that was about to break over their heads.

As chairman of the Senate Investigating Committee, Adam Warner received a steady stream of visitors at his home in Georgetown, and the sessions in his study often lasted until the small hours of the morning. There was little doubt that when this was over and Michael Moretti's Organization was broken, the presidential race would be an easy victory for Adam.

He should have been a happy man. He was miserable, facing the greatest moral crisis of his life. Jennifer Parker was deeply involved, and Adam had to warn her, to tell her to escape while she still had a chance. And yet, he had another obligation: an obligation to the committee that bore his name, an obligation to the United States Senate itself. He was Jennifer's prosecutor. How could he be her protector? If he warned her and it was discovered, it would destroy the credibility of his investigating committee and everything it had accomplished. It would destroy his future, his family.

Adam had been stunned by Colfax's mention of Jennifer having a child.

He knew he had to speak to Jennifer.

Adam dialed her office number and a secretary said, "I'm sorry, Mr. Adams, Miss Parker is not in."

"It's—it's very important. Do you know where I can reach her?"

"No, sir. Can someone else help you?"

No one could help him.

* * *

During the next week, Adam tried to reach Jennifer several times each day. Her secretary would only say, "I'm sorry, Mr. Adams, but Miss Parker is away from the office."

Adam was sitting in the study starting to call Jennifer for the third time that day when Mary Beth walked into the room. Adam casually replaced the receiver.

Mary Beth walked up to him and ran her fingers through his hair. "You look tired, darling."

"I'm fine."

She moved over to a suede armchair across from Adam's desk and sat down. "It's all coming together, isn't it, Adam?"

"It looks that way."

"I hope it's over soon, for your sake. The strain must be terrible."

"I'm bearing up under it, Mary Beth. Don't worry about me."

"But I do worry. Jennifer Parker's name is on that list, isn't it?"

Adam looked at her sharply. "How did you know that?"

She laughed. "Angel, you've turned this house into a public meeting place. I can't help but hear a little of what goes on. Everybody seems so terribly excited about catching Michael Moretti and his woman friend." She watched Adam's face, but there was no reaction.

Mary Beth looked at her husband fondly and thought, *How naïve men are.* She knew more about Jennifer Parker than Adam did. It had always amazed Mary Beth how brilliant a man could be in business or politics, and yet be so silly when it came to women. Look how many truly great men had been married to cheap little floozies. Mary Beth understood about her husband having an affair with Jennifer Parker. After all, Adam was a very attractive and desirable man. And like all men, he was susceptible. Her philosophy was to forgive and never forget.

Mary Beth knew what was best for her husband. Everything she did was for Adam's own good. Well, when all this was over, she would take Adam away somewhere. He *did* look tired. They would leave Samantha with the housekeeper and go someplace romantic. Perhaps Tahiti.

Mary Beth glanced out the window and saw two of the secret service men talking. She had mixed feelings about their presence. Mary Beth disliked the intrusion on her privacy, but at the same time, their being there was a reminder that her husband was a candidate for the presidency of the United States. No, how foolish of her. Her husband was going to *be* the next President of the United States. Everyone said so. The idea of living in the White House was so tangible that just thinking about it warmed her. Her favorite occupation, while Adam was busy with all his meetings, was to redecorate the White House. She would sit alone in her room for hours, changing furniture around in her mind, planning all the exciting things she was going to do when she became First Lady.

She had seen the rooms that most visitors were not allowed in: the White House Library with its almost three thousand books, the China Room and the Diplomatic Reception Room, and the family quarters and the seven guest bedrooms on the second floor.

She and Adam would live in that house, become a part of its history. Mary Beth shuddered at the thought of how close Adam had come to throwing away their chances because of that Parker woman. Well, that was all over, thank God.

She watched Adam now as he sat at his desk, looking drawn and haggard.

"Can I fix you a cup of coffee, darling?"

Adam started to say no, then changed his mind. "That would be nice."

"It will just take a jiffy."

The moment Mary Beth left the room, Adam picked up the telephone again and began to dial. It was evening and he knew Jennifer's office was closed, but there should be someone at the answering service. After what seemed an interminable period of time, the operator answered.

"This is urgent," Adam said. "I've been trying to reach Jennifer Parker for several days. This is Mr. Adams."

"One moment, please." The voice came back on the line. "I'm sorry, Mr. Adams. I have no word on where Miss Parker is. Do you want to leave a message?"

"No." Adam slammed down the receiver, filled with frustration, knowing that even if he did leave a message for Jennifer to call him, there was no way she could return that call.

He sat in his den, looking out at the night, thinking about the dozens of arrest warrants that would soon be drawn up. One of them would be for murder.

It would have Jennifer's name on it.

It was five days before Michael Moretti returned to the mountain cabin where Jennifer was staying. She had spent those days resting, eating, taking long walks around the paths. When she heard Michael's car drive up, Jennifer went out to greet him.

Michael looked her over and said, "You look a lot better."

"I feel better. Thank you."

They walked along the path leading to the lake.

Michael said, "I have something for you to do."

"What is it?"

"I want you to leave for Singapore tomorrow."

"Singapore?"

"An airline steward was picked up at the airport there, carrying a load of coke. His name is Stefan Bjork. He's in jail. I want you to bail him out before he starts talking."

"All right."

"Get back as fast as you can. I'll miss you."

He drew her close and kissed her very softly on her lips, then whispered, "I love you, Jennifer."

And she knew that he had never uttered those words to anyone before.

But it was too late. It was finished. Something had died in her forever, and she was left with only the guilt and the loneliness. She had made up her mind to tell Michael that she was leaving. There would be no Adam and no Michael. She had to go away somewhere, alone, and start over. She had a debt to pay. She would do this last thing for Michael and tell him her plans when she returned.

She left for Singapore the next morning.

53

Nick Vito, Tony Santo, Salvatore Fiore and Joseph Colella were having lunch at Tony's Place. They sat at a front booth, and every time the door opened they automatically glanced up to check out the newcomers. Michael Moretti was in the back room, and while there was no current conflict among the Families, it was always better to play it safe.

"What happened to Jimmy?" the giant Joseph Colella was asking.

"*Astutatu-morte*," Nick Vito told him. "The dumb son of a bitch fell for the sister of a detective. The broad was stacked, I'll give her that. She and her dick brother talked Jimmy into a flip. Jimmy arranged for a sit-down with Mike and he wore a wire hidden in his pants leg."

"So what happened?" Fiore asked.

"What happened was Jimmy got so nervous he had to pee. When he opened up his fly, the fuckin' wire came out."

"Oh, shit!"

"That's what Jimmy did. Mike turned him over to Gino.

440

He used Jimmy's wire to strangle him. He went out *suppilu suppilu*—very slowly."

The door opened and the four men looked up. It was the newspaper boy with the afternoon *New York Post*.

Joseph Colella called out, "Over here, sonny." He turned to the others. "I wanna check the lineup at Hialeah. I got a hot horse runnin' today."

The newspaper boy, a weather-beaten man in his seventies, handed Joseph Colella a paper and Colella gave him a dollar. "Keep the change."

That was what Michael Moretti would have said. Joe Colella started to open the paper and Nick Vito's eye was caught by a photograph on the front page.

"Hey!" he said. "I seen that guy before!"

Tony Santo took a look over Vito's shoulder. "Of course you have, shmuck. That's Adam Warner. He's runnin' for President."

"No," Vito insisted. "I mean I *seen* him." He furrowed his brow, trying to remember. Suddenly it came to him.

"Got it! He was the guy in the bar down in Acapulco with Jennifer Parker."

"What're you talkin' about?"

"Remember when I was down there last month deliverin' a package? I saw this guy with Jennifer. They was havin' a drink together."

Salvatore Fiore was staring at him. "Are you sure?"

"Yeah. Why?"

Fiore said slowly, "I think maybe you better tell Mike."

Michael Moretti looked at Nick Vito and said, "You're out of your fucking mind. What would Jennifer Parker be doing with Senator Warner?"

"Beats me, boss. All I know is they was sittin' in this bar, havin' a drink."

"Just the two of them?"

"Yeah."

Salvatore Fiore said, "I thought you oughtta hear about it, Mike. This Warner asshole is investigatin' the shit outta us. Why would Jennifer be havin' a drink with him?"

That was exactly what Michael wanted to know. Jennifer had talked about Acapulco and the convention, and she had mentioned half a dozen people she had run into. But she had not said a word about Adam Warner.

He turned to Tony Santo. "Who's the business manager of the janitor's union now?"

"Charlie Corelli."

Five minutes later, Michael was speaking to Charles Corelli on the telephone.

". . . The Belmont Towers," Michael said. "A friend of mine lived there nine years ago. I'd like to talk to the guy who was the janitor there then." Michael listened for a moment. "I appreciate it, pal. I owe you one." He hung up.

Nick Vito, Santo, Fiore and Colella were watching him.

"Haven't you bastards got anything to do? Get the fuck out of here." The four men hurriedly left.

Michael sat there, thinking, picturing Jennifer and Adam Warner together. *Why had she never mentioned him? And Joshua's father, who had died in the Viet Nam war. Why hadn't Jennifer ever talked about him?*

Michael Moretti began to pace the office.

Three hours later Tony Santo ushered in a timid, badly dressed man in his sixties who was obviously terrified.

"This is Wally Kawolski," Tony said.

Michael rose and shook Kawolski's hand. "Thanks for coming over, Wally. I appreciate it. Sit down. Can I get you anything?"

"No, no thank you, Mr. Moretti. I'm fine, sir. Thank you very much." He was doing everything but bowing.

"Don't be nervous. I just want to ask you a couple of questions, Wally."

"Sure, Mr. Moretti. Anything you want to know. Anything at all."

"Are you still working at the Belmont Towers?"

"Me? No, sir. I left there, oh, about five years ago. My mother-in-law has bad arthritis and—"

"Do you remember the tenants?"

"Yes, sir. Most of 'em, I guess. They was kind of—"

"Do you remember a Jennifer Parker?"

Walter Kawolski's face lit up. "Oh, sure. She was a fine lady. I even remember her apartment number. Nineteen twenty-nine. Like the year the market crashed, you know? I liked her."

"Did Miss Parker have a lot of visitors, Wally?"

Wally slowly scratched his head. "Well, that's hard to say, Mr. Moretti. I only saw her when she was comin' in or goin' out, like."

"Did any men ever spend the night in her apartment?"

Walter Kawolski shook his head. "Oh, no, sir."

So all this had been about nothing. He felt a sharp wave of relief. He had known all along that Jennifer would never—

"Her boyfriend might have come home and caught her."

Michael thought he must have misunderstood. "Her boyfriend?"

"Yeah. The guy Miss Parker was livin' with there."

The words hit Michael in the stomach like a sledgehammer. He lost control of himself. He grabbed Walter Kawolski by the lapels and jerked him to his feet. "You stupid cocksucker! I *asked* you if—what was his name?"

The little man was terrified. "I don't know, Mr. Moretti. I swear to God, I don't know!"

Michael shoved him away. He picked up the newspaper and pushed it under Walter Kawolski's nose.

Kawolski looked at Adam Warner's photograph and said

excitedly, "That's him! That's her boyfriend."

And Michael felt the world crashing down around him. Jennifer had lied to him all this time; she had betrayed him with Adam Warner! The two of them had been sneaking behind his back, conspiring against him, making a fool of him. She had put horns on him.

The ancient juices of vengeance stirred strongly within Michael Moretti, and he knew he was going to kill them both.

54

Jennifer flew from New York to London to Singapore, with a two-hour stopover in Bahrain. The almost-new airport at the oil emirate was already a slum, filled with men, women and children in native garb, sleeping on the floors and on benches. In front of the airport liquor store was a printed warning that anyone drinking in a public place was subject to imprisonment. The atmosphere was hostile, and Jennifer was glad when her flight was called.

The 747 jet landed at Changi Airport in Singapore at four-forty in the afternoon. It was a brand new airport, fourteen miles from the center of the city, replacing the old International Airport, and as the plane taxied down the runway Jennifer could see signs of construction still going on.

The Customs building was large and airy and modern, with rows of luggage carts for the convenience of passengers. The Customs officers were efficient and polite, and in fifteen minutes Jennifer was finished and headed for the taxi stand.

Outside the entrance, a heavy middle-aged Chinese man approached her. "Miss Jennifer Parker?"

"Yes."

"I am Chou Ling." Moretti's contact in Singapore. "I have a limousine waiting."

Chou Ling supervised the storing of Jennifer's luggage in the trunk of the limousine, and a few minutes later they were headed toward the city.

"Did you have a pleasant flight?" Chou Ling asked.

"Yes, thank you." But Jennifer's mind was on Stefan Bjork.

As though reading her thoughts, Chou Ling nodded to a building ahead of them. "That is Changi Prison. Bjork is in there."

Jennifer turned to look. Changi Prison was a large building off the highway, surrounded by a green fence and electrified barbed wire. There were watchtowers at each corner, manned by armed guards, and the entrance was blocked by a second barbed wire fence and, beyond that, more guards at the gate.

"During the war," Chou Ling informed Jennifer, "all British personnel on the island were interned there."

"When will I be able to get to see Bjork?"

Chou Ling replied delicately, "It is a very sensitive situation, Miss Parker. The government is most adamant about drug use. Even first offenders are dealt with ruthlessly. People who *deal* in drugs . . ." Chou Ling shrugged expressively. "Singapore is controlled by a few powerful families. The Shaw family, C. K. Tang, Tan Chin Tuan and Lee Kuan Yew, the Prime Minister. These families control the finance and commerce of Singapore. They do not wish drugs here."

"We must have some friends here with influence."

"There is a police inspector, David Touh—a most reasonable man."

Jennifer wondered how much "reasonable" cost, but she did not ask. There would be time enough for that later. She sat back and studied the scenery. They were passing through the suburbs of Singapore now, and the overwhelming impression was of greenery and flowers blooming everywhere. On both sides of MacPherson Road were modern shopping complexes alongside ancient shrines and pagodas. Some of the people walking along the streets wore ancient costumes and turbans, while others were smartly dressed in the latest western styles. The city seemed a colorful mixture of an ancient culture and a modern metropolis. The shopping centers looked new and everything was spotlessly clean. Jennifer commented on that.

Chou Ling smiled. "There is a simple explanation. There is a five-hundred-dollar fine for littering, and it is strictly enforced."

The car turned on to Stevens Road, and on a hill above them Jennifer saw a lovely white building completely surrounded by trees and flowers.

"That is the Shangri-La, your hotel."

The lobby was enormous, white and immaculately clean, with marble pillars and glass everywhere.

While Jennifer was checking in, Chou Ling said, "Inspector Touh will be in touch with you." He handed Jennifer a card. "You can always reach me at this number."

A smiling bellman took Jennifer's luggage and led her through an atrium to the elevator. There was an enormous garden under a waterfall, and a swimming pool. The Shangri-La was the most breathtaking hotel Jennifer had ever seen. Her suite on the second floor consisted of a large living room and bedroom, and a terrace overlooking a colorful sea of white and red anthuriums, purple bougainvillea and coconut palms. *It's like being in the middle of a Gauguin,* Jennifer thought.

A breeze was blowing. It was the kind of day Joshua loved. *Can we go sailing this afternoon, Mom? Stop doing that,* Jennifer told herself.

She walked over to the telephone. "I would like to place a call to the United States. New York City. Person-to-person to

Mr. Michael Moretti." She gave the telephone number.

The operator said, "I'm so sorry. All the circuits are busy. Please try again later."

"Thank you."

Downstairs, the operator looked for approval to the man standing next to the switchboard.

He nodded. "Good," he said. "Very good."

The call from Inspector Touh came an hour after Jennifer checked into the hotel.

"Miss Jennifer Parker?"

"Speaking."

"This is Inspector David Touh." He had a soft, indefinable accent.

"Yes, Inspector. I've been expecting your call. I'm anxious to arrange—"

The inspector interrupted. "I wonder if I might have the pleasure of your company at dinner this evening."

A warning. He was probably afraid of the phone being bugged.

"I would be delighted."

The Great Shanghai was an enormous, noisy restaurant filled, for the most part, with natives who were loudly eating and talking. There was a three-piece band on a platform, and an attractive girl in a *cheongsam* was singing popular American songs.

The maître d' said to Jennifer, "A table for one?"

"I'm meeting someone. Inspector Touh."

The maître d's face broke into a smile. "The inspector is waiting for you. This way, please." He led Jennifer to a table at the front of the room, next to the bandstand.

Inspector David Touh was a tall, thin, attractive man in his early forties, with delicate features and dark, liquid eyes. He was beautifully and almost formally dressed in a dark suit.

He held Jennifer's chair for her, then sat down. The band was playing a deafening rock song.

Inspector Touh leaned across to Jennifer and said, "May I order a drink for you?"

"Yes, thank you."

"You must try a *chendol*."

"A—what?"

"It is made with coconut milk, coconut sugar and little pieces of gelatin. You will like it."

The inspector glanced up and a waitress was at his side instantly. The inspector ordered the two drinks and *dim sum*, Chinese appetizers. "I hope you do not mind if I order your dinner for you?"

"Not at all. I would be pleased."

"I understand that in your country women are used to taking command. Here it is still the man who is in charge."

A sexist, Jennifer thought, but she was in no mood to get into an argument. She needed this man. Because of the incredible din and the music, it was almost impossible to carry on a conversation. Jennifer sat back and looked around the room. Jennifer had been to other Oriental countries, but the people in Singapore seemed extraordinarily beautiful, men and women both.

The waitress put Jennifer's drink in front of her. It resembled a chocolate soda with slippery lumps in it.

Inspector Touh read her expression. "You must stir it."

"I can't hear you."

He shouted, "You must stir it!"

Jennifer dutifully stirred her drink. She tasted it.

It was awful, much too sweet, but Jennifer nodded and said, "It's—it's different."

Half a dozen platters of *dim sum* appeared on the table. Some of them were odd shaped delicacies that Jennifer had never seen before, and she decided not to ask what they were. The food was delicious.

Inspector Touh explained, yelling over the roar of the room, "This restaurant is renowned for the *Nonya* style of food. That is a mixture of Chinese ingredients and Malay spices. No recipes have ever been written down."

"I'd like to talk to you about Stefan Bjork," Jennifer said.

"I can't hear you." The noise of the band was deafening.

Jennifer leaned closer. "I want to know when I can see Stefan Bjork."

Inspector Touh shrugged and pantomimed that he could not hear. Jennifer suddenly wondered whether he had chosen this table so they could talk safely, or whether he had selected it so they could not talk at all.

An endless succession of dishes followed the *dim sum* and it was a superb meal. The only thing that disturbed Jennifer was that she had not once been able to bring up the subject of Stefan Bjork.

When they had finished eating and were out on the street, Inspector Touh said, "I have my car here." He snapped his fingers and a black Mercedes that had been double-parked pulled up to them. The inspector opened the back door for Jennifer. A large uniformed policeman was behind the wheel. Something was not right. *If Inspector Touh wanted to discuss confidential matters with me,* Jennifer thought, *he would have arranged for us to be alone.*

She got into the back seat of the car and the inspector slid in beside her. "This is your first time in Singapore, is it not?"

"Yes."

"Ah, then, there is much for you to see."

"I didn't come here to sight-see, Inspector. I must return home as quickly as possible."

Inspector Touh sighed. "You Caucasians are always in such a rush. Have you heard of Bugis Street?"

"No."

Jennifer shifted in her seat so that she could study Inspector Touh. He had a face that was highly mobile and his gestures were expressive. He seemed outgoing and communicative, and yet he had spent the entire evening saying exactly nothing.

The car stopped for a *trishaw*, one of the three-wheeled carriages pedaled by natives. Inspector Touh watched with contempt as the *trishaw* carried two tourists down the street.

"We shall outlaw those one day."

Jennifer and Inspector Touh got out of the car a block away from Bugis Street.

"No automobiles are allowed in there," Inspector Touh explained.

He took Jennifer's arm and they started walking along the busy sidewalk. In a few minutes, the crowds were so thick it was almost impossible to move. Bugis Street was narrow, with stalls on both sides, fruit stalls and vegetable stands and stalls that sold fish and meat. There were outdoor restaurants with chairs set around small tables. Jennifer stood there, drinking in the sights and the sounds and the smells and the riot of colors. Inspector Touh took her arm and shouldered his way through the crowd, clearing a path. They reached a restaurant with three tables in front of it, all occupied. The inspector gripped the arm of a passing waiter, and a moment later the proprietor was at their side. The inspector said something to him in Chinese. The proprietor walked over to one of the tables, spoke to the guests, and they looked at the inspector and quickly rose and left. The inspector and Jennifer were seated at the table.

"Can I order something for you?"

"No, thank you." Jennifer looked at the teeming sea of people thronging the sidewalks and streets. Under other circumstances she might have enjoyed this. Singapore was a fascinating city, a city to share with someone you cared about.

Inspector Touh was saying, "Watch. It is almost midnight."

Jennifer looked up. At first she noticed nothing. Then she saw that all the shopkeepers were simultaneously beginning to close up their stands. In ten minutes, every stall was closed and locked and their owners had disappeared.

"What's happening?" Jennifer asked.

"You will see."

There was a murmur from the crowd at the far end of the street, and the people began to move toward the sidewalk, leaving a cleared place in the street. A Chinese girl in a long, tight-fitting evening gown was walking down the center of the street. She was the most beautiful woman Jennifer had ever seen. She walked proudly and slowly, pausing to greet people at various tables, then moving on.

As the girl neared the table where Jennifer and the inspector were sitting, Jennifer got a better look at her, and up close, she was even lovelier. Her features were soft and delicate, and her figure was breathtaking. Her white silk gown was slit at the sides so that one could see the delicately curved thigh and small, perfectly formed breasts.

As Jennifer turned to speak to the inspector, another girl appeared. She was, if possible, even lovelier than the first. Two more were walking behind her, and in a moment Bugis Street was filled with beautiful young girls. They were a mixture of Malaysian, Indian and Chinese.

"They're prostitutes," Jennifer guessed.

"Yes. Transsexuals."

Jennifer stared at him. It was not possible. She turned and looked at the girls again. She could see absolutely nothing masculine about any of them.

"You're joking."

"They are known as *Billy Boys*."

Jennifer was bewildered. "But they—"

"They have all had an operation. They think of themselves

as women." He shrugged. "So, why not? They do no harm. You understand," he added, "that prostitution is illegal here. But the *Billy Boys* are good for tourism and as long as they do not disturb the guests, the police close an eye to it."

Jennifer looked again at the exquisite young people moving down the street, stopping at tables to make deals with customers.

"They do well. They charge up to two hundred dollars. When they get too old to work, they become Mamasans."

Most of the girls were seated at tables now with men, dickering for their services. One by one, they began to rise and leave with their clients.

"They handle up to two or three transactions a night," the inspector explained. "They take over Bugis Street at midnight and they must be out by six in the morning so that the stands can open for business again. We can leave whenever you're ready."

"I'm ready."

As they moved along the street, an unbidden image of Ken Bailey flashed through Jennifer's mind and she thought, *I hope you are happy.*

On the drive back to the hotel, Jennifer made up her mind that, chauffeur or no chauffeur, she was going to bring up Bjork's name.

As the car turned on to Orchard Road, Jennifer said determinedly, "About Stefan Bjork—"

"Ah, yes. I have arranged for you to visit him at ten o'clock tomorrow morning."

55

In Washington, D.C., Adam Warner was summoned from a meeting to take an urgent telephone call from New York.

District Attorney Robert Di Silva was on the phone. He was jubilant. "The special grand jury just returned the indictments we asked for. Every one of them! We're all set to move." There was no response. "Are you there, Senator?"

"I'm here." Adam forced enthusiasm into his voice. "That's great news."

"We should be able to start closing in within twenty-four hours. If you can fly up to New York, I think we should have a final meeting tomorrow morning with all the agencies so we can coordinate our moves. Can you do that, Senator?"

"Yes," Adam said.

"I'll make the arrangements. Ten o'clock tomorrow morning."

"I'll be there." Adam replaced the receiver.

The special grand jury just returned the indictments we asked for. Every one of them!

Adam picked up the telephone again and began to dial.

56

The visitors' room at Changi Prison was a small, bare room with whitewashed stucco walls, containing one long table with hard wooden chairs set on either side. Jennifer was seated in one of the chairs, waiting. She looked up as the door opened and Stefan Bjork walked in, accompanied by a uniformed guard.

Bjork was in his thirties, a tall, sullen-faced man with protuberant eyes. *A thyroid condition,* Jennifer thought. There were vivid bruises on his cheeks and forehead. He sat down opposite Jennifer.

"I'm Jennifer Parker, your attorney. I'm going to try to get you out of here."

He looked at her and said, "You better make it soon."

It could have been a threat or a plea. Jennifer remembered Michael's words: *I want you to bail him out before he starts talking.*

"Are they treating you all right?"

He cast a covert look at the guard standing near the door. "Yeah. Okay."

"I've applied for bail for you."

"What are the chances?" Bjork was unable to conceal the hope in his voice.

"I think they're pretty good. It will be two or three days at the most."

"I have to get out of this place."

Jennifer rose to her feet. "I'll see you soon."

"Thanks," Stefan said. He held out his hand.

The guard said sharply, "No!"

They both turned.

"No touching."

Stefan Bjork gave Jennifer a look and then said hoarsely, "Hurry!"

When Jennifer returned to her hotel, there was a telephone message that Inspector Touh had called. As she was reading it, the phone rang. It was the inspector.

"While you are waiting, Miss Parker, I thought you might enjoy a little tour of our city."

Jennifer's first reaction was to say no, but she realized there was nothing she could do until she had Bjork safely on a plane out of here. Until then, it was important to keep Inspector Touh's goodwill.

Jennifer said, "Thank you. I would enjoy that."

They stopped to have lunch at Kampachi, and then headed for the countryside, driving north on Bukit Timah Road to Malaysia, going through a series of colorful little villages with a variety of food stands and shops. The people seemed well-dressed and prosperous looking. Jennifer and Inspector Touh stopped at the Kranji Cemetery and War Memorial, walking up the steps and through the open blue gates. In front of them was a large marble cross, and in the background an enormous column. The cemetery was a sea of white crosses.

"The war was very bad for us," Inspector Touh said. "We all lost many friends and family members."

Jennifer said nothing. Her mind could see a grave in Sands Point. But she could not let herself think about what lay beneath the small mound.

In Manhattan, a meeting of law enforcement agencies was in progress at the Police Intelligence Unit on Hudson Street. There was an air of jubilation in the crowded room. Many of the men had gone into the investigation with cynicism, for they had been through this kind of exercise before. Over the past years they had managed to accumulate overwhelming evidence against mobsters and murderers and blackmailers, and in case after case, high-priced legal talent had won acquittals for the criminals they represented. This time it was going to be different. They had the testimony of the *Consigliere* Thomas Colfax, and no one would be able to shake him. For more than twenty-five years he had been the linchpin of the mob. He would go into court, give names, dates, facts and figures. And now they were being given the go-ahead to move.

Adam had worked harder than anyone in the room to make this moment happen. It was to have been the triumphal carriage that would take him to the White House. Now that the moment was here, it had turned to ashes. In front of Adam was a list of people who had been indicted by the special grand jury. The fourth name on the list was Jennifer Parker, and the charges opposite her name were murder and conspiracy to commit half a dozen different federal crimes.

Adam Warner looked around the room and forced himself to speak. "You're—you're all to be congratulated."

He tried to say more, but the words would not come out. He was filled with such self-loathing that it was a physical pain.

The Spanish are right, Michael Moretti thought. *Vengeance is a dish best eaten cold*. The only reason Jennifer Parker was still alive was because she was out of his reach. But she would be returning soon. And in the meantime, Michael could savor what was going to happen to her. She had betrayed him in every way a woman could betray a man. For that he was going to see that she received special attention.

In Singapore, Jennifer tried again to put a call through to Michael.

"I'm sorry," the switchboard operator told her, "the circuits to the United States are busy."

"Will you keep trying, please?"

"Of course, Miss Parker."

The operator looked up at the man standing guard beside the switchboard, and he gave her a conspiratorial smile.

At his downtown headquarters, Robert Di Silva was looking at a warrant that had just been delivered. It had Jennifer Parker's name on it.

I've finally got her, he thought. And he felt a savage satisfaction.

The telephone operator announced, "Inspector Touh is in the lobby to see you."

Jennifer was surprised, for she had not been expecting him. He must have some news about Stefan Bjork.

Jennifer took the elevator down to the lobby.

"Forgive me for not telephoning," Inspector Touh apologized. "I thought it best to speak to you personally."

"You have some news?"

"We can talk in the car. I want to show you something."

They drove along Yio Chu Kang Road.

"Is there a problem?" Jennifer asked.

"None at all. Bail will be set for the day after tomorrow."

Then where was he taking her?

They were passing a group of buildings on Jalan Goatopah Road, and the driver brought the car to a stop.

Inspector Touh turned to Jennifer. "I'm sure this will interest you."

"What is it?"

"Come along. You will see."

The interior of the building was old and dilapidated-looking, but the overpowering impression was of the smell, wild and primitive and musky. It was like nothing Jennifer had ever smelled before.

A young girl hurried forward and said, "Would you like an escort? I—"

Inspector Touh waved her aside. "We won't need you."

He took Jennifer's arm and they walked outside into the grounds. There were half a dozen large sunken tanks and from them came a series of strange slithering sounds. Jennifer and Inspector Touh reached the first pen. There was a sign: *Keep Your Hands Off the Pool. Danger.* Jennifer looked down. The tank was filled with alligators and crocodiles, dozens of them, all in continuous movement, sliding over and under one another.

Jennifer shuddered. "What is this?"

"It is a crocodile farm." He looked down at the reptiles. "When they are between three and six years old they are skinned and turned into wallets and belts and shoes. You see that most of them have their mouths open. That is the way they relax. It is when they close their mouths that you must be careful."

They moved on to a tank with two enormous alligators in it.

"These are fifteen years old. They are used only for breeding purposes."

Jennifer shivered. "They're so ugly. I don't know how they can stand each other."

Inspector Touh said, "They can't. As a matter of fact, they do not often mate."

"They're prehistoric."

"Precisely. They go back millions of years, with the same primitive mechanisms they had at the beginning of time."

Jennifer wondered why he had brought her here. If the inspector thought that these horrible-looking beasts would interest her, he was mistaken. "May we go now?" Jennifer asked.

"In a moment." The inspector looked up toward the young girl who had met them inside. She was carrying a tray toward the first tank.

"Today is feeding day," the inspector said. "Watch."

He moved with Jennifer toward the first tank. "They feed them fish and pigs' lungs once every three days."

The girl began throwing food into the pen, and instantly it erupted into a churning, swirling mass of activity. The alligators and crocodiles lunged for the raw, bloody food, tearing into it with their saurian fangs. As Jennifer watched, two of them went for the same piece of meat, and instantly they turned on each other, savagely attacking, biting and slashing until the pen started to fill with blood. The eyeball of one was torn loose, but its teeth were sunk into the jaws of its attacker and it would not let go. As the blood began pouring out more heavily, staining the water, the other crocodiles joined in, savaging their two wounded mates, ripping at their heads until the raw skin was exposed. They began to devour them alive.

Jennifer felt faint. "Please, let's get out of here."

Inspector Touh put his hand on her arm. "One moment."

He stood there watching, and after a while he led Jennifer away.

That night, Jennifer dreamt of the crocodiles clawing and tearing each other to pieces. Two of them suddenly turned into Michael and Adam, and in the middle of her nightmare Jennifer woke up, trembling. She was unable to go back to sleep.

The raids began. Federal and local law-enforcement agents struck in a dozen different states and in half a dozen foreign countries, and the raids were orchestrated to take place simultaneously.

In Ohio, a senator was arrested while making a speech to a women's club on honesty in government.

In New Orleans, an illegal national bookmaking operation was shut down.

In Amsterdam, a diamond smuggling operation was halted.

A bank manager in Gary, Indiana, was arrested on charges of laundering Organization money.

In Kansas City, a large discount house filled with stolen goods was raided.

In Phoenix, Arizona, half a dozen detectives on the vice squad were placed under arrest.

In Naples, a cocaine factory was seized.

In Detroit, a nationwide automobile theft ring was broken up.

Unable to reach Jennifer by telephone, Adam Warner went to her office.

Cynthia recognized him instantly.

"I'm sorry, Senator Warner, Miss Parker is out of the country."

"Where is she?"

"The Shangri-La Hotel in Singapore."

Adam's spirits rose. He could telephone her and warn her not to return.

The hotel housekeeper walked in as Jennifer was getting out of the shower.

"Excuse me. What time will you be checking out today?"

"I'm not checking out today. I'm leaving tomorrow."

The housekeeper looked puzzled. "I was told to get this suite ready for a party coming in late tonight."

"Who told you to do that?"

"The manager."

Downstairs, an overseas call was coming in at the switchboard. There was a different operator on duty and a different man was standing over her.

The operator spoke into her mouthpiece. "New York City calling Miss Jennifer Parker?"

She looked at the man standing next to her. He shook his head.

"I'm sorry. Miss Parker has checked out."

The sweeping raids continued. Arrests were made in Honduras, San Salvador, Turkey and Mexico. The net swept up dealers and killers and bank robbers and arsonists. There were crackdowns in Fort Lauderdale and Atlantic City and Palm Springs.

And they continued.

In New York, Robert Di Silva was keeping close track of the progress being made. His heart beat faster as he thought about the net that was closing in on Jennifer Parker and Michael Moretti.

Michael Moretti escaped the police dragnet by sheer

chance. It was the anniversary of his father-in-law's death, and Michael and Rosa had gone to the cemetery to pay homage to her father.

Five minutes after they left, a carload of FBI agents arrived at Michael Moretti's house and another carload at his office. When they learned he was not in either place, the agents settled down to wait.

Jennifer realized that she had neglected to make a plane reservation for Stefan Bjork back to the States. She called Singapore Airlines.

"This is Jennifer Parker. I'm booked on your Flight One-Twelve leaving tomorrow afternoon for London. I'd like to make an additional reservation."

"Thank you. Would you hold the line, please?"

Jennifer waited and after a few minutes the voice came back on the line. Was that Parker? P-A-R-K-E-R?"

"Yes."

"Your reservation has been canceled, Miss Parker."

Jennifer felt a small shock. "Canceled? By whom?"

"I do not know. You have been taken off our passenger list."

"There's been some mistake. I'd like you to put me back on that list."

"I'm sorry, Miss Parker. Flight One-Twelve is full."

Inspector Touh was the one to straighten everything out, Jennifer decided. She had agreed to have dinner with him. She would find out what was happening then.

He picked her up early.

Jennifer told the inspector about the mix-up in her hotel and plane reservations.

He shrugged. "Our famous inefficiency, I am afraid. I will look into it."

"What about Stefan Bjork?"

"Everything is arranged. He will be released tomorrow morning.".

Inspector Touh said something to the driver in Chinese and the car made a U-turn.

"You have not seen Kallang Road. You will find it most interesting."

The car made a left turn on to Lavender Street, then one block later a right turn to Kallang Bahru. There were large signs advertising florists and casket companies. A few blocks later the car made another turn.

"Where are we?"

Inspector Touh turned to Jennifer and said quietly, "We are on the Street With No Name."

The car began to move very slowly. There were only undertakers on both sides of the street, row after row of them: Tan Kee Seng, Clin Noh, Ang Yung Long, Goh Soon. Ahead, a funeral was in progress. All the mourners were dressed in white and a three-piece band was playing: a tuba, a sax and drums. A body was laid out on a table with wreaths of flowers around it and a large photograph of the deceased sat on an easel facing the front. Mourners were sitting around, eating.

Jennifer turned to the inspector. "What is this?"

"These are the houses of death. The natives call them the *die houses*. The word death is difficult for them to pronounce." He looked at Jennifer and said, "But death is only a part of life, is it not?"

Jennifer looked into his cold eyes and was suddenly frightened.

They went to the Golden Phoenix, and it was not until they were seated that Jennifer had a chance to question him.

"Inspector Touh, did you have a reason for taking me to the crocodile farm and the die houses?"

He looked at her and said evenly, "Of course. I thought they would interest you. Especially since you came here to free your client, Mr. Bjork. Many of our young people are dying because of the drugs that are brought into our country, Miss Parker. I could have taken you to the hospital where we try to treat them, but I felt it might be more informative for you to see where they end up."

"All that has nothing to do with me."

"That is a matter of opinion." All the friendliness had gone out of his voice.

Jennifer said, "Look, Inspector Touh, I'm sure you're being well paid to—"

"There is not enough money in the world for anyone to pay me."

He stood up and nodded to someone, and Jennifer turned. Two men in gray suits were approaching the table.

"Miss Jennifer Parker?"

"Yes."

There was no need for them to pull out their FBI credentials. She knew before they spoke. "FBI. We have extradition papers and a warrant for your arrest. We're taking you back to New York on the midnight plane."

57

When Michael Moretti left his father-in-law's grave, he was already late for an appointment. He decided to call the office and reschedule it. He stopped at a telephone booth along the highway and dialed the number. The phone rang once and a voice answered, "Acme Builders."

Michael said, "This is Mike. Tell—"

"Mr. Moretti isn't here. Call back later."

Michael felt his body tightening. All he said was "Tony's Place."

He hung up and hurried back to the car. Rosa looked at his face and asked, "Is everything all right, Michael?"

"I don't know. I'm going to drop you off at your cousin's. Stay there until you hear from me.

Tony followed Michael into the office in the rear of the restaurant.

"I got word that the Feds are crawlin' all over your house and the downtown office, Mike."

"Thanks," Michael said. "I don't want to be disturbed."

"You won't be."

Michael waited until Tony walked out of the room and closed the door behind him. Then Michael picked up the telephone and furiously began to dial.

It took Michael Moretti less than twenty minutes to learn that a major disaster was taking place. As the reports of the raids and arrests began to filter in, Michael received them with mounting disbelief. All his soldiers and lieutenants were being picked up. Drops were being raided; gambling operations were being seized; confidential ledgers and records were being impounded. What was happening was a nightmare. The police had to be obtaining information from someone in his Organization.

Michael placed telephone calls to other Families around the country, and all of them demanded to know what was going on. They were being badly hurt and no one knew where the leak was coming from. They all suspected it was coming from the Moretti Family.

Jimmy Guardino, in Las Vegas, gave him an ultimatum. "I'm calling on behalf of the Commission, Michael." The National Commission was the supreme power that superseded the power of any individual Family when there was trouble. "The police are rounding up all the Families. Someone big is singing. The word we get is that it's one of your boys. We're giving you twenty-fours to find him and take care of him."

In the past, police raids had always netted the small fry, the expendables. Now, for the first time, the men at the top were being pulled in. *Someone big is singing. The word we get is that it's one of your boys.* They had to be right. Michael's Family had been the hardest hit, and the police were looking for him. Someone had given them solid evidence, or they never would have mounted a campaign this big. But who could it be? Michael sat back, thinking.

Whoever was tipping off the authorities had inside information that was known only to Michael and his two top lieutenants, Salvatore Fiore and Joseph Colella. Only the three of them knew where the ledgers were hidden, and the FBI had found them. The only other person who would have had the information was Thomas Colfax, but Colfax was buried under a garbage dump in New Jersey.

Michael sat there and thought about Salvatore Fiore and Joseph Colella. It was difficult to believe that either one of them could have broken *omertà* and talked. They had been with him from the beginning; he had handpicked them. He had allowed them to have their own loan-sharking operation on the side and to run a small prostitution ring. Why would they betray him? The answer, of course, was simple: the chair he was sitting in. They wanted his chair. Once he was out, they could move in and take over. They were a team; they had to be in it together.

Michael was filled with a murderous rage. The stupid bastards were trying to pull him down, but they would not live long enough to enjoy it. The first thing he had to do was arrange bail for his men who had been arrested. He needed a lawyer he could trust—Colfax was dead, and Jennifer—Jennifer! Michael could feel the coldness creeping around his heart again. In his head he could hear himself saying, *Get back as fast as you can. I'll miss you. I love you, Jennifer*. He had said that and she had betrayed him. She would pay for that.

Michael made a telephone call and sat back to wait, and fifteen minutes later Nick Vito hurried into the office.

"What's happening?" Michael asked.

"The place is still buzzin' with Feds, Mike. I drove around the block a couple of times, but I did like you said. I stayed away."

"I've got a job for you, Nick."

"Sure, boss. What can I do for you?"

"Take care of Salvatore and Joe."

Nick Vito stared at him. "I—I don't understand. When you say, *take care of them,* you don't mean—"

Michael shouted, "I mean blow their fucking brains out! Do you need a blueprint?"

"N-no," Nick Vito stammered. "It's just that I-I-I mean— Sal and Joe are your top men!"

Michael Moretti moved to his feet, his eyes dangerous. "You want to tell me how to run my business, Nick?"

"No, Mike. I—sure. I'll take care of them for you. When —?"

"Now. Right away. I don't want them to live to see the moon tonight. Do you understand?"

"Yeah. I understand."

Michael's hands tightened into fists. "If I had time, I'd take care of them myself. I want them to hurt, Nick. Make it slow, you hear? *Suppilu suppilu.*"

"Sure. Okay."

The door opened and Tony hurried in, his face gray. "There's two FBI agents out there with a warrant for your arrest. I swear to God I don't know how they knew you was here. They—"

Michael Moretti turned to Nick Vito and snapped, "Out the back way. Move!" He turned to Tony. "Tell them I'm in the can. I'll be right with them."

Michael picked up the telephone and dialed a number. One minute later he was talking to a judge of the Superior Court of New York.

"There are two Feds out here with a warrant for my arrest."

"What are the charges, Mike?"

"I don't know and I don't give a shit. I'm calling you to set things up so that I'm bailed out. I can't sit around in the slammer. I've got things to do."

There was a silence and the judge's voice said carefully,

"I'm afraid I won't be able to help you this time, Michael. The heat's on all over and if I try to interfere—"

When Michael Moretti spoke, there was an ominous note in his voice. "Listen to me, you asshole, and listen good. If I spend one hour in jail, I'll see to it that you're behind bars for the rest of your life. I've been taking good care of you for a long time. You want me to tell the D.A. how many cases you fixed for me? Would you like me to give the IRS the number of your Swiss bank account? Would you—"

"For God's sake, Michael!"

"Then move!"

"I'll see what I can do," Judge Lawrence Waldman said. "I'll try to—"

"Try to, shit! Do it! Do you hear me, Larry? Do it!" Michael slammed down the receiver.

His mind was working swiftly and coolly. He was not concerned about being taken to jail. He knew that Judge Waldman would do as he was told, and he could trust Nick Vito to attend to Fiore and Colella. Without their testimony, the government could not prove a thing against him.

Michael looked in the small mirror on the wall, combed back his hair, straightened his tie, and went out to meet the two FBI agents.

Judge Lawrence Waldman came through, as Michael had known he would. At the preliminary hearing, an attorney selected by Judge Waldman requested bail, and it was set at five hundred thousand dollars.

Di Silva stood there, angry and frustrated, as Michael Moretti walked out of the courtroom.

58

Nick Vito was a man of limited intelligence. His value to the Organization lay in the fact that he followed orders without question and that he carried them out efficiently. Nick Vito had been up against guns and knives dozens of times, but he had never known fear. He knew it now. Something was happening that was beyond his understanding, and he had a feeling that somehow he was responsible for it.

All day he had been hearing about the raids that were taking place, the sweeping arrests that were being made. The street talk was that there was a traitor loose, someone high up in the Organization. Even with his limited intellect, Nick Vito was able to connect the fact that he had let Thomas Colfax live and that, shortly afterward, someone had started betraying the Family to the authorities. Nick Vito knew that it could not be Salvatore Fiore or Joseph Colella. The two men were like brothers to him and they were both as fanatically loyal to Michael Moretti as he was. But there was no way he could ever explain that to Michael, not without getting himself chopped into small pieces; because the only other one who could be responsible was Thomas Colfax, and Colfax was supposed to be dead.

Nick Vito was in a dilemma. He loved the Little Flower and the giant. Fiore and Colella had done him dozens of favors in the past, just as Thomas Colfax had; but he had helped Colfax out of a jam, and look what it had gotten him. So Nick Vito decided he was not going to be softhearted again. It was his own life he had to protect now. Once he killed Fiore and Colella, he would be in the clear. But because they were like brothers to him, he would see that they died quickly.

It was simple for Nick Vito to determine their whereabouts, for they always had to be available in case Michael needed them. Little Salvatore Fiore was visiting his mistress's apartment on 83rd Street near the Museum of Natural History. Nick knew that Salvatore always left there at five o'clock to go home to his wife. It was now three. Nick debated with himself. He could either hang around the front of the apartment building or go upstairs and take Salvatore inside the apartment. He decided he was too nervous to wait. The fact that he was nervous made Nick Vito more nervous. The whole thing was beginning to get to him. *When this is over*, he thought, *I'm gonna ask Mike for a vacation. Maybe I'll take a couple of young girls and go down to the Bahamas.* Just thinking about that made him feel better.

Nick Vito parked his car around the corner from the apartment house and walked up to the building. He let himself in the front door with a piece of celluloid, ignored the elevator and walked up the stairs to the third floor. He moved toward the door at the end of the corridor, and when he reached it he pounded on it.

"Open up! Police!"

He heard quick sounds from behind the door and a few

moments later it opened on a heavy chain and he could see the face and part of the naked figure of Marina, Salvatore Fiore's mistress.

"Nick!" she said. "You crazy idiot. You scared the hell out of me."

She took the chain off the door and opened it. "Sal, it's Nick!"

Little Salvatore Fiore walked in from the bedroom, naked. "Hey, Nicky boy! What the fuck you doin' here?"

"Sal, I got a message for you from Mike."

Nick Vito raised a .22 automatic with a silencer and squeezed the trigger. The firing pin slammed into the .22 caliber cartridge, sending the bullet out of the muzzle at a thousand feet a second. The first bullet shattered the bridge of Salvatore Fiore's nose. The second bullet put out his left eye. As Marina opened her mouth to scream, Nick Vito turned and put a bullet in her head. As she fell to the floor, he put one more bullet in her chest, to make certain. *It's a waste of a beautiful piece of ass*, Nick thought, *but Mike wouldn't like it if I left any witnesses around.* .

Big Joseph Colella owned a horse that was running in the eighth race at Belmont Park in Long Island. Belmont was a one-and-one-half-mile track, the perfect length for the filly that the giant was running. He had advised Nick to bet on it. In the past, Nick had won a lot on Colella's tips. Colella always put a little money on for Nick when his horses ran. As Nick Vito walked toward Colella's box, he thought regretfully about the fact that there would be no more tips. The eighth race had just started. Colella was standing up in his box, cheering his horse on. It was a large-purse race and the crowd was screaming and yelling as the horses rounded the first turn.

Nick Vito stepped into the box behind Colella and said, "How you doin', pal?"

"Hey, Nick! You got here just in time. Beauty Queen's gonna win this one. I put a little bet on it for you."

"That's great, Joe."

Nick Vito pressed the .22 caliber gun against Joseph Colella's spine and fired three times through his coat. The muffled noise went unnoticed in the cheering crowd. Nick watched Joseph Colella slump to the ground. He debated for an instant whether to take the pari-mutuel tickets out of Colella's pocket, then decided against it. After all, the horse could lose.

Nick Vito turned and unhurriedly walked toward the exit, one anonymous figure among thousands.

Michael Moretti's private line rang.

"Mr. Moretti?"

"Who wants him?"

"This is Captain Tanner."

It took Michael a second to place the name. A police captain. Queens precinct. On the payroll.

"This is Moretti."

"I just received some information I think might interest you."

"Where are you calling from?"

"A public telephone booth."

"Go ahead."

"I found out where all the heat's coming from."

"You're too late. They've been taken care of already."

"*They?* Oh. I only heard about Thomas Colfax."

"You don't know what the hell you're talking about. Colfax is dead."

It was Captain Tanner's turn to be confused. "What are *you* talking about? Thomas Colfax is sitting at the Marine Base in Quantico right now, spilling his guts to everybody who'll listen."

"You're out of your mind," Michael snapped. "I happen to

know—" He stopped. What *did* he know? He had told Nick Vito to kill Thomas Colfax, and Vito had said that he had. Michael sat there thinking. "How sure are you about this, Tanner?"

"Mr. Moretti, would I be calling you if I wasn't sure?"

"I'll check it out. If you're right, I owe you one."

"Thank you, Mr. Moretti."

Captain Tanner replaced the receiver, pleased with himself. In the past he had found Michael Moretti to be a very appreciative man. This could be the *big* one, the one that could enable him to retire. He stepped out of the telephone booth into the cold October air.

There were two men standing outside the booth, and as the captain started to step around them, one of them blocked his way. He held up an identification card.

"Captain Tanner? I'm Lieutenant West, Internal Security Division. The Police Commissioner would like to have a word with you."

Michael Moretti hung up the receiver slowly. He knew with a sure animal instinct that Nick Vito had lied to him. Thomas Colfax was still alive. That would explain everything that was happening. *He* was the one who had turned traitor. And Michael had sent Nick Vito out to kill Fiore and Colella. Jesus, he had been stupid! Outsmarted by a dumb hired gunman into wasting his two top men! He was filled with an icy rage.

He dialed a number and spoke briefly into the telephone. After he made a second telephone call, he sat back and waited.

When he heard Nick Vito on the phone, Michael forced himself to keep the fury he felt out of his voice. "How did it go, Nick?"

"Okay, boss. Just like you said. They both suffered a lot."

"I can always count on you, Nick, can't I?"

"You know you can, boss."

"Nick, I want you to do me one last favor. One of the boys left a car at the corner of York and Ninety-fifth Street. It's a tan Camaro. The keys are behind the sun visor. We're going to use it for a job tonight. Drive it over here, will you?"

"Sure, boss. How soon do you need it? I was going to—"

"I need it now. Right away, Nick."

"I'm on my way."

"Good-bye, Nick."

Michael replaced the receiver. He wished he could be there to watch Nick Vito blow himself to hell, but he had one more urgent thing to do.

Jennifer Parker would be on her way back soon, and he wanted to get everything ready for her.

59

It's like some kind of goddamned Hollywood movie production, Major General Roy Wallace thought, *with my prisoner as the star.*

The large conference room at the United States Marine Corps base was filled with technicians from the Signal Corps, scurrying around setting up cameras and sound and lighting equipment, using an arcane jargon.

"Kill the brute and hit the inkies. Bring a baby over here . . ."

They were getting ready to put Thomas Colfax's testimony on film.

"It's extra insurance," District Attorney Di Silva had argued. "We know that no one can get to him, but it will be good to have it on the record, anyway." And the others had gone along with him.

The only person absent was Thomas Colfax. He would be brought in at the last minute, when everything was in readiness for him.

Just like a goddamn movie star.

Thomas Colfax was having a meeting in his cell with David Terry of the Justice Department, the man in charge of creating new identities for witnesses who wished to disappear.

"Let me explain a bit about the Federal Witness Security Program," Terry said. "When the trial is over, we'll send you to whichever country you choose. Your furniture and other belongings will be shipped to a warehouse in Washington, with a coded number. We'll forward it to you later. There won't be any way for anyone to trace you. We'll supply you with a new identity and background and, if you wish, a new appearance."

"I'll take care of that." He trusted no one to know what he was going to do with his appearance.

"Ordinarily when we set people up with a new identity, we find jobs for them in whatever field they're suited for, and we supply them with some money. In your case, Mr. Colfax, I understand that money is no problem."

Thomas Colfax wondered what David Terry would say if he knew how much money was salted away in his bank accounts in Germany, Switzerland and Hong Kong. Even Thomas Colfax had not been able to keep track of it all, but a modest estimate, he would guess, would be nine or ten million dollars.

"No," Colfax said, "I don't think money will be a problem."

"All right, then. The first thing to decide is where you would like to go. Do you have any particular area in mind?"

It was such a simple question, yet so much lay behind it. What the man was really saying was, *Where do you want to spend the rest of your life?* For Colfax knew that when he got to wherever he was going, he would never be able to leave. It would become his new habitat, his protective cover, and he would not be safe anywhere else in the world.

"Brazil."

It was the logical choice. He already owned a two-hundred-thousand-acre plantation there in the name of a Panamanian corporation that could not be traced back to him. The plantation itself was like a fortress. He could afford to buy himself enough protection so that even if Michael Moretti did finally learn where he was, no one would be able to touch him. He could buy anything, including all the women he wanted. Thomas Colfax liked Latin women. People thought that when a man reached the age of sixty-five he was finished sexually, that he no longer had any interest, but Colfax had found that his appetite had grown as he had gotten older. His favorite sport was to have two or three beautiful young women in bed with him at the same time, working him over. The younger the better.

"Brazil will be easy to arrange," David Terry was saying. "Our government will buy you a small house there, and——"

"That won't be necessary." Colfax almost laughed aloud at the thought of his having to live in a small house. "All I will require of you is that you provide me with the new identification and safe transportation. I'll take care of everything else."

"As you wish, Mr. Colfax." David Terry rose to his feet. "I think we've covered just about everything." He smiled reassuringly. "This is going to be one of the easy ones. I'll begin setting things in motion. As soon as you're finished testifying, you'll be on an airplane to South America."

"Thank you." Thomas Colfax watched his visitor leave and he was filled with a sense of elation. He had done it! Michael Moretti had made the mistake of underestimating him, and it was going to be Moretti's final mistake. Colfax was going to bury him so deep that he would never rise again.

And his testimony was going to be filmed. That would be interesting. He wondered whether they would use makeup on him. He studied himself in the small mirror on the wall. *Not bad*, he thought, *for a man my age. I still have my looks. Those young South American girls love older men with gray hair*.

He heard the sound of the cell door opening, and he turned. A marine sergeant was bringing in Colfax's lunch. There would be plenty of time to eat before the filming began.

The first day, Thomas Colfax had complained about the food that was served to him, and from then on General Wallace had arranged for all of Colfax's meals to be catered. In the weeks that Colfax had been confined at the fort, his slightest suggestion had become their command. They wanted to do everything they could to please him, and Colfax took full advantage of it. He had had comfortable furniture moved in, and a television set, and he received a daily supply of newspapers and current magazines.

The sergeant placed the tray of food on a table set for two, and he made the same comment he made every day.

"Looks good enough to eat, sir."

Colfax smiled politely and sat down at the table. Roast beef rare, the way he liked it, mashed potatoes and Yorkshire pudding. He waited as the marine pulled up a chair and sat down across from him. The sergeant picked up a knife and fork, cut off a piece of the meat and began to eat. Another of General Wallace's ideas. Thomas Colfax had his own taster. *Like the kings of ancient times*, he thought. He watched as the marine sampled the roast beef, the potatoes and the Yorkshire pudding.

"How is it?"

"To tell you the truth, sir, I prefer my beef on the well-done side."

Colfax picked up his own knife and fork and began to eat. The sergeant was mistaken. The meat was cooked perfectly, the potatoes were creamy and hot and the Yorkshire pudding was done to a turn.

Colfax reached for the horseradish and spread it lightly over the beef. It was with the second bite that Colfax knew something was terribly wrong. There was a sudden burning sensation in his mouth that seemed to shoot through his whole body. He felt as though he were on fire. His throat was closing, paralyzed, and he began gasping for air. The marine sergeant sitting across from him was staring at him. Thomas Colfax clutched his throat and tried to tell the sergeant what was happening, but no words would come out. The fire in him was spreading more swiftly now, filling him with an unbearable agony. His body stiffened in a terrible spasm and he toppled over backwards to the floor.

The sergeant watched him for a moment, then bent over the body and lifted Thomas Colfax's eyelid to make sure he was dead.

Then he called for help.

60

Singapore Airlines Flight 246 landed at Heathrow Airport in London at seven-thirty A.M. The other passengers were detained in their seats until Jennifer and the two FBI agents were out of the plane and in the airport's security office.

Jennifer was desperately anxious to see a newspaper to find out what was happening at home, but her two silent escorts denied her request and refused to be drawn into conversation.

Two hours later, the three of them boarded a TWA plane bound for New York.

In the United States Court House at Foley Square an emergency meeting was taking place. Present were Adam Warner, Robert Di Silva, Major General Roy Wallace, and half a dozen representatives from the FBI, the Justice Department and the Treasury Department.

"How the hell could this have happened?" Robert Di Silva's voice was trembling with rage. He turned to the general.

"You were told how important Thomas Colfax was to us."

The general spread his hands helplessly. "We took every precaution we could, sir. We're checking now to see how they could have smuggled prussic acid into—"

"I don't give a shit how they did it! Colfax is dead!"

The man from the Treasury Department spoke up. "How much does Colfax's death hurt us?"

"A hell of a lot," Di Silva replied. "Putting a man on a witness stand is one thing. Showing a lot of ledgers and accounts is something else. You can bet your ass that some smart attorney's going to start talking about how those books could have been faked."

"Where do we go from here?" a man from the Treasury Department asked.

The District Attorney replied, "We keep doing what we're doing. Jennifer Parker's on her way back from Singapore. We have enough to put her away forever. While she's going down, we're going to get her to pull Michael Moretti down with her." He turned to Adam. "Don't you agree, Senator?"

Adam felt ill. "Excuse me."

He quickly left the room.

61

The signalman on the ground, wearing oversized earmuffs, waved his two semaphores, guiding the jumbo 747 toward the waiting ramp. The plane pulled up to a fixed circle and, at a signal, the pilot cut the four Pratt & Whitney turbofan engines.

Inside the giant plane a steward's voice came over the loudspeaker, "Ladies and gentlemen, we have just landed at New York's Kennedy Airport. We thank you for flying TWA. Will all passengers please remain in their seats until a further announcement. Thank you."

There were general murmurs of protest. A moment later the doors were opened by the ramp crew. The two FBI agents seated with Jennifer in the front of the plane rose to their feet.

One of them turned to Jennifer and said, "Let's go."

The passengers watched with curiosity as the three people

left the plane. A few minutes later the steward's voice came over the loudspeaker again. "Thank you for your patience, ladies and gentlemen. You may now disembark."

A government limousine was waiting at a side entrance to the airport. The first stop was the Metropolitan Correctional Center at 150 Park Row, that connected into the United States Court House at Foley Square.

After Jennifer had been booked, one of the FBI men said, "Sorry, we can't keep you here. We have orders to take you out to Riker's Island."

The ride to Riker's Island was made in silence. Jennifer sat in the back seat between the two FBI men, saying nothing, but her mind was busy. The two men had been uncommunicative during the entire trip across the ocean, so Jennifer had no way of knowing how much trouble she was in. She knew that it was serious, for it was not easy to obtain a warrant of extradition.

She could do nothing to help herself while she was in jail. Her first priority was to get out on bail.

They were crossing the bridge to Riker's Island now, and Jennifer looked out at the familiar view, a view she had seen a hundred times on the way to talk to clients. And now *she* was a prisoner.

But not for long, Jennifer thought. *Michael will get me out.*

The two FBI men escorted Jennifer into the reception building and one of the men handed the guard the extradition warrant.

"Jennifer Parker."

The guard glanced at it. "We've been expecting you, Miss Parker. You have a reservation in Detention Cell Three."

"I have the right to one phone call."

The guard nodded toward the telephone on his desk. "Sure."

Jennifer picked it up, silently praying that Michael Moretti was in. She began to dial.

Michael Moretti had been waiting for Jennifer's call. For the last twenty-four hours he had been able to think of nothing else. He had been informed when Jennifer had landed in London, when her plane had left Heathrow, and when she had arrived back in New York. He had sat at his desk, mentally tracking Jennifer on her way to Riker's Island. He had visualized her entering the prison. She would demand to make a phone call before they put her in a cell. She would call him. That was all he asked. He would have her out of there in an hour, and then she would be on her way to him. Michael Moretti was living for the moment when Jennifer Parker walked through the door.

Jennifer had done the unforgivable. She had given her body to the man who was trying to destroy him. And what else had she given him? What secrets had she told him?

Adam Warner was the father of Jennifer's son. Michael was certain of that now. Jennifer had lied to him from the beginning, had told him that Joshua's father was dead. *Well, that was a prophecy that will soon be fulfilled*, Michael told himself. He was caught in an ironic conflict. On the one hand, he had a powerful weapon he could use to discredit and destroy Adam Warner. He could blackmail Warner with the threat of exposing his relationship with Jennifer; but if he did that, he would be exposing himself. When the Families learned—and they would learn—that Michael's woman was the mistress of the head of the Senate Investigating Committee, Michael would become a laughingstock. He would no longer be able to hold up his head or command his men. A cuckold was not fit to be a *don*. So the blackmail threat was a double-edged sword and, as tempting as it was, Michael knew that he dare not use it. He would have to destroy his enemies in another way.

Michael looked at the small, crudely drawn map on the desk in front of him. It was Adam Warner's route to where he was going to attend a private fund-raising dinner party that evening. The map had cost Michael Moretti five thousand dollars. It was going to cost Adam Warner his life.

The telephone rang on Michael's desk and he involuntarily started. He picked it up and heard Jennifer's voice on the other end. That voice that had whispered endearments into his ear, that had begged him to make love to her, that—

"Michael—are you there?"

"I'm here. Where are you?"

"They've got me at Riker's Island. They're holding me on a murder charge. Bail hasn't been set yet. When can you—?"

"I'll have you out of there in no time. Just sit tight. Okay?"

"Yes, Michael." He could hear the relief in her voice.

"I'll have Gino pick you up."

A few moments later Michael reached for the telephone and dialed a number. He spoke into the phone for several minutes.

"I don't care how high the bail is. I want her out *now*."

He replaced the receiver and pressed a button on his desk. Gino Gallo came in.

"Jennifer Parker's at Riker's Island. She should be sprung in an hour or two. Pick her up and bring her here."

"Right, boss."

Michael leaned back in his chair. "Tell her we won't have to worry about Adam Warner after today."

Gino Gallo's face brightened. "No?"

"No. He's on his way to deliver a speech, but he'll never get there. He's going to have an accident at the bridge at New Canaan."

Gino Gallo smiled. "That's great, boss."

Michael gestured toward the door. "Move."

District Attorney Di Silva fought Jennifer's bail with every stratagem at his command. They were appearing before William Bennett, a judge of the Supreme Court of New York.

"Your Honor," Robert Di Silva said, "the defendant is charged with a dozen counts of felony. We had to extradite her from Singapore. If she's granted bail, she'll flee to someplace where there is no extradition. I ask that Your Honor deny bail."

John Lester, a former judge who was representing Jennifer, said, "The District Attorney is guilty of gross distortion, Your Honor. My client did not flee anywhere. She was in Singapore on business. If the government had asked her to return she would have done so voluntarily. She's a reputable attorney with a large practice here. It would be inconceivable that she would run away."

The arguments went on for more than thirty minutes.

At the end of that time, Judge Bennett said, "Bail is granted in the sum of five hundred thousand dollars."

"Thank you, Your Honor," Jennifer's attorney said. "We'll pay the bail."

Fifteen minutes later, Gino Gallo was helping Jennifer into the back of a Mercedes limousine.

"That didn't take long," he said.

Jennifer did not reply. Her mind was on what was happening. She had been completely isolated in Singapore. She had no idea of what had been going on in the United States, but she was certain that her arrest was not an unrelated incident. They would not be after her alone. She badly needed to talk to Michael and find out what had been happening. Di Silva had to be very sure of himself to have had her brought back on a murder charge. He—

Gino Gallo said two words that caught Jennifer's attention.

". . . Adam Warner . . ."

Jennifer had not been listening.

"What did you say?"

"I said we won't have to worry about Adam Warner no more. Mike is havin' him took care of."

Jennifer could feel her heart begin to pound. "He is? When?"

Gino Gallo raised his hand from the wheel to glance at his watch. "In about fifteen minutes. It's set up to look like an accident."

Jennifer's mouth was suddenly dry. "Where—" She could not get the words out. "Where—where is it going to happen?"

"New Canaan. The bridge."

They were passing through Queens. Ahead was a shopping center with a pharmacy.

"Gino, will you pull up in front of that drugstore? I have to get something."

"Sure." He skillfully turned the wheel and swung into the entrance to the shopping center. "Can I help you?"

"No, no. I'll—I'll only be a minute."

Jennifer got out of the car and hurried inside, nerves screaming. There was a telephone booth at the back of the store. Jennifer reached into her purse. She had no change except for some Singapore coins. She hurried over to the cashier and pulled out a dollar.

"Could I have change, please?"

The bored cashier took Jennifer's money and gave her a handful of silver. Jennifer dashed back to the telephone. A stout woman was picking up the receiver and dialing.

Jennifer said, "I have an emergency. I wonder if I could—"

The woman glared at her and kept dialing.

"Hello, Hazel," the woman whooped. "My horoscope was right. I've had the worst day! You know the shoes I was going to pick up at Delman's? Would you believe they sold the only pair they had in my size?"

Jennifer touched the woman's arm and begged, "Please!"

"Get your own phone," the woman hissed. She turned back

to the receiver. "Remember the suede ones we saw? Gone! So you know what I did? I said to that clerk . . ."

Jennifer closed her eyes and stood there, oblivious to everything but the torment inside her. Michael must not kill Adam. She had to do whatever she could to save him.

The woman hung up and turned to Jennifer. "I should make another call, just to teach you a lesson," she said.

As she walked away, smiling at her little victory, Jennifer made a grab for the phone. She called Adam's office.

"I'm sorry," his secretary said, "but Senator Warner is not in. Do you wish to leave a message?"

"It's urgent," Jennifer said. "Do you know where he can be reached?"

"No, I'm sorry. If you would like to—"

Jennifer hung up. She stood there a moment, thinking, then quickly dialed another number. "Robert Di Silva."

There was an interminable wait and then: "The District Attorney's office."

"I have to speak to Mr. Di Silva. This is Jennifer Parker."

"I'm sorry. Mr. Di Silva is in a conference. He can't be dis—"

"You get him on this telephone. This is an emergency. Hurry!" Jennifer's voice was trembling.

Di Silva's secretary hesitated. "Just a moment."

A minute later, Robert Di Silva was on the telephone. "Yes?" His voice was unfriendly.

"Listen, and listen carefully," Jennifer said. "Adam Warner's going to be killed. It's going to happen in the next ten or fifteen minutes. They're planning to do it at the New Canaan bridge."

She hung up. There was nothing more she could do. A brief vision of Adam's torn body came into her mind and she shuddered. She looked at her watch and silently prayed that Di Silva would be able to get help there in time.

* * *

Robert Di Silva replaced the receiver and looked at the half-dozen men in his office. "That was a weird call."

"Who was it?"

"Jennifer Parker. She said they're going to assassinate Senator Warner."

"Why did she call you?"

"Who knows?"

"Do you think it's on the level?"

District Attorney Di Silva said, "Hell, no."

Jennifer walked through the office door and, in spite of himself, Michael could not help reacting to her beauty. It was the same way he felt every time he saw her. Outside, she was the loveliest woman he had ever seen. But inside she was treacherous, deadly. He looked at the lips that had kissed Adam Warner and at the body that had lain in Adam Warner's arms.

She was walking in saying, "Michael, I'm so glad to see you. Thank you for arranging everything so quickly."

"No problem. I've been waiting for you, Jennifer." She would never know how much he meant that.

She sank into an armchair. "Michael, what in God's name is going on? What's happening?"

He studied her, half admiring her. She was responsible for helping to bring his empire crashing down, and she was sitting there innocently asking what was going on!

"Do you know why they brought me back?"

Sure, he thought. *So you can sing some more for them.* He remembered the little yellow canary with its broken neck. That would be Jennifer soon.

Jennifer looked into his black eyes. "Are you all right?"

"I've never been better." He leaned back in his chair. "In a few minutes, all our problems are going to be over."

"What do you mean?"

"Senator Warner is going to have an accident. That'll cool off the committee pretty good." He looked at the clock on the wall. "I should be getting a phone call any minute."

There was something odd in Michael's manner, something forbidding. Jennifer was filled with a sudden premonition of danger. She knew she had to get out of there.

She stood up. "I haven't had a chance to unpack. I'll go—"

"Sit down." The undertone in Michael's voice sent a chill down her back.

"Michael—"

"Sit down."

She glanced toward the door. Gino Gallo was standing there, his back against it, watching Jennifer with no expression on his face.

"You're not going anywhere," Michael told her.

"I don't under—"

"Don't talk. Don't say another word."

They sat there waiting, staring at each other, and the only sound in the room was the loud ticking of the clock on the wall. Jennifer tried to read Michael's eyes, but they were blank, filled with nothing, giving away nothing.

The sudden ringing of the telephone jarred the stillness of the room. Michael picked up the receiver. "Hello? . . . Are you sure? . . . All right. Get out of there." He replaced the receiver and looked up at Jennifer. "The bridge at New Canaan is swarming with cops."

Jennifer could feel the relief flooding through her body. It became a sense of exhilaration. Michael was watching her and she made an effort not to let her emotions show.

Jennifer asked, "What does that mean?"

Michael said slowly, "Nothing. Because that's not where Adam Warner is going to die."

62

The twin bridges of the Garden State Parkway were not named on the map. The Garden State Parkway crossed the Raritan River between the Amboys, splitting into the two bridges, one northbound and the other southbound.

The limousine was just west of Perth Amboy, heading toward the southbound bridge. Adam Warner was seated in back, with a secret service man beside him, and two secret service men in front.

Agent Clay Reddin had been assigned to the senator's guard detail six months earlier, and he had come to know Adam Warner well. He had always thought of him as an open, accessible man, but all day the senator had been strangely silent and withdrawn. *Deeply troubled* were the words that came to Agent Reddin. There was no question in his mind but that Senator Warner was going to be the next President of the United States, and it was Reddin's responsibility to see that nothing happened to him. He reviewed again the precautions that had been taken to safeguard the senator, and he was satisfied that nothing could go wrong.

Agent Reddin glanced again at the probable President-to-be, and wondered what he was thinking.

Adam Warner's mind was on the ordeal that was confronting him. He had been informed by Di Silva that Jennifer Parker had been arrested. The thought of her being locked away like an animal was anathema to him. His mind kept returning to the wonderful moments they had shared together. He had loved Jennifer as he had never loved another woman.

One of the secret service men in the front seat was saying, "We should be arriving in Atlantic City right on schedule, Mr. President."

Mr. President. That phrase again. According to all the latest polls, he was far ahead. He was the country's new folk hero, and Adam knew it was due in no small measure to the crime investigation he had headed, the investigation that would destroy Jennifer Parker.

Adam glanced up and saw that they were approaching the twin bridges. There was a side road just before the bridge and a huge semitrailer truck was stopped at the entrance on the opposite side of the road. As the limousine neared the bridge, the truck started to pull out, so that the two vehicles arrived at the bridge at the same time.

The secret service driver applied his brakes and slowed down. "Look at that idiot."

The shortwave radio crackled into life. "Beacon One! Come in, Beacon One!"

The agent in the front seat next to the driver picked up the transmitter. "This is Beacon One."

The large truck was abreast of the limousine now as it started across the span. It was a behemoth, completely blocking out the view on the driver's side of the car. The limousine driver started to speed up to get ahead of it, but the truck simultaneously increased its speed.

"What the hell does he think he's doing?" the driver muttered.

"We've had an urgent call from the District Attorney's office. Fox One is in danger! Do you read me?"

Without warning, the truck veered to the right, hitting the side of the limousine, forcing it against the bridge railing. In seconds, the three secret service men in the car had their guns out.

"Get down!"

Adam found himself pushed down onto the floor, while Agent Reddin shielded Adam's body. The secret service agents rolled down the windows on the left side of the limousine, guns pointed. There was nothing at which to shoot. The side of the huge semitrailer blotted out everything. The driver was up ahead, out of sight. There was another jolt and a grinding crash as the limousine was knocked into the railing again. The driver swung the wheel to the left, fighting to keep the car on the bridge, but the truck kept forcing him back. The cold Raritan River swirled two hundred feet below them.

The secret service agent next to the driver had grabbed his radio microphone and was calling wildly into it, "This is Beacon One! Mayday! Mayday! Come in all units!"

But everyone in the limousine knew that it was too late for anyone to save them. The driver tried to stop the car, but the truck's huge fenders were locked into it, sweeping the limousine along. It was only a matter of seconds before the huge truck would edge them over the side of the bridge. The agent driving the car tried evasive tactics, alternately using the brake and the accelerator to slow down and speed up, but the truck had the car cruelly pinned against the bridge railing. There was no room for the car to maneuver. The truck blocked off any escape on the left side, and on the right side the limousine was being pushed against the iron railing of the bridge. The agent fought the wheel desperately as the truck pressed hard into the limousine once again, and every-one in the car could feel the bridge railing start to give way.

The truck was jamming harder now, forcing the limousine over the side. Those in the car could feel the sudden list as the front wheels broke through the railing and went over the edge of the bridge. The car was teetering on the brink and each man, in his own way, prepared to die.

Adam felt no fear, only an ineffable sadness at the loss, the waste. It was Jennifer he should have shared his life with, had children with—and suddenly Adam knew, from some-where deep within himself, that they had had a child.

The limousine gave another lurch and Adam cried out once aloud at the injustice of what had happened, what was hap-pening.

From overhead came the roar of two police helicopters as they swooped down out of the sky, and a moment later there was the sound of machine guns. The semitrailer lurched and all motion suddenly stopped. Adam and the others could hear the helicopters circling overhead. The men remained motion-less, knowing that the slightest movement could send the car over the bridge, into the waters below.

There was the distant scream of police sirens drawing nearer, and a few minutes later the sound of voices barking out commands. The engine of the truck roared into life again. Slowly, carefully, the truck moved, inching away from the trapped car, removing the pressure against it. The limousine tilted for one terrible instant, and then was still. A moment later, the truck had been backed out of the way and Adam and the others could see out of the left-hand windows.

There were half a dozen squad cars and uniformed police-men with drawn guns swarming over the bridge.

A police captain was at the side of the battered car.

"We'll never get the doors open," he said. "We're going to bring you out through the windows—real easy."

Adam was lifted out of the window first, slowly and carefully, so as not to upset the balance of the car and send it over the side. The three secret service men were next.

When all the men had been removed from the car, the police captain turned to Adam and asked, "Are you all right, sir?"

Adam turned to look at the car hanging over the edge of the bridge, and then at the dark water of the river far below.

"Yes," he said. "I'm all right."

Michael Moretti glanced up at the clock on the wall. "It's all over." He turned to face Jennifer. "Your boyfriend's in the river by now."

She was watching him, her face pale. "You can't—"

"Don't worry. You're going to have a fair trial." He turned to Gino Gallo. "Did you tell her that Adam Warner was going to be blown away in New Canaan?"

"Just like you told me, boss."

Michael looked at Jennifer. "The trial's over."

He rose to his feet and walked over to where Jennifer was sitting. He grabbed her blouse and pulled her to her feet.

"I loved you," he whispered. He hit her hard across the face. Jennifer did not flinch. He hit her again, harder, then a third time, and she fell to the floor.

"Get up. We're taking a trip."

Jennifer lay there, dizzy from the blows, trying to clear her head. Michael hauled her roughly to her feet.

"You want me to take care of her?" Gino Gallo asked.

"No. Bring the car around the back."

"Right, boss." He hurried out of the room.

Jennifer and Michael were alone.

"Why?" he asked. "We owned the world, and you threw it away. *Why?*"

She did not answer.

"You want me to fuck you once more for old times' sake?" Michael moved toward her and grabbed her arm. "Would you like that?" Jennifer did not respond. "You're never going to fuck anyone again, you hear? I'm going to put you in the river with your lover! You can keep each other company."

Gino Gallo came back into the room, his face white. "Boss! There's a—"

There was a crashing sound from outside the room. Michael dived for the gun in his desk drawer. He had it in his hand when the door burst open. Two federal agents came through the door, guns drawn.

"Freeze!"

In that split second, Michael made his decision. He raised the gun and turned and fired at Jennifer. He saw the bullets go into her a second before the agents started shooting. He watched the blood spurt out of her chest, then he felt a bullet tear into him, and then another. He saw Jennifer lying on the floor, and Michael did not know which was the greater agony, her death or his. He felt the hammer blow of another bullet, and then he felt nothing.

63

Two interns were wheeling Jennifer out of the operating room and into Intensive Care. A uniformed policeman followed at Jennifer's side. The hospital corridor was a bedlam of policemen, detectives and reporters.

A man walked up to the reception desk and said, "I want to see Jennifer Parker."

"Are you a member of her family?"

"No. I'm a friend."

"I'm sorry. No visitors. She's in Intensive Care."

"I'll wait."

"It could be a long time."

"That doesn't matter," Ken Bailey said.

A side door opened and Adam Warner, gaunt and haggard, entered, flanked by a team of secret service men.

A doctor was waiting to greet him. "This way, Senator Warner." He led Adam into a small office.

"How is she?" Adam asked.

"I'm not optimistic. We removed three bullets from her."

The door opened and District Attorney Robert Di Silva hurried in. He looked at Adam Warner and said, "I'm sure glad you're okay."

Adam said, "I understand I owe my thanks to you. How did you know?"

"Jennifer Parker called me. She told me they were setting you up in New Canaan. I figured it was probably some kind of diversionary ploy, but I couldn't take a chance, so I covered it. Meanwhile, I got hold of the route you were taking and we sent some choppers after you to protect you. My hunch is that Parker tried to set you up."

"No," Adam said. "No."

Robert Di Silva shrugged. "Have it your way, Senator. The important thing is that you're alive." As an afterthought he turned to the doctor. "Is she going to live?"

"Her chances are not very good."

The District Attorney saw the look on Adam Warner's face and misinterpreted it. "Don't worry. If she makes it, we've got her nailed down tight."

He looked at Adam more closely. "You look like hell. Why don't you go home and get some rest?"

"I want to see Jennifer Parker first."

The doctor said, "She's in a coma. She may not come out of it."

"I would like to see her, please."

"Of course, Senator. This way."

The doctor led the way out of the room, with Adam following and Di Silva behind him. They walked a few feet down the corridor to a sign that said INTENSIVE CARE UNIT — KEEP OUT.

The doctor opened the door and held it for the two men. "She's in the first room."

There was a policeman in front of the door, guarding it. He came to attention as he saw the District Attorney.

"No one gets near that room without written authorization from me. You understand?" Di Silva asked.

"Yes, sir."

Adam and Di Silva walked into the room. There were three beds, two of them empty. Jennifer lay in the third, tubes running into her nostrils and wrists. Adam moved close to the bed and stared down at her. Jennifer's face was very pale against the white pillows, and her eyes were closed. In repose, her face seemed younger and softer. Adam was looking at the innocent girl he had met years ago, the girl who had said angrily to him, *If anyone had paid me off, do you think I'd be living in a place like this? I don't care what you do. All I want is to be left alone.* He remembered her courage and idealism and her vulnerability. She had been on the side of the angels, believing in justice and willing to fight for it. What had gone wrong? He had loved her and he loved her still, and he had made one wrong choice that had poisoned all their lives, and he knew he would never feel free of guilt for as long as he lived.

He turned to the doctor. "Let me know when she—" He could not say the words. "—what happens."

"Of course," the doctor said.

Adam Warner took one long last look at Jennifer and said a silent good-bye. Then he turned and walked out to face the waiting reporters.

Through a dim, misty haze of semiconsciousness, Jennifer heard the men leave. She had not understood what they were saying, for their words were blurred by the pain that gripped her. She thought she had heard Adam's voice, but she knew that could not be. He was dead. She tried to open her eyes, but the effort was too great.

Jennifer's thoughts began to drift . . . Abraham Wilson came running into the room carrying a box. He stumbled and the box opened and a yellow canary flew out of it . . . Robert Di Silva was screaming, *Catch it! Don't let it get away!*

. . . and Michael Moretti was holding it and laughing, and Father Ryan said, *Look, everybody! It's a miracle!* and Connie Garrett was dancing around the room and everyone applauded . . . Mrs. Cooper said, *I'm going to give you Wyoming . . . Wyoming . . . Wyoming . . .* and Adam came in with dozens of red roses and Michael said, *They're from me,* and Jennifer said, *I'll put them in a vase in water,* and they shriveled and died and the water spilled onto the floor and became a lake, and she and Adam were sailing, and Michael was chasing them on water skis and he became Joshua and he smiled at Jennifer and waved and started to lose his balance, and she screamed, *Don't fall . . . Don't fall . . . Don't fall* . . . and an enormous wave swept Joshua into the air and he held out his arms like Jesus and disappeared.

For an instant, Jennifer's mind cleared.

Joshua was gone.

Adam was gone.

Michael was gone.

She was alone. In the end, everyone was alone. Each person had to die his own death. It would be easy to die now.

A feeling of blessed peace began to steal over her. Soon there was no more pain.